Sticks and Stones

A novel about bullying

Claire H Wood

**Copyright 2023 by Claire H Wood.
All rights reserved.**

ISBN: 9798399769233

Dedication

I dedicate this book to anyone who has suffered from bullying in their life and who understands the long-lasting effects that it can have. Stay strong, keep the faith and always remember how important you are.

Claire x

Part one: Julia
Prologue

February 2002

I remember it being one of those uncharacteristically warm days for the middle of February, almost as though spring had burst into bud a few weeks early. The sound of birdsong was amplified and pretty bulbs were beginning to open up between blades of dewy grass. My face glowed from the warmth of the sun and the air smelt fresh and clean. It was one of those beautiful days that cut through the bleakness of winter and awakened everyone from hibernation.

It was one of those beautiful days that would have put a smile on my face and a spring in my step had it not have been for the sheer hell of the situation in which I had found myself in. Because rather than a warm, soft glow in my cheeks, they were burning red hot with fever. My entire body trembled uncontrollably as I slipped in and out of consciousness. Two paramedics gently lifted me onto a stretcher and carried me to where an ambulance was waiting for us, and I found myself aware of lots of people standing around watching as my eyelids started to become heavy again.

"Stay with us Julia," urged a voice, but all I could make out as I squinted to identify its owner, was a blurry outline of a dark haired young man, with a round friendly face and a wide smile.

"I'm Andy," he then explained, gripping my hand tightly as he spoke. His voice was soft and kind. "I'm a trainee paramedic and I'm here to look after you. Everything's going to be alright."

As my eyes opened and closed again, I could see the bright blue lights from the ambulance flashing through my eyelids, and before I was able to make sense of what was happening I had been lifted into the back of it and the doors were slammed shut. The sound of all the concerned voices from the crowd outside were immediately replaced by sirens, as the ambulance began to move.

"It hurts," I croaked, swallowing hard and raising my right arm – the one that wasn't in excruciating pain – and feeling on my face for where my glasses should have been, in the hope of being able to focus on the kind paramedic more closely.

"Your glasses got broken when you collapsed," Andy explained, when he realised what I was doing. "Try not to move, you've got a nasty infection and we need to keep your arm nice and still."

I licked my dry lips and swallowed again. The pain in my left arm was unbearable and I could hear my heart pounding in my ears as the ambulance swayed from side to side.

"What happened?" I sobbed, as he gripped hold of my hand again and brushed a few stray strands of hair away from my tear tracked face. Deep down I knew what had happened though. I just didn't want to admit it to myself. Before we arrived at the hospital I lost consciousness again.

Chapter one

Friday 26th April 2019

"And how did that make you feel?" Dr Jules asked, as she peered over the top of her reading glasses.

Her client shifted about uneasily in her seat, doing her best not to look the inquisitive psychologist directly in the eye.

"Is that a trick question?" her client then clarified. "How do you *think* it made me feel?"

"Well, you're here to tell me," replied Dr Jules. "It's up to you to use the time we have together to talk about your experiences and to try and make sense of them."

Jules could tell that Caitlin didn't entirely approve of the school's initiative to introduce counselling to the students at the beginning of last term. She had gone along anyway because the alternative would have resulted in suspension and possibly even expulsion. Caitlin couldn't bear to think about the expression on her stepfather's face if she had been obliged to go home and announce that outcome. Pinewood Secondary, the comprehensive school that she had been attending for the past three years, had recently pioneered a brand new anti-bullying initiative. They had appointed Dr Jules as their new pastoral support officer, who had invited Caitlin in to talk to her about her experiences with bullying. Clearly Caitlin didn't claim to actually *have* any experiences as far as that was concerned. She was very popular at school. She had simply been trying to put one of the other, less popular, students in her place by asserting her authority in the lunch queue on Tuesday.

"She pushed in front of me. I was really angry," she explained, looking Dr Jules straight in the eye. "She deserves everything she gets!"

"And you think it's OK to express your anger by getting aggressive and confrontational?" asked Dr Jules, sliding her reading glasses back up her nose and making a few notes on the pad of paper that was perched on her knee.

"That boffin thinks she's better than me. Just because she's a straight A student, doesn't mean she can push in front of me in the lunch queue."

"Can you think of any other ways of dealing with a situation like that?" Jules nodded, resisting the strong urge to overstep her professional boundaries by reminding Caitlin that shouting and using violence were not the answer.

Dr Jules had studied psychology at university, before training to be a counsellor. She had worked with a cross-section of clients with varying issues, including alcoholism and bereavement, but this was the first time she had counselled children. When she found out about the pastoral support officer role at Pinewood, she was compelled to apply for it straight away because she knew that she would end up tackling some issues that were very close to her heart, like bullying and low self-esteem. But her experiences in the past were also proving to be a bit of a handicap because her professional head and her emotional heart were often at loggerheads with each other. Of course, she knew that she should always deal with situations in a professional manner, but that didn't stop her from allowing her feelings and emotions to get the better of her from time to time.

When Dr Jules qualified as a counsellor five years ago, she didn't expect to form such a personal attachment to some of her cases, but bullying was one of the reasons why she decided to become a counsellor in the first place. She wanted to try and make a difference, a *real* difference, to the lives of both the victims *and* the bullies. And the Pinewood secondary school initiative seemed like the perfect opportunity to try and implement this. Some of the students were proving to be quite a challenge though, particularly Caitlin Murphy, who seemed to be at the root of the majority of 'incidents' involving the girls in year 10. Jules had hoped that the Easter holidays would have given Caitlin the opportunity to reflect on her behaviour, but they were only three days into the new school term and she had already been reprimanded for upsetting Louisa again.

Caitlin was sitting slumped back in her chair with her legs crossed and her arms folded. She was chewing a piece of gum and staring out of the window, trying to pretend that she wasn't really there. There was no doubt that she had agreed to this meeting under duress, and couldn't wait until it was over so that she could go outside and join the rest of her 'pack' for a cigarette behind the bike sheds. Her skirt was too short, her blouse was un-tucked, her tie had been loosened around her collar and her jagged bobbed hair was black all over with a single streak of blonde along the front. She was wearing heavy eye make-up and purple lipstick, and her high platform heels persisted on kicking the leg of the table next to her every time she considered the answer to one of Dr Jules' questions.

During her sessions with Caitlin, Jules couldn't help but feel as though Caitlin wasn't fully concentrating on what was going on because when she wasn't staring out of the window, she had her nose buried in her phone at every available opportunity. She was still able to answer Jules' questions when it came to multi-tasking, but it was very difficult to 'read' her because her answers were rather robotic. The smart phone generation were a bit of an enigma to Jules. She didn't get her first mobile phone until she was in her late teens and even then it couldn't take photos or connect to the internet. Social media was only just becoming a craze, and young people were still going out and socialising with their friends in person rather than electronically.

Jules wondered why it was referred to as 'social' media when it appeared to be anything but. Everyone had forgotten how to interact with each other socially, and even when they were actually in the same room as one another, their devices seemed to take priority. It made her wonder how relationships could be sustained or even exist in the first place. Young people in particular were constantly inaccessible or distracted, and the urge to check their phone was unbearably compelling, almost addictive in fact.

They were sitting in a medium sized office with a desk in the far right-hand corner next to the window. The space felt a lot smaller than it actually was though because the walls had been painted in a dark olive colour and there were no less than seven filing cabinets surrounding the desk which the teachers used for all their overflow paperwork. But Jules knew that she was lucky to have any kind of office at all and really tried to make the most of what little space she did have by draping a couple of patterned throws over the top of the filing cabinets to try and make the room feel less clerical and more relaxed for her students. There were hard chairs opposite her desk for them to sit in and she had even brought a couple of brightly coloured scatter cushions in to make the chairs seem comfortable. She believed that the more relaxed her students felt, the more likely they were to open up to her during their sessions together. Or so she hoped. Her flat mate Amy had tried to persuade her to light some incense as well, forcing Jules to remind her that the students were there to talk to her about their experiences with bullying and not to do meditation. Unfortunately, Caitlin didn't even appear to be prepared to do that today.

"Caitlin, I would like us to continue these sessions without any distractions," she tentatively suggested, reaching her hand out.

Caitlin hesitated, looked up from her phone for the briefest of moments, and then continued scrolling. Jules was unperturbed and edged closer to where Caitlin was sitting. This time Caitlin rolled her eyes and begrudgingly placed the device into Jules' outstretched hand. Now that Caitlin no longer had her phone, Jules knew that she wouldn't be able to use it as a comfort blanket anymore. She was all too aware that many young people who found themselves in social situations that made them feel uncomfortable, would be compelled to scroll through their phone instead, but one of Jules' most significant roles at the school was to encourage the children to communicate and open up more. Having studied social anxiety amongst many other areas of psychology, she was determined to try and implement a phone-free policy within the school grounds, but the head teacher was still keen to allow the students to have access to their devices when they weren't in any classes.

Social anxiety was of particular interest to Jules due its close links with bullying. And because bullying was such a primitive behaviour, often motivated by an instinctive desire to mask that person's own vulnerability by controlling other people, it was more than likely that Caitlin had a few vulnerabilities of her own which needed exploring.

It had felt like a really long session with very little engagement, but as their time together eventually drew to a close, Jules decided to set some more time aside for Caitlin on a separate occasion in the hope that she might end up being a little more receptive next time.

"Shall we conclude things here?" she suggested, looking at the clock on the wall behind her.

Caitlin let out a big sigh as she snatched her phone and the appointment slip from Dr Jules and then slammed the door of the office on her way out. Dr Jules flinched as the walls of the office shook with the sound, and she closed her eyes and sighed. Just at that moment, her own phone rang causing her to flinch again. She rummaged around in her handbag to find and answer it and then swallowed hard when she heard that it was the hospital.

"I'll be right there," she replied to the voice at the other end, before flinging her handbag onto her shoulder, grabbing her keys from the desk, and leaving the office almost as quickly as Caitlin had.

❖

"She wouldn't agree to let me call anyone but you," explained the nurse when Jules arrived at the hospital. "Her parents don't even know she's here yet."

Jules was more than used to making emergency visits to the hospital whenever one of her clients had decided to take matters into their own hands. This afternoon, Louisa, who was one of Caitlin's victims from the school, had been found truanting at lunch time and had fallen over during her attempt to escape from one of the teachers.

"I'll take over from here," Jules insisted, relieving the teacher from his bedside vigil. "I'll make sure she gets home safely."

The teacher simply huffed in reply. It seemed that many of the staff at the school had developed a very cynical opinion of the new anti-bullying initiative, and in particular the new pastoral support officer, who was clearly expected to resolve the tension between Caitlin and Louisa overnight.

"We *are* making progress by the way," Jules reassured the teacher, as he reluctantly agreed to leave Louisa in her care. "She trusts me. Why do you think she asked the nurse to contact me?"

Louisa swung her legs over the side of the bed and stood up. Her right knee had a large dressing on it from where she had fallen over, and her school uniform was badly torn.

"Are you taking me home now?" she smiled. Jules couldn't help but wonder whether Louisa had deliberately staged what had happened at lunchtime in order to avoid going back to school that afternoon because she knew that she had a double period with Caitlin after lunch.

"We'll talk about this later," replied Jules, trying to remain as two dimensional as she could about the situation. It was important not to show any kind of bias, without coming across as unsupportive or uncaring towards any of her students. And that could be quite a difficult balance to strike sometimes.

The Accident and Emergency department was a hub of activity as usual. She looked around for the nurse who had contacted her, but she had already disappeared into one of the other cubicles. She needed to get Louisa discharged as soon as possible so that they could return to the school and get to the bottom of why Louisa had felt the need to truant in the first place. Just at that moment, she caught sight of a doctor, and he appeared to be between patients because he was standing in the middle of the department scratching his head and looking around, as if he was trying to decide which case to tackle next. As Jules started to walk towards him, his gaze fell upon her and he smiled. The tall, dark and handsome doctor sounded like such a cliché, but in his case it was true. And he had such a warm smile to match. Jules actually found herself feeling quite giddy at the sight of him. Their rather intense eye contact was making her embarrassed, so she tried to regain her professional composure by looking down at his name badge instead.

'Dr Drew Trent, Senior Registrar' it read.

"Hello, I'm Dr Jules Croft, Louisa's school pastoral support officer," she explained, looking up again. "I was wondering whether you could discharge her now please?"

"Of course, I apologise for keeping you waiting," replied Dr Trent, without realising that Jules had only just arrived.

As he walked over to Louisa's bed and picked up her discharge papers, Jules couldn't seem to take her eyes off him. He really was very good looking, but not in a conventional way. Jules didn't really find herself attracted to conventionally good looking men. This dark haired doctor on the other hand, definitely seemed to be having quite an effect on her.

"So can we go now?" complained Louisa, as Jules thanked him for being so efficient in what can only be described as a very lame attempt at flirtation. Flirting never came naturally to her. She was far too self-conscious. She also had absolutely no confidence whatsoever when it came to relationships with the opposite sex.

Louisa was looking at her with a very unimpressed expression on her face. Jules regained her composure once more and then reluctantly dragged herself away from her new muse.

"I'm contacting your parents and then we're going straight back to school," she asserted as they made their way to the exit. "Allowing your grades to slip is one thing, but truanting! I thought we were trying to work through this?"

"You sound like the teachers" groaned Louisa, dragging her feet behind her. "A couple of counselling sessions aren't going to make Caitlin go away. If anything, it's making her worse."

When Jules arranged to see Caitlin following the incident in the lunch queue the day before, she feared that Louisa might end up bearing the brunt of it. She didn't know exactly what had happened to encourage Louisa to run away from school, but she fully intended to find out. As Louisa very slowly limped her way to Jules' car, Jules observed that she started to look very vulnerable again. She sank into the passenger seat with an extremely deflated expression on her sallow face. Her blond hair hung limply over her shoulders, and her eyes looked dark and sunken behind her glasses.

"Everything's going to be OK," Jules attempted to reassure her, but deep down she knew that Louisa's experiences with bullying could very easily get worse before they got better. After all, if anyone knew what that was like, Jules did.

Chapter two

October 1995

"Sticks and stones may break my bones, but words will never hurt me."

I've never completely understood what the point to that children's rhyme is. Apparently, according to Wikipedia, it's supposed to 'persuade the child victim of name calling to ignore the taunt, to refrain from physical retaliation, and to remain calm and good-living'. Well what about another well-known saying: "The pen is mightier than the sword"? Sometimes what you write or say about another person can be more powerful, more painful even, than any other kind of weapon. And emotional scars can take a lot longer to heal than physical ones.

I am ashamed to admit that I in fact am the bearer of both kinds of scars, which is the main reason why I decided to study psychology and become a counsellor. I wanted to be able to provide support to other people so that they wouldn't be obliged to make the same mistakes as I have over the years. Because for better or for worse, taunting and bullying has shaped me into the kind of person that I am today. And it all started as long as 24 years ago, when a boy called Barry Harper decided to retrieve a twig and a pebble from the ground of Acornfields primary school's playground, and threaten me with them. I remember running as fast as I could towards the sports field behind our classroom, and searching frantically for an effective hiding place. I couldn't quite work out how I had managed to run that far or that fast, but the cool autumn air stung my tear tracked face as I went, and my heart was hammering so hard, I felt as though my chest was about to explode.

Eventually I managed to find a small gap in the bottom of one of the hedgerows that surrounded the perimeter of the sports field, and I anxiously slid my way underneath, snagging my skirt on some brambles and getting my hair caught in a branch above my head. Barry was on the heavy side so he would never have managed to fit into such a tight gap compared with my short, 9 year old frame. I stared at the floor, praying that he wouldn't be able to find me.

"Where did she go?" complained Barry, as he and his little following of so-called friends managed to reach the opposite side of the sports field where the hedgerows were.

I held my breath and tried to remain as quiet as I possibly could as Barry paced up and down looking for me. And just as his dirty trainers got to the gap where I was hiding, the teacher's whistle blew, signalling the end of lunchtime. Barry kicked at the ground in frustration and then reluctantly admitted defeat before slowly dragging his friends back towards the school building. As soon as I was certain that they had gone, I started to breathe normally again. Warm tears continued to roll down my cheeks and my entire body began to shake from the relief of not being found. I was safe, for now at least.

Barry Harper was absolutely vile. He and his friends had been making my life a misery for what seemed like forever and I had been able to just ignore it until then, but that afternoon, something inside me just snapped and I decided not only to retaliate, but to run away. Up until a few months prior to that incident, I had really enjoyed going to school. Everyone in my class used to play together at lunchtimes and there were no divisions whatsoever. But then everything started to change and Barry decided to assert his authority over everyone. Some of the more confident children in my class managed to distance themselves from him completely and form their own alliances, and others decided that they would be in a far stronger position if they joined his gang. I, on the other hand, found that I had become a bit of a loner, and I was therefore the perfect target for his bullying.

Lunchtimes were the worst because I didn't seem to have any choice but to go out into the playground and just wait for him to find me. And if I sat in the dining hall, he would deliberately sit next to me and ridicule me to the point where I couldn't even eat my lunch, so I had more or less given up on eating, just so that I could avoid him for a little bit longer. One of the dinner ladies would try and sit me somewhere else, but Barry always seemed to track me down. In fact, I had often spent many a lunch hour hiding in the girls toilet because it was about the only place that Barry wasn't allowed to go, but then my teacher Mrs Greaves found me in there and insisted that I went outside, claiming that lunch breaks were for eating and exercising, and that I should try to stand up for myself a bit more from then on. But just look where that had got me.

A conflicting piece of advice that I was often being offered by 'responsible adults' whenever they realised that I was a little more vulnerable than some of the other children was to "just ignore them". But that seemed to make Barry even more determined than ever. The theory behind this resolution is that the bully will get bored because they are no longer getting any kind of reaction from you. But they are still getting a reaction from their little gang of followers, and as long as they have an audience to 'perform' in front of, bullies will maintain their position of power over both the victim and their so-called friends. Even as a 9 year old, I was emotionally mature enough to know that I would rather be on my own, than in a friendship that was based around intimidation and popularity. The decision to spend the rest of my school life in what felt like complete isolation was quite a bold one though because after I squeezed out through the little gap in the hedgerow and bravely went to confront the consequences of my actions, little did I know then that Barry Harper would be the least of my problems.

I had always been a shy child, often described as a bit of a 'leg hugger'. I would glue myself to my mum's side whenever we were out in public because I was too afraid to discover what life would be like if I managed to venture as far as the other children did. Everyone would praise my mum and dad for raising such a well behaved little girl, before running off to the opposite end of the supermarket in order to remove their own child's grubby little hands from the contents of the pick 'n' mix display. In hindsight, it would have helped if I had been able to stand up for myself a bit more, but there's a very fine line between confidence and precociousness and I still maintain that I would rather be a subservient wimp with no genuine friends, than a spoilt little brat with lots of fake ones.

As well as being a very shy little girl, I was also very pretty, with big almond shaped eyes and long strawberry blonde hair. But during the summer holidays between my transition from infants to juniors, I had to go and have my eyes tested because the words on the white board were beginning to look out of focus. And my strawberry blonde hair, which was gradually becoming darker and darker, was also starting to get a little 'unruly' as my mum termed it, so she took me to have it cut into a more practical bob. Unfortunately, the hairdresser ended up getting rather carried away, and before I knew it, I was looking at what felt like someone else's reflection in the mirror. Any degree of prettiness had just vanished beneath my short dark hair and thick plastic rimmed glasses, and I returned to school in September feeling very deflated.

This transformation also happened to coincide with when all the divisions in our class started forming. Everyone just seemed to sort themselves out into categories of either 'popular' or 'unpopular' and I had no choice but to go along with it. Prior to that, we were all too young to form any kind of genuine and long lasting bonds with each other. Children are very fickle, they don't really base their relationships on anything other than their ability to play together, although I continue to be fascinated by this particular phase in a child's life because at a certain point, everything changes. Personalities begin to define who they are and the type of children who they choose to associate with and relate to. In fact, personalities really begin to take over. Shy and subservient children become withdrawn and quiet, whilst the more wilful children find themselves taking charge of everybody else, almost to the point of intimidating them. I often wonder what bullies like Barry were like as a toddler. What shapes young people into junior versions of the adults whom they later grow into? And how much of the 'nature and nurture' phenomenon is responsible?

That incident out on the school field was just the beginning. Barry Harper had exposed a weakness in me that was rather like tearing a plaster off a wound, and every time we saw each other he was compelled to rub salt into it so that it never had the chance to heal properly. It felt as though I spent the next three years of junior school bracing myself for his potential attacks, a knot of adrenalin so deeply entangled inside my stomach that it would never seem to disappear. I remember feeling so fearful of lunchtimes in particular because he would make a point of tracking me down. Sometimes I was tempted to spend the period between leaving the dining hall and queuing to go back into class, stooped in the same position as I had ended up in that day out on the school field. Seeking solace beneath the thorny branches of a hedgerow and praying for the lunch break to be over. The longest 40 minutes of my life. 40 minutes, five days a week, isolated and alone, wishing I had someone to play with, someone who could stick up for me whenever Barry and his gang approached.

If I could have chosen one of the girls in my class who I would like to have been best friends with it would have to be Kylie Sinclair. She was pretty and popular and always seemed to command respect from everyone, wherever she went. All the boys wanted to marry her and all the girls wanted to be her. In fact, even the teachers thought she was something rather special because she used to excel at everything regardless of which subject it was, particularly sport and performing arts.

Sport was quite a sore point for me because I wasn't in the least bit athletic. I didn't even enjoy visiting playgrounds as a child because the swings made my stomach flip over and the slide was always that little bit too steep for my liking. I remember standing at the foot of the climbing frame and staring longingly up at all the other children as they swung about like a load of acrobatic chimpanzees. It was hard to believe that I was just as close a descendant to the ape as they were because any natural instinct to climb and explore, or push my adventurous tendencies to their limits, completely eluded me. Not only that but whenever I exerted myself in the vaguest possible way, my face would turn the deepest shade of beetroot. So at the end of year 4, when the time came for our annual sports day, I was absolutely petrified. And it was that particular sports day that drew Barry Harper's attention to me for all the wrong reasons.

Of course no climbing was required, but we did have to try and run the length of our running track whilst balancing an egg on a spoon. And it was a real egg and a real spoon back in those days as opposed to the plastic ones that they use for school sports days now. Not only that but as well as being divided up into our house teams, we were also obliged to run the egg and spoon race as a relay along with three other members of our class. Barry was in the green team with me.

My mum came to watch me as she did every year and as she tentatively slid her way to the front of the crowd of parents and stood on the side lines, she looked particularly concerned. It was obvious that she had even less faith in my abilities than I did. In fact, 'cautious' might as well have been her middle name whilst I was growing up because it seemed as though everything was either too high, too fast or just too plain dangerous, which was probably why I ended up with such a profound fear of playgrounds, amongst many other things. Mum liked to wrap me in cotton wool all the time. And rather than pushing me to feel the fear and do it anyway, she had a tendency to just avoid things altogether so that I would very rarely be obliged to step outside of my comfort zone.

That egg and spoon race was such a daunting prospect for me and I remember looking around at all the other children in my class, envying them for coming across as so relaxed and happy whilst I was being consumed by inner turmoil. All those children, parents and teachers watching and waiting for me to screw up, which I inevitably did, although there was always a microscopic part of me that retained a glimmer of hope for the alternative outcome. The outcome that involved me sprinting across the finish line ahead of everyone else and receiving a rapturous applause.

Once the whistle had been blown and I had watched the other three members of our relay team complete their lengths of the track, I suddenly realised that the greens were in first place. As the egg and spoon were passed to me I took a deep breath and stumbled slightly before I managed to remember how to actually place one foot in front of the other. Eventually I was able to gain a bit more momentum and speed as the other members of the relay team jumped up and down and cheered from the side lines. Hearing them chanting my name actually made me feel quite popular for the first time in my life, and as the finish line drew closer, and my closest opposing team member started to gain on me over my shoulder, I held the spoon rigid in my hand and continued to motor forward as best I could. That was until I felt my left knee buckle underneath me causing me to fall forwards and drop the egg on the ground. My right foot plummeted towards the egg before I had a chance to pick it up and put it back on my spoon. As the shell shattered beneath the rubber sole of my trainer and its slimy contents leaked out, I skidded dramatically across the slippery grass and fell onto my bottom with a hard thud as all the other children overtook me and reached the finish line.

The other members of my relay team were shouting at me for letting them all down, their supportive chants turned to heckles of disgust and displeasure. The other house teams in contrast were laughing and teasing me for being so clumsy. And as I looked back at where my mum was standing, I realised that she had her hand over her mouth in pure horror. Everything felt as though it was closing in around me and I was incapable of standing up.

"Clear the running track!" shouted the head teacher. "We need to set up for the obstacle race."

But my bottom felt glued to the spot. I was literally rigid with fear. Eventually my mum had to come over and help me back onto my feet again stimulating the heckles from the crowd to get even louder, and as I looked at the mortified expression on mum's face and thought about how disappointed she must have been in me, I burst into tears.

"I want to go home," I blubbed feeling utterly humiliated, not only at having fallen over and lost the race, but at my inability to get up from the ground by myself. But going home early simply

postponed the inevitable because when I returned to school the following day, no one, particularly the other members of the green house team, had forgotten about what had happened the day before. And whilst the novelty of sports day was quickly replaced by the excitement of the last week of term, it seemed that my reputation as 'Egg Girl' would stick around for some time to come.

Chapter three

Friday 26th April 2019

"How was your day?" enquired Amy, as Jules eventually returned home a few hours later.

Amy was Jules' house mate. They lived in a very characteristic two bedroom Victorian terrace, which they had been renting together since leaving university. It had a cosy sitting room with a bay window, high ceilings and an original fireplace, and the kitchen to the rear was small but functional. They had met at university when Jules was taking her psychology degree, and although Amy had followed an entirely different career path, she still ended up providing a counselling service for Jules at the end of a difficult day.

"Not great," replied Jules, pouring herself a large glass of red wine before she had even taken her coat off. Fortunately it was Friday though so this was practically compulsory in their house.

"It's only the first week back after the Easter holidays and I've already ended up in Accident and Emergency with one of my students," she explained, before resisting the urge to elaborate in the fear that this would be classed as 'breaching patient confidentiality'.

"I've ordered us an Indian takeaway," replied Amy, rubbing Jules' back reassuringly as she followed her through to the sitting room.

"She's OK, it was just a minor injury," added Jules "And on the plus side, I met someone."

Amy's ears pricked up and she almost spilt her wine as she turned to face Jules on the sofa. This was the first time Jules had 'met anyone' in what felt like forever. In fact, with the exception of Greg, her boyfriend from university who had left her heart shattered into a thousand pieces, Jules had never really spoken of another male in a potentially romantic sense before.

"Tell me more," she insisted "I want to hear *all* the details!"

"There's not really much to tell," replied Jules, as a smirk started to creep across her face.

"But you're smirking," continued Amy "You *never* smirk. Where did you meet and when are you seeing him again?"

"We met at the hospital today," Jules explained before allowing her smirk to develop into a fully blown smile. "He's a doctor and he's absolutely gorgeous. His name's Drew but I'm afraid we won't be seeing each other again because I only spoke to him very briefly when he was discharging my student from A&E and I just wasn't brave enough to ask him out. He's probably got a girlfriend anyway."

Amy's excited facial expression dropped and she placed her glass of wine down on the coffee table in front of her in disappointment. She was hoping that Jules had actually agreed to go on a date with someone at the very least. Just as she was about to interrogate her further, their front door bell rang and Jules disappeared into the hall in order to collect their bag of takeaway food from the delivery boy on the doorstep. How could Amy persuade her to have more confidence in her ability to attract members of the opposite sex? She had always suffered from low self-esteem, particularly following her break up with Greg. But that was four years ago now. Would she ever feel comfortable enough to put herself out there again, and to leave herself open to potential rejection?

"I think we should go speed dating," suggested Amy, as Jules re-entered the sitting room carrying two dinner plates stacked high with their cartons of Indian food. "You need to remind yourself how to partake in a little bit of harmless flirtation, instead of just shutting down all the time in the fear that no one will fancy you."

Jules considered the concept for a moment as she started peeling the cardboard lids from all the foil cartons and laying them out on the table in front of them.

"You really do mean harmless, don't you?" she clarified before reminding herself that Amy was already in a long term relationship and was therefore very unlikely to do anything that could jeopardise that.

Whether Amy being there could jeopardise Jules' *own* chances of attracting anyone on the other hand, would remain to be seen. After all, Amy was stunning. She had long blonde hair, a size 8 figure and big green eyes that seemed to just draw men towards her wherever she went. When they were at university, Jules often felt like the insignificant friend who was just there to keep Amy company while she flirted with every red blooded male in the room. Jules often ended up getting very drunk and emotional before disappearing into the ladies toilets and staring at her pathetic reflection in the mirror. She wasn't exactly unattractive. In fact, if anything, she had really managed to transform herself from the ugly duckling of her teenage years into a beautiful swan in her early twenties. Her chocolate brown hair hung neatly around her shoulders, and her almond shaped eyes and wide smile were often described as very warm and welcoming. But as soon as she found herself in a potentially romantic situation, she just put her barriers up because she couldn't bear the thought of being rejected again.

The following morning, after rolling out of bed with what felt like a bit of a hangover, Jules pulled on an old pair of jogging bottoms and a sweatshirt, and snuck out of the house to buy some milk at the local shop. She and Amy had ended up getting through almost two bottles of wine the night before as they attempted to put Jules' relationship status to rights, and it was only after the first bottle had been finished that she eventually agreed to go speed dating at their local pub the following weekend. A decision that she was beginning to regret already as she rubbed her tired eyes and tied her rather unruly looking hair out of her face with an elastic band.

"Good morning Mr Shah," she smiled at the shop keeper as she pinged the door open and went straight to the milk fridge.

"Good morning Miss Croft," replied Mr Shah from the top of his step ladder, as he continued to stock up the top shelf of groceries. "What can I do for you today?"

"I just need some semi-skimmed," explained Jules, before stopping to look at the irresistible display of 'reduced to clear' Easter eggs by the till. Just as she was about to help herself to one, she managed to get the sleeve of her sweatshirt caught in the Perspex price holder underneath and the entire display became dislodged. Before she knew it, the floor in front of the till point was covered in chocolate foil wrapped eggs. She sensed that someone was stooping down next to her in order to pick them up, and before she could react fast enough, their hands touched by mistake.

"I'm so sorry" she apologised, feeling her face flush as she looked up at the kind gentleman opposite her on his hands and knees. But it was only once he had looked up too that she discovered who he was.

"Hello again," smiled Drew, "Didn't we meet at the hospital yesterday?"

Jules remembered that her hair was a mess, that she was wearing her old jogging bottoms and that she had absolutely no makeup on whatsoever, and she just wanted the ground to swallow her up.

"That's right," she replied, trying to sound laid back about their encounter, almost as though she had barely spared him a moment's thought ever since. "Thanks again for looking after Louisa for me."

"I was just doing my job," replied Drew, placing the final few Easter eggs back on their display. "It was nice to see you again."

Jules' stomach was doing somersaults as he left the shop, particularly once he had caught her eye again through the window and smiled. He really was gorgeous. As she counted out enough loose change to pay for the milk and chocolate and slid it across the counter to Mr Shah, he recognised the infatuated expression on her face and laughed.

"Knocking that display over was a very clever way of getting his attention. I just hope you haven't damaged any of my stock!"

"Is he new to the neighbourhood?" Jules enquired "I would definitely remember if I'd seen him around here before."

"He's just got a job at the hospital," explained Mr Shah, confirming what she already knew. "I'm afraid I don't know where he lives though. Perhaps you should follow him home?"

"Very funny!" laughed Jules, collecting her shopping from the counter. Now that she had some milk, she could go home and have a bowl of cereal. It wasn't even breakfast time yet and she had experienced more than enough drama for one Saturday morning already.

When Jules got home, Amy was sitting at the breakfast bar in their kitchen looking at one of their old university friend's Facebook profiles on her tablet. Jules was one of the few people she knew who refused to use Facebook, mainly because she was a firm believer in living in the present as opposed to the past. She just failed to see the point of keeping up to date with people who she hadn't seen in years. After all, if they were meant to remain a part of her life then they would still be friends with her now.

"Tania's getting married next year," announced Amy, as Jules flicked the kettle on to make them both a cup of tea. "And Sarah's having a baby."

It would seem that Jules didn't even need to have a Facebook profile of her own in order to keep up to date with what everyone from university was doing now because Amy always persisted on filling her in anyway, whether she liked it or not. And who cared what Tania and Sarah were doing now? Jules hadn't heard from either of them in years. Amy was rather fascinated with how many engagements and pregnancies there were though because she and her boyfriend Tim had been together for four years and he still hadn't even so much as hinted at a potential proposal.

"I really don't understand why you're always looking at that. I'm just not interested in making contact with anyone from my past," explained Jules. "People you haven't seen or spoken to in years just start coming out of the woodwork and prying into your personal life as though it's some kind of competition. Who's got the most successful career or the best looking spouse or the cutest children... it's so conceited."

"Who are you so afraid of?" replied Amy, looking up from her tablet briefly. "I don't understand why you always have such strong views about it". She then glanced down at Jules' left arm and stopped talking immediately.

"You won't believe who I've just bumped into in Mr Shah's shop." announced Jules, happily changing the subject. Amy spun round on her bar stool so that she was fully facing her, and studied her facial expression.

"Not Dr Dish?" she concluded immediately. "It must be fate."

"What, fate that he sees me looking like *this*?" complained Jules. "At least yesterday I was wearing makeup and I had my best suit on."

"Don't worry about it," insisted Amy, putting her tablet down and pouring the tea. "Men don't even notice these things."

"That's easy for you to say," Jules observed. "Are you sure this speed dating is such a good idea?"

"Definitely," replied Amy without any hesitation. "Just as long as you don't wear your jogging bottoms!"

Jules was mortified at the thought; of all the times to bump into him again. She wouldn't be able to leave the house anymore without being on constant red alert for him roaming the streets of their neighbourhood. As if he didn't have anything better to do of course, but now that she knew he lived locally, there would always be the possibility and that was enough for her to become a paranoid mess. Paranoia was another one of her less attractive personality traits, thanks to the unfortunate experiences in her past. She was convinced that other people were persistently watching her and judging her every move. And she was also prone to over analysing everything after it had happened. Amy liked to refer to Jules' analyses as 'post mortems' and she just knew that Jules would be picking apart the incident in Mr Shah's shop for many weeks to come, even though Drew probably hadn't even given it a second thought.

Friday 3rd May 2019

Jules had studied 'nature and nurture' as part of her psychology degree. She was hoping to try and draw from her experiences in this field in order to make sense of the situation between Caitlin and Louisa, but until she could find out a little more about each of her clients, she would be unable to base her conclusions on anything rock solid. So during her next counselling session with Caitlin that Friday, she ventured to delve into her personal life a little. And she was pleasantly surprised with how receptive Caitlin was on this occasion.

"My mum and dad aren't together anymore," explained Caitlin, softening her expression slightly, as she began kicking the leg of Jules' desk again. Without wishing to think of Caitlin's situation as an open and shut case, Jules was determined to hear the full story before she jumped to any conclusions or judgements. After all, 'broken homes' were a lot more common place *now* than they were when she was at school.

"I live with my mum and my step dad and I visit my dad every other weekend."

Jules had a great deal of sympathy for single parent families and was wholeheartedly in agreement of the fact that a couple should never stay together just for the sake of the children. But she couldn't help but sympathise with all the disruption it caused.

"How is your relationship with your parents?" she casually enquired, trying not to sound too intense.

Caitlin simply shrugged her shoulders in reply. Jules should have been able to answer that question for herself. Teenagers, after all, were notorious for not getting on with their parents. So she tried to re-phrase the question slightly:

"Do you talk to them about anything?"

"Not really," explained Caitlin, before opening her mouth again as though she was about to elaborate. Jules sat upright in her chair expectantly, but then Caitlin decided to stare out of the window instead.

Jules usually used to feel as though she could talk to her mum and dad. It was just unfortunate that the teachers weren't quite as supportive towards her situation. And she certainly didn't have a pastoral support officer who she could confide in. She was just about to probe Caitlin further when there was a knock at the door. Mr Ellington, one of the science teachers was hovering outside in the corridor holding a handful of paperwork which he reluctantly passed over to her with an embarrassed expression on his face.

"It's Louisa's biology homework," he explained. "We were talking about reproduction last week and I asked her to hand write her class notes as punishment for missing the lesson on Friday."

It had been a while since Jules had seen any hand written school work, everything seemed to be done on the computer these days. It was clear to see why Mr Ellington was showing the papers to her though because they had been completely defaced in a particularly inappropriate way.

"Caitlin?" she concluded, lowering her voice and then feeling the disappointment wash over her. She really felt as though she was making progress today by getting her to open up about her family, but this kind of behaviour was totally unacceptable.

"She will be disciplined," he explained. "Her mother's being summoned to the school as we speak. Perhaps you could keep Caitlin here until she arrives and then we can all have a meeting together? It's probably best to keep Louisa out of it at this stage though."

Jules nodded in approval and then quietly closed her office door feeling deflated. On the plus side, at least she would have the opportunity to meet Caitlin's mum.

Chapter four

September 1995

Even the summer holidays, six entire weeks for everyone to forget about what had happened on that fateful sports day, wasn't long enough for me to shake off my new nickname. Particularly thanks to Barry Harper who hid an egg inside my plimsoll on our first day in year 5 so that when I stepped into it before morning registration, my foot became covered in sticky egg white, slimy yellow yolk and sharp crunchy fragments of shell. Maybe I should have told Mrs Greaves about it but I was too afraid that Barry would accuse me of being a 'grass' so I simply limped off to the girls toilets to clean myself up and then crept into the classroom wearing my outdoor shoes in the hope that no one would notice.

"You're supposed to be wearing your plimsolls when you're inside Julia," Mrs Greaves observed.

"I need new ones Miss," I replied, stealing a glance in Barry's direction. "My feet have grown over the summer holidays and my mum hasn't got around to buying me a new pair yet."

"Well, see that she does," instructed Mrs Greaves. "Outdoor shoes bring lots of dirt into the classroom."

"Yes Miss," I mumbled under my breath as she began to address the whole class by asking us if we had all enjoyed our summer break.

Mrs Greaves seemed a lot older than she actually was and she certainly didn't do anything to help this fact because her clothes were particularly old fashioned. She usually wore a brightly coloured floral print skirt with a patterned top that always clashed, and her greying hair was fastened into a beehive bun with long metal hair pins.

Unfortunately Mrs Greaves' impression of me continued to deteriorate throughout the course of my time in year 5, and Barry was largely responsible for that because he knew that the more trouble he caused for me, the less likely I was to tell anyone about it in the fear that things would end up getting even worse. Looking back, junior school, as it was known then, and in particular years 5 and 6, were an extremely negative time in my life. Generally speaking, I suppose I probably had my good days and my bad days but there are a number of specific incidents that remain etched in my memory for all the wrong reasons, including the year 4 sports day and the hedgerow hideout, and these affected me quite profoundly. When you're repeatedly bullied at primary school you're not emotionally mature enough to understand how damaging it can be to your self-esteem. But if you get treated as though you're utterly worthless often enough, you do start to actually believe it after a while and it can be very difficult to learn how to trust people. I know now that I should have trusted Mrs Greaves but I found it almost impossible to open up to anyone at the time. And Mrs Greaves was a firm believer in 'tough love' which completely went against all of my mum's beliefs. So I didn't really find her very approachable and I suppose I probably convinced myself that she was likely to choose Barry's word over mine anyway.

The only time she was actually a witness to one of his attacks was when he referred to me as 'Egg Girl' in the dining hall one lunchtime because I had foolishly chosen to try and eat one of my egg sandwiches that my mum had packed for me in my lunchbox.

"Egg Girl!" he teased, once he had managed to confirm what my sandwich filling was, compelling me to force it back into my lunchbox and click the lid shut before anyone else could notice.

"Just ignore him, he'll soon get bored," advised Mrs Greaves who was standing behind Barry at the time. As soon as he realised she was there he scurried away to join his mates at the table by the window. Suffice to say I felt very hungry for the rest of the afternoon and was not at all happy with my mum for her insensitive choice of sandwich filling.

❖

I've always been one of those overly conscientious people, constantly fearful of getting in everybody else's way when I'm walking down the street, or steering my shopping trolley around the supermarket, terrified of saying or doing anything that might offend anyone. I tend to try and put myself in somebody else's shoes and then look at me through their eyes, speculating about how they feel and what they think and endlessly analysing every last little conversation we had in the fear that it might have been misconstrued. But the chances are many of the concerns that keep me awake at night are completely unjustified, because other people don't think about these things at all. And in some ways this usually ends up disappointing me because if everybody else was that little bit more conscientious, the world would be a far nicer place.

It's no great surprise that I'm so anxious of other people's opinions of me because I spent a large percentage of my childhood being told that I simply wasn't worth the effort. So now I'm just a pathological 'people pleaser', agreeing to things that I don't even want to do so that everybody else is happy even if I'm not, because I can't possibly run the risk of disappointing anyone or not stepping into the gutter when they're walking down the street towards me.

I suppose I ought to try and remember that I'm important too, but when you are as shy and socially anxious as I am, it isn't always as easy as that. Mud sticks and I've really had my fair share flung at me over the years. Even after I left school and eventually went on to university, I managed to find myself involved in the wrong kind of relationships. Men who broke my heart, and women who gained my trust and then trampled all over it once they had managed to get what they wanted out of me, which was usually a sympathetic ear and a shoulder to cry on, or something rather more materialistic like a financial loan. I had even been used as a cover story for some of the other students that I shared a Halls of Residence with to avoid them getting into trouble with the Dean. A consequence of which resulted in me getting into trouble myself.

Fortunately, in my second year at university, I had met Amy who was three years younger than me, because rather than having a gap year after I left school, I actually ended up having three 'gap years' in which I summoned up the courage to take the A-levels that I was unable to go and work towards when I was 17. These A-levels included psychology, a subject that I was inspired to pursue following the months of counselling that I arranged for myself to have during my GCSEs. So when I later went on to do a degree in it at university, it became increasingly clear where my career path would lead.

Amy, on the other hand, was studying some rather different areas of Science in order to become a physiotherapist. We got chatting in the student union bar one evening at the end of our first year, and she told me that she was looking for someone to share a house with her in September. Three months later we moved in together and we haven't looked back since.

Chapter five

Saturday 4th May 2019

Saturday evening seemed to come around so quickly and before she knew it, Jules was getting herself ready to go speed dating with Amy.

"Remind me why I agreed to this again?" she groaned, frowning at her reflection in the full length mirror in her bedroom. Amy was lying on her bed waiting for the bright red varnish on her fingernails to dry; she was looking absolutely stunning as usual.

"Because you need to learn how to actually talk to members of the opposite sex without spontaneously combusting with embarrassment," she replied, before adding "And because you had just drunk the best part of a bottle of wine!"

"I feel like I could do with one of those now!" laughed Jules, as she turned around and tried to scrutinise the back of her outfit. Amy gauged that she was in need of a compliment and declared that she looked beautiful. But Jules never felt very beautiful when she compared herself with Amy, even in spite of her ability to 'scrub up well' as her dad described it. It was amazing what a spray tan, a manicure and a cut and blow dry could do. Jules didn't often agree to treat herself to any kind of pampering whatsoever but she decided that she needed all the confidence boosters she could get before embarking on her speed dating ventures, so she had booked herself in to the local salon for a full top to toe treatment.

"Is my make-up alright?" she enquired, fiddling with one of her contact lenses. "I don't usually wear eye shadow."

"You've got absolutely nothing to worry about," insisted Amy, sliding off the bed and squirting Jules with some perfume.

"That's easy for you to say," replied Jules, slipping into a long sleeved black cardigan with sequins around the neckline. "You've already got a boyfriend."

In spite of the fact that Tim seemed to be incapable of picking up on any of Amy's engagement hints, he was clearly very much in love with her, so much so in fact that he had agreed to let her go speed dating while he sat on his own in their flat with a takeaway pizza and a four pack of beer. Although Amy suspected that he was just hoping to ensure that she didn't go home with anyone else.

"Wow Jules, you look gorgeous!" Tim exclaimed, admiring her little black dress as she entered the sitting room looking for her handbag. Jules looked at him and blushed.

"Thanks," she smiled, stealing a sip of beer from the opened can on the coffee table. "I'm so nervous."

"Just enjoy it," insisted Tim. "And remember to be yourself."

❖

When they arrived at the pub, Jules wasted no time in ordering herself a large glass of white wine from the bar. Not only was she extremely nervous about the prospect of trying to initiate small talk with over a dozen different men during the course of the evening, but she had also had another very difficult week at work. Caitlin's mother had failed to turn up to their meeting at the school, prompting Mr Ellington to suspend Caitlin until further notice. In a desperate attempt to try and salvage the situation for fear of failing *both* of her students, Jules resolved to go and visit Caitlin and Mrs Murphy at home first thing on Tuesday morning, straight after the bank holiday weekend. And this was a prospect that she was looking forward to even less than the speed dating.

"Try not to look so nervous," insisted Amy, perching herself on a bar stool. "Your shoulders are all hunched; just relax."

Jules remained rooted to the spot and simply stared at the specials board in front of her as one of the staff rubbed out the 'soup of the day' and replaced it with the words 'love is in the air...' Meanwhile, Amy, who seemed to exude confidence from every pore as she sat and waited for the speed dating to commence, decided to take the opportunity to have a look around the pub at all the various different men who were arriving, in the hope of finding someone suitable for Jules. Many of them seemed to look quite business-like. Presumably they were young professionals who were just too busy to find romance in the conventional way, although why they had chosen to wear a suit on a Saturday night was puzzling and could also be construed as rather vain and arrogant. So she then tried to pick out any men who were wearing smart trousers and a shirt, which implied that they had made just the right amount of effort to look nice without trying too hard. And by the time she had ruled out anyone who appeared to be either too young, too old, too short, too fat or too bald, she finally settled on a tall, dark and handsome 'thirty something' who was standing on his own by the door and staring uncertainly at his score card.

She was just about to point him out to Jules when the bell rang, reminding all the women to take a seat at separate tables for two, ready for their first 'date'. Jules took a seat by the window, where she then proceeded to look longingly outside, wishing she could escape this unbearably embarrassing scenario. Social situations had always been a challenge for her because she was extremely self-conscious. Whenever she stepped foot into a public place it felt as though everyone was staring at her and just waiting for her to humiliate herself by doing something wrong. Of course she had studied social anxiety as part of her psychology degree and she was painfully aware of what was primarily to blame for it, which was why she was determined to try and help other people to overcome the effects of bullying before they had a chance to become too deeply rooted.

Eventually the bell rang again and all the men went to find the table number that corresponded with the number on the badges that they had been given when they arrived. Jules found herself opposite a 'forty something' business type with a sharp suit and slicked back hair.

"I'm Fraser" he smiled, introducing himself and then looking down at Jules' cleavage.

"Jules" she replied, feeling her invisible defence field shoot up as he tucked his legs so far under the table that she could actually feel his knees touching hers. She slid her seat back tentatively and then crossed her legs towards the window instead as he continued to admire her outfit with an unnerving expression on his face.

"You're beautiful Jules; if you don't mind me saying," he grinned. "Tell me about yourself. What do you do for a living?"

Jules *did* mind, but she knew that if she was going to put herself through something like this, she needed to enter into the spirit of the occasion wholeheartedly. After all, it wasn't as though she was ever going to see this man again after tonight, whether *he* actually wanted to or not.

"I'm a pastoral support officer," she replied, trying to soften her expression slightly. "I've recently started working with some of the young people at the local secondary school, offering counselling amongst other things. What do you do?"

"I'm a banker," announced Fraser, rather boldly. "I work in Canary Wharf." He sounded quite proud of his profession, which, Jules concluded, was something to be admired, particularly as bankers were always getting such a hard time from everyone. But Jules also knew that anyone working in Canary Wharf was probably too busy to have a relationship because they were renowned for working a 60 hour week, in which case speed dating was probably the only way that Fraser could actually meet anyone.

In the three minutes that followed, Jules felt as though she was glazing over a bit and she had already made her mind up that

Fraser deserved no more than a 2 or 3 out of 10. It was clear that he was far more in love with himself than he could ever be with a member of the opposite sex, but she decided to indulge him in some harmless banter anyway and massaged his ego with anecdotes about the stock market. He didn't appear to be particularly interested in her, but Jules was rather relieved about that to a certain extent because she hated having to talk about herself. Not wanting to be the centre of attention was one of the reasons why she was friends with someone as outgoing as Amy.

Three minutes seemed to tick by at an unbearably slow pace, but no sooner had she escaped from Fraser's mental undressing, than another man had taken his place. And this 'date' was just as uncomfortable for entirely different reasons. His name was Martin and he was tall, skinny and red haired. He appeared to be extremely shy and unassuming and could barely manage to maintain eye contact with her for more than a couple of seconds before staring down at the table instead. Jules actually felt quite sorry for him.

"I'm an IT manager," he explained when she asked him what he did for a living. A computer nerd seemed to suit him although she couldn't quite fathom how he was able to actually 'manage' anyone. They ended up passing the time of day by talking about the weather for the next couple of minutes as Martin seemed to have quite an in depth knowledge about the Met Office. He also gave a bit of a history lesson about the pub they were in. The conversation flowed quite effortlessly after that because neither of them was obliged to talk about themselves anymore, although it was clear that their mutual interest in each other was virtually non-existent so Jules marked her scorecard with another 3 out of 10 as soon as he had vacated her table.

She found herself feeling fairly indifferent as far as her following two 'dates' were concerned. They both seemed perfectly nice and normal, although one of them was a little on the immature side and persisted with making jokes all the time. Julia couldn't decide whether he was using his sense of humour as a defence mechanism because he felt embarrassed about the situation, but she scored him a 6 out of 10 anyway, just in case. Amy would have been quite impressed with the other one because he was young and athletic looking like Tim and seemed to know what the right thing to say was. Jules felt that he was probably a little *too* smooth for her liking, she preferred the more 'wholesome' type, but he earned himself a 7 out of 10 as he went sauntering off towards Amy's table encouraging Jules to lean over and smile at her behind his back.

Jules stared at her score card and sighed. She knew that she wasn't really here in the hope of actually meeting 'Mr Right', she simply needed to try and brush up on her social skills a little bit. But there was a small part of her that was hoping that she might end up meeting the man of her dreams anyway, so that she could curl up in his warm arms on a Saturday night and smile smugly at the thought of all these other single girls out on their speed dating ventures.

Date number 5 was even more of a disappointment than the first 4 and he gave Jules a very uneasy feeling as he sat down opposite her. He was a little on the overweight side with greasy unwashed looking hair and dark circles under his eyes. He certainly wouldn't score very much for attractiveness, she thought to herself as she half-heartedly shook hands with him. His palms were warm and clammy and she wiped her hand discreetly on her dress afterwards. Perhaps his personality would manage to win her over.

"You seem familiar," she then frowned as he flicked his mop of greasy hair out of his eyes. "Have we met before?"

"I think I would remember someone as stunning as you," he smiled suggestively revealing a large mouth of nicotine stained teeth which looked as though they had been straightened by a brace at some point. Jules tried not to grimace at the smell of stale cigarette smoke on his breath as he leaned towards her across the table. First Fraser and now this guy; how many more creeps would she be obliged to waste three minutes of her life with this evening?

"Do you fancy coming to a party with me after this?" he continued, ignoring the distasteful expression on Jules' face.

"You don't even know anything about me yet," Jules retorted.

"You're gorgeous," replied her date. "I don't need to know anything else."

Come back Fraser, all is forgiven, Jules thought as she tried really hard to work out why this creep looked so familiar. He made her feel very uneasy and that was without the addition of all his lecherous comments.

"What's your name?" she frowned as a feeling of panic started to rise inside her.

"Craig," he replied, forcing Jules to slam her hand over her mouth.

"Craig Riley?" she then verified feeling her legs turn to jelly, and not in a good way.

"That's right," he beamed. "And you are?"

"Julia," revealed Jules firmly, starting to stand up from the table "Julia Croft. You used to use my head as target practice when you and your mates were playing football together at secondary school."

"Did I?" frowned Craig. "Sorry about that. So how about you come to this party with me and we can get to know each other again." He was smiling suggestively once more.

"I wouldn't agree to go to a party with you if you were the last man on earth!" Jules snapped. "You made my life a misery."

As her voice became raised, Amy realised that Jules was standing up and then mouthed "Are you OK?" at her from across the pub.

When Jules shook her head, Amy gestured for her to sit back down, but when Jules reminded herself of how vile Craig was, she was filled with an overwhelming urge to run home. The past 17 years hadn't been particularly kind to him. When she was 16 he was the school heart throb and all the girls fancied him, including her. Now he just looked scruffy and haggard, almost unrecognisable in fact.

"Are you sure I used to bully you at school?" he frowned scratching his head, and then something dawned on him.

"Hang on a minute," he announced. "You're the girl who ended up in hospital!"

Just as she was about to be saved by the bell, Jules felt as though she was going to faint. The room started spinning and then everything went out of focus as the heat rose in her body and her pulse began to pound rapidly in her ears. She wobbled a little but managed not to lose consciousness, stumbling instead into the arms of date number 6.

"We really should stop meeting like this," he smiled, helping her back into her chair and passing her a glass of water. "It's a good job I'm a doctor!"

"Dr Dish..." she gushed, as soon as she was able to identify who the muscular arms which had caught her belonged to.

"...erm, I mean Dr Drew..." she then amended before feeling her face flush.

"Just Drew will do," he smiled, encouraging her entire body to flush as well. Her heart continued beating rapidly in her chest and her stomach started doing somersaults but it was definitely in a good way this time. It never ceased to amaze her what an effect he seemed to have on her.

"I'm so sorry," she insisted. "It's just a stupid name that my friend made up."

"You've been talking to your friends about me?" Drew clarified, before smiling again. "That does sound promising."

Jules wanted the ground to swallow her up. What on *earth* was she thinking telling him something like that? She had just managed to make an embarrassing situation about a thousand times worse. But what was he doing here? He must have been providing some moral support to one of his friends, just like Amy was. He couldn't possibly be single, he was far too gorgeous.

"Are you OK now? You looked like you were about to pass out."

Jules nodded and then looked across at Amy's table where Craig now appeared to be completely oblivious to the scornful expression on her face as he attempted to chat her up.

"I used to know that guy and he wasn't very nice to me. But let's not waste the next three minutes talking about him."

"You look lovely by the way," Drew observed, changing the subject and trying to pay Jules a compliment at the same time.

"At least I'm not wearing jogging bottoms this time," laughed Jules, running a nervous hand through her hair and gripping the stem of her wine glass tightly. "I was a bit of a mess that morning. Not to mention hung-over."

What did she want to go and tell him something like that for? He would probably think she was some kind of alcoholic now.

"I thought you looked rather lovely then as well," replied Drew. "I'm just sorry I couldn't stay and talk to you. I was on a late shift at work and I had a million errands to run that morning. It's good to see you again now though."

"I hear you're new to the area," smiled Jules, allowing herself to relax a little. "Have you and your girlfriend moved here to be closer to family?"

"I don't have a girlfriend," confirmed Drew. "I moved here because of my job; to be closer to the hospital."

Jules observed that he was not wearing a wedding ring and decided to conclude that he probably was single after all. She still wasn't prepared to consider asking him out though because he was completely out of her league and was probably just paying her compliments because he felt sorry for her.

"So apart from almost passing out, how are you enjoying the evening?" he asked, allowing a big smile to spread across his face. "I've never done anything like this before; have you?"

"No, never; it was my friend Amy's idea," explained Jules, pointing towards Amy's table. "She's hoping I might gain a bit more self-confidence."

Drew's eyes observed her with interest. "But I thought you were a psychologist? Shouldn't you know all about that sort of thing?"

"I do," replied Jules. "I'm just not very good at practising what I preach."

"Well that's a real shame," smiled Drew, before reaching across the table and gently placing his hand on top of hers. "Because you seem like a very beautiful person, inside and out."

Jules wasn't used to being complimented so much and she started to question Drew's sincerity. Were his motives entirely honourable or was he just another smooth talker like Fraser? It felt very nice holding hands with him though, and she had to admit, there was something very genuine about him. She just found it so hard to trust people, particularly members of the opposite sex. It felt as though she had been let down or hurt so many times in the past. Putting her barriers up was merely an act of self-preservation.

When Jules failed to respond to Drew's advances, he decided to pull his hand away and change the subject again. They were both more than happy to make small talk with each other for the remaining few minutes of their date because the conversation just seemed to flow so effortlessly. When Drew wasn't paying her compliments, he was actually one of the most easy going people

Jules had ever met, and in spite of her attraction to him, Jules felt extremely comfortable in his presence. And it was only after he had vacated her table in order to go and introduce himself to her jaw droppingly beautiful friend that she realised she was insanely jealous of Amy, and wasn't in the least bit interested in her own date number seven. Amy smiled at her again as Jules unfolded her score card and discreetly scribbled a 10 out of 10 next to Drew's name. She was really beginning to fall for him now and there was nothing that she could do about it.

❖

"Remind me never to go along with any more of your crazy dating suggestions," Jules complained, as she and Amy staggered home arm in arm.

"*I* really enjoyed it!" exclaimed Amy, shoving Jules towards the curb in order to avoid walking through a puddle in her new pair of heels.

"Well that's because you get to go to bed with Tim tonight," replied Jules. "*My* bed, on the other hand, will feel even emptier than ever."

"I had no idea that you were hoping for a one night stand!" Amy teased her.

"You know what I mean," Jules cringed. "I needed to prove to myself that I'm capable of meeting someone, but all the speed dating has proved is that I can't even pull anyone who I'm not actually interested in."

"That's because they *know* you're not interested," explained Amy, stopping to pull her shoes off altogether so that she could hobble along the pavement in bare feet. "And besides, if you don't fancy them anyway, who cares?"

Jules hesitated at that point. She was desperate to tell Amy that 'Dr Dish' had been her sixth date of the evening, but the fact that Amy had failed to mention it first, just proved that Drew obviously hadn't bothered to make himself known to her, and that was the only indication that Jules needed in order to confirm to herself that he wasn't genuinely interested in taking their chance encounters any further. After all, Drew knew that Amy was her best friend before he went to sit at her table. If he was in the least bit attracted to Jules then he could have taken that opportunity to introduce himself properly, because he was aware that they had been talking about him.

Not only that, but he had also failed to hang around in the bar after the speed dating had finished. And Jules felt so ashamed for believing that anything could possibly happen between them, that she ordered herself another large glass of wine, deciding there and then that she would keep his identity to herself, and that she wouldn't even tell Amy about it.

"Are you OK? You've gone quiet," Amy interrupted her thoughts, as they turned the corner into their street.

"You're not thinking about Creepy Craig are you?"

Jules shuddered at the memory. "I'm just tired. I could do with an early night."

"Well it's a bit late for that!" laughed Amy, checking the time on her phone as she rummaged in her handbag for the house keys. "Can I tempt you with a hot chocolate before you go upstairs?"

"Just a hug will do," Jules replied, as they hobbled up to their front door and let themselves in. They stood in their hallway and held each other, and Jules was suddenly struck with the overwhelming urge to cry. She often found herself feeling very emotional after a few drinks, but this was different. This reminded her of a feeling that she had experienced many times when she was standing in the corner of the playground as a child. And as she kissed Amy goodnight and made her way up the stairs to her empty bed, she realised what the feeling was. It was the feeling of being alone.

Chapter six

Tuesday 7th May 2019

Before Jules knew it, the bank holiday weekend was over and it was the beginning of another working week again. Sunday and Monday seemed to have passed her by like some kind of trance, as she had ended up hibernating in her bedroom for two days, watching 'chick flicks' and eating chocolate. She hadn't even managed to change out of her pyjamas, and she had cancelled her usual visit to her parent's house for Sunday lunch, claiming that she was in bed with a bad headache. But it wasn't a hangover that was causing her to feel so bad. In fact she felt completely and utterly empty inside, almost as though Drew had opened up her chest and ripped her heart out. Amy had tried hard to entice her downstairs several times by tempting her with all kinds of suggestions, but she wasn't even interested in walking down to the local park on Monday to watch Tim and his equally athletic friends playing football in the spring sunshine.

"It's a beautiful day out there," insisted Amy, climbing on to the bed next to Jules. "And some of Tim's friends are very nice."

Jules pulled the bed covers up over her head and groaned when she recalled the fact that she had once snogged one of them because she thought he reminded her of her ex-boyfriend, Greg. But then she had discovered that they were all even more vain and shallow than Tim was, and Jules preferred her men to have a little more 'substance' than that. She wanted to go out with someone who she could take home and meet her parents. Someone who was thoughtful without being possessive; well-presented without feeling the need to spend more time in the bathroom than she did; and sufficiently laid back without being in danger of taking her for granted. Someone like Drew.

As she pulled up in the car park outside the school and picked her handbag up from the passenger seat, she was confronted by Mr

Ellington who was loitering outside her car with an uneasy expression on his face. And she knew exactly what he was going to say before she had even managed to get her car door open.

"Caitlin Murphy."

"Good morning to you too Mr Ellington," Jules smiled, trying to make light of the situation. "How was your weekend?"

Mr Ellington's expression softened slightly as he adjusted his glasses and assured her that it had been very pleasant. But then he continued to remind her that Caitlin had been suspended and that she had agreed to go and visit her at home that morning.

"I haven't forgotten," replied Jules, reassuringly. "I just need to speak to Mr Langley first, but I'll make sure I let you know how I get on."

"That would be very much appreciated," replied Mr Ellington as he followed Jules to the building in which her temporary office was located. "And do let me know if there's anything I can do to help."

"I doubt it," Jules muttered under her breath as she smiled and waved at Mr Ellington from the refuge of her office doorway before slowly closing the door in his face. And as she reminded herself of the large pile of case notes on her desk, she thought about her warm bed and her big bar of chocolate, and wished that it was yesterday all over again.

Mr Langley was the deputy head, who had been keeping the position of Pinewood's regular head teacher filled during her maternity leave. He had arranged to come and see Jules after morning assembly so she decided to take the opportunity to check her emails first. As her computer began to fire itself up, she rummaged in her handbag for her phone and then came across her score card from Saturday night. 'Is love in the air for you?' it read. 'Remember to register your scores online and find out who you're compatible with'. Jules' enthusiasm wavered when she thought about all the 2s, 3s and 4s out of 10 who she had met in the bar that night. Other than Drew, the highest score she had given was a 7 and she had already decided to mark that down to a 6 because he belonged on the football pitch with Tim. So was there really any point in finding out what her dozen disappointing dates thought of her? On the one hand, it might give her a bit of a confidence boost. But on the other hand, it could have the opposite effect. After all, even Fraser hadn't bothered to go and talk to her after the speed dating had finished because he was too busy trying to chat all the other women up instead. And it was obvious that Drew wasn't interested. Or was he? There was only one way to find out...

"Sorry to interrupt you," announced Mr Langley, bursting into her office and encouraging her to drop her score card into the waste paper bin under her desk.

"I thought I would come and speak to you *before* morning assembly. The sooner you can go and visit Caitlin, the better."

"Of course," agreed Jules, closing down her computer again and giving Mr Langley her undivided attention.

❖

An hour later, Jules had arrived at Caitlin's house. It was a mid-terrace, separated from its left-side neighbour by a narrow, ground floor passageway and it had a very untidy garden that was in much need of some weeding and pruning. The concrete path was cracked and uneven, and the brown paint on the front door was peeling off. There didn't appear to be a doorbell so she decided to knock instead, at which point a huge Bull Terrier came bounding towards her from the side passageway, barking aggressively.

"Sid, come back here!" commanded a voice. Jules breathed a big sigh of relief as the dog immediately retreated back to where he had come from, and was replaced with an equally intimidating looking woman instead. "Can I help you?"

"Mrs Murphy?" confirmed Jules, holding her hand out. "I'm Dr Jules Croft. I work at the school."

Mrs Murphy dismissed Jules' attempt to shake her hand and simply frowned at her instead, causing her hard features to appear even more severe. Jules concluded that she obviously hadn't been expecting any visitors and attempted to explain.

"I'm here to talk to you about Caitlin. She was suspended last week for defacing another pupil's school work. It's clear that they have some unresolved issues with each other and I've been trying to provide them both with some support."

"So what do you want me to do about it?" sniffed Mrs Murphy, defensively.

"Perhaps I could come in?" suggested Jules. "We could talk about everything in more detail. Is Caitlin here?"

"I've sent her to the shops to buy me some fags," replied Mrs Murphy, crossing her arms in front of her chest. "We could do without you lot sticking your snooty noses in where they're not wanted."

Jules was beginning to wish she was confronted with the dog again instead. She hated confrontational people. She had always assumed the role of 'peace maker' whenever any kind of conflict was imminent. And before she became a psychologist and was obliged to deal with these kind of situations for a living, she just used to retreat altogether.

"Please Mrs Murphy; I can assure you that I am here to help. I really do have Caitlin's best interests at heart."

Mrs Murphy looked Jules up and down disapprovingly and then reluctantly led her down the side passageway of the house, encouraging Jules to feel relieved that she had managed to persuade Mrs Murphy to invite her inside, but terrified of what might be awaiting her when she got there. If the passage was anything to go by, there was rubbish and dog excrement everywhere. She could barely put one foot in front of the other. And the smell of stale cigarette smoke was overwhelming as she gradually approached the back door and stepped into the house.

"I suppose you'll be expecting a cup of tea," complained Mrs Murphy, shoving the kettle underneath the kitchen tap.

"Only if it's no trouble," smiled Jules, standing uneasily in the doorway, as the dog sniffed the bottom of her suit trousers.

"Sid, BED!" bellowed Mrs Murphy, causing Jules to jump as the enormous jawed animal whimpered and then retreated to his very stained looking cushion in the corner of the kitchen. Jules definitely favoured dogs over cats, but there was something about the unpredictable nature of stereotypically dangerous breeds like Bull Terriers that made her feel very uncomfortable.

"So what exactly did Caitlin do to this other student's school work?" Mrs Murphy enquired, confrontationally. "Because whatever it was, she didn't deserve to be suspended for it."

"It was biology homework and she defaced it with inappropriate images," explained Jules, as Mrs Murphy handed her some very milky looking liquid in a dirty mug. She didn't have the heart to tell her that she drank her tea black. "But it was the most recent in a long line of incidents with this particular girl, and we decided to take firmer action this time in order to try and prevent it from happening again."

"How do you know the other girl didn't deserve it?" complained Mrs Murphy, chucking the tea bag into an already overflowing bin and then leading Jules through into a very tired looking living room with a brown carpet and peeling wallpaper.

"The school doesn't tolerate intimidation of any kind, regardless of who was responsible for starting the conflict," explained Jules, perching on the very edge of the sofa and placing her mug of tea down on the coffee table next to an ash tray full of cigarette ends.

"Dr Jules!" announced Caitlin, at that moment, as she entered the room and handed the packet of cigarettes to her mother. "What are you doing here?"

She didn't exactly look pleased to see Jules, almost as though she had been caught doing something she shouldn't.

"I'm here because you and your mother failed to turn up to our meeting on Friday," replied Jules. "We tried to contact you to make another appointment, but Mr Ellington and Mr Langley felt that I ought to pop round and offer you some support at home."

"Support for WHAT?" demanded an extremely aggressive sounding male voice from the hall. "What have you been up to now Caitlin? Why aren't you at school?"

Caitlin looked absolutely terrified as a broad shouldered monster of a man emerged through the other door into the living room and slammed his fist down on the sideboard. He had a shaved head and a large tattoo running up the side of his neck. In fact, he was so intimidating that he reminded Jules of a human version of Sid. It was true: dogs really *do* look like their owners.

"I'll make you some tea Steve," smiled Mrs Murphy, before retreating to the kitchen again. Jules couldn't believe that she was actually capable of smiling, although it was clear that her uncharacteristically happy facial expression was simply an attempt to mask how she was really feeling about her husband's arrival.

"You have to go," pleaded Caitlin quietly, looking at Jules in pure desperation. Jules swallowed hard and then frantically started trying to come up with an alternative excuse as to why she was there.

"I've not been feeling well," Caitlin explained, trying not to look her stepfather in the eye. "Dr... I mean, Miss Croft was just popping round to make sure I'm OK."

"That's right," stammered Jules, nervously, before sneaking one of her business cards into Caitlin's hand and mouthing the words "call me" when she was certain that Mr Murphy wasn't watching.

"I'll show you out," he grumbled, encouraging Jules to follow him into the hall. "We don't need your sort or any of your posh friends coming over here again!"

And just as Jules was about to apologise for fear of getting Caitlin into even more trouble, he opened the front door and practically shoved her out onto the broken path. Her heart was racing as she attempted to compose herself, but as soon as she reached the safe sanctuary of her car, her entire body started to shake and tears began to prick the back of her eyes again.

❖

"What happened?" asked Mr Ellington, once Jules had returned to her office. She couldn't help but wonder why he wasn't making himself useful by teaching GCSE science to a class of enthusiastic teenagers, as opposed to darkening her door again.

"It wasn't a convenient time," Jules explained, in the hope of getting him off Caitlin's case a little bit. He had been on a vendetta to get her expelled ever since she first started causing trouble in his classroom, but now that Jules had met her family, she could tell that expulsion was the last thing Caitlin needed, or for that matter, deserved.

"Believe me Mr Ellington, I am dealing with this," she insisted. "Now if you don't mind, I've got a pile of paperwork to get through."

Mr Ellington sensed Jules' rather hostile tone and sloped away with his metaphoric tail between his legs. She couldn't help but feel ever so slightly guilty for offending him, but he was notorious for sticking his prehistoric nose in where it wasn't wanted. And Jules had a duty of care for the students she was counselling, whether he liked it or not. She knew that he wasn't the only teacher at Pinewood School who viewed the new anti-bullying initiative rather sceptically. She particularly struggled to gain the approval of the more 'traditional' members of the teaching staff. But Mr Langley believed in her role as pastoral support officer, and it wasn't as though they had any other solutions. Jules was just about to begin working her way through all the case notes that had been building up when her phone started to vibrate across the desk. When she looked at the display and discovered that Amy's name was flashing up, she was tempted to press the 'cancel' button, but her conscience persuaded her otherwise.

"Have you checked the speed dating website yet?" asked Amy enthusiastically. "I scored an average of 9 out of 10."

"Only 9?" replied Jules, sarcastically. "You must be disappointed!"

"Very funny," retorted Amy. "Besides, I've already got a boyfriend. I want to know how *you* got on."

"I haven't had time to look yet," complained Jules. "Some of us have got work to do."

"I have another client coming over in half an hour," smiled Amy, defensively. Amy was a freelance physiotherapist and tended to work quite flexible hours at the clinic. "And besides, its lunchtime."

She had alerted Jules to the fact that she was entitled to take a break, although Jules had to admit that a small part of her was actually relieved when Mr Langley had interrupted her that morning because it meant that she could put her dating fate on hold for a bit longer. But she couldn't put it off forever, and lunchtime did seem like the most opportune moment to do it.

"I'll have a look now and then let you know."

Amy hung up on her as quickly as possible so that she could get on with it. She was just about to rescue the speed dating score card from the bin under her desk when her phone started vibrating again.

"Give me a chance!" she laughed, without looking at the name on the display this time and assuming it was Amy again.

"Dr Jules?" said a shaky sounding voice at the other end.

"Caitlin, is that you? Are you OK?" replied Jules, desperately.

"No, not really," complained Caitlin, swallowing the lump in her throat. "My step dad's just found out that I've been suspended and he's so angry."

"Are you at home?" pressed Jules, in the hope of being able to go back and pacify the situation.

"Not anymore..." replied Caitlin before being interrupted by some interference on the phone line "...I had to get away...I..." and just at that moment the line went dead.

Chapter seven

December 1995

Mrs Greaves remains to this day to have been one of the most influential teachers I have ever had, for good reasons as well as bad. In fact, she reminds me of a double-edged sword. On the one hand she was a bit of a bully. On the other hand she encouraged many positive developments and achievements for me whilst I was at primary school, like allowing me to actually step out from beneath the shadows and shine, even when my shy nature and subservient tendencies towards my peers tried their very best to sabotage her efforts. I didn't want to stand out at first. It was a lot easier to just hide – both physically and metaphorically, whenever the spotlight shined in my direction. But Mrs Greaves wasn't one of those teachers who invested all her attention in the likes of Kylie Sinclair and ignored the quiet underachieving children. If anything, she was quite the opposite because she went out of her way to give everyone in the class, particularly the likes of me, as many opportunities to shine as possible, whether we liked it or not.

She was always taking risks rather than relying on the children with the very obvious talents to step up and take the lead part in the school play, for example. But more often than not her risks paid off and she was able to uncover another future star in the making. I remember her telling me once that self-confidence and belief were far more important than popularity and the superficial kind of talents that Kylie Sinclair and some of her friends possessed. She was quite a reckless and impulsive teacher who didn't think too hard about anything before doing it, claiming that it was possible to over-think things and then talk yourself out of them, resulting in lost or wasted opportunities.

My mum on the other hand was completely the opposite. She was always over thinking everything, risk assessing situations to the point where all the fun was taken out of them so that I never actually felt compelled to do anything. I was certainly never challenged to step out of my comfort zone. To break free from the cotton wool that I was so tightly wrapped in and try something a little less predictable for a change. Of course, she wasn't like that with my elder brother, Christian. He was allowed to get away with doing whatever he wanted to do, because he was three years older than me and he was a boy. I was treated like some kind of porcelain doll – too fragile to be exposed to anything difficult or different. And I was too afraid to object because I had grown so used to it over the course of my childhood. Even if my mum had decided to loosen her apron strings a little, I probably would have remained glued to her side anyway.

So when Mrs Greaves made the rather radical decision to cast me as the lead part in the year 5 festive production that Christmas, I was absolutely petrified. I had no singing, acting or dancing experience whatsoever. And during infant school I never even got the chance to play an angel in the Nativity like the rest of the girls in my class. I was usually just a sheep or a tree. Of course, Kylie Sinclair was Mary every single year, so when the parts for The Wizard of Oz were announced and Mrs Greaves happily declared that I would play the part of Dorothy, Kylie was particularly disgruntled. I don't believe to this day that Kylie would have punished me so wickedly for Mrs Greaves' casting decision, had it not been for Barry Harper's encouragement, but I guess I'll never know. What I do know is that my big appearance in the spotlight was never quite going to live up to anyone's expectations, least of all my own. And for that I will never be able to forgive Mrs Greaves because she provided Barry and Kylie with so much ammunition that Christmas, when she should have just been protecting me from them instead.

The rehearsals had all managed to go relatively well, although it quickly became clear that I needed to work on the projection of my voice. I had an extraordinary recollection of the script and managed to learn my lines virtually word for word within a couple of weeks, but my stage presence left an awful lot to be desired because my nerves tended to get the better of me so that my timid little voice was swallowed up by the knot of anxiety in my stomach. Mrs Greaves was, however, quite impressed with my characterisation. Apparently my portrayal of Dorothy was unexpectedly convincing and believable. I just needed to really immerse myself in the part because I would then stand a greater chance of letting go of my inhibitions. After all, Dorothy Gale was a great deal more confident and relaxed than Julia Croft, even when confronted with the Wicked Witch of the West, as well as the upsetting realisation that whilst there was 'no place like home', she may never be able to actually make it back there again.

Synonymously, the part of the witch was played by Kylie, and Barry was her goblin monkey sidekick. I don't know whether this was a deliberate casting decision on Mrs Greaves' part, but it certainly left me more vulnerable to their tormenting. As well as the convenient opportunities that this presented them with, they also had the perfect excuse to get away with it because they were able to claim that they were simply playing their parts or 'getting into character'.

It started off quite subtly at first with an apple juice stain on some of the pages of my script, but luckily I didn't stumble across any of my lines because I had learnt them all off by heart already. Then Barry played his usual trick of putting a raw egg in my shoe, only this time it was of course one of my red sparkly shoes that Dorothy removes from the feet of the Wicked Witch of the East after she's crushed by Dorothy's house in the storm. So I had to spend the rest of the dress rehearsal slopping about the stage in bare feet. Mrs Greaves demanded Barry to take the shoe home with him that afternoon so that he could scrub it clean for me. I was amused when I discovered that his prank wasn't going to go unpunished this time, but unfortunately Mrs Greaves' punishment simply succeeded in making him all the more determined to get his own back on me.

So on the day of the actual performance, as all our parents and grandparents started to gather in our school hall and we all

55

waited anxiously backstage as year 4 finished their performance of A Christmas Carol, I could feel my nerves creeping up on me. I wasn't entirely sure whether I was more nervous about my starring role or about the outcome of Barry's potential prank, but as I checked my shoes for eggs and then clip clopped along the corridor to where our backstage entrance was, I could hear the applause from the audience on the other side of the curtain, prompting me to start running through my lines in my head one last time.

"Break a leg," Kylie whispered as we quickly made our way up onto the stage and nervously waited for the curtains to open. Her features were obliterated by heavy green face paint and a long plastic nose with a wart on the end, but I could still tell that she was smirking at me. I smoothed down the apron on my blue gingham dress and took a deep breath as the curtains began to slide across the stage and reveal our audience. Mum, Dad and Christian were all sitting in the very front row. Many of the parents were smiling encouragingly and blowing kisses to their children. My family, on the other hand, looked almost as terrified as I was. Particularly my mum, who was cupping her hand over her mouth and frowning already, and I hadn't even delivered my first line yet. I desperately wanted her to just smile at me and put my nerves at ease a little, but it was almost as though she was finding the entire experience physically painful to watch. Then the music started.

Everything was going just fine for about the first ten minutes. Because the junior school had four different year group performances to get through, each one had been scaled down so that year 5 was only on stage for no longer than 30 minutes in total. The Wizard of Oz was quite a long production so many of the more integral parts of the story, like when Dorothy meets the scarecrow, tin man and lion, were portrayed over the course of just one piece of music, during which the four of us had to link arms with each other, skip across the stage and sing "We're off to see the wizard, the wonderful wizard of Oz". I was really beginning to enjoy myself by this point, and even my mum's facial expression was starting to soften a little too. But then the scene where Dorothy has to throw water all over the witch was upon us and I suddenly started to feel my stomach plummeting in fear as Kylie and Barry joined me on the stage.

The bucket of water that I was holding as a prop was full of blue confetti as opposed to water, and as Kylie started chasing me around the set with her goblin monkey in tow, I was supposed to turn around suddenly and throw it at her. But as I held the bucket in the air and pivoted my body slightly in order to face her, Barry nudged me sideways causing me to lose my footing completely and stumble backwards into the enormous Christmas tree at the side of the stage. Blue confetti went everywhere – everywhere that is except in Kylie's direction – and the Christmas tree wobbled dramatically before crashing to the floor in what felt like slow motion. Surprisingly, unlike on the year 4 sports day, I actually managed to remain upright, my feet glued to the spot in horror as members of the audience got up and fled from their seats in order to avoid the broken shards of baubles that were ricocheting through the air towards them.

❖

There were still two more weeks of school left until the end of term, which I remember spending in complete isolation because I couldn't bear to have to re-live the humiliation of looking like an absolute klutz in front of all those people. Not only that but many of my class friends were annoyed with me for ruining the entire performance so that year 6 had to come on and take over from us before we had finished, whilst the caretaker frantically swept up piles of broken Christmas tree ornaments and pine needles in front of the stage.

"It wasn't my fault," I would whinge in my defence every time anyone else managed to corner me about it. "Barry pushed me."

"You're just clumsy, Egg Girl!" heckled a group of Kylie's friends in the dining hall one lunchtime.

"Leave me alone," I retaliated before abandoning my tray of food and running towards the girls' toilets again. I was safe from any further condemnation until the lunch break was over, but I was also very hungry. And I hadn't even taken a packed lunch with me that day because the dinner ladies had prepared a special Christmas dinner for everyone.

Year 5 didn't really get any easier after that because by the time I had managed to alienate myself from the rest of the class it seemed there was no going back. I guess I managed to get used to it to a certain extent, and spending lots of time on my own did have its advantages sometimes, but I was very lonely, particularly at break and lunch times when I watched all the other girls in my class happily playing together in their little friendship groups. There were the rough and tumble sporty types who always tried to challenge the boys to a game of football out on the field. There were the Kylie Sinclair clones that stood around braiding each other's hair and talking about nail varnish – I'm ashamed to admit that many of these girls were the ones I used to play with when I was in Infants. And there were the more studious, nurturing types of girls who liked to spend their playtimes helping the younger children in the Junior playground.

In some ways I wish I could have been looked after by someone like them when I was in year 3 because it might have helped me to deal with the difficult transition between Infants and Juniors. It's called Key Stage 1 and Key Stage 2 these days, and a friend of mine who works at a primary school tells me that specific members of the year 5 and 6 classes are sent into the Key Stage 1 playground at lunchtimes in order to ensure that all the children have someone to play with. They organise games and comfort you if you fall over, until a teacher is able to come and apply first aid.

It does feel as though children have things a lot easier these days. When I was at primary school, we were just expected to get on with it whether we liked it or not. Discipline was a lot stricter and sympathy and understanding were virtually non-existent. If the teacher wanted you to do something that you really didn't want to do, no amount of crying or grovelling would make any difference. And mental health issues like anxiety and depression didn't even exist. If children were anxious about anything and objected to doing it, they were disciplined for being defiant. And that's exactly what happened to me when I was in year 6 and it was time for our residential field trip. But that's another story.

Chapter eight

Tuesday 7th May 2019

When Caitlin had failed to call her back again, Jules was beginning to get really worried. And every time she attempted to dial the number that had appeared on her screen, it went straight through to voicemail. She wasn't sure whether to go back round to the house in case Caitlin was in some kind of danger. She sounded so shaky and scared; Jules was convinced that something bad must have happened. But Caitlin had told her that she wasn't at home, in which case her second visit to the Murphy's house in less than two hours would probably cause more harm than good. She had to do *something* though. She couldn't just sit in her office and hope that Caitlin called her again because what if she didn't? She must have phoned Jules because she needed her help, so Jules needed to try and find a way of tracking her down. But how?

Perhaps one of Caitlin's friends would be able to shed some light on the situation. Maybe Caitlin had contacted one of them. Or maybe they knew of a favourite place that Caitlin might be likely to retreat to. Jules rummaged through the pile of case notes on her desk in the desperate hope of finding Caitlin's file, but the closest she came to it was Louisa's, and that didn't seem to have any information about Caitlin in it whatsoever. Then it suddenly dawned on her. She had left the file in her bedroom. She had taken it home with her on Friday so that she could do some work on it over the weekend, in preparation for her home visit this morning. But it must have got buried by her pile of chick flick DVD cases and she had forgotten all about it.

Ten minutes later she was sat back behind the steering wheel of her car and was motoring towards her house as quickly as she could without deliberately breaking the speed limit. Every single set of traffic lights seemed to turn red on her approach, and she almost ended up having a collision with a Mini Copper whose driver had failed to indicate right at the roundabout into her street.

But she managed to make it home in one piece and was frantically retrieving her handbag from the passenger seat when she heard her phone ringing.

"Caitlin?" she answered, sounding out of breath from having searched around in her handbag trying to find her phone before it cut off again.

"No, it's your mum," replied Jules' mother. Jules slumped back against the passenger door of her car in defeat, her hand still shaking as she held the phone to her ear.

"I'm just calling to find out how your headache is today and to make sure that you'll be able to come to Sunday lunch *next* weekend instead. Your brother's got something to tell us all."

"I'll be there," replied Jules, rolling her eyes at the thought of what Christian's big announcement could be. "Can I speak to you about it later though mum; I'm just in the middle of an important case for work."

Mrs Croft was by no means impressed with her daughter's inability to make time to have a conversation; in spite of having phoned her during her lunch break, but she vacated the line nonetheless as Jules was very anxious to keep it clear in case Caitlin called back. And without giving Christian's potential news a second thought, Jules hastily let herself in through the front door of her house and darted up the stairs. But when she got to the landing, she stopped dead in her tracks as she was confronted by a half-naked man, who definitely wasn't Tim, making his way from the bathroom to Amy's bedroom with nothing but a towel wrapped around his muscular waist. The man turned around as he heard Jules approach, at which point they were able to identify each other properly, and Jules could barely believe her eyes.

"Drew!"

"Hi Jules, I thought you would be at work," smiled Drew awkwardly, as Jules tried to compose herself long enough to draw her attention away from his gorgeous body and look him in the eye.

"I just needed to pop home for something," she explained feeling her face redden. "I'm sorry if I've disturbed you."

"That's OK," replied Drew, following her through to her bedroom as she frantically unearthed Caitlin's case notes from the bottom of her pile of chick flick DVDs. Her room was an absolute mess, and when she thought back to how deflated she had been feeling about Drew and the speed dating event the previous day, she couldn't believe that he was standing half naked in her doorway less than 24 hours later.

"Please don't take any notice of the mess," she insisted, as she knocked the DVD cases and a collection of chocolate bar wrappers onto the floor. Why was she always so clumsy around him? "I've been really busy at work and I haven't had a chance to tidy yet."

As she stood up from the foot of the bed where she had been collecting the fallen chocolate wrappers from, she found herself face to face with Drew's naked torso and ended up blushing again. He really did have the most exquisite physique. It was toned and muscular with a light tan and just the right amount of chest hair, including a line that ran from the bottom of his belly button to the top of his towel. She followed it with her eyes and then realised that he was smiling at her.

"Anyway, I need to go," she then concluded, and before Drew was given the chance to say anything else, she had brushed past him in the doorway and had disappeared back down the stairs.

Once she had escaped through the front door again, she took a deep breath and then allowed the realisation of what had just happened to completely overwhelm her thoughts. Amy and Drew had only just met and they were already having an affair. She couldn't believe that her oldest friend could betray her like that. Her entire body started shaking as she made her way back towards her car and continued thinking about the impact of the situation; Drew and Amy; Amy and Drew. Everything was ruined now; her feelings for him; her friendship with her. Even her home was ruined because she couldn't possibly carry on living there now. Not anymore.

It was so unfair. She hadn't met anyone like Drew in a really long time and now Amy had stolen him away from her. Not that he was ever actually interested in Jules in the first place of course, but there was always a chance. She shouldn't have been surprised though. Amy was younger, prettier and sexier than she was. And she had been getting fed up with Tim's inability to commit for a while now. Perhaps that was the *real* reason why she arranged for them to go speed dating on Saturday. Jules never returned home from work in the middle of the day so it was the perfect opportunity for them to spend time together without being caught. It was all so deceitful though because Amy had given her the impression that she would be in and out of appointments at the clinic all day. And what about Tim? Jules dreaded the thought of telling him but she knew that it was her responsibility to let him know what was going on. Amy and Drew's plans had backfired and they would be obliged to face the consequences.

She opened the window of her car and allowed the cool spring air to freshen her thoughts as she opened Caitlin's file and flicked through it, trying as hard as she could to banish any thoughts of Drew and Amy from her mind. But the pages of notes simply passed her by in a bit of a haze and she seemed to find it impossible to focus on any of the words that were in front of her. Looking up at the house, she decided that she needed to drive somewhere else first because the scene of the crime was currently overshadowing her ability to concentrate on Caitlin, and she needed to put her vulnerable student far above her non-existent love life. Starting the engine, she manoeuvred out of her parking space and drove a few hundred yards down the road until she had pulled up outside Mr Shah's shop. She then opened Caitlin's file again and began reading one of Mr Ellington's reports in as much detail as she possibly could before her mind was given the opportunity to start wandering again. There seemed to be no reference to any of Caitlin's friends, and Jules just hadn't been working at the school long enough to familiarise herself with the student's social network, so it was impossible to try and come up with someone who Caitlin may have confided in or bunked off school with on a previous occasion.

She then decided to try calling Caitlin's number again, in the hope that she might pick up this time, but the number continued to go straight through to voicemail. Jules was reluctant to leave a message in case her phone was intercepted by Mr Murphy, so she simply hung up in defeat and bashed her head back against the car head rest with frustration.

"Bad day?" smiled Mr Shah, through the open window of her car as he stepped outside the shop to replenish the newspaper stand.

"You could say that," replied Jules, softening her screwed up forehead and smiling back at him.

"I may have to come in and treat myself to some chocolate," she then added, trying to ignore all the chocolate that she had already managed to consume during her slumber the day before.

"I saw that new doctor this morning," Mr Shah explained. "The one you were asking me about last week. He came in here and bought a big box of chocolates. I wonder who the lucky lady is."

Jules decided not to disclose Amy's identity because she knew how much Mr Shah liked to gossip to the locals. She couldn't help but feel a little bit disappointed on Amy's behalf though because a box of chocolates from Mr Shah's shop was hardly the most romantic gesture of the century. But it was only their first date. And besides, they had already slept together anyway. When Jules' response was particularly unforthcoming, Mr Shah simply waved and then went back into the shop again, leaving her to think about what he had said. It just didn't make any sense. Amy and Tim had been together for such a long time that she could barely remember what Amy was like when she was single. She was very flirtatious and always ended up coming home with a string of phone numbers, but she had never had a one night stand; it just wasn't her style. And she must have heard Jules and Drew talking just now; why didn't she come out onto the landing and defend herself, instead of hiding away in her bedroom, feeling ashamed? Just at that moment, Jules' phone rang again, only this time it was Mr Langley.

"Louisa's in your office," he explained. "She seems to think you have a meeting with each other after lunch."

Jules looked at the car clock and then remembered that she had arranged another session with Louisa after she collected her from the hospital the week before.

"I'll be straight back," she assured him, before throwing Caitlin's case notes onto the passenger seat and starting her engine again.

❖

Back at the school, Jules discovered that Louisa had decided to get engrossed in her latest English Literature text while she waited for her counselling session to commence. She was extremely studious and conscientious about her school work, particularly English Literature which was her favourite subject. When Jules commented on how impressed she was with Louisa's commitment, Louisa was more than happy to explain that she was hoping to become an author once she had finished her studies.

"Fantastic," smiled Jules, placing her handbag under her desk as she slid into the swivel chair behind it and picked up her notepad from the tray next to her. In doing so, she was also careful to place her phone where she could see it and Louisa couldn't, just in case Caitlin attempted to make contact during their session. She had switched it to silent again because she didn't want Louisa to think that she wasn't entitled to have her undivided attention for the next half an hour; but at least she would be able to see whether the display was lighting up, as well as the identity of the caller at the other end.

"It's great to have ambition at such an early age. And an author is a wonderful profession. I will look forward to reading your first novel one day."

"Thanks," smiled Louisa modestly, looking down at her hands in her lap. "Why did you decide that you wanted to be a counsellor?"

"I can't really remember now," replied Jules, feeling a little uncomfortable. "I was always quite fascinated with psychology and after I studied it at A Level, I decided that I would like to go on to university and do a degree. I guess it just went from there really."

Jules wasn't being completely honest with Louisa because she knew exactly what had motivated her to study psychology, particularly one that specialised in counselling school children who were involved in bullying, and that was her own experiences when she was a child. She felt the need to turn those very difficult and unpleasant memories into something positive. Not only that, but she had also earned herself a bit of a reputation at university as being the person who everyone turned to with their problems. Her subservient side meant that she would never have the heart to turn anyone away, even at the expense of her own problems, and that she would enjoy nothing more than the opportunity to gain people's trust, affection, and, in some cases, approval. She had spent far too many years of her life feeling isolated and unpopular. Feeling needed and liked was a lot more agreeable, even if it wasn't necessarily sincere.

"How's your knee?" she then smiled, changing the subject.

"Much better," replied Louisa. "I've taken the dressing off now and it appears to be healing well."

There was an uneasy pause before Louisa continued.

"Thanks for coming to meet me at the hospital. I'm sorry about bunking off."

"You don't need to apologise to me," insisted Jules. "I was just worried about you. It was so unlike you. What did your parents say?"

Louisa tucked her hair behind her ears nervously, before sliding her glasses up her nose.

"They've promised to support me," she explained. "They were disappointed when my grades started slipping so I've agreed to knuckle down again now, particularly with English Literature."

"And are you going to tell me why you decided to run out of school in the first place?" replied Jules, making some notes on her notepad.

Louisa shrugged and then looked out of the window in the hope of avoiding the question. Jules still hadn't managed to get to the bottom of what had happened immediately before Caitlin's counselling session with her that day, but she knew that if the science work defacing incident wasn't bad enough, this was guaranteed to be worse. When Louisa refused to answer the question, Jules knew that she couldn't press her too hard, but what she *did* know was that if Louisa did eventually decide to confide in her, she would be obliged to consider whether to share the information with Mr Langley. And that could affect whether Caitlin would be allowed to return to school or not.

"Caitlin's suspended until next week," she reminded her, taking a more gentle approach. "If you decide that you feel the need to come and talk to me before then, my door is always open."

"I know," replied Louisa, as Jules reached over her desk and located Louisa's case file.

"I have a few exercises that I would like us to work on together over the next few sessions," Jules explained. "Some of them are self-esteem boosting techniques and others are a little more challenging. It's important to try and step out of your comfort zone every once in a while, rather than avoiding things or relying on what we call safety behaviours."

Louisa simply snorted in reply before turning to face her. "I do that every time I come to school," she complained. "Every time I'm in a class with Caitlin, or standing in the lunch queue just minding my own business. Why do you think I spend so much time in the library? Because it's the only place where Caitlin doesn't bother to come and find me."

Jules felt crushed. She knew exactly what Louisa was going through but she needed to try and remain as professional as possible by putting her owns opinions and feelings to one side. She thought for a moment and then took a deep breath before her next line of questioning:

"Let's try and look at it another way," she explained, tilting her head to one side. "Why do you think Caitlin picks on you?"

"Because she's evil!" exclaimed Louisa without any hesitation. "Because it makes her feel like she's better than me; like she's got some kind of power over me. An ego boost I suppose."

Jules was determined not to put words into Louisa's mouth because her training had taught her that trying to influence her clients in any way was strictly forbidden. So she continued with another leading question:

"But why do you think she feels the need to boost her ego?"

Louisa took some time to consider the question carefully, at which point Jules was hopeful that she might reach the same conclusion as Jules had. And what Jules had concluded as a result of meeting Mr and Mrs Murphy that morning, was that deep down, Caitlin was just as unhappy and vulnerable as Louisa was. Eventually Louisa just shrugged and looked down at her lap again.

"How can I possibly try and relate to her?" she mumbled.

"Because you might find that you have more in common with each other than you realise," replied Jules, feeling a little disappointed with Louisa's response. "How would you feel if I arranged a session with Caitlin next week so that you can talk everything through with each other in a safe and controlled environment?"

Louisa shrugged again and then laughed uncomfortably. "I just can't imagine trying to have a civil conversation with her," she explained. "But I suppose it's worth a try."

"Excellent," replied Jules encouragingly, taking her diary from her tray so that she could pencil a date in. Just as she was about to pick it up, the display screen on her mobile phone started flashing to indicate that she had a text message, and she was only just able to make out what it said without drawing Louisa's attention to the fact that she was reading it:

'Sorry we got cut off earlier. I'm OK, nothing to worry about. C U soon. Caitlin.'

Jules wasn't certain whether to be reassured by that or not. She would have preferred to have spoken to Caitlin in order to find out why she had bothered to contact her in the first place, if nothing else. And how could she ensure that Caitlin had sent the text message herself? It could have been her stepfather, posing as Caitlin. Jules' imagination was beginning to run away with her just as it had done after she had walked in on Drew and Amy earlier, and she really had to shake herself back to reality in order to concentrate on Louisa again.

"How does next Wednesday lunch time suit you?" she suggested, flicking through her diary.

"Are you sure this is such a good idea Dr Jules?" replied Louisa, with a concerned expression on her face.

If Jules was completely honest with herself, she wasn't sure at all. But she wasn't prepared to tell Louisa that. And besides, it had to be worth a try.

Chapter nine

When Jules eventually arrived home from work, it felt as though she had endured one of the longest and most difficult days of her career so far. It was only the beginning of the working week, and all she wanted to do was to curl up on the sofa with a glass of wine and share all her problems with Amy. But on this occasion, Amy was one of the reasons why everything else had felt more challenging than usual, because of what had happened with Drew. And at one point Jules had even considered going to stay with her parents, in the hope of postponing their confrontation for as long as possible, but then she thought about her mum's reaction and she couldn't face the thought of having to explain everything to her. Besides, the sooner she and Amy could have it out with each other, the better.

As she let herself in through the front door and hung her jacket on the hook in the hall, Jules peered into the living room and spotted an open box of chocolates on the coffee table. She kicked her shoes off aggressively when she thought about what Mr Shah had told her, and slammed her handbag down on the floor, at which point Amy suddenly appeared at the kitchen doorway.

"Another bad day?" she smiled sympathetically, reaching forward and grabbing Jules by the hand so that she could drag her through into the living room.

"Why don't you have a chocolate to cheer you up?"

"It's going to take a lot more than chocolates to make me feel better," protested Jules, pulling her hand out of Amy's clutch and shoving the box of chocolates onto the floor. Amy took a step back in surprise and then decided to give Jules the benefit of the doubt, in the fear that something terrible had happened.

"What's wrong Jules? This isn't like you at all."

And she was right. Jules didn't usually react so aggressively towards anyone, least of all her best friend. But the events of the past few hours had really managed to get on top of her, and she decided that she was fed up with being taken for a mug, particularly by the one person who she was supposed to be able to trust the most.

"How can you act so innocently?" she exclaimed, as Amy perched uneasily on the side of the arm chair in the hope that if Jules sat down as well, she would be forced to calm her mood a little. Jules remained standing and tried not to look Amy directly in the eyes as she continued:

"You know exactly what's wrong; I came home and found you together at lunchtime."

Amy's facial features relaxed slightly when she realised what Jules was referring to.

"You mean Drew?" she clarified, before attempting to continue, at which moment Jules cut her off.

"You're not even going to deny it!" she screamed, feeling the blood rush to her face in fury "What about me? What about Tim?"

Amy stood up again and held her hands up innocently. "Now hang on a minute; it's not what you think." she insisted .

"I found him going into your bedroom half naked when you should have been at work," continued Jules. "And you didn't even bother to confront me about it at the time. You just hid in your bedroom like a coward."

"I wasn't hiding from anyone because I had nothing to feel guilty about," explained Amy, whilst drawing Jules' attention to the white tunic top that she was wearing. "What does this say?"

"What are you asking me that for? It's your work uniform." scowled Jules, calming down a little as Amy forced her to read what was written on her badge.

"Physiotherapist!" she announced. "It says physiotherapist."

Amy didn't need to say anymore after that because it soon became clear that Jules was able to work out what had *really* been going on at lunchtime. She sank down onto the sofa feeling defeated, as Amy eventually decided to explain:

"When I met Drew at the speed dating event on Saturday night, and he asked me what I did for a living, he told me that he suffered from back pain. I offered to give him some treatment but he didn't feel comfortable coming to the clinic because some of his colleagues from the hospital do locum work there from time to time..."

"So you invited him to the house instead," concluded Jules, cutting Amy off again. "I'm *so* sorry I jumped to conclusions. I'm a paranoid idiot."

"It's OK," replied Amy, unconvincingly. "I understand how paranoid you can get after what happened with Greg. I just wish you had trusted me enough to know that I would never betray you in the first place."

Jules put her face in her hands and filled them with warm tears as Amy moved over to the sofa in order to comfort her.

"You need to have more faith in yourself instead of assuming that everyone's out to get you all the time" Amy explained, putting her arm around her and rubbing her shoulder. "I know you've had a difficult time in the past but you can't keep finding reasons to push other people away. Greg was just one person. Don't base everybody else's commitment to you on what he did."

"Except it's not just him, is it," insisted Jules. "I've been treated badly by other people too."

"Barry Harper," nodded Amy. "He was just a petulant child."

"Not *just* Barry," Jules explained. "I was treated badly at secondary school too. By Craig Riley for starters. I was even bullied by one of my best friends."

Jules had never really confided in Amy about what had happened to her at secondary school. Or why she had such a bad scar on her left arm. And Amy knew better than to probe her about it.

"Well I would never do anything like that to you. I care about our friendship too much" Amy assured her.

"It's a defence mechanism" replied Jules, wiping her face with the back of her sleeve. "Self-preservation."

"I know what it is, Doctor!" Amy teased, as the two of them embraced each other properly. "But it's time you started practising what you preach and taking a few risks. You never know, you might end up making yourself happy."

"Maybe *you* should be the counsellor instead," Jules smiled, pulling away from Amy's embrace and composing herself.

"And maybe *you* should offer to give Drew his next massage!" laughed Amy, giving her a nudge. "Why didn't you tell me that 'Dr Dish' was at the speed dating event? I only found out who he really was after I heard you talking to each other at lunchtime."

"He's not interested in me anyway," insisted Jules, looking at the box of chocolates on the living room carpet. "He didn't even hang around after the speed dating had finished."

"He told me that he was on call that evening and had just received a message from the hospital," explained Amy, encouraging Jules' heart to form a lump of anticipation in her throat. "Have you bothered to check your scores yet? He might have left you a message."

"I doubt it," replied Jules, feeling embarrassed. "Besides, he knows where I live now. If he's interested then he can just pop round."

"Stop putting it off," continued Amy, collecting her tablet from the dining table. "You've got to find out sooner or later. Remember what I said about taking a few risks?"

"OK, OK," sighed Jules, eventually deciding to succumb to Amy's persuasive nature. "What have I got to lose?"

❖

"With extra marshmallows, just the way you like it," smiled Amy, placing a large mug of steaming hot chocolate in front of Jules on the coffee table.

"I would have preferred a large glass of wine instead, but it *is* only Tuesday!" laughed Jules in reply, as she tentatively accessed the speed dating website once more. She took a deep breath and then clicked on the 'Is love in the air for you?' icon in the top right-hand corner of the web page, before turning away from the screen in dread.

"Would you like to know what your average score was?" insisted Amy, leaning over her to look at the screen.

"Do I have any choice in the matter?" Jules teased, knowing full well that Amy was about to tell her anyway. Amy hesitated and then composed herself long enough to try and gauge Jules' reaction.

"What would you *like* it to be?" she then smiled, refusing to give anything away.

"9 out of 10," replied Jules, sarcastically, failing to elaborate on the fact that only girls like Amy ever managed to achieve scores that high.

Amy frowned a little and then curled the side of her mouth in an encouraging kind of way, giving Jules the immediate impression that the outcome was obviously a bit of a 'glass half empty or half full' situation. And at that point she decided that she just couldn't be bothered to play the guessing game any longer so she turned to face the screen herself and confirmed her long awaited fate.

"You're disappointed aren't you?" clarified Amy, continuing to try and gauge Jules' facial expression. It was extremely difficult though because being a psychologist, Jules had become very good at learning not to give anything away in her face.

"No, not really," she replied, taking a sip of hot chocolate and licking a soft sticky piece of marshmallow from her top lip, "6 out of 10 is nothing to be ashamed of."

"And you looked really stunning on Saturday," insisted Amy, trying to make her feel better.

"So it must have been my sparkling personality that let me down!" concluded Jules, pretending to laugh it off.

"I *knew* you were disappointed," replied Amy, grabbing the tablet and accessing the 12 men's individual comments.

There was only one comment that Jules was interested in and that was Drew's, but she pretended to listen to the various other responses first in order to maintain the open mind that she had gone along to the speed dating event with in the first place. Amy scrolled down the page and then started to read them out loud;

"Fraser: 'Jules is a beautiful girl who needs to have a bit more confidence in herself. She seems to take life too seriously and could do with letting her hair down every once in a while.'"

Jules smiled when she reminded herself of Fraser's arrogant and overbearing nature as Amy continued;

"Martin: 'I enjoyed talking to Jules about the Met Office and the pub's history, but she wasn't particularly forthcoming as far as talking about herself was concerned.'"

"Neither was he!" exclaimed Jules, shrugging his comments off. "Besides, I can't imagine that he managed to get a very high score either; he was far too geeky."

"Some women like the computer nerd type," insisted Amy, defensively, completely overlooking her *own* very sporty and athletic choice in boyfriend. "In fact you could do with someone like Martin to drag you out of the dinosaur age."

She was referring to Jules' inability to embrace anything technology related, including Facebook and Twitter. Amy had attempted to persuade her to join up on several occasions, but Jules was terrified of being contacted by any of the people from her past; people who she had done her best to forget over the years. After all, she had made the effort to keep in touch with the people who really mattered, and as far as she was concerned, the negative influences from her past deserved to *stay* in her past. Particularly the likes of Craig Riley, who, mercifully, had failed to leave a comment on the speed dating website. He was probably too ashamed to when he remembered how badly he had treated her in the past.

Amy rattled through a few of the other men's comments and then slid the tablet across the coffee table as though she didn't want Jules to see what was written next.

"What is it?" Jules frowned, suspiciously. "Has Drew written anything?"

Amy hesitated again as though she wasn't quite sure how to break the news to her. "Well…" she began before retrieving the tablet from the other end of the table. "Drew doesn't appear to have left a comment at all, but he probably just hasn't got around to it."

"Why not, because he was too busy buying boxes of chocolates for attractive physiotherapists?" smiled Jules, nudging her gently as she clutched her mug of hot chocolate with both hands.

"You haven't written anything either!" retorted Amy.

"And neither have you," replied Jules, prompting Amy to remind her that she already had a boyfriend and that she had only bothered to go along to the speed dating event in order to provide Jules with some moral support.

The two women sat in silence for a moment and pondered what to do next. Eventually Amy decided to log out of the speed dating website altogether so that she could check her Facebook page, giving Jules the opportunity to scrutinise her text message from Caitlin.

"Do you think I'm cut out to be a counsellor?" she asked, out of the blue.

Amy looked up from the tablet and smiled encouragingly. "Of course you are. What makes you say that?"

Jules knew that she couldn't really share any of the details about her situation with Caitlin and Louisa, so she chose to justify her fears by observing that people like Amy seemed to be far better equipped to deal with other people's problems because they didn't have any issues of their own.

"It may not seem like I have any issues," replied Amy. "But maybe I'm just better at hiding them than you are." Jules reminded herself of Amy's resentment towards Tim's inability to commit, as she continued;

"Wearing your heart on your sleeve can be a good thing because it prevents you from bottling things up. And having 'issues' means that you have life experience and empathy which are two very important qualities in a counsellor."

"You know that saying; 'Sticks and stones may break my bones but words will never hurt me'," explained Jules "Broken bones heal but emotional scars never do. Bullying can have a lasting effect because it doesn't just make you feel self-conscious and unhappy when it's actually happening; it can stay with you for the rest of your life."

"I do understand why you feel so afraid of getting into a relationship," Amy soothed. "But it's time to try and put the past behind you and just go for it with Drew. Otherwise you might regret it."

Chapter ten

June 1997

It was unusual for a class teacher to stay with the same year group for two consecutive years, and when I first found out that Mrs Greaves would be moving up to Year 6 with us, I wasn't particularly happy about it. But I eventually managed to convince myself that 'better the devil you know' was a well-known saying for a very important reason, and by the time I moved onto secondary school I concluded that I would have quite willingly sold my right arm in order to be taught by Mrs Greaves again. Secondary school is an entirely different matter, and year 6 is everybody's opportunity to prove to the teaching staff that they are ready to make that transition. SATs and '11-plus' exams, helping the infants at break times, and going on the residential field trip are just three examples of how year 6 pupils are expected to step up and prove their worth.

But nothing really prepares you for secondary school, particularly when you're used to going to a primary school with as few as 200 pupils, like I was. Year groups are more than tripled and there are different class teachers for each and every subject. The building is about four times the size, with a labyrinth of corridors and a sports field the length of a football stadium with a full-sized running track around the outside. I remember going to look round my secondary school for the very first time and feeling utterly overwhelmed. I also remember talking to Mrs Greaves about it at the year 6 parent's evening, when she decided to raise concerns with my parents about how unprepared she felt I was.

"I thought we were supposed to be discussing Julia's academic abilities," my dad frowned, sounding a little defensive.

"You will see from my report that she's doing just fine in all her core subjects," replied Mrs Greaves sliding an A4 envelope across the table to us and revealing a sheet of paper underneath that

made my stomach sink. "It's her social skills that she really needs to work on. But I understand from our head teacher that you have refused to sign the consent form giving your permission for her to come on the residential field trip."

"She couldn't possibly cope," my mum explained. My dad opened his mouth to speak too but promptly closed it again as soon as he realised that mum's defence mode had kicked in.

"She's shy and vulnerable and she would be unbearably homesick. Particularly if she ends up falling victim to some of the other children's ridicule again, which she inevitably will."

It was more than twenty years later and I could still replay this conversation in my head almost as though it happened yesterday. I could vividly recall the look on Mrs Greaves' face as she diverted her attention towards me, desperately willing me to try and contradict my mum's justification in some way. But I couldn't, because I knew it was true. And no matter how much I wanted it not to be, I also wanted to bury my head in the sand because it would have been a lot easier to just pretend that the residential trip wasn't even happening. After all, I knew deep down that I had no choice but to go on it, and that the sheet of paper that had been concealed underneath my school report, was the unsigned consent form.

"Mrs Croft; I'm sorry to tell you that this field trip simply cannot go ahead unless all our students are there," explained Mrs Greaves, as my mum looked at the consent form and sighed in a way that could only suggest that she was at a complete loss as to what to do for the best. Her hand was forced. If she refused to give her consent for me to go on the field trip to Wales then she would prevent all the other children in my class from going as well. I didn't realise it at the time because 11 year olds aren't really capable of such a concept, but this was nothing short of blackmail. Of course, these days children are given the option as to whether they feel able to go or not. If I was sitting with my parents across the desk from Mrs Greaves during a modern day parent' evening, my mum's concerns would have been taken very

seriously indeed. In fact, I probably would have been diagnosed with anxiety and sent to the pastoral support officer for counselling.

"Well it sounds like I don't really have any choice then," she concluded, reluctantly hovering her pen above the signature line. My mum was quite a subservient character. She was always motivated to do things for the good of others, and more assertive people were often taking advantage of her kind nature. I had inherited many of my personal attributes from her, but unfortunately this often meant that I ended up being used as some kind of 'door mat' for children like Barry Harper to wipe their filthy feet on all the time.

This wasn't the first time that my mum or dad had made an effort to speak to Mrs Greaves about the painful reality that I was being bullied. It seemed that their concerns were falling on deaf ears though because whether I liked it or not, I was obliged to spend a week away in Wales with Barry and his gang and there was absolutely nothing that I could do about it.

❖

I remember feeling utterly miserable when we arrived at our destination. My mum and I had spent several days preparing my suitcase with everything I would need, and my mum had labelled it all in the hope of trying to feel as though she was taking as much control of the situation as she possibly could. But every time I removed anything from my suitcase after I had hauled it up two flights of stairs at the youth hostel, the sight of her neatly written labels made my insides contract because I missed her so much, and I had to swallow several times before the lump in my throat subsided sufficiently in order for me to suppress any tears. The dormitory smelt musty, almost as though something damp had been left in there over the winter. Every time I smell anything like that now, it feels like I'm transported back to that dormitory all over again and I have to shudder at the memory. There were as many as seven bunk beds in our dormitory to accommodate the 13 girls in my class, but all the others girls had inevitably paired up with each other, leaving me to claim the seventh bunk by myself. Kylie Sinclair and some of her friends were standing in a group at the other end of the room and I have a vivid recollection of what Kylie was wearing. It was a bright mauve shell suit, and her blonde wavy hair was tied up in a pineapple ponytail on top of her head, using a matching mauve scrunchy. She was always dressed in the latest trends with the most fashionable hair styles that the rest of us could only dream of. Her friends were a little more understated but they all had matching bum bags and they visibly tightened any gaps amongst the circle in which they were standing when they saw me looking across the room at them. I sighed and continued with my unpacking, although a large part of me wanted to keep most of my belongings in the suitcase because unpacking them would have been like admitting that I was actually obliged to stay there for longer than a few hours.

Barry Harper and the other boys in our class were in a dormitory across the corridor, and because my bunk was closest to the door, I could hear them laughing and shouting together every night when we were all supposed to be settling down and going to sleep. The teachers didn't seem to do anything about it, not even Mrs Greaves who was always such a stickler for discipline.

I decided on our first night there that if I tried to keep a low profile all week then I probably wouldn't leave myself too susceptible to any kind of ridicule, but this approach actually ended up having completely the opposite effect because the other girls in the dormitory persisted on asking me why I was being so quiet. Kylie immediately jumped to the conclusion that I must have been crying because my covers were pulled right up over my head like a protective cocoon. The more she and her friends taunted me about how subdued I was behaving, the more I felt like crying for real, until eventually I was reduced to a blubbering heap in a blanket. My body was quivering uncontrollably and stifling my sobs became completely impossible.

One particularly loud squeak of emotion prompted Kylie to jump out of her own bunk in protest and storm down the corridor to the teachers' dormitory, and when she returned she had Mrs Greaves in tow.

"What's the matter Julia?" demanded Mrs Greaves pulling my bed covers back. I had my back to her and my knees were pulled up tightly into my chest as I clung onto my favourite bedtime teddy.

"Your crying is disturbing the other girls. Unless you can learn to control your emotions you will have to come and spend the night in the teachers' dormitory with myself and the other grownups."

And that is exactly what I had to do. But I was particularly disgruntled about it because my parents had gone to the trouble of warning Mrs Greaves about how homesick I would be when they met with her but she had completely refused to listen.

Of course these days no such thing would be allowed to happen. A child like me certainly wouldn't have been subjected to further anxiety provoking experiences such as a dormitory full of unsympathetic girls, or some of the trauma and torment that was to be inflicted on me throughout the course of the 5 days that followed. But anxiety didn't even exist in those days. Everyone believed in the 'put up and shut up' approach. And there is a certain amount of sense in that because many therapists discourage avoidance tactics when they are trying to deal with specific anxiety provoking situations. But those fateful five days in Wales completely tipped the balance for me. It was simply too much for me to cope with. In fact, even an emotionally strong person probably would have struggled at times.

Shyness is often viewed as quite a positive trait, particularly in the UK where being reserved is highly regarded. Shy children are endearing, as well as being calm and thoughtful and generally well behaved, which, when compared with their more impulsive or destructive counterparts, can be a welcome blessing. But because my extreme shyness resulted in me being unable to fully engage in social activities, I actually presented quite a challenge for my parents and many of the other adults who were responsible for me when I was growing up. It was clear that Mrs Greaves resented me for feeling like that, and she actually ended up compounding my problems even further as a result. In fact, she became even more of a bully to me on that fateful field trip than Barry or Kylie did.

Chapter eleven

Sunday 12th May 2019

That weekend, Jules found herself driving to her parents' house for Sunday lunch with an almighty hangover. She and Amy had stayed up until as late as 2am the night before and they had also managed to consume about a bottle and a half of wine throughout the course of the evening, enabling her to numb the memory of Drew a little more. But now she would be obliged to endure one of her mum's less than satisfactory Sunday roasts whilst listening to Christian and his equally pretentious girlfriend Suzy rambling on about how wonderful their life was.

She pulled up in her parents' driveway just as Christian and Suzy were getting out of their convertible sports car. Predictably, the slightest glimpse of sunshine had encouraged Christian to put the roof down, in spite of the fact that it was a particularly chilly spring morning. Suzy was very attractive. She was of mixed race origin with chocolate brown hair extensions and immaculately applied make-up. Her finger nails were always beautifully manicured and her clothes boasted a range of designer labels. Jules looked down at her own Marks & Spencer's outfit and sighed before grabbing her handbag from the passenger seat and opening her car door.

"Hello," she smiled, leaning in to receive an air kiss on each cheek from Suzy, as her equally expensive perfume wafted in her direction. Jules swallowed the stale taste in her mouth and tried to ignore how nauseous she was feeling, as Christian threw his arm around her shoulders and squeezed her tightly;

"You look a bit peaky little sis," he teased. "Have you been out on the town again? Mum tells me you went speed dating last week!"

"It was just a bit of fun," Jules replied, trying to make it sound as though she lived a very eventful existence. It was obvious that Christian wasn't in the least bit interested in Jules' social life though because no sooner had he asked the question, than he was ringing their parents' front door bell and smothering Suzy's neck with kisses while they waited for Mr Croft to let them in. Jules knew that her dad would be on door-answering duty as her mum would no doubt be up to her elbows in roast potato peelings and Yorkshire pudding batter.

"I'm just basting the beef," Mrs Croft shouted from the kitchen, as Jules, Christian and Suzy followed Mr Croft straight through into the living room in order to keep out of her way. Christian and Suzy collapsed onto the comfortable sofa together, leaving Jules to perch uneasily on the edge of the not-so comfortable arm chair opposite them, and as they continued to smoother one another with kisses, Jules' nausea started to return with a vengeance.

Jules' parents had lived in their house for almost 40 years, and whilst it was a charming detached property with a beautifully manicured garden, the inside looked as though it hadn't been redecorated since the day they moved in. There was thick floral wallpaper in every room and the floors were covered throughout with brightly coloured carpets, including the bathroom. Jules dreaded to think how many years' worth of urine stains there were hidden amongst the thick pile of the carpet around the toilet pan. Having said that, her mum kept the entire house immaculately clean and tidy, and her dad was a very keen gardener. It had been eight years since she had moved out of home, and they still appeared to have no intension of downsizing.

"Your mother tells me that I need to prepare a toast," smiled Mr Croft, passing everyone a champagne flute and then waiting for his wife to join them. Jules had completely forgotten that Christian was due to be making some kind of announcement today and reluctantly stood up again as soon as her mum entered the room, so that she could raise a glass and pretend to look happy for him.

"Have I missed anything?" said Mrs Croft, looking hot and flustered as she untied her apron and accepted a glass of champagne from the bottle that her husband had just uncorked.

"Not yet," smiled Christian, without taking his eyes off Suzy for a single second. "But as you know, I do have an announcement to make."

Jules rolled her eyes discretely as her brother continued to try and milk his big moment for as long as possible, before eventually confessing;

"Last week I asked Suzy to marry me and I'm very pleased to report that she said yes!"

Jules' parents wasted no time in congratulating them both with what felt like a particularly long drawn-out series of hugs and kisses, during which Jules couldn't help but wonder why they had decided to wait an entire week to break the news to everyone. A simple phone call just wouldn't have been enough for Christian though. He needed to build the suspense up for as long as possible, giving their parents the opportunity to buy the most expensive bottle of champagne that they could lay their hands on, and then make an official, public announcement in front of everyone in order to try and inflate his oversized ego even further. But at least he hadn't chosen to invite the extended family along too.

Jules and Christian had always taken sibling rivalry to the extreme. They really were like chalk and cheese. Jules was withdrawn and subservient while Christian was outgoing and brash. Jules was unpopular at school while Christian seemed to have a harem of friends, and was always far too busy enjoying his social life to concentrate on his school work. But he was also extraordinarily academic, a trait that he appeared to have inherited from their father, because his exam grades were exceptional and he had gone on to carve a very successful career as a Marketing Executive, which had enabled him to live such a luxurious lifestyle.

While Jules had struggled both socially and academically, Christian had just taken everything in his stride. He always seemed to fall on his feet, and Mr and Mrs Croft were in awe of his achievements. They were in the middle of admiring Suzy's enormous diamond ring when Mr Croft looked up and managed to catch his daughter's eye. She smiled at him reluctantly, encouraging her dad to break away from the champagne circle and put his arm around her;

"You'll get engaged one day too," he smiled reassuringly. "Besides, Christian's a couple of years older than you are."

"It's not the same for men," replied Jules, trying not to talk loud enough for anyone else to hear. "I'm 33 years old and I haven't even got a boyfriend."

"The right man's out there for you somewhere," her dad insisted, as she took one sip from her champagne flute and then decided to stay off the alcohol for the rest of the weekend. "You just haven't met him yet."

Jules thought for a moment before smiling and looking in to her father's eyes assertively. "Or maybe I *have*!"

❖

Monday 13th May 2019

Jules couldn't quite believe that she had actually arrived at the hospital where Drew worked, and she wasn't even nursing an injury, or visiting one of her students. On this occasion, she was there to go and visit *Drew* instead, in order to then undergo the single most nerve-wracking decision of her entire life; to ask him out. It was Monday lunch time and she had thought about nothing else ever since Christian and Suzy's engagement announcement the day before.

The Accident and Emergency department was heaving with people as usual, and Jules knew that she would need to wait until Drew was between patients before he would be able to deal with a personal visitor, so she notified the receptionist that she was there, and then went to sit nervously in the waiting area. Every time the double doors in front of her swung open and someone in a pair of blue scrubs emerged, her heart started pounding in her chest. But almost 45 minutes ended up ticking past and there was still no sign of him. She looked at her watch again and then started to remove her coat from the back of the chair next to her, reminding herself that the lunch hour was almost over and that she was due to spend the rest of the afternoon preparing for her meeting with Louisa and Caitlin on Wednesday. Just as she was about to stand up and put her coat on, a tall figure appeared beside her, causing her stomach to start doing somersaults.

"Hi Jules," frowned Drew. "Is everything OK?"

"Yes, fine thanks," replied Jules, rather hurriedly, as the nerves took over her vocal chords. "I just came to apologise for being so abrupt when I bumped into you at our house last week. I was stressed about work."

"I see," Drew smiled, as he processed what Jules was telling him. "You don't need to explain yourself to me."

"Don't I?" Jules replied, sounding a little disappointed, before side-tracking slightly in the fear of making a fool of herself. "What I mean is, no, of course I don't. I was just saying; that's all. So how was your weekend?"

Drew avoided the question and looked deep into Jules' eyes, spurring her face to flush again. "Was there another reason for your visit? I'm pretty sure you haven't come here just to find out how my weekend was."

They both stared at each other for what felt like an eternity before Jules managed to scrape enough courage together to speak again, but just as she was about to open her mouth, Drew's pager went off.

"I'd better go," he explained, apologetically, unclipping it from the waistband of his trousers. Jules' enthusiasm drooped and she swallowed hard as Drew smiled again and then started to walk away. She had been waiting here for over three quarters of an hour and had only managed to fumble her way through a 30 second conversation with him before they had been interrupted. She couldn't waste this opportunity and she desperately wanted him to ask her out so that she wouldn't have to be the one to say it instead. She just didn't want to risk the possibility of being rejected again.

"Drew!" she called after him, as he made his way towards the double doors and back beyond the point of no return. "There *was* something else I wanted to ask you actually."

Drew turned around expectantly as Jules caught up with him in the doorway and then handed him one of her business cards, upon which she had circled her mobile phone number and scribbled 'fancy a drink?' alongside it. But before Drew had been given the opportunity to actually look at what she had placed in his hand, Jules turned around and ran as fast as she could towards the exit, determined not to look behind her.

Chapter twelve

June 1997

One of the most horrifying examples of that traumatic trip to Wales was when I returned to my own bunk bed the morning after I had stayed awake sobbing in the teachers' dormitory. I pulled the duvet back and discovered that my bed sheets were completely soaked through, almost as though someone had poured an entire bucket of water over my bed. The mattress had absorbed most of the moisture, but some of it was running through the base of the bed and onto my suitcase underneath. I grabbed as many of my belongings as I could and started dabbing them frantically with the underside of my pyjama sleeve, but it was a futile exercise. Everything was ruined; even my mum's neatly written labels were practically illegible from where the ink had run. I was devastated.

Even though I knew that one of the other girls in my dormitory must have been responsible, my instinct was to conceal what had happened to avoid any further embarrassment. But Kylie didn't even give me the chance to throw my duvet back over the mattress before she strutted across the room to where I was standing, initially oblivious to what I had been trying to do.

She actually apologised for making me cry the night before, but I remember finding it very difficult to put any degree of faith in the sincerity of her remorseful confession. Ever since our year 5 Christmas production she had purposefully made it her mission to alienate me from the rest of the girls in our class, even the nurturing ones who chose to turn a blind eye to what was going on between us because they were afraid of becoming a 'victim' like me. I used to look over at them pleadingly whilst we were at school, and as such, during that field trip, they managed to perfect the art of avoiding eye contact with me at all costs. I could tell that they felt guilty though because their instinct was to help people. And to this day, I maintain that if there were more people like them in the world, children like Kylie Sinclair and Barry Harper wouldn't stand a chance.

Nowadays school children have PSHE lessons: Personal, Social and Health Education. And as part of that they're taught how to respect and care for each other. Society can be incredibly uncaring and selfish. People don't seem to know how to behave around each other anymore. Everything's computerised, including most forms of communication. In fact, even self-service checkouts in shops no longer require you to actually interact with another human being. And as a result of this, everyone's too wrapped up in themselves and they simply can't be bothered to think about anyone else; a sad fact reflected in the number of occasions that I am obliged to step into the gutter whenever I encounter anyone walking in the opposite direction to me down the street. And why nobody ever seems to take responsibility for anything anymore; to pick up their own litter, to wait patiently in a traffic jam, or to apologise when they do something wrong.

I accepted Kylie's apology that morning because I wanted her to leave me alone, but unfortunately my attempt to conceal my wet mattress was hopeless, and before I knew it she had attracted her entire entourage to my end of the room, including Barry Harper who had been skulking outside in the corridor. He burst into the dormitory and marched straight up to my bed, practically rubbing his hands together with glee. I'll never forget the malicious tone in his voice as he uttered the immortal words that have remained etched in my memory ever since;

"Have you wet your bed Egg Girl?" he laughed. "I'll have to start calling you 'Wee Wee Girl' from now on instead!"

I tried so hard to tell him that it wasn't me, but my throat had closed up in fear and all I could focus on was the continuous drip of liquid that was still running through my mattress and onto the floor.

"Wee wee girl!" Barry sang wildly, drawing an even larger crowd of onlookers towards us from the corridor as well as from the other end of the dormitory. "Julia's wet the bed!"

'Wee wee girl', 'Wee wee girl' was all I could hear, and the slow and steady dripping of the water that was seeping out from underneath my mattress was all I could look at. The pressure was so unbearable that eventually I felt my bladder constrict. I hadn't been to the toilet all night because I was afraid of getting out of bed whilst I was staying in the teachers' dormitory, and before I was able to make sense of what was happening, I could feel something warm and moist running down the inside of my thighs. I would have made a hasty retreat to the bathroom but for some reason I found myself frozen to the spot, just like I did on the year 4 sports day. Only this time it was a lot more humiliating than skidding on an egg. Barry had accused me of wetting myself and now his accusations had become a devastating reality.

❖

The part of the brain that controls memory can actually block certain traumatic events out as a way of protecting itself from Post Traumatic Stress Disorder. Although some forms of PTSD can simply conjure up a feeling as opposed to an event because that's the only bit that you remember anyway; the feeling. In fact, sometimes it doesn't necessarily depend on what *you experience; it's more to do with* how *you deal with it. It was over twenty years ago and my memory of what happened immediately after I wet myself that morning is a complete blur. But I don't believe that my poor recollection of it has anything to do with how long ago it was because I can still remember my year 6 parent's evening with Mrs Greaves virtually word for word. And I can vividly describe what Kylie Sinclair was wearing when we arrived at the youth hostel. So I believe that my subconscious has blocked it out because it was simply too traumatic for me to come to terms with.*

I know that Mrs Greaves was summoned again and I know that fresh bed linen was provided, even though I was obliged to spend a further two nights in the teachers' dormitory whilst my mattress dried out. I couldn't understand why they wouldn't just let me sleep on the top bunk instead, and I was actually left questioning whether I had in fact wet the bed the night before, but despite my somewhat sketchy memory, I knew in my heart of hearts that someone had poured water over it, and if it wasn't one of the other girls then it must have been Barry. To this day, I still don't know for sure that it was him, but that dreadful boy was at the root of everything bad that happened to me in my life back then, and he had been loitering outside our dormitory the following morning, almost as though he was waiting for something humiliating to happen to me.

I also don't recall how I got to the bathroom to clean myself up, or what the activity was that day. But what I do know is that each and every individual element of that field trip was like another nail in my coffin, and they have all clung to my memory as a series of unbearable incidents, culminating in what later proved to be one of the worst weeks of my entire childhood. Amongst other things, our itinerary included mountain biking, pony trekking, canoeing, and orienteering. I could not have created a less suitable or desirable list of activities for Julia Croft to embark on. But my mum had signed the consent form; and staying at the youth hostel by myself whilst the rest of my class went out and enjoyed themselves, was simply not an option. Mrs Greaves was absolutely adamant that I should join in with every excursion and I was forbidden from complaining about any of it because I had caused everyone more than enough trouble already. In fact the only activity that I was vaguely able to cope with was the pony trekking, despite my itchy eyes and streaming nose due to the horse hair allergy that I had inherited from my mum.

Everything else was a living hell, particularly with the addition of Mrs Greaves' stern facial expressions bearing down on me at every available opportunity. Up until that trip to Wales I had managed to console myself with the possibility that she always had my best interests at heart, even if it didn't actually feel like it most of the time. She gave me that part in the Christmas play because she wanted to encourage me to shine, and because she knew that if it went well, it would boost my confidence a little bit. And for a while there I was convinced that she had forced me to come away on the field trip for the same reasons. To boost my confidence and to give me the opportunity to prove to myself that I could do anything I put my mind to. But she wasn't just strict, she was unkind. And her methods were a catalyst for the likes of Barry Harper, who took immense pleasure in quite literally 'rocking the boat' out on the river, causing me to cling onto the sides of my canoe in terror as the water viciously lapped around me. Every time I protested about something, Mrs Greaves told me off for complaining, much to Barry's amusement. And every time Mrs Greaves told me off, my eyes erupted with tears. I felt completely powerless and alone. No one understood and no one cared. My parents were hundreds of miles away and there was absolutely nothing that I could do about it.

On the day of the mountain biking I had been given a bike which had a seat that was too high for me. I had miraculously managed to pass my cycle proficiency test in year 5, but I didn't like the feeling of not being able to put my feet on the ground. So in order to prove a point, rather than simply lowering the seat a little, Mrs Greaves deliberately traded it for another bike which was far too small, and every time I peddled, my knees bashed the handle bars. I was so covered in bruises by the end of it that I sobbed myself to sleep again, sinking my fingernails into the soft flesh on my forearms in order to distract myself from the pain.

On the penultimate day of the field trip, we were divided into groups according to our house teams, and given some maps and a compass. Because I knew that Barry was in the same team as me, I went up to Mrs Greaves whilst she was waiting for everyone to climb into the minibuses, and I begged her to let me go in a different group. But she dismissed me immediately and simply told me to get on with it. Remarkably, rather than using this situation as a convenient excuse to play yet another prank on me, Barry simply chose to exclude me from the activity altogether, and he wouldn't even give me a copy of the map. I was so afraid of spending time with him that I actually felt quite relieved when I ended up getting left behind, but my sense of direction was pretty poor at the best of times because I had always been so used to allowing my mum and dad to drag me around by the hand everywhere they went. I had never even possessed the ability to navigate my way around our local supermarket unaided. So at eleven years old, when I found myself embarking upon an orienteering exercise in the middle of the Welsh countryside with not even so much as a compass to help me work out which way was North, I didn't quite appreciate at first, how serious the situation was.

No one appeared to have realised that I was missing, until they all reassembled back at base and took the register. Meanwhile, I remained hunched beneath a tree just a few hundred metres away from where the minibuses had dropped us off because I knew that everyone would be likely to assemble there again once their orienteering was complete. But rather than being relieved to find me, or concerned for my welfare, Mrs Greaves was furious. I suspect her fury was simply trying to mask any semblance of guilt that she may have been experiencing for demonstrating such negligence, because misplacing a child, particularly a primary school child, was an extremely serious offence.

Of course, nothing further was done about it and she returned to the youth hostel in stony silence before instructing us all to pack our suitcases and assemble in the dining hall for supper. Once everyone had eaten, we were invited outside to toast marshmallows on the camp fire. It was early evening but the sun was still high in the sky at that time of year and I remember wishing that it would get dark as quickly as possible so that I could go to bed, fall asleep and then wake up the following morning knowing that this nightmare field trip was finally over. As we gathered around the camp fire, Mrs Greaves stood up and gave a speech about how proud she was of all of us for making the year 6 residential such a success. But just as she was about to sit back down on the log that she had been perched on before her little announcement, she decided to add the immortal words;

"I also want to take this opportunity to congratulate Julia for making it all the way through to the end of the week. Can we all give her a round of applause?"

Everyone sniggered and reluctantly clapped their hands together as I stared at the camp fire feeling utterly mortified. I couldn't help but surmise that she had simply said that in order to humiliate me even further, as punishment for all the challenges that I had provided her with over the past seven days. As I tentatively looked up at the satisfied expression on her face, it became clear that my suspicions were correct. And the final three weeks at Acornfields JMI couldn't be over quickly enough for me after that.

Chapter thirteen

Wednesday 15th May 2019

Jules had spent the past two days feeling completely elated about her visit to the hospital on Monday lunchtime, because Drew had wasted no time in responding to her rather tentative attempt to ask him out, by sending her a text message that very same afternoon. They had arranged to meet for a drink on Saturday evening, at the pub where the speed dating event had taken place. It was the first date that Jules had been on since her break up with Greg, and she was overcome with a powerfully emotional mixture of both nerves and excitement. She really liked Drew and she was determined to try and pursue a proper relationship with him without scaring him off completely. Besides, he couldn't possibly be accused of being an even bigger commitment-phobe than *she* was.

She was just about to prepare for her facilitated meeting between Caitlin and Louisa when her phone rang, causing her heart to leap into her throat. Now that Drew had her mobile number, she was terrified of the prospect of receiving an actual call from him, in the fear that she would end up suffering from an embarrassing case of verbal diarrhoea. Text messages were a lot safer because she could read them back to herself at least a dozen times before eventually pressing the send button. She picked her phone up from the desk and discovered that it was her mum's name on the display screen instead, before experiencing a combination of relief and disappointment.

"Hi mum" she said, unenthusiastically, looking at the clock on the wall in her office in order to confirm that she only had 5 minutes until Caitlin and Louisa were due to arrive.

"Hello Julia," her mum replied. "I'll make this quick because I know you're at work. I've just spoken to your brother."

Jules rolled her eyes and then braced herself for what her mother was about to say;

"He and Suzy have decided to have a bit of an engagement party at that lovely new Thai restaurant in town and he wanted me to let you know when it is."

Jules located her diary in her handbag and started flicking through the pages in the assumption that it would probably end up being in a few weeks' time, when Mrs Croft suddenly dropped the bombshell;

"It's on Saturday evening."

"*This* Saturday evening?" Jules confirmed, reminding herself of her date with Drew. "I already have plans this Saturday"

"Well you'll just have to rearrange them," replied her mum, unsympathetically. "You can't miss Christian's engagement party; you're his sister."

Just as Jules was about to try and find a way to wriggle out of it, there was a knock on her office door.

"I can't talk now mum," she sighed, feeling defeated. "Some of my students have just arrived for a counselling session."

Unsurprisingly, Louisa was the first of the two girls to arrive, and she entered the office very nervously as Jules smiled warmly and placed her phone in her handbag under her desk, so as to resist temptation. This was a very important meeting for both Louisa *and* Caitlin, and Jules needed to give their situation her full and undivided attention. She would just have to sort her predicament about Saturday night out later.

"There's no need to look so nervous," Jules insisted, as Louisa pulled up one of the chairs opposite her. "Try and think of today as a positive step forward. Caitlin's agreed to attend this meeting too so she obviously wants to try and resolve your situation just as much as you do."

"Assuming she turns up of course," replied Louisa, sceptically, reminding Jules that she and Caitlin had failed to actually speak to each other throughout the duration of her suspension. Ever since last Monday, Jules had repeatedly called her and left messages, and every so often Caitlin would text her back in order to let Jules know that she was OK. But she was determined to discourage Jules from visiting her at home again, insisting instead that she would come along to the mediation with Louisa today.

"I expect she's just running a bit late," smiled Jules, looking up at her clock again and then trying to put Louisa at ease by changing the subject;

"How's your English Literature coursework going?"

"Really well thanks," replied Louisa, brightening up a little. "I've even started working on a short story."

"That's great," Jules beamed. "What's the story about?"

Louisa crossed her legs, placed her hands in her lap and looked down hesitantly before replying;

"It's about bullying," she explained, sheepishly. "I find it helps me to write about my experiences from someone else's point of view."

Jules raised her eyebrows encouragingly. "That's quite an effective way of dealing with your problems. Writing things down acts as an outlet for them, and putting yourself in the shoes of your main character enables you to see the situation from an alternative perspective, which is exactly what I'm hoping to help you to achieve during this session today."

Just as Louisa was about to tell Jules a little more about her story, the office door swung open and Caitlin wandered in. Louisa's shoulders hunched as Caitlin pulled up a chair next to her. Caitlin flung her school bag on the floor in front of Jules' desk, and sank down into her seat with her arms folded and her eyes down. Jules looked up at the clock again, hoping that Caitlin would at least acknowledge the fact that she was late even if she had no intension of apologising for it, but Caitlin simply chewed a piece of gum dismissively and pretended that Jules and Louisa weren't even there.

"Thank you for joining us Caitlin," Jules smiled, trying to encourage her to look up. "I'm really pleased that you and Louisa have both agreed to meet up today in order to discuss your situation. Would either of you like to begin?"

There was a very long and very uncomfortable silence as the two girls both sat opposite Jules refusing to speak. Caitlin's dyed hair hung so far in front of her face that Jules could barely manage to work out what her expression was doing underneath it all, but it was obvious that she was trying to be as uncooperative as possible. And whilst it was clear that Louisa was perfectly willing and able to contribute to the meeting, Caitlin's demeanour had left her feeling even more introverted than she was already. So Jules resolved to take a different approach to the proceedings;

"OK, I would like you both to stand and face each other please," she instructed, urging Louisa to reluctantly push herself up from her seat and turn towards Caitlin with a look of pure trepidation on her face.

"Caitlin, that includes you," insisted Jules, when Louisa remained the only one standing.

Caitlin sighed and pushed her chair out from underneath herself aggressively, whilst continuing to stare at the floor. Jules tried not to react in the fear that Louisa would decide not to cooperate either, and simply continued to introduce them to one of her rather unorthodox communication techniques;

"Think of this as a word association exercise," she explained "If I were to say the word 'apple', one of you might respond by saying 'fruit' or 'tree'..."

"Or iPad!" sniggered Caitlin, enticing Louisa to laugh too. Jules excused Caitlin's facetious interruption because it had confirmed to her that both the girls were paying attention to what she was saying, as well as taking the opportunity to share a joke with one another.

"OK, well I think you get the gist," she smiled. "So how many other words can you each come up with relating to the word 'school'?"

There was another long pause as Louisa swallowed nervously and waited for Caitlin to speak first. Caitlin simply started tapping her foot on the floor and chewing her gum even more vigorously than she had been doing before, as her jagged bobbed dark hair continued to encase her face protectively and mysteriously. Eventually the silence was broken as Louisa drew a deep breath in and whispered;

"Exams," at which moment Jules turned her attention towards Caitlin again, hoping that she would decide to follow suit. When there was no response, Jules then suggested that Louisa could continue to come up with as many words as she was able to think of, before inviting Caitlin to interrupt her at any time. Caitlin simply snorted as if to suggest that she had no intention of joining in, persuading Louisa to make the bold decision to take the lead again;

"Teachers," she continued. "Homework. Revision. Assembly. Classroom. Playground..."

"Bike sheds!" Caitlin smiled, snidely. "Detentions. Friends. Lunch breaks. Boring lessons. Boffins!"

"Bullies!" retorted Louisa, defensively, aware that Caitlin's 'boffins' comment was aimed at her, at which point the two girls stood and stared at each other maliciously.

"Very good," insisted Jules, encouragingly, trying not to place any direct emphasis on the tension between them. "Now how many words can you each think of which are associated with the word 'bully'?"

"Ridicule," replied Louisa, without hesitation. "Intimidation. Hatred. Isolation. Loneliness..."

"Fear," interrupted Caitlin, beginning to mirror Louisa's vulnerable demeanour. "Pain. Misery. Entrapment..." her voice trailed off as her throat became choked with tears, prompting Louisa to look at Jules in surprise.

"Thank you girls," smiled Jules awkwardly, before pointing towards her office door and inviting Louisa to leave the room while she spoke to Caitlin alone. "You've both done really well today but I think we'll leave it there for now."

"Of course," smiled Louisa softly, retrieving her school bag from the floor next to her and respecting Jules' wishes. It had been a particularly enlightening experience for Louisa. Not only because of how articulate Caitlin was, but because of how emotional she had ended up. She couldn't help but wonder whether there was anything else going on, and concluded that she would just have to wait until their next session to find out more. Assuming there was going to *be* a next session of course.

As soon as Louisa had closed the door behind her, Jules made her way across the office to where Caitlin was standing and placed her hand on her shoulder reassuringly;

"What's *really* going on Caitlin?" she asked. "Why did you feel the need to phone me last week?"

Caitlin slowly lifted her head for the first time since she had entered the office, and revealed the *real* reason why she had been determined to spend the entire session looking down at the floor. Jules gasped in disbelief as Caitlin reluctantly tucked her hair behind her ears and exposed the most enormous bruise along the left side of her face. The skin around her left eyelid was swollen and her upper lip was split.

"Who did this to you?" Jules insisted. "Was it Mr Murphy?"

Caitlin refused to answer as a tear cascaded down her cheek, but her silence spoke volumes and told Jules exactly what she needed to know. 'Caitlin the class bully' was being bullied herself and by none other than her own stepfather.

"Did he find out about your suspension?" continued Jules, determined to try and get to the bottom of the situation.

"It wasn't Steve!" shouted Caitlin, defensively. "I just fell down the stairs and banged my face on a wall."

"Tell me the truth Caitlin," Jules insisted. "You can trust me. I promise I won't tell anyone; not even Mr Langley."

"I *am* telling you the truth," replied Caitlin, raising her voice again and then making her way towards the door. "It was an accident. Steve had nothing to do with it. Now please leave me alone!" and with that, she stormed out of Jules' office and slammed the door behind her.

❖

Jules could think of nothing else after her session with Caitlin and Louisa. She just didn't know what to do. She knew that she wasn't allowed to breach confidentiality by sharing Caitlin's revelation with the rest of the teaching staff, but she also knew that she couldn't just sit back and allow her situation at home to continue. Involving Social Services would cause all kinds of problems, particularly if Caitlin wasn't prepared to tell anyone how she had *really* managed to sustain her injuries. But doing nothing would give her stepfather the opportunity to beat her up again, and next time she might not be lucky enough to get away with just a few cuts and bruises. When Jules agreed to take on this role, she had no idea what she was letting herself in for. She felt completely out of her depth and was desperate to talk to someone about it. But rather than confiding in her mum or one of her oldest friends like Amy, she found herself dialling Drew's phone number for the very first time.

"Hi, it's Jules," she announced, as the hand that was holding the receiver started shaking uncontrollably and her voice was overcome with nerves.

"Hello you" replied Drew, warmly, putting her straight at ease. "Are you OK?"

"I'm afraid there's a bit of a problem about Saturday night," Jules explained, starting to relax. "My brother's having an engagement party meal and I really need to be there."

She was determined to call and explain the situation properly, in the fear that a series of text messages would give the wrong impression. After all, she had finally managed to arrange a date with 'Dr Dish'; the last thing she wanted to do now was mislead him into thinking that she was the kind of girl to pull out of things at the drop of a hat.

"I understand," Drew replied, reassuringly. "So are you allowed to take a 'plus one' to the party?"

"Of course!" laughed Jules in surprise. "But are you sure you want to spend our first date with my entire family?"

"Why not?" exclaimed Drew. "I've been looking forward to seeing you on Saturday, and it will save you from having to make small talk with your extended family all evening. Besides, I'm sure we'll be able to sneak off and spend some time alone together after the meal."

Jules' stomach started doing somersaults again as an enormous smile spread across her face, at which point she reminded herself of the *other* reason why she had phoned him.

"Can I ask your advice about something?" she enquired, reluctantly, after a short pause. "It's completely confidential but I just don't know what to do and I really need to talk to someone."

"Of course," insisted Drew, empathetically. Being a doctor meant that he understood all about confidentiality.

Jules hesitated again and then decided to tell him everything, taking care not to disclose any of Caitlin's personal details. Drew listened attentively, causing goose bumps to prickle the surface of the skin around the back of her neck. She was actually confiding in a man who she had the potential to really care about. It was an unfamiliar feeling but it was also extremely comforting.

After she had finished explaining, Drew sighed reflectively before trying to come up with the appropriate response;

"We see this sort of thing in the hospital all the time," he replied. "You need to report it to Social Services so that they can investigate her injuries. I have a couple of good contacts if you want me to look them up?"

"Thanks," smiled Jules, softly, reaching across her desk and sliding her notepad towards her so that she could write the contact details down.

"Try not to worry about it," insisted Drew, sensing Jules' anguish. "You're doing the right thing."

"I hope so," Jules replied, tapping her pen on the desk nervously. "I really do hope so."

❖

Saturday 18th May 2019

"You look gorgeous" declared Amy glancing up from her tablet, as Jules joined her in the living room half an hour before Drew was due to pick her up for their date. She was wearing an electric blue dress with matching eye shadow and her hair had been lightly curled at the ends.

"I can't find my black cardigan though," grumbled Jules, lifting up the cushions on the sofa in the hope of finding it under one of them.

"Don't spoil your outfit with that," replied Amy. "You'll look a lot better without it."

"But the dress has short sleeves," Jules insisted. "And you know I have to cover my scar up."

"I know," sighed Amy, softly. "I think it might be in my room."

"Thank you," smiled Jules in relief, whilst turning to make a dash up the stairs. She sensed that Amy was a little deflated though and decided to rein herself in long enough to make sure she was OK.

"Are you looking at Facebook again?" she established, encouraging Amy to nod dejectedly.

"Megan's pregnant now too and I'm not even engaged yet. In fact, I don't even *live* with my boyfriend and we've been going out together for five years."

"Tim's asked you to move in with him loads of times," Jules reminded her. "You just prefer our house to his bachelor flat, and you know you can't afford to buy anywhere together yet."

"I know," mumbled Amy, looking down at her tablet again and allowing her facial expression to brighten up a little. "This is a piece of news that will make you smile. Apparently Barry Harper is in prison!"

"Since when have you been following ex Acornfields pupils on Facebook?" frowned Jules, whilst processing what Amy had just said.

"Since you refused to do it yourself," smiled Amy. "Don't you want to know what Barry's in prison for?"

"Not really," replied Jules, trying not to think about it too much. "I need to finish getting ready for the engagement party."

She hesitated before venturing to leave the room again. "That is unless you want me to stay at home tonight and talk about Tim?"

"Definitely not," insisted Amy. "You're not missing your big date with Dr Dish for anything."

By the time Jules had rescued her black cardigan from Amy's bedroom and given herself an extra spray of perfume, the doorbell rang, causing her stomach to turn inside out. She stared at her nervous reflection in the bathroom mirror and tried to compose herself before descending the stairs and making her way towards the front door. She could see Drew's tall silhouette through the frosted glass and took a deep breath as she leaned forward to open the door and let him in.

"Does the sister of the groom-to-be live here?" he smiled, putting her at ease straight away. He seemed to have a knack of doing that. He then presented Jules with a small posy of pink tulips and kissed her softly on the cheek, making her legs turn to jelly.

"You look beautiful," he observed, as she invited him into the hallway long enough for her to put the tulips in a vase of water.

"I bet you can't wait to see what she'll be wearing at the wedding!" teased Amy, appearing in the doorway of the living room with a huge smile on her face.

Jules cuffed her lightly on the arm with embarrassment and then gave her friend a hug. "Are you sure you're going to be OK tonight?"

"Of course I am," replied Amy. "And I'll try not to spend too long on Facebook."

Drew frowned as he and Jules left the house, prompting Jules to fill him in on Tim's commitment issues as they started to make their way down the street.

"Five years is a long time," he agreed. "I'm not surprised she's getting fed up with waiting."

There was a brief pause before he decided to continue. "So how come no one's managed to snap *you* up yet?"

In spite of the time of year, it was late enough for the early evening dusk to disguise the colour of Jules' cheeks as she deliberated how to respond.

"I just haven't met the right man yet," she then replied, before changing the subject. "So have you been to this new restaurant before?"

Drew sensed that Jules obviously wasn't ready to confide in him about any of her past relationships yet, particularly as they were still only less than half an hour into their first date, so he decided instead to go along with her segue.

"Not yet," he confessed, as they strolled alongside each other awkwardly. "But I've heard lots of good things about it."

"I like Thai food," smiled Jules, clutching onto the thin strap of her handbag and trying not to pay too much attention to Drew's right hand as it swung lightly with each step, occasionally brushing her left thigh if he got too close. She then started to laugh;

"I still can't believe you've agreed to be my 'plus one'. Can I apologise in advance for my family; I fear you won't be interested in having a second date with me by the time you've met them all!"

She then realised what she had said and blushed.

"It's going to take a lot more than that to put me off," he smiled, giving her a nudge. "Besides, who's going to be your 'plus one' at the wedding?"

Jules erupted into giggles and clutched onto Drew's arm affectionately, before realising what she was doing and pulling away.

"You're getting a bit ahead of yourself aren't you," she smiled, as they approached the door of the Thai restaurant and then hesitated.

Drew laughed, inviting Jules to walk through the door ahead of him;

"Well I guess we're about to find out."

Chapter fourteen

Jules' pulse started racing as she reluctantly entered the restaurant. The open door had unleashed a burst of warmth and noise as waiters rearranged tables and chairs, and Suzy, who was wearing a rather stunning silver evening dress, fussed around them with silver balloons and white floral table arrangements. Each of the tables had been decorated in silver and white, and there were pretentious looking photos of the happy couple beaming down on them from large wall canvases. Jules despised wall canvas photos, particularly of her smug brother and his super model fiancée. Drew rubbed her arm reassuringly as she waited for various members of her family to descend on them, at which point Mrs Croft came scurrying towards them through the crowd.

"Hi mum," Jules smiled, giving her a kiss on the cheek. "I'd like you to meet Drew."

Mrs Croft's eyebrows shot so far up her forehead, that Jules feared they would disappear below her hairline altogether.

"Are you and my daughter a couple?" she smiled, composing herself a little as Drew gently shook her hand.

"He's my date," replied Jules, determined not to let anyone know that this was actually the *first* time she and Drew had been out together.

"We've been seeing each other for a while now," agreed Drew, referring to the fact that they had spent the past three weeks bumping in to one another; not that Jules' mother needed to know that of course.

"And what do you do for a living Drew?" beamed Mrs Croft, as Christian and Suzy came to join them.

"I'm a doctor," replied Drew, making Jules feel very smug. "I work in the A&E department at the local hospital."

"So you're a 'proper' doctor then," confirmed Christian, shaking his hand. "Not just a boring GP; way to go sis!"

"This is my brother," Jules sighed, introducing them.

"Ah, the groom-to-be," smiled Drew, enthusiastically. "Congratulations; is this the blushing bride?"

"I'm Suzy," smiled Suzy, awarding him with a pair of air kisses. Jules cringed at the thought of how insincere this looked, before managing to catch her father's attention from across the other side of the restaurant. As her dad came to greet them, Jules could feel herself relaxing a little because she knew that he and Drew would probably manage to pass the time of day with each other by discussing any manner of different subjects, particularly anything sports related. Drew was polite enough to do his best to include Jules' mum in the conversation as well though, which definitely seemed to go down well;

"I don't know the first thing about cricket," Mrs Croft smiled, as her husband presented her with a Martini and tonic from the bar.

"A lot of the doctors from the hospital play it; it's a very civilised sport," insisted Drew, as Jules observed the scene and smiled to herself. He appeared to have both her parents eating out of the palm of his hand within only ten minutes of meeting them, and she couldn't help but imagine him as their future son-in-law, immediately reminding herself that this was still only their first date.

Christian and Suzy meanwhile, had spent less than 30 seconds introducing themselves to him before disappearing to the back of the restaurant in order to finalise the seating plan.

"How did they manage to secure such a large booking at short notice?" frowned Jules, following her parents to the long table in the very centre of the restaurant, that had been decorated with silver and white balloons and 'Congratulations on your engagement' banners.

"You know what your brother's like," replied Mr Croft, taking a sip from his pint of Guinness. "He always seems to find a way around these things."

"Doesn't he just," sighed Jules, enticing Drew to raise his eyebrows at her with interest as they started to scour the place settings for their names.

"So what's the deal with you and Christian?" enquired Drew, when they eventually located their seats and sat down next to each other. The rest of the party guests were talking loudly but Jules was still convinced that someone would be able to overhear their conversation so she leant across to whisper in Drew's ear. As she did so, the delicious smell from his neck distracted her momentarily and she almost forgot what they were talking about.

"We're just very different," she eventually explained sipping her glass of wine. "Christian's very outgoing and I'm quite shy."

Drew smiled in agreement when he thought about how long it had taken Jules to admit that she was attracted to him.

"There's nothing wrong with being shy," Jules insisted, noticing the cheeky expression on Drew's face and then cuffing him lightly with the back of her hand.

"I never said there was," whispered Drew, leaning in even closer so that he was almost brushing her earlobe with his bottom lip as he spoke. "In fact, I think it's rather endearing."

His warm breath tickled Jules' neck and she felt her entire body flush as she tried to compose herself;

"Anyway, as I was saying," she then laughed, distractedly, as Drew eventually leaned back in his chair and smiled at the couple who were taking their seats opposite them "Christian can be a little too 'over-confident' sometimes, to the point of being cocky. And he always seems to excel in absolutely everything he does, without even trying that hard. School, friendships, career... even his fiancée is practically a super model!"

"She's alright I suppose," agreed Drew, looking across the room at Suzy as she greeted a few more of their engagement party guests.

"Only alright?" quoted Jules in amazement. "She's absolutely stunning!"

"Well I guess she's not really my type," insisted Drew, draining his wine glass and then reaching across the table to fill it up again. He hovered the bottle over Jules' glass but she waved it away in the fear that she would end up getting too tipsy.

"What about Amy?" she continued, determined to try and establish exactly what type of woman Drew really *was* attracted to.

"She's alright too, I suppose," he replied, nonchalantly. "Although she's a little too full of herself really. She's got a good sense of humour, but she can come across as a bit crass sometimes."

"Really?" gasped Jules incredulously. She had always assumed that Amy was just one of those women who *every* man was attracted to, regardless of whether they had a 'type' or not. After all, she was blonde, beautiful and confident; what wasn't to like about her?

"If I had to describe my perfect woman," smiled Drew, putting his hand on Jules' knee "I would have to say; shy, sweet, thoughtful, funny, down to earth..."

Jules couldn't help but look down at the table with embarrassment at that point because it quickly became obvious by the way he was looking at her that Drew was describing her. He brushed a strand of hair away from her face, stimulating her to look up again

"...and I particularly like clumsy brunettes!"

Jules cuffed him again and laughed when she thought about the incident with the chocolate bar display in Mr Shah's shop, not to mention the mess she had made in her bedroom when she was looking for Caitlin's file. Drew always made her feel so nervous, particularly when she had bumped into him half naked on their landing. He was wearing a black shirt to the engagement party but she could still see his broad shoulders and his muscular arms rippling through it. They stared at each other intensely for a second, at which point they were interrupted by one half of the couple who had taken their seats opposite them;

"I thought I ought to introduce myself as we're going to be sitting with each other this evening," he announced, as Jules managed to suppress her feelings for Drew long enough to look across at him and smile politely. "I'm Leroy," the man continued. "I'm Suzy's brother."

"Julia," Jules replied, stretching her right hand across the table in order to shake his. "I'm Christian's sister."

"So this is the sibling's part of the table," concluded Leroy, flashing a wide smile of brilliant white teeth, and then taking the opportunity to introduce his wife Rebecca to them as well. Rebecca was every bit as stunning as Suzy and her long black afro Caribbean hair had been beautifully braided using turquoise beads that matched the maternity tunic she was wearing. Drew smiled and shook their hands too, just as the waiting staff started presenting each table with a basket of prawn crackers.

"My favourite," announced Rebecca, delving into the basket before anyone else had a chance to help themselves.

"She's pregnant" explained Leroy, drawing their attention to Rebecca's bump. Jules clasped her hands together excitedly.

"Congratulations!" she beamed, looking as though she was about to give them both a round of applause. "Is it your first baby?"

Rebecca nodded as she finished her mouthful of prawn cracker. "We only got married last autumn so it came as a bit of a surprise. How long have you two been together?"

"Not very long at all by the looks of it," laughed Leroy. "I can spot a new relationship from a mile off. You've barely been able to take your eyes of each other since we sat down!"

Jules tentatively glanced sideways at Drew before blushing, prompting Rebecca to change the subject for fear of giving her husband the opportunity to embarrass either of them even further.

"So what do you do for a living Julia?"

"I'm a psychologist," Jules replied, feeling her face cool down again. "I've recently started working as a pastoral support officer at one of the local secondary schools, providing counselling to some of the children who are being bullied."

"I bet you're a natural at it," Drew smiled, putting his hand on her knee again.

"Thank you," smiled Jules, bashfully. "It's a brand new initiative and its early days still but I'm really enjoying it."

"I'm sure it will be brilliant," Drew assured her, as the sound of someone tapping their knife against the side of their wine glass interrupted them.

"May I have everyone's attention," announced Christian from the other end of the table, whilst Jules rolled her eyes. "Suzy and I would just like to say a huge thank you to each and every one of you for being here this evening, and for celebrating our engagement with us. I would also like to ask you all to raise a glass and toast my beautiful fiancée. She's the best thing that's ever happened to me and I can't wait to marry her."

"Your brother's so sweet," gushed Rebecca, as everyone held their glasses up in front of them.

"Yes, everyone loves Christian," agreed Jules, with a bitter undertone to her voice that only Drew seemed to pick up on.

"Where's the wine bottle?" she then insisted before draining her glass. "Maybe I *will* have that top up after all."

❖

"So what about your mum and dad?" enquired Drew, after they had finished their meal. "Do they think of Christian as a bit of a 'golden boy'?"

They had decided to retreat outside for some privacy while the rest of the engagement guests were saying their goodbyes to the happy couple, because Mr and Mrs Croft had invited some of the family back to their house for coffee and a slice of engagement cake afterwards.

"I suppose they do," Jules explained. "But they've always let him do what he likes. I, on the other hand, have been wrapped in cotton wool so many times that I've lost count."

"Well you're their little girl," teased Drew, giving her a nudge. "And you're the youngest. My parents are exactly the same with my sister."

"So why aren't *you* married yet?" smiled Jules, allowing the cool evening air to amplify how tipsy she was already feeling.

"I was," admitted Drew, causing Jules to stumble a little in surprise and then grab onto him for support "But it was a really long time ago; we were very young. We thought we were in love but then we ended up outgrowing each other. I'm 38 now and I have much more of an idea about the kind of woman I want to be with."

"And who's that?" replied Jules, as they turned to face each other.

"How much more obvious do you want me to be about it?" Drew confessed, before gently cupping her chin in his right hand and pulling her waist towards him with his left.

Jules felt herself melt into his embrace as his lips met hers, and clung onto his broad shoulders intensely as he slowly slipped his tongue into her mouth. This was the first time she had ever kissed anyone she really fancied and she was overcome with desire. That was until they were interrupted by a very familiar sounding voice which made Jules' blood run cold. She pulled away from Drew and looked behind her, at which point her worst suspicions were confirmed. Emerging from the restaurant was none other than her ex-boyfriend Greg, and he appeared to be walking straight towards them.

Chapter fifteen

"Hello Jules; long time no see," Greg smiled, as he approached the tree under which Jules and Drew had been embracing each other.

"What are you doing here Greg?" replied Jules, sounding uncomfortable, as Drew placed his hand on her shoulder protectively.

"Christian invited me," explained Greg, defensively, before looking Drew up and down. "I saw his engagement announcement on Facebook and he asked me if I fancied coming along for a drink with him after the meal."

"Bloody Facebook," Jules cursed, under her breath. "And bloody Christian!"

"Just because we're not together anymore doesn't mean that I'm not entitled to stay in touch with your brother," complained Greg, reminding Jules of how well Greg and Christian used to get on with each other. Looking at the snide expression on Greg's face now, she couldn't believe that she had managed to string a relationship out with him for as many as four years. The fact that he and Christian were such good friends ought to have been enough of a warning sign that she and Greg weren't suited to one another, but she just couldn't seem to see it at the time.

"So why aren't you in there having a drink with him?" snapped Jules, whilst turning to look up at Drew apologetically.

"Because I wanted to let you know that I was here," replied Greg. "In case it was weird for you."

"Why would it be weird for me?" retorted Jules, feeling the blood rush to the surface of her skin in rage. "We broke up more than four years ago."

Drew rubbed Jules' shoulder supportively as it became clear that Greg was beginning to regret his decision to go outside and speak to her. And as Greg slowly backed away from them and retreated inside the restaurant again, Jules started shaking uncontrollably.

"What happened between you two?" frowned Drew, wrapping his arms around her and holding her tightly.

"He made me remember how I used to feel when I was a child," Jules explained. "After our relationship ended, I felt completely and utterly worthless. The one person who was supposed to care about me the most in the world, had betrayed me in the worse possible way, and he actually managed to make *me* feel responsible for it."

"Did he cheat on you?" asked Drew, kissing the top of her head. Jules buried her face in his shoulder and nodded;

"I was very insecure," she explained. "Even at university. Greg used to flirt a lot and go out with his friends without telling me. It made me feel extremely paranoid. Eventually I became absolutely convinced that he was having an affair. So much so that I ended up driving him to cheat on me anyway. So from that point of view, I suppose you could say I *was* responsible."

"Don't say that," insisted Drew, squeezing her even tighter. "He was the one who was unfaithful, not you. And he doesn't even appear to feel any remorse."

"That's because he's an arrogant arsehole," concluded Jules, laughing a little and releasing herself from their embrace again. "Shall we go for a walk?" she then suggested. "If some of Christian's old Facebook friends have just turned up, it will be a while before any of the family will be ready to head back to Mum and Dad's house."

"Only if I can hold your hand," smiled Drew, inviting Jules to kiss him softly on the lips;

"That would be *more* than acceptable," she replied.

They walked down the road until they reached the entrance of the local park and then decided to take a more scenic route. As she felt Drew's warm fingers entwine with hers, Jules couldn't believe how at ease she was with him.

"I'm sorry I got so angry when I saw Greg," she insisted. "That's not a side of me that I wanted you to see tonight; or *ever* for that matter. I'm pleased to say that I don't show my angry side all that often."

"You don't need to apologise," replied Drew, as they approached the deserted children's play area. "I just can't believe he treated you like that."

Jules nodded solemnly, before deciding to snap them both out of what had happened outside the restaurant by jumping feet first onto the carpet of bark chippings and running across to one of the swings;

"Will you give me a push?" she then laughed, persuading Drew to gently shove her onto the seat of the swing and kiss her passionately.

"Why are you so perfect?" she whispered, as he softly moved his lips down to the bare skin around her neck. "What's the catch?"

"Why does there have to be a catch?" smiled Drew.

"Because there's *always* a catch!" Jules laughed, straightening her legs and then propelling herself forwards with her feet. Drew ran around to the back of her so that he could shove the swing even higher before declaring;

"I have an ex-wife!"

"Well I suppose that will have to do." concluded Jules, reminding herself that he had been married before. An ex-wife wasn't really the kind of catch that she had been concerned about though. Besides, bumping into Greg that evening had taught her that everyone has a past, even Drew. It depends on how you allow your past to affect your future that *really* matters. And that was something that Jules was aware of only too well.

❖

It was almost midnight by the time the Croft family eventually decided to retreat to Jules' parents' house for coffee, by which point Drew was beginning to look at his watch at regular intervals;

"I ought to be heading home soon," he announced. "I'm supposed to be on call tomorrow."

Jules couldn't help but feel a little relieved that he obviously had no intension of inviting himself back to her house for the night, because she felt as though she had bared more than enough of her soul to him already that evening; without having to explain the scar on her arm as well. As everyone made their way through to Mr and Mrs Croft's living room, Drew wasted no time in sinking down onto the comfortable double sofa that was usually reserved for Christian and Suzy, and rubbing the seat cushion next to him as an invitation for Jules to sit down too. Jules smiled smugly as Christian and Suzy perched uneasily on the edge of the armchair that she would normally be obliged to sit in, and then rested her head on Drew's shoulder.

"You two really do make a wonderful couple," gushed Mrs Croft, as she placed a tray of coffee cups on the low level table in the middle of the room and started filling some of them from the large cafetiere that Mr Croft had just handed to her.

"I can't believe Julia didn't tell us about you."

"We haven't been together for very long," insisted Jules. "Drew only agreed to be my plus one because we were supposed to be seeing each other this evening anyway. I wouldn't usually introduce a boyfriend to my entire family after only 3 weeks."

"It depends if you were hoping to scare him off!" laughed Christian, helping himself to a large slice of engagement cake.

"Well being confronted by Greg didn't help," complained Jules, staring at Christian pointedly.

"You know what Facebook's like sis," Christian replied, as he passed her a slice of cake that was barely half the size of his own.

"No actually, I don't" Jules retorted.

"Of course, I forgot; you're too scared of your past to run the risk of actually getting in contact with anyone from it," remarked Christian, snidely, as the rest of the room fell silent.

"Drew needs to make a move now," Jules eventually announced, awkwardly. "So I think I'll head home too."

"Are you alright love?" enquired Mr Croft, catching her by the arm as she made her way towards to door of the living room. "You've only just got here. You haven't even eaten your cake yet."

"I'm fine Dad, I'm just a bit tired that's all. I'll speak to you during the week."

As Jules handed the plate of rejected cake to her father and gave him a kiss on the cheek, Drew took a quick gulp of coffee and then thanked everyone for a pleasant evening before joining her in the hallway.

"Are you sure you're alright?" he whispered, as they let themselves out of the front door and escaped into the street.

"It's just Christian," replied Jules, slipping her arm through his. "He always seems to have a knack of making me feel completely inferior."

After a short pause, Jules felt the pit of her stomach sinking when she thought about whether Drew would be inclined to ask her on a second date. After all, during the course of the evening, she had managed to have a confrontation with her ex-boyfriend, *and* a disagreement with her family; she wouldn't be surprised if he never wanted to see her again.

"I should apologise," she insisted. "This has been a bit of a disastrous first date!"

"It's certainly been a little unorthodox," Drew laughed. "And as first dates go, it will definitely be one of my more memorable ones, but for all the *right* reasons."

"Thank you for being my 'plus one'," Jules smiled, turning to face him. "Believe it or not, I've really enjoyed myself tonight too."

"You know I've fancied you ever since we first met each other in the hospital a few weeks ago," explained Drew.

"Well why didn't you ask me out?" frowned Jules, trying not to blush.

"Because I wasn't sure whether *you* fancied *me*," Drew replied. "When we had our speed date, I was making a really big effort to flirt with you, but you didn't seem to want to know."

Jules thought back to the speed dating event two weeks ago and then remembered how defensive she had felt when Drew was complimenting her. She couldn't tell whether he was being genuine, or whether he was just trying to be like Fraser by saying what he thought she wanted to hear. And being reunited with Craig Riley hadn't helped.

"Well why didn't you stick around afterwards to talk to me?"

"I was on call," explained Drew. "And then I didn't know whether to send you a message through the speed dating website or not because you didn't seem that interested."

"I'm sorry," smiled Jules, before kissing him softly on the mouth. "I'm shy. And thanks to Greg, I have trouble trusting people sometimes."

Drew hesitated, took Jules' hands in his and stared deep into her eyes for a moment;

"Is there anything else you're not telling me?" he enquired, reticently. "I get the feeling that there's more to your past than you're letting on."

Jules pulled her hands away abruptly and then looked down at the ground. "That's not really any of your business." she snapped.

"I know it isn't, and I never should have asked you," insisted Drew, apologetically. "But you should know that you can talk to me about a*nything*; anything at all."

"I know," replied Jules, remorsefully, as they continued to walk down the street. Jules was desperate for Drew to ask her on another date before they parted, but she knew that she probably didn't deserve it, particularly after her latest outburst, so she decided not to say anything to encourage him either way and simply walked alongside him in silence until they eventually reached her house.

"Thank you for walking me home," she smiled, hesitating as she removed her front door key from her handbag and placed it in the lock.

"Are you sure you're OK?" clarified Drew, looking concerned. Jules nodded and opened the door, before planting a kiss on Drew's cheek and then escaping inside. Drew loitered on the doorstep for a few seconds, but made no attempt to embrace her more passionately, or to ask her whether he would be able to take her out again, prompting Jules to simply close the door behind her and then sink down onto the hall floor in tears.

"What's happened?" asked Amy, appearing at the top of the stairs.

Jules looked up ready to explain but then realised by the redness around her eyes that Amy had been crying too. She rushed up the stairs towards her and the two friends gave each other a much needed hug.

"Never mind about me," Jules insisted. "Why have you been crying?"

Amy led Jules through to her bedroom and they both collapsed in a defeated heap onto the bed together.

"Tim and I had a row," she explained, rubbing her eyes. "He rang me and I told him that I wanted us to buy our own place and move in together"

"I take it he wasn't too keen on the idea?" clarified Jules, grabbing one of Amy's scatter cushions and cradling it against her chest.

"You could say that," replied Amy, her facial expression brightening a little. "And I don't think he appreciated me trying to talk to him about it during the middle of his mate's stag do."

The two girls erupted into fits of giggles when they reflected on how inappropriate that was. Then Amy decided to take the opportunity of asking Jules how her date with Drew had gone.

"Well taking him to Christian and Suzy's engagement party was a *big* mistake," explained Jules. "And he hasn't asked me out again so I think I've completely blown it."

"You don't know that," smiled Amy, rubbing Jules' back reassuringly. "For him to have agreed to go out with your family in the first place is a really good sign."

"But he wasn't expecting to meet my ex-boyfriend as well!" laughed Jules, encouraging Amy to sit bolt upright in surprise;

"*Greg* was there?"

"Christian invited him," replied Jules, nodding. "Apparently they've been in contact with each other ever since we broke up."

"Unbelievable," criticised Amy. "So that's the end of that then; you didn't even get a snog?"

Jules' mouth melted into an enormous smile, spurring Amy to clout her with her pillow.

"It was amazing," gushed Jules. "And I really, really like him. I just hope he gives me a second chance."

"Try not to worry," insisted Amy. "I expect he'll call you tomorrow and ask you out again."

"Maybe," replied Jules, reflectively, before lying back on Amy's bed and staring up at the ceiling. "I really hope you're right."

Chapter sixteen

Barry Harper was the sort of bully who enjoyed seeing the reaction of other people just as much as he enjoyed seeing the reaction of his 'victim'. All his taunts were very audience friendly and usually consisted of some kind of prank or practical joke. He obviously took great pleasure in watching and being inspired by slapstick comedy sketches starring black and white movie icons like Laurel and Hardy, because if his victim ended up flat on their bottom in front of a crowd of onlookers then it was a job well done in his eyes. But whilst his taunting made me very unhappy during primary school, there was still something rather harmless about it. He was just an ignorant 10 year old boy who felt the need to make himself feel better by keeping his pointless group of cronies amused at all times. I don't believe that he ever had anything against me personally. He simply took advantage of my shy nature because it made me an easy target.

When I was at secondary school, I fell victim to a far more malicious type of bully than Barry Harper. She didn't indulge in audience friendly pranks in order to improve her social status. She was a lot more vindictive and underhand than that because her taunting tended to go unnoticed by everybody else. And it had a far more damaging effect on me because she was very calculated in her approach. She would use psychological taunts and insults to try and undermine and belittle me when nobody else appeared to be listening, almost as though she was training me up to do all the hard work for her, by convincing me that I was completely and utterly worthless.

Physically speaking her approach was very different to Barry's. There were small examples of abuse like forcing me to take a drag from her cigarette so that I was coughing violently in order to catch my breath again. On one occasion she removed her chewing gum from her mouth and squeezed it into my ponytail until it was welded so tightly to each and every strand of hair that I had to go to the staff room and have a clump of my brown locks cut off. I remember feeling so grateful that it wasn't any closer to my scalp otherwise I might have been obliged to have yet another rather unflattering haircut. When the teacher asked me who had done it, during which time he held an ice pack against my hair in the hope that the chewing gum would solidify sufficiently in order for him to break it off, I decided to shrug my shoulders and tell him that I didn't know. I thought that if I told him the truth, she would try and punish me even more harshly. And besides, no one would have believed me anyway, because as far as they were all concerned, she was my best friend. And that's the worst type of bully of them all.

Looking back now, it feels strange to think of me and Melanie as friends because our relationship was practically unrecognisable by the time we left secondary school. But we really were close during our first three years at Heathmount Comp. In fact, it was probably fair to say that we were inseparable. And meeting Melanie was the best thing that could have happened to me at the time because after my experiences during the junior years of Acornfields JMI, I was severely lacking in confidence, particularly when it came to forming any kinds of friendships. But Melanie and I ended up sitting next to each other on the school bus one morning during year 7 and we just seemed to hit it off straight away. We discovered that we had all kinds of things in common. Like me, Melanie was extremely academic, excelling at English and maths in particular. And she didn't enjoy anything remotely related to sport or PE, even though our PE teacher, Mr Parker was particularly attractive.

We enrolled in an after school art club together in year 8, whilst the rest of the girls in our year were trying out for the netball team. And at weekends we would meet up and go shopping together in town, or hang out at the local park in the hope of catching a glimpse of Craig Riley the school heart throb, who liked to play football there with his mates. We both fancied him like mad but we knew that he would probably never be interested in either of us, so we decided to just admire him from afar.

When I hit puberty my skin broke out in a bad case of acne, so along with my particularly unflattering glasses and greasy brown shoulder length hair, I certainly wasn't likely to attract the attentions of someone as popular as Craig Riley. Melanie's hair was long and blonde but it seemed to have the uncontrollable urge to turn into one big mass of frizz during our humid bus ride to school every morning, and her teeth were encased in a pair of train track braces, earning her the nickname 'Metal Mouth'. Melanie spent a lot of time at my house after school because her parents worked long hours and she would often find herself at home on her own. My mum enjoyed having an extra mouth to feed because Christian was virtually never at home anymore. As soon as he started 6th form he seemed to be out with his friends all the time, and every time Mum thought about the permanently empty chair around the dining room table, she just felt compelled to fill it because she knew that it wouldn't be long before he went off to university and deserted her for good. Christian was a real mummy's boy.

After dinner Melanie and I would sit and do our homework together and then my dad would drive her home. More often than not we would find her house in complete darkness because her parents still hadn't returned from work, and with no brothers or sisters to keep her company either, I always felt very sorry for her as she let herself into an empty house, switching on the hall light and turning to wave us off from the front door.

"What sort of a parent leaves their 13 year old daughter at home on her own at 8'oclock in the evening?" my dad would complain, as he reluctantly drove away.

He knew that there was nothing he could do about it though, and that Melanie would refuse to let us help her any further. On one occasion he even tried talking to Melanie's mother about it as she returned home from work a little earlier than usual, but she was extremely defensive and practically slammed the front door in his face. I started writing Melanie letters so that she could read them once she got home. They included all kinds of teenage angst and anecdotes, as well as some magazine cuttings of the boy bands that we were both into at the time. It wasn't long before she started writing back to me, and sometimes she would include a little gift in the envelope; either some stickers or a chocolate bar, and even a friendship bracelet which she had made from some old bits of purple thread. I wore it on my wrist every day for nearly two years, but the day it broke off was the day that a girl called Fran joined our school, and that was also the day that my friendship with Melanie changed forever.

Chapter seventeen

Sunday 19th May 2019

Jules and Amy ended up spending most of Sunday morning checking their phones in the hope of receiving text messages from Drew and Tim. But by 2pm, they were both beginning to give up hope. That was until the doorbell rang, interrupting them from their very late brunch of eggy bread and potato waffles. They looked at each other and hesitated before attempting to talk themselves out of having to actually answer the door because they were both still dressed in their onesies.

The doorbell rang again, spurring Amy to take a deep breath and drag herself into the hall. Jules panicked when she thought about the possibility of it being Drew, but when Amy led their visitor through to the living room, she was amazed to discover that it was in fact *Christian* who emerged behind her.

"Nice onesie sis!" he smiled, looking her up and down. "You do realise its two o'clock in the afternoon don't you?"

"Amy and I felt like a 'duvet day'" replied Jules, self-consciously as Christian sank down onto the sofa and put his feet up on the coffee table arrogantly.

"What are you doing here Christian?" frowned Jules, waiting for an explanation as to why her brother had decided to pay her a visit at home for the first time in almost 18 months.

"Mum asked me to drop a box of your stuff round," he explained. "She was going to give it to you last night but you left before she had the chance."

"What stuff?" Jules frowned, looking perplexed. "You don't appear to have anything with you."

"I left it in the hall," replied Christian, at which point Amy burst into the room wearing a white apron with a blue gingham waistband.

"How do I look?" she beamed, twirling around.

Jules snatched the apron from her and retreated to the hall, denying Amy of the chance to remove anything else from the box.

"I'm taking this all upstairs to my bedroom," she then announced, her stomach churning as she began to realise what the rest of the contents of the box may have consisted of.

Her hands were shaking as she placed it onto her bed and then returned to the living room again where Amy and Christian were happily chatting together as though they didn't have a care in the world. Meanwhile, a box containing some of the most painful reminders of Jules' past was sitting waiting for her upstairs, ready to send her world crashing down around her shoulders. And Christian was completely oblivious.

"Why did Mum want me to have that?" Jules enquired, interrupting him from his conversation with Amy.

"Because it belongs to you," he replied, nonchalantly. "Why else?"

"But I haven't used any of that stuff in years. I didn't even realise that they still had it."

"Neither did they," explained Christian "But Suzy sent Dad up to the loft last week to bring down some embarrassing photos of me for the wedding book that she's making, and Dad found it amongst a few boxes of my things."

Jules was silent, inspiring Amy to escape to the kitchen in order to make them all a cup of tea.

"Mum could've just given it to me the next time I go over there. Why the urgency? You haven't been to my house in over a year."

"I also came to apologise," replied Christian, removing his feet from the coffee table and maintaining a more remorseful stance. "I shouldn't have invited Greg to the engagement party and then teased you about your past in front of Drew. It was really out of order of me."

Jules raised her eyebrows in disbelief and then relaxed down onto the sofa next to him.

"Thank you," she conceded "You don't know how much that means to me," and before she was able to get a grip of her own emotions, her head unexpectedly collapsed onto her brother's shoulder.

"Are you about to cry?" panicked Christian, slipping his arm around her. "Because I didn't mean to upset you even more!"

"You haven't" insisted Jules, sitting up again and attempting to compose herself. "I'm just feeling a bit emotional today, that's all" she paused slightly before continuing to explain;

"I think I've completely blown it with Drew and I really, really like him."

"Because of Greg?" clarified Christian, as a cue for Jules to shake her head reassuringly.

"No, because of *me*!" she exclaimed. "I don't think I'll ever be able to have a relationship with anyone; I'm too messed up."

Amy snuck in with two mugs of tea at that point and then disappeared again in time for Christian to squeeze his sister comfortingly;

"I don't think you give yourself enough credit sis," he insisted. "You have a great career and some lovely friends who obviously really care about you."

Jules smiled bashfully as her brother continued;

"You've had to overcome a lot in your young life but you're definitely a lot stronger as a result. In fact, you remind me of the ugly duckling who turned into a beautiful swan!"

Jules looked at Christian and they both laughed.

"Seriously though; Drew's a lucky man to have you."

As Jules leant forward to take a sip of tea from her mug, she turned to her brother again and frowned;

"Why are you being so nice to me all of a sudden?"

There was another long pause as Christian shifted uneasily in his seat and then persuaded himself to look Jules straight in the eyes.

"Because I've never forgiven myself for not being there for you when you when you ended up in hospital."

"But it was your gap year," insisted Jules, pulling the sleeves of her onesie down so that they covered the scar on her arm. "You were away travelling the world; there was nothing you could have done."

"I could have been more supportive of you afterwards," replied Christian, shaking his head. "But I just flounced off to university without a second thought for what you had been going through."

Jules looked down at the floor as she cradled her mug of tea in her hands.

"It doesn't matter now anyway," she concluded, lowering her voice a little in the hope of drawing the conversation to a close. "What matters now is how I sort the mess with Drew out."

"Well that I *can* help you with," smiled Christian, leaning forward and grabbing Jules' phone from the coffee table in front of them before she had managed to realise what he was doing. As she tried to snatch it off him, Christian selected Drew's number in her contacts list and started dialling it. Jules completely went to pieces.

"Just ask him out again," insisted Christian, holding his hand over the mouth piece as he passed her the phone. Jules felt as though she had no choice but to at least *speak* to Drew, in the fear that if she hung up on him instead, he would accuse her of being even more unhinged than ever.

"Hello," she eventually croaked, holding her phone to her ear with a shaking hand.

"Hello you," replied Drew, warmly. "I was planning to call you tonight."

"You were!" Jules squeaked in surprise, before reining herself in a little. "Why?"

"Because I was wondering whether you're free for dinner tomorrow evening; I'll cook."

"So you want me to come over to your place?" Jules clarified, as Christian started nudging her and smiling.

"That's if you're willing to try my cooking!" laughed Drew. "I'll text you my address. Is 7pm OK?"

"7pm is perfect; see you then," smiled Jules, ending the call and placing her phone back on the table just as Amy re-entered the living room.

"We've got a second date!" Jules exclaimed, leaping into her friend's arms and jumping up and down excitedly. "Drew's invited me round for dinner tomorrow."

"So he called you then; I knew he would," concluded Amy, once they had both calmed down a little.

"Actually, *I* called *him*," replied Jules, persuading Christian to interrupt them.

"I think you'll find it was *me* who called him," he reminded her, sounding disgruntled. "And besides, I thought he was already your boyfriend. What's all this about a 'second date'?"

❖

Monday 20th May 2019

The following morning at school, Jules had arranged through Louisa and Caitlin's form tutors, for them to attempt another facilitated counselling session. She felt that her word association exercise had really helped Caitlin to open up to her, and that Louisa had taken some comfort from Caitlin's honesty and vulnerability, encouraging her to feel a little less intimidated by Caitlin's strong character. It was a bit of a risky strategy though; particularly considering Caitlin's facial injuries and her volatile relationship with her stepfather. But Jules was finally beginning to get through to them both, and she was determined not to give up; on *either* of the girls.

As she opened her case files out onto the desk in front of her, there was a knock on her office door. Confirming by the clock on her wall that it was too early for either of the students to arrive for their appointment, she closed the files again and walked over to the door to open it.

"Good morning Miss Croft," Mr Langley smiled, from the hallway. "I'm afraid Caitlin's form tutor has just informed me that she won't be joining you for the session; she hasn't turned up to school today."

Jules' heart fell to the pit of her stomach when she reminded herself of the call she had made to Drew's friend in Social Services last week. She smiled uncomfortably in order to try and reassure Mr Langley that Caitlin's absence was probably nothing to worry about, and then thanked him for letting her know.

"I expect she's just truanting again," concluded Mr Langley. "I'll try and arrange another meeting with her mother."

"Leave it with me," Jules insisted, whilst feeling her phone vibrate in her suit trouser pocket.

"Are you sure?" clarified Mr Langley, frowning, as Jules removed her phone from her pocket and stared at it distractedly.

"Absolutely," she replied. "Now if you'll excuse me, I'll need to contact Louisa and let her know."

"Of course," smiled Mr Langley, stepping out of the doorway as she began to swing it closed. "Keep up the good work."

Jules frantically unlocked her phone and opened up her text messages in the hope of having received one from Caitlin, but the message was simply from Amy instead, asking her if she was free to meet up for lunch. She replied by telling her that she would meet her in the park in half an hour, and that she would need to call in on one of her students on the way. She then closed her text messages and immediately dialled Caitlin's number. It went straight through to voicemail, and she started to convince herself that something terrible must have happened to her. Just as she was about to look Caitlin's home phone number up in her file, there was another knock at the door, and this time Jules discovered that it was Louisa out in the hallway.

"I'm a bit early Dr Croft; I hope you don't mind?" she smiled, sheepishly. "I was hoping you could have a look at the story I'm writing before Caitlin arrives."

"Caitlin won't be joining us today," replied Jules, sounding a little abrupt. "So I've decided to postpone this morning's session in order to take an early lunch as there's something urgent I now need to do. We could meet up for a chat tomorrow though if you'd like?"

Louisa's shoulders sunk in disappointment and then she nodded understandingly; "I'll come back tomorrow at the same time."

"Thank you," Jules smiled, softly, feeling a little guilty for letting her down. "And perhaps I could borrow what you've written in the meantime so that I can make a start on it before our meeting?"

"Of course," replied Louisa, enthusiastically, her facial expression brightening a little as she removed a thick binder of word processed pages from her school bag and laid it on Jules' desk.

"See you tomorrow," Jules smiled. She then grabbed her car keys from her desk and followed Louisa out of the office.

❖

Less than half an hour later, Jules and Amy were walking around the park arm in arm.

"So where was it that you needed to be before you came to meet me?"

"I was planning to call in on one of my students who didn't turn up to school today," explained Jules. "But I drove over to her house on my way to the park and there was no one at home."

They stopped and sat down at a bench, where Jules removed her lunch from her bag.

"You look worried," observed Amy, as Jules carefully unwrapped her sandwich and bit into it.

"It's a very long and complicated story, and I'm not really allowed to talk about it" replied Jules as Amy's phone started ringing.

"Sorry Jules but I'm afraid I'll have to go," Amy explained once she had spoken to the person at the other end. "One of my clients has turned up early and there's no one else to cover."

"No worries, I'll catch up with you at home later," Jules insisted, hugging her friend goodbye and then continuing to consume the rest of the sandwich, comforted by the soft sounds of birdsong and the light spring breeze in the trees around her.

She was just about to close her eyes and put her head back against the bench, when another sound interrupted her thoughts. It was the sound of someone weeping, but Jules couldn't seem to work out where it was coming from. She looked along the path at Amy, just as she was about to vanish from view, and then stood up suddenly when she eventually managed to locate the source of the crying. There, underneath one of the trees behind the bench that she was sitting on, was a young woman in school uniform, with her knees hugged to her chest and her dyed black hair hanging down around her face.

"Caitlin; what are you doing here?"

"You can't tell anyone I'm here," insisted Caitlin, as Jules lowered herself onto the ground next to her, and placed a reassuring arm around her shoulder.

"Of course I won't," replied Jules, "You can trust me; I told you that."

Caitlin looked up at her, as two fresh streaks of diluted mascara went trickling down her cheeks;

"Thank you Miss," she sobbed. "It really helps having someone to talk to."

"So how did you end up at the park?" questioned Jules, leaning back against the tree trunk that they were both sitting under.

"Steve and I had an argument and it was the first place that I could think of to hide from him. He usually manages to track me down at the playing fields opposite our house; some friends and I go there to smoke sometimes."

Jules' ears pricked up at the mention of her stepdad's name, and as soon as Caitlin had picked up on Jules' reaction, she insisted that her assumptions were dumbfounded;

"It was just an argument," she explained. "We have them all the time. But he didn't hit me; I swear."

"Then how did you get these injuries?" enquired Jules, referring to Caitlin's black eye and split lip.

"It was an accident," persisted Caitlin, hugging her knees protectively. "Will you please stop asking me about it."

"I have a duty of care towards you," replied Jules.

"I thought your duty of care was towards the likes of Louisa," snapped Caitlin, defensively, shrugging Jules' arm away and then standing up. "After all, she's the one who's being bullied."

"Bullying doesn't just affect the victim; it affects the bully as well," Jules explained, trying to sound as un-confrontational as possible. "Often people choose to bully because they're going through some personal problems of their own. It's a bit like a defence mechanism."

"Where did you learn that?" spat Caitlin, looking away from her in disgust. "At the 'psychologist's convention' where you learnt all your other bullshit!"

Jules stood up and shook her head disappointedly, before persuading Caitlin to look at her again. "Let's just say that you're not the only one who's had a difficult adolescence," she replied.

"You mean *you* were a bully?" retorted Caitlin, allowing a smile to break out across her face.

"Not exactly, no," explained Jules. "But I have been deeply affected by bullying in the past and I didn't have anyone to confide in in the same way that you do; so why don't you just take advantage of the fact that we've bumped into each other today, and actually *talk* to me?"

"Some things can't be fixed by talking about them," replied Caitlin, walking over to the bench that Jules and Amy had been sitting on, and jumping feet first onto the seat slats.

After a short silence spent watching Caitlin as she paced up and down the bench a few times, receiving disapproving looks from an elderly couple walking their Cocker Spaniel, Jules decided that she was probably never going to persuade her to open up about her stepfather, so she decided to follow an entirely different line of enquiry;

"So these friends that you go smoking with; do they go to Pinewood?"

"Not anymore," replied Caitlin, jumping down from the bench at last. "They used to be in the year above me but they dropped out after they failed their exams."

Jules thought back to the fact that she had been unable to find any information about Caitlin's friends on her case file, and then gently probed a little further; "So other than smoking, what else do you do for fun around here?"

"Not a lot!" laughed Caitlin, as the elderly couple's dog ran over and wagged its tail at them. "But as long as I'm not at home, I don't really care."

"What's wrong with being at home?" Jules enquired, raising her eyebrows and leaning forward to stroke the Spaniel's long, soft ears.

"You've been there," Caitlin complained, reminding Jules of her very intimidating visit to the Murphy household the week before. "My parents are a nightmare."

"What parents aren't?" laughed Jules as the dog belted off again to re-join its owners. "Particularly when you're 15."

"What are your parents like?" asked Caitlin, as they both sat down on the bench together.

"They're a little overbearing," Jules replied. "They used to be very overprotective when I was your age."

"Did you rebel?" Caitlin smiled, expectantly.

Jules started to feel a little uncomfortable about where the conversation appeared to be leading. "We're supposed to be talking about *you.*"

The fact was, Jules had rebelled against her parents' over-protectiveness in the worst way possible, and it was an element of her past that she was never in much of a hurry to revisit, particularly not with one of her vulnerable students.

"I'd better go," Caitlin suddenly announced when it became clear that Jules was reluctant to share any personal stories of her own anytime soon. "Thanks for the chat."

"But where are you going?" panicked Jules, standing up. "You need to come back to school with me."

"Goodbye Miss Croft," replied Caitlin, ignoring her suggestion and removing a cigarette from her blazer pocket. And before Jules was able to try and think of an effective way of enticing Caitlin to stay with her, she had disappeared down the same path that Jules had watched Amy walk along, with a small grey cloud of cigarette smoke following her as she went.

Chapter eighteen

When Jules arrived home later that afternoon, Amy had already returned from work and was slumped in front of the television in the living room with a tub of butterscotch ice cream balanced on her knee.

"Still no word from Tim?" Jules clarified, leaning across the coffee table and kissing her friend on the forehead. "Why don't you call him? It worked for me and Drew."

Amy shook her head, placed the ice cream tub on the table in front of her and lay down on the sofa;

"What time's your date tonight?" she then enquired, conveniently changing the subject.

"7 o'clock," replied Jules, looking at her watch. "I've got plenty of time to get ready; perhaps I'll have a quick look at my work emails first."

As she slumped down onto the sofa next to Amy and opened up the emails on her phone, she discovered that she had received another reply from someone called 'M Williams', who had contacted her earlier in the day in order to ask for some support for her son. She read the original email exchange back to herself again first so that she would be able to compose an appropriate reply to her most recent message:

M Williams: *'I've recently discovered that my son, who is in year 7 at Pinewood, is being bullied. I just don't know how to deal with it. Every time I try and talk to him about it, he completely shuts down. I could really do with some advice and I'm hoping that you might be the right person to help me.'*

Dr Jules: *'Thank you so much for your email. You've already made the first step by contacting me. Why don't you begin by telling me a bit more about it?'*

'M Williams: *'What sort of details do you need?'*

Dr Jules: *'How did you find out that your son was being bullied? Do you know what kind of bullying he's experiencing? Have you noticed any changes in his behaviour recently?'*

The most recent reply which Jules hadn't yet read said:

M Williams: *'My housekeeper told me that he was being bullied and suggested that I checked his computer. Apparently other children have been posting nasty comments about him all over his Facebook page. But it wasn't until today that one of his teachers confirmed what has been going on and gave me your contact details. I'm ashamed to admit that I hadn't been aware of anything until my housekeeper told me about it. I've been really busy at work recently.'*

Jules felt that it would be best for her to begin with a more gentle approach in order to earn the client's trust, so she decided to reassure her as much as possible, and then asked her a few general questions:

Dr Jules: *'Every mother blames themselves but what's happening to your son isn't your fault. And it certainly isn't your son's fault. In fact, it's not even the bullies' fault. It's just important to remember that he will get through this and that you'll always be there for him. So what do you do for a living?'*

As Jules sat and waited for a further reply, Amy suddenly snatched the phone from her and instructed her to stop thinking about work and go and get herself ready for her big date with Drew.

"She sounds really worried about her son," urged Jules trying to grab her phone out of Amy's grasp.

"You can have it back once you've finished making yourself look beautiful," insisted Amy.

Jules sighed heavily in defeat and then retreated upstairs to get ready. As she opened the door to her bedroom, her breath caught in her throat when she remembered that the box from her parents' loft was still waiting for her in the corner underneath the window. She had resisted the urge to look through it after Christian had left the day before, and had moved it off her bed last night with the intention of sorting through it as soon as possible, but something was preventing her from being brave enough to actually explore what was inside.

She looked at her watch again and decided that if she had a quick look through it now, she would still have plenty of time to get ready for her date afterwards. And then she could just tip it all into a black bin bag and forget about it whilst she went to enjoy her romantic evening at Drew's house. Perhaps she should just tip it straight into the bin bag now, rather than actually bothering to torture herself with its potentially painful contents. After all, ignorance was bliss. And she had endured more than enough reminders of her difficult past over the last three weeks already; Craig Riley, Greg, the Facebook update about Barry Harper, even the situation between Caitlin and Louisa. It was almost as if the universe was trying to tell her something. In fact, it was probably telling her to actually deal with some of the demons from her past once and for all, so that they wouldn't persist on coming back to haunt her all the time.

She took a deep breath and opened the box. As she lifted out the apron that Amy had tried on; the apron that she had worn in her year 5 Christmas production as Dorothy in the Wizard of Oz, she discovered that the only other item which appeared to be in there was a thin beige folder labelled 'school reports'. Her chest loosened as she began to breathe normally again, overcome with relief when she thought about how many painful reminders that *could* have been in the box. Perhaps her mum had got rid of them all because she didn't want Jules to start dwelling on the past again. She opened the folder of school reports and rather misguidedly decided to read the one that Mrs Greaves had written in year 6:

'Julia has been a challenge to teach over the past two years. She is very bright, and has excelled in English and maths again in her final term at Acornfields, but she has a very defiant personality and caused a lot of disruption during our residential field trip in Wales at the end of term.'

Jules threw the report down onto the bed without venturing to read any further because she could feel her blood pressure going up. How could someone who claimed to be an experienced and well respected teacher, have such a complete lack of compassion and understanding for one of her most vulnerable students? As Jules stood up from the bed, the folder, which was perched on the very edge of the mattress, slid onto the floor and emptied its contents everywhere, prompting her to sigh heavily before stooping down to pick it all up. But as she did so, she discovered that it didn't *just* contain school reports after all; because tucked between the paperwork for year 6 and year 5 was a postcard that made her heart plummet. It was the postcard that she had sent to her parents during the field trip and it had a photo of the youth hostel on the front.

There was something rather spine chilling about the photo, almost as though it was a haunted house that had featured in some kind of horror film. Her hands started shaking again as she slowly turned it over and began reading the faded handwritten message from her 11 year old self on the back:

'Dear Mummy and Daddy,

I am really enjoying myself in Wales. The youth hostel is very nice and we have been doing some fun activities every day. Today we went pony trekking and tomorrow we are going canoeing, which I'm looking forward to trying. See you when we get back.

Love from Julia x'

It had all been lies of course because she had been trying to protect her parents from the truth until she got back home. She didn't want them to worry about her when she was still hundreds of miles away; particularly her overprotective mother, who immediately made an appointment to go and speak to the Head Master about Mrs Greaves' negligent behaviour as soon as Jules had filled her in on what had really happened during the field trip.

According to Kylie Sinclair's mother, who often bumped into Mrs Croft in their local supermarket, and who had a younger daughter in year 4 at Acornfields, Mrs Greaves retired the following year and moved down to the south coast. Jules never actually found out whether she was encouraged to take early retirement though, or whether it was entirely her own decision. Meanwhile, Mrs Sinclair took great pleasure in updating Jules' mother about how well Kylie was getting on at the rather prestigious girls' school that they had decided to send her to across town; Head Girl; Captain of the netball team; Chair of the school council. She was almost like the female equivalent of Christian.

And as for Barry Harper; he dropped out of school completely when he was 15 and got a job at the local fish and chip shop for a while. He appeared to spend most of his time hanging around on street corners with some very unsavoury looking teenagers, rolling joints and vandalising things. Fortunately, Jules only managed to cross paths with him once during their secondary school years, whilst she and Melanie were out shopping together one weekend. He and his gang had their hoods pulled up even though it wasn't cold or raining, and Barry didn't appear to have recognised her as she subtly crept her way past. She couldn't help but feel a little bit sorry for him for getting into the wrong crowd, and she feared for the future that lay ahead of him once it had become clear that his seemingly harmless behaviour as a 10 year old boy, had by that point turned into something rather more serious.

Jules shuddered at the memory and then threw the postcard, folder of school reports and the apron back into their box. It was almost 5.45pm and she needed to start getting ready for her date with Drew, otherwise she would have Amy to answer to. Just as she bent down to reach under her bed for the pair of black strappy shoes that she intended to wear that evening, she noticed an A5 envelope on the floor. It must have fallen out of the folder without her realising. She was about to investigate it further when Amy knocked on her bedroom door, forcing her to shove the envelope into her handbag.

"Aren't you changed yet?" tutted Amy peering her head around the door. "I need to do your hair and makeup and the taxi will be here in less than an hour!"

Chapter nineteen

As Jules' taxi pulled up outside Drew's house, her heart was beating so rapidly that it felt as though it was about to explode through her chest cavity. She handed her fare to the taxi driver, her hands shaking uncontrollably encouraging her to smirk diffidently at him whilst he counted out her change.

"Thank you," she smiled, opening the taxi door and placing an equally unsteady foot onto the pavement outside. "Have a good evening."

She had decided to order a taxi in the hope that the benefit of a couple of alcoholic drinks would steady her nerves a little. This was the first time she had been completely alone with Drew and she was really hoping to enjoy a certain amount of intimacy with him in the privacy of his home. But she was terrified of exposing too much of herself too soon; both of her soul, and of the scar on her arm. She clung onto the buttons of her trusty black cardigan protectively as she hobbled up his driveway on wobbly legs. High heels were definitely a mistake on this occasion. And as she rang the doorbell, she filled her lungs with air and tried to breathe as normally as she could so that Drew wouldn't realise how nervous she was. While she was waiting for Drew to answer the door, she finally received a reply from her new email contact;

M Williams: *'I'm an accountant. I'm currently being considered for a promotion, which is why I'm having to work such long hours at the moment. My boss is a bit of a task master. He's been telling me to put the rest of my life on hold recently. He won't even give me permission to travel down to the south of France for my father's funeral at the end of this week.'*

Dr Jules: *'I'm sorry to hear about your father. Were you very close to him?'*

"Hi," Drew smiled, interrupting Jules' train of thought as he opened the front door and invited her inside. "Can I take your cardigan?"

"No thanks, I'll keep it on," insisted Jules, a little too abruptly, sliding her phone into her handbag and slipping off her shoes. Drew's smile crumbled slightly, persuading Jules' initially defensive stance to become apologetic.

"I'm sorry," she explained. "I just feel the cold, that's all."

"I'll keep you warm," Drew smiled, leaning forward and delicately pressing his soft lips towards hers.

He pulled away for a second and looked deep into her eyes, before replacing his lips on hers and then softly slipping his tongue into her mouth. Jules allowed her handbag to fall to the floor and then slid her hands up Drew's arms, gripping onto his muscular shoulders tightly as they continued to kiss each other.

"Do you feel a bit hotter now?" Drew then laughed cheekily, gently pulling away from their embrace.

"A little," replied Jules, feeling embarrassed, as he led her into his kitchen. "So what's on the menu tonight?"

Drew looked at her and smiled again. Jules cuffed him lightly with the back of her hand. "I meant for dinner!"

"I've made a lasagne," he eventually replied. "But I'm keeping the dessert a surprise. Would you like a glass of wine?"

"Yes please!" insisted Jules, overenthusiastically, causing Drew to raise his eyebrows at her suspiciously.

"I hope you're not planning to get drunk tonight," he teased. "I'm not that difficult to be around, am I?"

"Not at all," Jules replied, as he passed her a glass of wine. "I'm sorry; I keep putting my foot in it this evening."

Drew's house was larger than hers, although it boasted very similar Victorian features which Drew had clearly spent a lot of money having restored before he moved in; one of the advantages of owning your home as opposed to just renting it. The ground floor had been opened up so that the kitchen and sitting room flowed into each other, and there was a dining table along the right-hand wall of the kitchen which Drew had adorned with a single red rose in a vase, a bottle of chilled champagne, and two cream taper candles which were burning softly.

The house was very clean and tidy; a quality in a man that Jules always admired, particularly as she was frequently obliged to put up with Tim's wet towels on the bathroom floor, toenail clippings on the coffee table, and muddy football boots in the hall. He even persisted on leaving the toilet seat up, causing Jules to almost fall down it in the middle of the night on more than one occasion. For some reason, Jules couldn't imagine Drew leaving the toilet seat up even though he lived on his own.

"Is everything OK?" Drew confirmed, opening the oven door to check on the lasagne and then offering her a slice of garlic bread.

Jules pulled herself up onto one of the stools at the breakfast bar and tore the steaming hot slice of garlic bread in half, before licking the butter from her hands.

"Christian came over to see me yesterday," she explained. "He wanted to apologise to me for what happened at the engagement party."

"That's great," smiled Drew, finding himself a little distracted by Jules as she continued to lick the hot garlic butter from her fingers.

"It's certainly a first for Christian," she exclaimed, choosing not to mention anything about the fact that her brother was actually responsible for contacting Drew on her behalf.

At that moment her phone flashed again with another email. Jules wiped her greasy hands on a napkin and scrolled through the message whilst Drew was busy draining a pan of new potatoes into the sink.

M Williams: *'Not particularly, no. When I was growing up, he was always working and so was my mum. I ended up having to just look after myself most of the time.'*

Dr Jules: *'That must have been tough. I hope you managed to make it up with him though. I'm sure he was very proud of you. Becoming a successful accountant, and settling down to have a family'*

"Who are you busy messaging?" Drew smiled, as he tipped the potatoes into a dish.

"Sorry," Jules apologised. "One of the year 7 parents has been in contact with me. I'm just getting a bit of background information from her before we arrange to meet."

"You really love your job don't you," he stated whilst enticing Jules towards the table.

Jules admired the rose and the candles more closely and beamed. "This looks lovely."

Drew removed a pair of champagne flutes from the sideboard and uncorked the bottle. He then filled her flute glass to the brim with plenty of frothy bubbles and selected some mellow sounding music on the iPod.

"You're very romantic," Jules gushed, placing her glass of wine on the table before finding the courage to lean over and kiss Drew passionately. They stared at each other for several seconds afterwards, and Jules felt as though she was about to burst with desire, persuading her to eventually step away from him and then return to her mission to get tipsy.

Drew smiled in defeat before fetching the dish of new potatoes from the kitchen worktop and placing it on a mat in the centre of the table. Jules watched him as he removed the lasagne from the oven and presented her with it, along with a big wooden bowl of fresh green salad.

"This looks delicious," she smiled, over the rim of her wine glass. "Almost as delicious as the chef!"

"Are you flirting with me Miss Croft?" retorted Drew, dimming the lights a little and taking a seat opposite her at the table.

"I think this drink's going to my head already," Jules giggled in reply, as she attempted to serve herself some of the mouth-watering spread. "So how did you learn to cook?"

"I've been living on my own since I was at university," Drew explained. "I just taught myself as I went along."

"This is a really nice house," Jules insisted admiring her surroundings. "I thought registrars didn't earn very much."

"We don't earn as much as consultants do," laughed Drew, helping himself to a large spoonful of lasagne. "But we don't do too badly."

❖

By the time they had reached the end of the main course, Jules was beginning to feel very tipsy indeed. But she couldn't decide whether it was the alcohol, or whether it was simply Drew's intoxicating company that was making her feel so light-headed. He was so easy to talk to, and Jules really felt as though she could be herself around him. He was warm and sensitive, with a very wicked and flirtatious undertone that Jules found utterly irresistible. He was ambitious and level-headed, and absolutely drop-dead gorgeous to look at. She just couldn't quite believe that she was actually sharing a romantic candlelit dinner with someone so perfect, and that he seemed to like *her* just as much. As he stood up to clear the table, she took the opportunity to check the latest email from her new client and then composed a reply:

M Williams: *'Not exactly. I fell pregnant with my son just after I finished university and I was about to begin my accountancy exams. As I'm sure you can probably imagine, my parents were not very pleased about that and they had very little to do with me while my son was a baby. My dad had a heart attack and they decided to move to France. I wasn't with the baby's father anymore so I was forced to look after him all on my own; life was pretty tough.'*

Dr Jules: *'I realise I haven't really spent very long getting to know you yet but reading between the lines, I can't help but conclude that your son isn't the only person who is being bullied. Has it occurred to you that you yourself have in fact been suffering at the hands of a bully over the past few months and years? And not just one bully but two; your father and your boss.'*

"So what's the surprise dessert?" she smiled, as Drew finished stacking the dirty dishes into the dishwasher.

"Well I gave it a lot of thought," he replied with a smirk. "And I concluded that I probably couldn't go wrong with chocolate fudge cake."

"Chocolate's my favourite," replied Jules enthusiastically, draining her wine glass and refilling it again. "How did you know?"

"Well, apart from the fact that I'm yet to meet a member of the female human species who *doesn't* like chocolate," Drew explained, presenting her with the most mouth-wateringly delicious looking fudge cake dessert Jules had ever seen. "I picked up a couple of clues before we were going out together; like the Easter eggs in Mr Shah's shop, and the empty chocolate bar wrappers in your bedroom!"

Jules was hoping that Drew hadn't been paying that much attention to her clumsiness, but he was obviously a lot more interested in her than she had initially realised, because he had actually made the effort to not only *notice,* but subsequently *remember* that chocolate was one of her favourite foods.

"Thank you," she gushed, trying to brush over how embarrassed she had felt on both of the occasions that he had just reminded her about. "This is really thoughtful."

"Would you like to eat it somewhere more comfortable?" Drew suggested, pointing through to his living room.

Jules' stomach flipped, urging her to drain her wine glass again;

"Okay," she then croaked, nervously pushing herself up from the table and following him through to the sofa. Her legs almost buckled beneath her as she stood up and she started to feel extremely light-headed again.

"Are you alright?" Drew frowned, looking concerned, as he served her a big slice of chocolate fudge cake.

"Too much wine I expect," smiled Jules unconvincingly as Drew lowered himself down onto the sofa next to her. "I'm a bit of a liability, aren't I."

"Not at all," insisted Drew. "I'm just worried about you. You were obviously really upset after I left you on Saturday night."

"I didn't expect you to ask me out again," confessed Jules. "I was convinced that I must have put you off."

"Of course not," replied Drew, as Jules took a mouthful of dessert. "I really like you Jules; what do I need to do to prove that to you?"

"I'm sorry; I'm just not used to it, that's all," blushed Jules. "I haven't been in a relationship for a really long time, and the last one ended very badly."

"Greg didn't deserve you," insisted Drew, putting his hand on Jules' knee. "You're one of the sweetest and most considerate women I've ever met. You're constantly putting the needs of others before your own."

"That's my job," replied Jules. "Besides, *you* save lives for a living."

Drew laughed before continuing to make his point;

"But it's not just a job to you is it. What about that student who you contacted Social Services about?"

Jules thought back to her conversation with Caitlin in the park earlier that afternoon, but then decided not to share any of the other details with Drew, as tempting as it was.

"And you're always popping over to someone's house when you're off duty, or paying them a visit in the A&E department."

It was Jules' turn to laugh this time, at which point another email from 'M Williams' sprang up on her phone:

M Williams: *'Would it be alright if we meet to discuss this further?'*

"Are you still emailing that new client of yours?" retorted Drew, as Jules attempted to compose yet another suitable reply, despite feeling rather tipsy.

Dr Jules: *'Of course. A face to face chat about your son would be a lot easier. When did you have in mind?'*

"Sorry," she apologised, taking her phone through to the hall and filing it away in her handbag so that she would be able to resist the temptation of checking it.

"I've just arranged to meet up with her face to face so I promise I won't allow myself to be distracted by it anymore. I just find it really difficult to ignore her messages; it sounds as though she's in a very challenging situation."

Drew stroked her hair affectionately.

"Is it possible to care *too* much?"

"It shouldn't be," he replied, reassuringly. "In fact I wish more people could be as compassionate as you are. You're beautiful; inside and out."

There was a long silence as Drew brushed the corner of Jules' mouth with his thumb.

"You had some fudge cake on your lip," he smiled, placing his dessert bowl on the table beside him and caressing her cheek tenderly.

Jules' stomach started doing cartwheels as she decided to place her own bowl on the floor next to her, so that she could lean towards him in return. Before she knew it, they were kissing again, only this time it felt a lot more passionate than any of their previous embraces, and she knew that it was likely to go a little further than just a kiss. She just couldn't seem to help herself though. Drew was incredibly sexy, and he had gone to so much effort to provide her with an unbelievably romantic second date. She knew that his affection for her was genuine, and that she really liked him as well, but she was terrified of exposing her agonising past to him too soon, and of running the risk of having her heart broken again. As their kissing intensified further, Drew slid the palm of his hand across her cleavage and attempted to unbutton her black cardigan, persuading her to pull away suddenly.

"May I use your toilet?" she announced, folding her arms across her chest self-consciously. "The wine's gone right through me."

"Straight ahead of you at the top of the stairs" nodded Drew, sitting back on the sofa looking disappointed.

"Thank you," she stumbled, grabbing her handbag along the way. "I won't be long."

"Take as long as you need," insisted Drew. "I'm not going anywhere."

When she got to the bathroom, she locked the door behind her and let out a deep sigh, staring disapprovingly at her reflection in the mirror on the wall opposite her. As predicted, Drew's bathroom was just as immaculate as the rest of his house. No wet towels on the floor; even the lid of the toilet was down. He really was perfect, so why on earth was she up here hiding from him? She should have been down on that sofa enjoying the weight of his warm muscular body on top of hers, but instead she found herself thinking about the A5 envelope that she had discovered on her bedroom floor, and before she could get control of her senses, she was removing it from her handbag and opening it.

The envelope contained a letter from Melanie which she scan read briefly and then stuffed back into her handbag, because it was the other item in the envelope that intrigued her the most, and that was a little broken bracelet made of purple thread. The feel of it between her fingers made her throat tighten when she remembered wearing it on her wrist every day for nearly two years. But then she also remembered what had happened the day it eventually broke apart because that was the same day that her friendship with Melanie started to break apart too.

She looked at her reflection in Drew's mirror again and started crying.

"I know I told you to take as long as you need, but I just wanted to make sure that you're OK," called Drew tapping lightly on the locked door.

"I can't do this, I'm sorry," Jules complained, unlocking the bathroom and brushing past him in the doorway.

"I'm sorry if I came on too strong for the second date," insisted Drew, following her down the stairs. "We can take this as slowly as you like."

"It's not that," snapped Jules, crying. "I just can't be with you; I'm really sorry."

And before Drew was able to take the opportunity to convince her otherwise, she had disappeared out through the front door.

Drew didn't even attempt to try and run after Jules as she escaped into the dark night. Part of her wanted him to follow her, or to at least call after her down the street, but he just closed his front door in defeat as though he had already exhausted himself of all the many different ways to convince her that his feelings were genuine. After all, it was only their second official date and she was proving to be a lot of effort. She ran far enough out of his reach in order to be able to collapse onto a nearby wall and recover from her ordeal, at which point she removed her phone from her pocket in the hope that he might have attempted to call or text her instead. But all that was awaiting her was another email from M Williams:

'Are you free first thing tomorrow morning?'

Part two: Melanie
Chapter twenty

Friday 26th April 2019

Melanie crouched on the floor of the toilet cubicle and stared at the inside of the door as one of her work colleagues with particularly hollow sounding high-heeled shoes, clip clopped over to the sinks, unzipped her handbag, rummaged around in her make-up case, and then left, enabling Melanie to let out a deep sigh of relief. Nobody knew she was in there. And if they did, then they had no idea that she was hiding, as opposed to simply using the facilities.

"This is ridiculous," she muttered, under her breath. "I'm 33 years old. Why on earth am I cowering in a toilet cubicle?"

She knew that she wouldn't be able to get away with staying in there for too long before one of her colleagues realised that she was missing, so she straightened herself up and tentatively unlocked the cubicle door. As she emerged, the mirror above the sink opposite confirmed that her cheeks were stained with two lines of diluted mascara, and her eyes looked puffy and red. She frantically retrieved her own make-up case from her handbag and attempted to remove the evidence before anyone else came to join her in the ladies toilets. Philip's 61 year old PA, Gill for example, who always seemed to look down her nose at Melanie every time they were obliged to be civil to one another in the workplace.

Philip Delaney was Melanie's boss at the accountancy firm where she worked. He had been a partner there for over 25 years, and was currently in the process of trying to recruit someone to take over from his co-partner, who was due to retire at the end of the year. Melanie was a senior manager at the firm and was one of the most likely contenders for the promotion, but she had been obliged to spend the past 6 months jumping through hoops in order to try and earn herself a worthy place on the shortlist, and the entire process was proving to be extremely demoralising. This was the fourth time in less than two months that she had found herself in floods of tears in a toilet cubicle, and she was beginning to wonder whether she was really cut out for the job. After all, she was putting in at least 10 hours of unpaid overtime every week, and hadn't managed to get home from work before 9pm since the beginning of the new financial year. If these hours were a taste of things to come, Melanie wasn't sure whether she wanted to be a partner there anyway, but thanks to her particularly pushy parents, she had always been extremely ambitious, and she wasn't about to change the habit of a lifetime now. She would simply pull herself together and get back out there.

The hustle and bustle of the open plan office on the other side of the door felt overwhelming as she emerged from the toilets and strutted back towards her work station, trying not to make eye contact with anyone on the way past. But when she looked down at the enormous pile of paperwork on her desk, she discovered that a handwritten note had been laid on top of it with the words 'Mr Delaney wants to see you urgently' scrawled across it. Melanie's heart sank. What on earth did he want to see her about now? She had almost finished working on the latest assignment that he had set her, and many of the junior accountants had agreed to help her out. This morning had just been a bit of a wobble but she had assured him that it was all under control, even if she didn't truly believe it herself.

"You wanted to see me?" she announced as she approached his office door and tried to sound as bright and breezy as possible in front of Gill.

"Come in Ms Allsopp," Philip replied, without even looking up from his computer screen. "Take a seat."

Mr Delaney was in his early sixties with a grey receding hairline and neatly trimmed beard and moustache. He was of medium height with a rather round waistline, and he always wore very expensive looking suits. Melanie pulled the swivel chair out from behind the meeting table in the corner of the room and wheeled it in front of Philip's desk. After what felt like an eternity, he eventually looked up, his dark blue eyes bearing into hers.

"What's wrong with your face?" he then observed in an equally abrupt tone. Empathy was not one of his strong points.

"Hay fever," Melanie lied, cursing herself for not applying more concealer. "What was it that you wanted to see me about?"

"I need you to stay behind tonight and finish working on the assignment that the juniors have been dealing with," he explained. "We're presenting the figures to the CEO on Monday morning and a manager needs to sign them off."

"But I thought we had until the end of May?" Melanie retorted, feeling a fresh set of tears well up inside her. "I'm supposed to be leaving at 6pm tonight so that I can spend the evening with my son; it's his Birthday today."

"They've brought the deadline forward by three weeks," replied Philip, scratching his bald forehead and leaning back in his chair arrogantly. "And if you want this promotion, you'll just have to celebrate your son's Birthday over the weekend instead."

"But he's with my husband this weekend," protested Melanie, encouraging Philip to raise his eyebrows at her in disbelief.

"And of what concern is that to me?" he then remarked, before looking down at his computer screen again. "Close the door on your way out."

As she left Philip's office, Melanie hung her head in defeat and sloped past Gill's desk as inconspicuously as she could. But Gill was far too partial to a slice of office gossip and seemed to have a sixth sense when it came to other people's negative body language.

"Is something the matter Melanie?" she enquired, pretending to sound genuinely concerned. But Melanie wasn't prepared to fall for it and simply shook her head persuasively.

"I'm just tired, that's all" she insisted. "Everything's fine."

When she returned to her desk, she discovered that it was approaching 5.30pm, and that her housekeeper Ursula was due to be finishing her shift in just over an hour. She frantically shoved her pile of paperwork to one side and reached for her phone so that she could call and explain that she would be tied up at work for a little longer tonight, and that Ursula would need to stay at the house with Josh until she got home.

"That's the fourth time this week," complained Ursula, once Melanie had finished explaining her predicament. "And what about Josh's Birthday? He's been really looking forward to spending some time with you this evening."

"There's nothing I can do about it," sighed Melanie, gazing longingly at the photo of Josh on her desk. "Perhaps you could call Richard and ask him if we can swap round this weekend? I'll take Josh out to celebrate tomorrow instead."

Richard was Melanie's estranged husband. They had been separated for four months and Richard was hoping to gain custody of Josh due to the fact that their housekeeper, who wasn't even a qualified childminder, was increasingly obliged to spend more time with Josh than his own mother was. Even during the Easter holidays Melanie had barely seen him, and Richard and Ursula had rather reluctantly agreed to take it in turns to make sure that Josh didn't spend too much time on his own. But Richard wasn't even Josh's biological father. Melanie had fallen pregnant following a one night stand while she was still at university, preventing her from graduating until Josh was old enough for her to resume her studies and become a qualified accountant. And ever since then Melanie had thrown herself into her career to such an extent that she had ended up driving Richard away.

"Leave it with me," replied Ursula, before putting the phone down.

Melanie stared across the office at the toilet door and then swallowed the lump in her throat before removing the first sheet of paperwork from the pile and kicking herself back into accountancy mode. It was going to be a long evening.

❖

Melanie lived in a large detached house with five bedrooms and a double driveway. The house was fairly modern in appearance with a generous sized hallway which led into an even bigger living room on the left. The living room had dual aspect windows and patio doors which opened out onto the back garden, in front of which stood a beautiful grand piano that had been passed onto her by a wealthy great-aunt who had no children of her own.

The house felt even bigger than ever now that Richard was no longer living there, and there were reminders of him everywhere because, being a builder, he had worked hard to turn it into their dream home over the past few years; including of course, the enormous kitchen-diner complete with all the mod cons. Melanie never had time to actually cook in it though. Since splitting up with each other, Richard had moved into a small rental flat on the far side of town. It had a box room which Josh always stayed in but it was only a little bigger than a single bed and it certainly wouldn't do for Josh full time if Richard ended up gaining custody of him.

"You can't keep expecting everyone to change their plans at the very last minute just to suit you," complained Richard, as Melanie stepped out of the doorway in order to allow Josh to escape inside the house. In spite of the fact that it was almost 9.30pm, she was still wearing her coat because she had only just returned home herself, and Richard looked at her suspiciously as she attempted to conceal this fact by hiding two thirds of her body behind the front door.

"There was nothing I could do about it," she explained. "You know what my job's like sometimes; Mr Delaney didn't give me any choice in the matter."

"You always have a choice," replied Richard, sounding disappointed. "But you just seem to choose work over everything else."

A year ago she and Richard had been really happy, but then she started working late and putting her boss' needs before her husband's, and before she knew it, following a particularly unpleasant Christmas, Richard was packing his bags and walking out on her. She still loved him, and she desperately wanted them all to be a family again, but Richard had made it perfectly clear that whilst he would continue to spend time with Josh, he wasn't prepared to attempt any form of reconciliation with Melanie unless she drastically re-assessed her priorities, and that wasn't about to happen anytime soon.

"Thank you for dropping Josh home," she smiled weakly, as Richard started to make his way down the path. "Will we see you next weekend?"

"I knew you wouldn't remember," replied Richard abruptly, stopping dead in his tracks and turning around. "I'm taking Josh camping."

"Camping?" Melanie frowned, before starting to panic about how something like that might affect Richard's chances of gaining custody. "That all sounds very cosy; are you hoping to score a few brownie points?"

"I just want to spend some proper time with my step son," explained Richard, defensively. "I'm the closest thing he's ever had to a dad and I don't see why he should be forced to suffer just because we're not together anymore. We talked about the trip a couple of weeks ago; you told me you were okay with it."

"Do what you like!" retorted Melanie, before slamming the front door behind him and storming up the stairs to her bedroom.

"I hate it when you two argue," complained Josh, sheepishly from the bedroom doorway.

"We weren't arguing darling, we were just talking. But it's nothing you need to worry about." Melanie smiled feeling guilty. "Did you have a nice evening?"

"It was brilliant," replied Josh, looking animated. "Dad took me to my favourite pizza restaurant and then we went to see the new sci-fi film at the cinema."

"How did he manage to get tickets at such short notice?" Melanie frowned.

"He booked them in advance," continued Josh. "I can't wait to tell my mates at school on Monday; they're going to be so jealous."

It was only after Josh had returned to his own bedroom again that Melanie realised what Richard had done. He had obviously predicted that she would end up working late this evening and had booked the cinema tickets in order to compensate for the fact that Josh wouldn't be able to see his mum on his Birthday. Was she really that predictably unreliable? The realisation made her feel sick to her stomach as she buried her face in her hands, at which point a text message appeared on the screen of her phone, which was lying next to her on the bed. It was from Philip;

'I need you in the office by 6.30am on Monday' it said, encouraging her heart to start pounding in her chest when she thought about what she had done wrong. He was obviously disgruntled with the assignment that she had been working on all evening, and whilst it wouldn't have surprised her to discover that she had made one or two mistakes due to her mind being elsewhere, she couldn't help but feel extremely angry with her boss for failing to appreciate the sacrifices she had made in order to get it completed on time.

Josh was sitting at his laptop when Melanie went in to wish him goodnight a few minutes later, determined to try and forget about Mr Delaney's demands over the weekend. As she appeared in his bedroom doorway unannounced, Josh slammed his laptop shut suddenly and then looked up at her shamefacedly.

"What are you up to?" she smiled, playfully.

"Nothing!" snapped Josh in reply, persuading her to take a step back in surprise.

"Is everything alright darling?" Melanie clarified, feeling a little concerned about her son's particularly defensive response.

"Everything's fine," replied Josh. "I just don't like it when you sneak up on me."

"I wasn't sneaking up on you," insisted Melanie. "I just came to say goodnight, and to assure you that we'll do something special for your Birthday tomorrow, OK?"

"OK," Josh smiled weakly. "Good night mum."

Chapter twenty one

Monday 29th April 2019

"You're late," barked Mr Delaney, as Melanie joined him in his office on Monday morning. She looked at her watch. It was 6.34am. She was 'late' by only 4 minutes, and she wasn't even due to start work for another two hours. Not only that, but she had been forced to make special arrangements for Ursula to begin her shift early, so that she could ensure that Josh was able to get himself ready for school on time. Melanie usually gave him a lift to breakfast club on her way to work, but she had arranged for a taxi to collect him from the house instead, and all so that she could be at her boss' beck and call once again.

"Is there something wrong with the work I did last week?" Melanie enquired, nervously, as Philip invited her to sit down by pointing aggressively towards the chair opposite him.

"It was fine," he simply replied, much to her relief. "I just need you to put a few more hours in."

"More hours?" replied Melanie in surprise, realising that whilst the work she had produced last week was satisfactory, she would obviously be obliged to begin work at this unearthly hour on a regular basis from now on. "But I've been staying in the office until 9pm on most days. When am I supposed to see my family?"

"You can see your family at weekends" retaliated Philip, slamming his pen down on the desk. "Do you want this promotion or not?"

"Of course I do," insisted Melanie. "I wouldn't be doing all this if I didn't; you don't need to keep asking me."

"Then prove it," Philip snapped, making her jump a little.

"But I thought that's what I've been doing over these past few months," Melanie complained, surprising herself with how honest and forthright she was being. "I've been working so hard it's cost me my marriage."

"I had no idea your husband was so fickle," smirked Philip. "It sounds like you're better off without him."

Melanie swallowed and then slowly stood up from her seat. "Is that all you wanted to see me about?" she clarified, trying not to allow her emotions to overcome her.

"That's all for now," replied Philip. "But I've left some work on your desk and I'll be keeping a very close eye on you over the next few weeks."

Nodding wearily, Melanie edged her way out of Mr Delaney's office and closed the door. When Richard walked out on her, she was so angry at him for giving up on their marriage so easily, but what she hadn't appreciated at the time was that he was the only one who had actually been putting any work into their relationship for all those months, and that it hadn't been an easy decision for him at all. Now that they had separated, it became clear that *he* was better off without *her*, not the other way around.

"Morning dear," shouted one of the office cleaners, interrupting Melanie's thoughts as she slid the vacuum cleaner along the walkway behind her.

"Morning," replied Melanie, flicking the desk light on and picking up her mug of strong coffee.

"You're here early today," the cleaner observed, as she switched the vacuum cleaner off and then reached under Melanie's desk in order to empty her waste paper bin.

"I thought I'd try and get a head start on a few things before everyone else arrives," explained Melanie, feeling a little dishonest. "It's nice and peaceful at this time of day."

"It's peaceful," agreed the cleaner. "But I don't think I'll ever get used to getting up at 5.30am."

Melanie decided to make the effort to look down at the cleaner's name badge so that she could address her properly;

"Brenda," she smiled, softly. "Do you enjoy your job?"

"Well I'll never be a millionaire!" replied Brenda, laughing "But starting this early means that I can finish at lunchtime and then spend the afternoons with my grandchildren which is really wonderful."

Melanie felt a sudden twinge of guilt but then she reminded herself that Brenda was twice her age and on the verge of retirement.

"Spending time with family is important," she insisted. "But providing for them is too."

"Of course it is dear," Brenda smiled, sensing the defensive tone in Melanie's voice. "I wish I could have been as bright as you are; you all do an amazing job in this office."

Melanie laughed; she had never heard an accountant be described as 'amazing' before, but she accepted the compliment nonetheless.

"You cleaners do a pretty amazing job too," she agreed. "Every morning the place looks immaculate until we all come along and trash it again!"

"Well I guess every profession has its place," chuckled Brenda, before turning Melanie's question around "So do *you* enjoy *your* job?"

Melanie thought for a moment, at which point Gill entered the office with the usual air of authority around her.

"Very much so," Melanie then smiled, a little too insincerely, turning her attention to the huge pile of work on her desk. Brenda sensed that the conversation was over and immediately switched her vacuum cleaner on again before shouting "It was nice talking to you."

"You too," replied Melanie under her breath, so that Gill wouldn't overhear.

❖

Saturday 4th May 2019

"Fran, you're such a bad influence on me!" Melanie laughed, reluctantly holding her wine glass out and accepting another top up.

It was Saturday evening and she had invited her two best friends round for wine and pizza in order to compensate for such a difficult week at work, as well as for Josh's absence of course.

"I have been since the day we first met," replied Fran. "But how often do you have the house to yourself? You should make the most of it."

"My estranged husband and my impressionable son have gone camping together for the weekend," Melanie reminded her. "I'm not really in the mood for partying. Who knows what ideas Richard could be putting into Josh's head?"

"Richard's not like that, you know he isn't," insisted Melanie's more level headed friend, Rebecca. "Anyway, you and Fran have never really filled me in on what the two of you got up to at school. I'm intrigued."

Melanie and Fran looked at each other sheepishly.

"It was years ago," Melanie replied, before changing the subject. "So how's the pregnancy going?"

"Slowly," complained Rebecca, rubbing her bump. "I'm dying for a glass of wine."

"I'm sure one glass won't do any harm," Fran insisted.

Melanie knew that Rebecca was far too sensible to actually give in to her craving though, despite Fran's persuasive personality.

"I see what you mean about being a bad influence!" Rebecca laughed, waving the wine bottle away and helping herself to a glass of tap water instead. "I bet you two were an absolute nightmare at school."

Melanie had met Rebecca at accountancy college and introduced her to Fran three years ago at her 30th Birthday party. The two of them had hit it off straight away, but Melanie and Fran had never indulged Rebecca in the details of their somewhat 'shady' past because they had both done their best to put their secondary school days well and truly behind them. Rebecca observed the uneasy expressions on the other women's faces and then turned her own smile into a look of concern;

"Seriously though, did something happen?"

"Just leave it will you," snapped Melanie, slamming her wine glass onto the kitchen worktop.

"Of course, sorry," replied Rebecca, apologetically, taking a step back, at which point the doorbell rang.

"That will be the pizza," Melanie then concluded, before leaving the room.

"I'm sorry if I put my foot in it," Rebecca whispered, turning to Fran.

"It's OK," replied Fran, squeezing her shoulder reassuringly. "It was just a long time ago."

When Melanie re-entered the room, the silence was unbearable as she slowly opened the cardboard box and encouraged each of her friends to tear themselves a slice of pizza. She hated thinking about the past. There was nothing about her childhood that evoked positive memories for her. School life aside, her parents had been particularly aloof throughout the course of her adolescence. Her dad had then suffered a massive heart attack just after Josh was born and Melanie was never quite sure whether the shock of becoming a grandfather at such a young age was to blame. But the doctors assured her that he had just been overdoing things; working long hours, not eating properly and exposing himself to all kinds of unnecessary stress.

When Melanie was 22, her parents had decided to take early retirement and moved to the South of France. Until Melanie met Richard, she was obliged to raise Josh completely on her own. She employed a full-time child minder so that she could re-launch her career and prove to her parents that having a baby straight out of university wasn't a waste of a life after all. But even though they had given up their own careers and were sunning themselves abroad, she still felt as though they were constantly looking over her shoulder and scrutinising her every move, judging her decisions and belittling her choices; waiting for her to fall flat on her face.

"You look like you're miles away Mel," smiled Rebecca, breaking the silence. "Is everything OK?"

"I'm fine," replied Melanie before giving her friend a hug. "And I'm sorry I snapped at you just now; I just don't enjoy talking about my past very much."

"Are you thinking about Josh as well?" confirmed Fran, picking the slices of mushroom off her segment of pizza and passing them to Rebecca. "I'm sure he'll be alright."

"Of course he will," smiled Melanie, weakly. "He's with Richard."

There was another brief silence as each of her friends observed the hopeless expression on her face.

"Do you still love him?" Fran then ventured, before receiving a kick in the shins from Rebecca who was perched on one of the bar stools nursing her bump.

Melanie looked down at the floor and then felt the blood rush to the surface of her face;

"Yes," she confessed. "I think I do. He's the best thing that's ever happened to me and I just forced him away."

"Maybe he shouldn't have given up on you so easily" replied Fran, defensively.

"I don't think he did though," continued Melanie, gnawing on a crust of pizza. "I think he gave our relationship everything he had. It was me who gave up on it."

"So what are you going to do?" frowned Rebecca, sympathetically.

"I wish I knew," Melanie sighed, before laughing, much to the surprise of the others. "I just can't believe that my parents are still together. They used to work twice as hard as I do. They lived for their jobs. I was convinced that they would get divorced as soon as they retired because they would actually end up having to spend some time together!"

"But I guess your dad's heart attack put things into perspective," explained Fran. "Perhaps they finally realised that there really is more to life than work."

Melanie decided not to say anything in reply. But deep down she couldn't help but wonder what would have happened to her if they had only realised that sooner.

Chapter twenty two

September 2000

The first time I met Fran, it was as though I had been put under some kind of spell. She was utterly mesmerising, with wavy red hair that reached as far as the bottom of her blazer, and piercing green eyes. She always wore a hat at school even though we weren't supposed to wear anything that wasn't part of the school uniform. She had a vast collection of hats, but her favourite was a rainbow coloured beanie which enabled me to spot her from a mile away, as she strode towards me baring a mouthful of perfectly straight teeth.

"Are you in year 10?" she smiled, winding a piece of chewing gum around her mouth. She was quite well-spoken and I could smell the spearmint on her breath. Nodding distractedly she then linked her arm through mine and offered me a stick of gum. I told her that we weren't allowed gum in school, or hats, for that matter.

"Like I give a shit!" laughed Fran, forcing me to look down at my feet with embarrassment.

Quoting the school rule book to someone as self-assured as Fran wasn't exactly the best way of creating a good first impression, and I remember feeling quite intimidated by her colourful use of language, even though we had only just met. It was almost as colourful as her beanie. She told me that she was supposed to be meeting the head of music, and asked me if I could point her in the right direction, but I was actually heading that way anyway and I offered to take her there. It turned out that we were both musical. Fran played the guitar and I played the piano. Her commitment to her music didn't seem to suit the rest of her image but it was a relief to find someone who was as enthusiastic about it as I was. Julia and I had many other things in common including English, maths and art, but she was completely tone deaf and couldn't even tell the difference between a crotchet and a quaver.

It wasn't long before I found myself spending more time with Fran than I was with Julia. We formed a school band together with a couple of other girls in year 10, and once our after school jamming sessions in Heathmount Comp's music department were over, Fran would come round to my house for a sandwich and a smoke. I had never tried smoking before I met her, but the more I did it, the easier it became to inhale the smoke without coughing. And my parents were nearly always late home from work so they never had the chance to find out what we were up to out on the patio, as long as I remembered to dispose of our dog ends sufficiently well.

One of the other things that Fran and I had in common were the type of parents that we both had the misfortune to be saddled with. Her mum and dad were a pair of workaholics too. I asked her if we could go back to her house for a change, but she always managed to make an excuse. Eventually, one day, about two months after we had first met, she decided to take me there, and I had never seen anything quite so spectacular in all my life. It was practically a mansion.

"Why were you ashamed to bring me here?" I beamed, staring up at the double-fronted town house in disbelief. Fran told me that she didn't want me to accuse her of being some kind of spoilt little rich girl. It turned out that she had been to a private school before she came to Heathmount Comp, and that her parents had decided to start sending her to a state comprehensive school instead because they felt that she needed to 'integrate' with a few different classes of people for a change. It was only after this revelation that I realised how plummy her accent was despite her eclectic use of swear words and blasphemies. It had never really occurred to me before.

"So am I a different class?" I smiled as she led me out into her enormous garden and passed me a cigarette.

"Of course not!" Fran laughed. "You're my soul sister."

And from there our friendship grew, until eventually Julia and I were practically strangers. Sometimes I would stare across the classroom at Julia and wish that we were still 13 years old; talking about boy bands and making bracelets together. But I had done a lot of growing up since then. My parents had forced me to whether I liked it or not, by creating more and more opportunities for me to prove my independence. Or at least that's what they preferred to refer to it as. Julia and her dad would complain about how it was nothing short of 'child neglect' when they used to give me a lift home to an empty house almost every evening.

Sometimes I missed Julia's mum's cooking, particularly when I was obliged to scrape a sandwich together for Fran and I to share, using stale bread and rancid tasting butter, because my mum had been too busy to buy any groceries for ages. I was surprised she didn't just pay someone to get the food shopping for her. After all, she paid for practically everything else to be done in her absence, including the cleaning, laundry and gardening. Of course, these days you can just get groceries delivered to your house. Not that she would have had time to sit down at the computer and order it all. In fact, she should have just hired someone to look after me. Either that, or not even bothered to have children in the first place. Fran didn't have any siblings either which was something else that we had in common, although she did have two step-sisters from her father's previous marriage. Julia of course had Christian, and her mother absolutely worshipped him. Whenever he decided to grace the family with his presence during meal times, Mrs Croft would practically roll the red carpet out for him.

I suddenly realised that I had been staring across the classroom at Julia all that time, because she eventually turned to look over in my direction, snapping me out of my trance with a jolt. My face flushed a little and we both exchanged an awkward smile, before continuing with our work. But at the end of the lesson Julia tentatively approached my desk and asked me if I would like to go round to her house after school. It had been several weeks since I had last done that because my jamming sessions with Fran had somehow managed to completely take over, but Fran had been off sick for the past couple of days, which is probably what had spurred Julia to invite me. I smiled again and nodded, before agreeing to meet her at the school bus stop at 3.15pm, the thought of her mum's cooking encouraging my stomach to flip over with excitement.

Later that day, back at Julia's house, it should have felt like the good old days, but for some reason it just didn't, almost as though we had managed to outgrow each other over the past couple of months. It was clear that I had certainly outgrown her anyway. She hadn't changed a bit as she flicked through back copies of what used to be our favourite teen magazine, and talked about how fit Craig Riley had looked that day. And she didn't even seem to notice when I failed to respond with any real amount of enthusiasm like I would have done a few months previously. She did however notice the tattoo on my ankle as I stretched my legs out in front of me on her bed and pulled my socks off in order to cool my feet down.

"You've got a tattoo!" she gasped, clapping her hand to her mouth whilst she stared at the lower part of my leg in horror.

"Just a little one," I replied, sliding my feet towards me and hugging my knees into my chest protectively. "It was Fran's idea. She's got two."

Julia reminded me that I wasn't even 16 yet, and asked me what my parents thought about it. Of course I hadn't told them, because it was my body and I could do what I liked with it.

"Did Fran bully you into having it done?" continued Julia, causing me to feel more and more defensive as each minute passed. "Because I heard that she was expelled from her previous school for bullying."

"You don't know what you're talking about!" I snapped, pushing myself up off the bed and grabbing my socks from the floor where I had dropped them. I needed to escape Julia's interrogation as quickly as possible.

"Fran's cool," I continued. "You're only saying that because you're jealous of our friendship."

I remember practically spitting my last comment in her face as I made a reach for her bedroom door handle, but as I did so her mum managed to open it from the other side, prompting Julia and I to both snap our mouths shut suddenly. Mrs Croft looked a little concerned about the sound of raised voices and asked us if we were alright. Julia simply nodded dejectedly as her mum informed us that dinner was ready. I hadn't intended to stay for a minute longer than was absolutely necessary, following my altercation with Julia, but as soon as the delicious aromas from downstairs started to curl their way up to us in the air, I was simply unable to resist the urge to stay. It had been several weeks since I had enjoyed a home-cooked meal, and as Julia reluctantly followed me downstairs to the dining room, I couldn't help but feel rather angry and resentful towards her. After all, she had two loving parents who would do anything for her. I, on the other hand, was lucky if I actually got to see my mum and dad, never mind have a meal cooked by them.

Most of the meal time had been unbearably tense, although I was quite content to simply blame my lack of small talk on my rather overly zealous eating technique instead. I must have looked like a homeless person in a soup kitchen on Christmas Eve. Mr Croft eventually observed that I hadn't been round to their house for a while, causing Julia to visibly bristle all over. I told him that I had recently started playing the keyboard in a band, whilst doing my best to avoid eye contact with Julia across the table.

"Is that with the girl who was expelled from a private school?" confirmed Mrs Croft, compelling me to throw my cutlery down in defence.

"She wasn't expelled!" I protested, looking at Julia at last. She had obviously been filling her parents' heads with all kinds of rubbish. Despite my hostility, Julia was resolute, reminding me that I couldn't possibly say that for sure because I didn't really know anything about Fran.

"She's probably just using you. People like that don't have any genuine friends," Julia remarked, bitterly.

"Fran's not the one who doesn't have any friends, you are!" I screamed, standing up from the dinner table. Before I knew it, I had battled my way through their tightly locked front door and out onto the street. And as well as not sustaining my right to a lift home that evening, I didn't even have a chance to enjoy any of the dessert.

Chapter twenty three

Monday 6th May 2019

"So how was the camping trip?" Melanie smiled, as Josh and Richard arrived back from their bank holiday weekend away together.

"It was really great!" replied Josh, animatedly. "We took some amazing photos; can we put them on the big screen to show you?"

Richard hesitated slightly; he found being around Melanie extremely painful and was tempted to make his excuses so that he wouldn't be obliged to spend any more time in her company than was absolutely necessary. But he didn't want to disappoint Josh so he eventually agreed to collect his camera from the car and then followed Josh into the living room in order to set it up. Josh jumped into the armchair, leaving the sofa vacant. Melanie and Richard looked at each other uncomfortably, and then reluctantly sat down together. Melanie longed to sit close to him and to feel the warmth of his body next to hers, but there was an invisible wall between them that was impossible to knock down, so she decided to keep her distance in the fear that she would end up pushing him away altogether.

The photos of their camping trip left a very bitter-sweet taste in her mouth. It was heart-warming to see how much fun they had together, and how fond they had grown of each other even though Josh wasn't Richard's biological son, but it was equally heart-wrenching to be excluded from their adventures, and to realise how happy they both were without her around. She was just about to look down at her lap solemnly when Josh suddenly started laughing;

"I took that photo just after the spider came into our tent," he explained, pointing at the screen. "Dad was terrified!"

Melanie smiled when she remembered how terrible Richard was with creepy crawlies, particularly spiders. She had never seen a man react so strongly to one and was constantly obliged to come to his rescue when they were living together, even though she didn't really care for spiders herself. But it was humbling to see his vulnerable side and it made her all the more attracted to him.

Just at that moment, Richard looked over at her from the other end of the sofa and smiled. He must have been recalling some of the same memories as she had. As he turned away to look at the screen again, Melanie swallowed hard and then tentatively slid her hand across the gap in-between them so that she could place it on top of his. For a split second, Richard turned the palm of his hand upwards and slowly interlocked his fingers with hers, encouraging her stomach to turn inside out. She knew he still had feelings for her too; she just needed to find a way to get through to him, and thinking about their relationship *before* everything started to go wrong, was always a very promising place to start. Melanie stroked the palm of his hand seductively with her fingertips and got ready to slide the rest of her body across the sofa towards him when her phone beeped. When Richard realised what was happening he pulled his hand away suddenly. Melanie's hopes deflated. It was a message from Mr Delaney, asking her to go into the office early again the following morning.

"It's from *him* isn't it," clarified Richard, turning cold.

"If by 'him' you mean Philip, then yes, it is," replied Melanie defensively. "But he's my boss; you don't need to refer to him as though we're having some kind of affair!"

"You might as well be," snapped Richard in reply, standing up from the sofa and giving his stepson a hug. "I need to go home."

"Please stay," insisted Josh, sounding disappointed. "We were having such a great time looking at the photos."

"I'm sorry," Richard continued, picking up his camera and walking over to the living room door without even bothering to give Melanie a second glance. "This was a mistake; I should never have stayed."

As Richard closed the door behind him, Josh stood up from his seat and grabbed Melanie's phone from her hand in a rage. "Now look what you've done!" he shouted, throwing it across the room. "You always have to ruin everything."

❖

"Can I come in?" whispered Melanie, through Josh's bedroom door. "I'm really sorry."

"Go away," replied Josh, before switching his music on loudly. Melanie sighed, slid down onto the floor outside his room and looked at the remnants of the broken phone that were in her hand. If anyone should have had cause to barricade themselves in their bedroom and sulk, it should have been *her*. After all, Mr Delaney would be furious when he found out that her company mobile had been broken, particularly if he was still trying to get messages through to her on it.

Josh's music vibrated against the door as she gently rested her head on it and closed her eyes. Since when had her life resorted to a series of grovelling tactics outside her 12 year old son's bedroom? The look on Richard's face as he stormed out of the living room sent a chill up her spine. He really did despise her sometimes. But the element of the evening that bothered her the most was the fact that they had actually held hands with each other. It may have only been for a split second, but it was enough to reassure her that Richard still cared about her. Besides, why else would he have reacted so strongly to Mr Delaney's text?

Since she and Richard had split up, she had tried to reach a reconciliation with him, she really had. But it genuinely seemed as though he was not prepared to give their relationship a second thought unless she resigned from her job, and she just wasn't prepared to be held to that kind of ransom; it wasn't fair. She had trained long and hard to reach the level of accountant that she was now. She could just imagine what her parents' reaction would be, particularly as they had never really approved of her marriage to Richard. He was in the building trade, and that simply wasn't 'high-flying' enough for them.

And it wasn't fair of Josh to accuse her of ruining everything, when she had been trying a lot harder than Richard had to reconcile their differences. In fact, she wouldn't be surprised if Richard hadn't spent the entire camping trip trying to brainwash Josh into thinking the worst of her. She stood up from where she had slumped herself and looked at the broken phone again. She needed to talk to her son and she needed to talk to him now. Without even bothering to knock first, she grabbed the door handle and forced her way into his bedroom. The loud music masked the sound of the door opening, so that Josh didn't have enough time to shut his laptop down before her approach, and as she peered over his shoulder and was confronted with a wall full of abuse all over his Facebook page, she put her hand up to her mouth in disbelief.

"I told you to go away!" Josh screamed, slamming his laptop shut and trying not to look her directly in the eye.

"Not until you tell me what's been going on," insisted Melanie. "Are you being cyber-bullied?"

"It's none of your business," Josh shouted, before reluctantly turning to face her. And it was at that point that she discovered he had been crying.

❖

Tuesday 7th May 2019

"Have you noticed anything unusual about Josh's behaviour recently?" whispered Melanie as she sat at her desk at work the following morning. She was on the phone to Ursula, who had been called in to give Josh a lift to breakfast club again so that Melanie could get to the office early. Just as Ursula was about to reply, a large male frame with a designer suit appeared at the desk next to her. She immediately slammed the phone down onto the receiver and sat bolt upright in her chair.

"Mr Delaney," she smiled nervously. "I was hoping to come and speak to you this morning."

"Well I've saved you the bother," snapped Philip abruptly, making Melanie jump a little. "Do you care to tell me what happened to your company mobile?"

Melanie's stomach leapt at the thought of its broken remains lying on the living room floor after Josh had thrown it there the night before. How on earth had he found out about it so quickly? Damaging company property would be more than her job's worth.

"It was my friend's dog," she suddenly replied, trying to think of an effective enough excuse. There was no way she was about to tell him that her own son had thrown it across the room during an argument about work.

"It grabbed it off the coffee table and tried to treat it like a chew toy; I'm so sorry."

Philip simply stood there staring down at her as though he was still waiting for her to start explaining. She thought about offering an alternative excuse but then decided to just keep quiet altogether until he eventually moved away from her desk, leaving her in no doubt that this would not be the last she would hear of it. Besides, Gill was probably already in the process of notifying the entire office that Melanie was some kind of vandal.

Melanie was just about to carry on with her work, when her desk phone rang. Assuming Ursula was about to have a go at her for hanging up on their previous conversation, she braced herself for an angry Eastern European accent, and was surprised when she discovered that it was her mother's voice at the other end of the phone.

"Melanie, its mum," she announced rather shakily. "I'm afraid I have some bad news. Your father's had another heart attack."

Chapter twenty four

October 2000

Unsurprisingly, that was the last time I ever got invited to have dinner with the Croft family. From that day onwards, my friendship with Julia completely fell apart, and I remained really angry with her for throwing such unreasonable accusations about Fran around, particularly when she was so much luckier than Fran was. Fran may have lived in an enormous house with the most expensive version of everything inside it, but it was one of the loneliest houses I had ever stepped foot in. There were no voices of family members all busily chatting and laughing together. In fact, even bickering would have been an improvement on the silence. And there were no cooking smells to entice you into a warm kitchen. It was just cold, empty and quiet, and the only smell was the one wafting from our cigarettes as we sat and enjoyed another sneaky smoke together outside on Fran's equally enormous patio.

It was the Monday after half term and I had finally got around to telling Fran about my altercation with Julia as she had been absent from school for the rest of that week. To this day, I never actually found out the reason for Fran's absence. It was the end of October by that point and the house was in complete darkness when we returned home from band practice, even though it was only 4.30pm. I pulled my scarf up around my neck as we huddled together beside the terracotta flower pot that Fran used as an ashtray, and took a long deep suck on my cigarette.

After as little as two months, smoking had become second nature to me, and it's only now, when I look back at the 15 year old version of myself all those years ago, that I begin to appreciate how irresponsible I was. I was polluting my lungs with nicotine and pushing all the people who really meant anything to me away, just so that I could try and maintain the approval of someone who I believed to be a positive influence; someone to boost my self-

esteem. After all, since becoming friends with Fran I had joined a band, got a tattoo and started smoking. And I had even managed to tame my unbearably frizzy mop of long blonde hair by allowing Fran to work her magic on it. She had all kinds of weird and wonderful beauty products in her bedroom, and after we had finished our cigarettes that afternoon, we ran upstairs to douse ourselves in perfume in order to disguise the smell of smoke on our clothes.

"I think we should teach Julia a lesson for spreading rumours about me," Fran suggested as I started trying on a few of her hats and posing at myself in the mirror. She passed me a stick of chewing gum and as I pushed it into my mouth, I also took the opportunity to admire my perfectly straight set of teeth now that my train track brace had been removed, relieving me of my 'metal mouth' status at last.

"You're looking good these days," Fran continued, peering over my shoulder in the mirror. "I think it's about time you got yourself a boyfriend."

I asked Fran how me getting a boyfriend was going to teach Julia a lesson, and before I knew it she had fixed me up on a date with none other than Craig Riley. I should have questioned why Fran wanted me to go out with Craig, when it was her who Julia had been spreading the rumours about. But because Julia and I used to be friends, I knew that it would be a tougher punishment. And besides, I still fancied Craig like rotten, and I knew that for the first time in my life, I would actually stand a decent chance of being with someone as popular as him. As well as my sleek and silky hair and my lack of 'metal mouth', my friendship with Fran had given me a new found confidence. However it's only now that I am able to comprehend that Fran was a bit like the puppet master who was pulling my strings. At the time, I genuinely believed that she had my best interests at heart, but she was simply looking for someone to manipulate so that she could continue to bully some of her weaker peers in a far less conspicuous way.

My big date with Craig took place at the Halloween disco later that same week. Most of the people in year 10 had been planning to go to it anyway, but Fran managed to arrange for Craig and I to go together. And to make matters worse – for Julia at least – I was forced to give Julia the impression that I wanted to call a truce at the disco, in order to ensure that she definitely showed up. Fran had prepared something for me to write and pass onto her in class, telling her that I had been thinking about our argument all over half term. I remember Fran standing over me whilst I wrote it, almost as though she didn't trust me to copy what she had planned for me to write, word for word.

"But it has to sound like me," I protested, when I attempted to change the wording slightly.

It would have been easy for Julia to decide not to go to the disco, but the note clearly had the desired effect because when Fran and I eventually arrived at the school that evening, she was patiently waiting for me outside the hall, just as we had arranged. Fran had managed to smuggle some vodka into the school grounds in an Evian bottle. She tried to entice me to share it with her, but I managed to resist, even though I had never been so nervous in all my life as Craig sidled up to me and casually slipped his arm around my shoulder. Julia stiffened slightly at the sight of us together, and my heart started hammering against my rib cage as Craig slowly leaned forward and practically suffocated me with the force of his mouth against mine.

I hadn't expected us to snog each other quite as quickly as that because I had barely even spoken to him before that night, but as soon as his free hand started groping my right breast, it became obvious that Fran's little match making arrangement would be of mutual gain. As he forced his tongue into my mouth, I remember trying so hard to relax, but I wasn't actually enjoying it very much, particularly as I could taste cheese and onion crisps on his breath. Julia and I had been infatuated with him for nearly two academic years and I had frequently tried to imagine what it would be like to kiss him, but the reality was extremely disappointing, and since then I have tried to ensure that I allow myself to get to know someone before I decide whether I'm attracted to them or not, as opposed to the other way around. It only took me as little as three hours to fall head over heels in love with Richard. And he is by far the best kisser I have ever had. Craig, on the other hand, was sloppy and awkward, and he was squeezing my breast so tightly at one point that I literally had to bat his hand away. By the time I broke free from his embrace, Julia had run inside in floods of tears, leaving her billowy witches cape in a heap on the ground.

Julia's fancy dress costumes were always so impressive. Her mum was an expert with the sewing machine. But in the absence of either of our own mother's sewing skills, Fran and I had simply been obliged to buy two pairs of cats ears and some matching tails from Poundland, which we each wore to accompany a pair of black leggings and a top, although Fran had gone to the effort of drawing some whiskers on our faces using an eye liner pencil. And Craig had simply strapped a Frankenstein's monster mask to his head. He hadn't even bothered to change his clothes. As we started to make our way towards the entrance of the hall, he pulled his mask down over his face and slipped his arm around my shoulder again. And as the doors of the hall opened, we were welcomed with the deafening tones of Michael Jackson's 'Thriller', which oscillated through the entire room.

I hated school parties so much, and being in the 'popular' crowd hadn't seemed to improve my opinion of them at all even though I was on the arm of one of the best looking boys in the whole of Heathmount Comp. Nowadays teenagers have school proms to contend with too. I don't think I could have coped with anything as high profile as that when I was at school. Everything seems to be about image, personal perception and social status; having the best outfit, the coolest dance moves and the most eligible date. And it all gets splashed across social media for further scrutiny afterwards; embarrassing photos, social faux pas. At least binge drinking doesn't seem to be as popular as it was when I was youthful enough to drink my own body weight in alcohol. Young people these days are far too busy posting updates on their smart devices to bother staggering to the bar to buy another drink.

That night at the Halloween disco, when Fran successfully managed to smuggle an entire litre of vodka onto the school premises, I was very tempted to share it with her in order to enable me to survive another snog from Craig. But I resisted because I decided that at the tender age of 15, I would draw the line at smoking and tattoos. Regrettably however, I ended up getting into trouble for it anyway because within less than half an hour of us arriving in the hall, Mr Parker our PE teacher had confiscated the Evian bottle from Fran's possession, sniffed its contents and escorted all three of us to the door.

"Leave the party immediately," he demanded. "And report to Mrs Jenkinson first thing in the morning."

"But I haven't even done anything!" I protested as he grabbed onto me by my elbow and forced me onto the street. The gate was closed behind us and that was the end of the matter, until we got to school the next day of course, at which point Mr Parker practically frogmarched us all the way to the Head Mistresses' office. Mrs Jenkinson told us that she would arrange for our parents to go into school and speak to her about the three of us being suspended. When it was my turn to report to her individually later that same day, I didn't know how likely she would be to make contact with my mum and dad, but I knew that I didn't have anything to feel guilty about anyway because I hadn't actually consumed any of the vodka. But rather than concentrating on trying to think of a way to prove my innocence, I was far more preoccupied in working out who had been responsible for telling Mr Parker what was in the Evian bottle. It had been at that moment that I happened to look out of Mrs Jenkinson's office window, where I spotted Julia on her way back from afternoon registration, and suddenly all the evidence began to fall into place.

I remember feeling compelled to bang on the window and shout at her for getting me into trouble for something that I didn't even do, but for some reason my vocal chords had closed up so that no sound was coming out. Meanwhile, Mrs Jenkinson had picked her phone up and appeared to be dialling my father's number. I can still close my eyes and picture the look of disappointment on her face as she held the phone up to her ear and waited for someone to eventually answer.

"Mr Allsopp; I really need you and your wife to come down to the school immediately," she had explained, sounding most insistent. "There was a serious incident involving your daughter at the Halloween disco last night and I need to discuss it with you in person."

I couldn't hear my father's reply but it soon became obvious that he had no intention of leaving his important work meeting in order to come and speak to my head teacher, giving Mrs Jenkinson no option but to inform him over the phone that I had been caught drinking vodka on school premises and that I was going to be suspended. Eventually she explained that one of my parents would be coming to collect me, but that they were unable to get away from their individual work commitments straight away, so I was obliged to wait in Mrs Jenkinson's office with her until they eventually materialised. It was so humiliating. Mrs Jenkinson tried to assure me that they probably wouldn't be very long, but I knew better than to believe that. I told her that their jobs always came first, regardless of whether anything else was going on. I remember the sickeningly over-sympathetic look on her face as she tilted her head on one side and asked me what they each did for a living. She was obviously desperate to try and make conversation with me. Perhaps she thought she might be able to break a few of my defence barriers down, although I didn't fancy her chances. When I told her that my father was in banking and my mother had her own PR company, Mrs Jenkinson nodded understandingly before concluding that their long working hours can't have been very easy for me.

"I can look after myself," I insisted, defensively. "I'm used to it."

I was still waiting in her office nearly two hours later. School had finished and Mrs Jenkinson persisted on looking at the clock on her office wall pointedly, whilst sighing loudly. She asked me what time my mum and dad usually got home from work, and whether I had to cook my own dinner. 9pm wasn't unusual but I remember

193

deciding not to tell her that in the fear that she might have invited me back to her house for a meal. She asked me if I wanted her to try calling them again. She was obviously beginning to feel sorry for me. I shook my head and offered to get the bus home instead, but she told me that she needed one of my parents to sign my suspension form before she could release me from the school premises. I could feel myself starting to panic when I thought about being suspended. Up until that point I had never even had a detention before. I also started to wonder what had happened to Fran and Craig. Apparently they had both been collected over three hours ago, although Fran's parents had sent their Personal Assistant to pick her up because they were out of the country on business.

I asked Mrs Jenkinson what would happen to me and she explained that I would be reinstated after a brief period of leave, but that another incident similar to this one would result in my immediate expulsion. It was so unfair. I hadn't even drunk any of the vodka anyway. I thought about which one of my parents would be most likely to come and collect me. I remember thinking what a close-run call it was, but I was secretly hoping that it would be my father. Not because he was likely to go more easy on me for getting suspended, but because it would prove that he was actually bothered enough to care about me in the first place. I suddenly felt very vulnerable as I continued to sit and stare at the clock on the wall, willing the time to pass quickly enough for me to be collected. Mrs Jenkinson continued with what she was doing and part of me was hoping that she would actually look up long enough for me to catch her attention. After all, I just wanted to be noticed. I just wanted to feel as though someone actually gave a damn about me.

Eventually she announced that she needed to make a quick phone call using her secretary's phone outside in the Reception area. As the office door closed behind her, I jumped up and pressed my ear against it so that I could listen to what she was saying. She was clearly talking to her husband because she referred to the person on the other end of the phone as 'darling' and then apologised for being late home for dinner. There was a slight pause as she listened to her husband's reply, after which the tone of her voice became very defensive.

"Well her mother and father are busy people; they're not able to get away from work very early, and I can't let her go home until they've signed the suspension form. They're obviously too self-important to put their daughter's needs before their jobs, which could help to explain why she misbehaved in the first place."

I had no option but to conclude that she was accusing me of being some kind of attention seeker, and I wasn't prepared to listen to a single second more of their conversation. If she wanted to go home and have dinner with her precious husband then I decided that I wasn't about to stand in her way. I opened the office door and stormed through the Reception area towards the main exit, prompting Mrs Jenkinson to slam the phone back onto its receiver in a panic. But she was too slow because I had already bolted, denying her the chance to catch up with me even though I knew that my punishment would probably be extended as a result.

Sure enough, my suspension period was increased, despite Fran's decision to come forward and take full responsibility for the vodka. It was too late by then because I had already broken another school rule by running away from my head teacher. So I was suspended from Heathmount Comp for two very long and lonely weeks, with nothing at home to keep me company apart from some trashy daytime TV programmes and half a loaf of stale bread for me to make my sandwiches with at lunchtimes. I remember thinking it was the most unbearably boring fortnight of my entire life. My parents were out at work every day, and because I was under 'house arrest' I couldn't even go and visit Fran for a jamming session. Besides, it wasn't actually in my nature to break the rules. I had simply seen red when I overheard Mrs Jenkinson on the phone that day, and all I wanted to do was run away. Part of me actually felt quite exhilarated by it all because I knew that my parents would be obliged to actually acknowledge my existence for a change. But admitting to myself that Mrs Jenkinson may have been right to accuse me of being an attention seeker, was simply too unbearable to contemplate, so I really tried my best to remain as unaffected as possible when my father's particularly underwhelming reaction to my suspension was being played out in front of me.

"I really don't have time for this, Melanie," he sighed when I was eventually given the chance to cross paths with him two days after the Halloween disco. "You know how busy I am at work at the moment. How can you be so selfish?"

And that was that. Mediocre disappointment and not a raised voice to be heard; I actually felt rather deflated afterwards. Why didn't he and my mother care about me in the way other people's parents cared about their children? In the way Julia's parents cared about her? I spent a lot of time thinking about Julia during my two week suspension. Not because I was dwelling on our failed friendship; but because I was unbelievably angry with her for telling Mr Parker about Fran's water bottle. And as the anger slowly started to build inside me, along with the bitter aftertaste of her thriving relationship with her mum and dad, I decided that as soon as Fran and I returned to school, it would be our mission to make her life as miserable as possible.

Chapter twenty five

Tuesday 7th May 2019

"I need to request some compassionate leave," confessed Melanie sheepishly, as she approached Gill's desk.

"Has someone died?" bristled Gill, peering over the top of her glasses.

"Not yet, no," replied Melanie. "But my dad's seriously ill in hospital and I need to go and visit him."

"You can only take compassionate leave for bereavements and funerals I'm afraid," announced Gill, unsympathetically, before looking back at her computer screen as though she wasn't expecting Melanie to say anything further.

"But he's had a heart attack," protested Melanie, trying not to disclose the full extent of her frustration. "And this isn't the first time. He's in a critical condition."

Gill sighed and sat back in her chair. "Well can't you just go and visit him after work tonight, or over the weekend?"

"No actually, I can't," retorted Melanie, raising her voice. "He lives in the south of France!"

There was a long silence as the two women attempted to work out whether Philip had been able to overhear their conversation. His office door was slightly ajar so Gill leaned across to pull it shut and then tapped her long red fingernails on the desk.

"Philip won't be very happy; you've got a lot of important assignments on the go at the moment."

"I know," admitted Melanie, looking down at the floor. "But I don't know how much longer he's likely to hang on for. My mum says the doctors aren't very hopeful."

She could sense Gill's expression soften slightly but then Philip opened his door suddenly and jerked her back into ice-maiden mode again.

"What's going on out here?" he complained. "Is this about your vandalised company phone?"

Melanie discreetly scoffed at his use of the word 'vandalised' and then waited for Gill to explain the situation on her behalf. There was another long silence.

"Well, is anyone going to tell me what the two of you have been plotting about outside my office door?"

"My father's had another heart attack," explained Melanie reluctantly, as Gill started tapping away at her computer keyboard nonchalantly. "He lives in the south of France and I would like to go and visit him in hospital..."

"Out of the question!" snapped Philip, cutting Melanie off in mid-sentence. "I need you here. We're far too busy; the last thing I can afford to do is send one of my most senior members of staff off on some glorified holiday."

Melanie felt her entire body stiffen at the word 'holiday' and then swallowed deeply in order to try and control her emotions.

"But he's seriously ill," she insisted, trying to sound as reasonable as possible, although she could sense quite a shaky and vulnerable tone to her voice which encouraged her to swallow again before continuing. "I don't know if he has much longer to live."

"If he's been living in the south of France for the past few years, he'll be absolutely fine," replied Philip. "You'll probably find that it was just a bad case of indigestion from all the cheese and wine he's been knocking back. Do you want to make partner in this firm or not?"

Melanie nodded unenthusiastically and looked down at the floor.

"Well that's the last I want to hear of it. Now can you go and prepare those accounts that the juniors have been working on; I need them on my desk by close of business today."

"But I'll need longer than a day to prepare those!" Melanie protested, as Philip turned to retreat back to his office again.

"I'll have a coffee when you're ready please Gill," he then requested, pretending he hadn't even heard what Melanie had just said.

Melanie suddenly felt the overwhelming urge to burst into tears and turned to flee from Gill's desk as abruptly as she could, encouraging Brenda the cleaner to drop the tube of her vacuum cleaner on her way past.

"Are you alright love?" she enquired, as Melanie made a hasty retreat in the direction of the toilets. Melanie was too choked up to respond and simply shut herself in her favourite cubicle as warm tears began to cascade down her cheeks. She really needed to stop making a habit out of this.

"Tell me to leave you alone if you like," urged Brenda's kind voice from the other side of the door. "I just can't bear to see anyone so upset."

Melanie opened her mouth to speak but only sniffles and squeaky sounds came out.

"Between you and me, your boss doesn't seem very friendly," Brenda observed. "He complained that I hadn't emptied his bin last week when there was only one ball of scrunched up paper in it."

Melanie managed to stop crying long enough to smile weakly at the thought, and then slid down onto the toilet floor feeling exhausted.

"It's my dad," she eventually managed. "He's had a heart attack and I need to go and visit him in hospital but I can't get the time off work."

"Oh love, I'm so sorry to hear that; are you very close to your father?" asked Brenda, pretending to wipe one of the sinks down with a cloth in the fear that she would get accused of not working hard enough by one of the other members of the office staff.

Melanie removed a tissue from her suit pocket and dabbed her face with it before replying;

"Not particularly, no. He's the reason why I'm so ambitious, but he's never really been there for me. In fact, in a funny sort of way, if I can't manage to get away from my work for long enough to go and see him, he's only got himself to blame, because if it wasn't for him, I wouldn't have ended up working somewhere like this in the first place."

Brenda wasn't really sure how to respond to that and simply nodded sympathetically even though Melanie couldn't actually see that she was nodding.

"I have the hugest amount of respect for my dad," continued Melanie. "I just don't happen to like him very much."

She felt very guilty for saying that but she couldn't overlook how insecure her relationship with her father had made her feel over the years, and how she had spent most of her life just trying to gain his approval. Her behaviour at school, her unplanned pregnancy, her choice in husband, her career path; no matter how hard she tried, everything had fallen short of his expectations. And it seemed that she would be obliged to disappoint him yet again by failing to go and visit him when he needed her the most.

But what about all the occasions when she had needed him; all the important and significant times in her life when he was just too busy to be a dad to her? She was constantly trying to get his attention but nothing ever seemed to be enough. He and her mother were devoted to their jobs, and having a child was just one big inconvenience as far as they were concerned.

"Maybe he won't even care whether I go to visit him or not," she then concluded, before reluctantly emerging from the cubicle. "Maybe I'll just have to tell my mum that I'm too busy to go over there."

Brenda put the cloth down and then turned to face her with a stern expression on her face.

"Don't do anything you might regret love," she insisted. "This could be your last chance to make amends."

"But if I can't get the time off work, there's nothing I can do about it anyway; I just need to find a way of not feeling guilty about that."

Deep down, Melanie knew that it wasn't going to be easy though.

❖

Wednesday 8th May 2019

Melanie sat at her piano the following evening, softly running the tips of her fingers across the keys in deep thought. Her parents had forced her to take music lessons when she was at primary school, and her ability to play the piano to such a high standard as an adult, was one of the few things that she was truly grateful to them for. Her father in particular had never managed to make it along to a single one of her recitals though, and she had never really forgiven him for that. But perhaps, now that he was critically ill, it was finally time for her to forgive and forget.

Her thoughts were interrupted by a gentle knock at the door. She looked at her watch and then frowned when she discovered that it was almost 9.30pm. Who on earth could be visiting her at this hour? She was even more perplexed when she opened the door and discovered that Richard was standing on the doorstep holding a small bunch of tulips. Tulips had always been her favourite.

"Josh told me about your dad," he smiled, sadly. "Are you OK?"

Melanie gazed into his dark brown eyes and became overwhelmed with emotion, encouraging him to wrap his arms around her in a deep embrace.

"I don't know how I'm supposed to feel," she sobbed, burying her face in his shoulder. "I've spent so much of my life trying to gain his approval but I'm not sure he's ever really loved me. And I'm so angry with him for getting ill; does that make me a bad person?"

Richard stroked a tear away from her cheek with his thumb and then kissed her softly on the forehead.

"You've got no reason to feel guilty," he insisted, stepping into the hall and closing the front door behind him. "You and your dad have never had the most straight-forward of relationships. But he's still your dad. And you need to go and make peace with him before it's too late."

"I know you're right," agreed Melanie, as Richard leant forward to kiss her forehead again, only this time his lips ended up on her mouth instead, and before she knew it they were kissing each other passionately. Melanie knew he still loved her. Why else would he have come over to comfort her about her dad? Just as she was about to melt into their embrace, Richard pulled away suddenly.

"I'm so sorry," he insisted. "You're feeling vulnerable and I should never have taken advantage."

As he started to step backwards, Melanie grabbed his arm. "Please don't go."

"I'm sorry Melanie," Richard repeated, before opening the front door again and disappearing into the night.

Chapter twenty six

Sunday 12th May 2019

Four days later, Melanie and Richard had failed to make any form of contact with each other following their kiss, and Melanie felt as though she had the weight of the world on her shoulders. As well as thinking about Richard's feelings towards her, she had also been agonising over her situation with her father, whose condition appeared to be deteriorating by the day. But Mr Delaney was continuing to pile the pressure on at the office, so much so that she had even been obliged to spend most of Saturday at her desk working, encouraging Richard and Josh to take the opportunity to do even more 'stepfather/stepson bonding' with each other. But when Richard came to the house to collect and then return Josh home, he wouldn't even get out of his car. Melanie tried to get his attention by loitering on the doorstep a little longer than necessary, but he simply sat and stared ahead of him out of the windscreen as though she wasn't even there.

So on Sunday afternoon she decided to meet Rebecca and Fran for afternoon tea at one of her favourite tearooms in town. It had pink gingham table cloths, fresh vases of yellow, pink and mauve tulips on every table, and the smell of freshly baked scones welcomed them as they opened the door.

"I love it here!" Melanie exclaimed as she sat down. "This is exactly what I need right now."

"I think I would have preferred a cocktail in that new bar over the road," Fran scoffed. "But I suppose this will have to do."

Melanie and Rebecca both looked at each other and rolled their eyes, at which point one of the staff appeared to take their order.

"I'll have a cream tea please," smiled Melanie. "And an extra-large slice of your lemon drizzle cake."

The thought of it made her salivate, and she was equally impressed with Rebecca's order, which included a toasted teacake and a big slab of fruity flapjack.

"I'll just have a black coffee please," instructed Fran when it was her turn to order. The other two looked at each other again.

"What?" replied Fran defensively. "I don't like tea."

"Well it was Melanie's choice to come here," Rebecca insisted. "And it's up to us to try and cheer her up. She's had a really difficult week."

"Thank you," smiled Melanie weakly. "It has been pretty horrendous. Richard wouldn't even ring the front door bell when he came to collect Josh yesterday. He just stayed in his car and sent him a text message to let him know he was outside."

"What an idiot!" complained Fran.

"He's *not* an idiot," replied Melanie. "He's a good man. I should never have blown it with him."

"It's obvious he still has feelings for you," Rebecca assured her as a large pot of tea and two floral patterned cups were placed on the table in front of them. "He's probably just embarrassed about the kiss."

"Maybe," pondered Melanie, looking down at the table in deep thought, during which there was a long silence.

"So how's your dad?" enquired Fran, in an attempt to get the conversation flowing again.

"Still critical," Melanie replied. "I spoke to my mum again yesterday and she's really angry with me for not making arrangements to visit him yet."

"But *you* have a life too," Fran replied "And it was their choice to move to the south of France. You can't be expected to just drop everything and go and sit vigil at his bedside!"

Rebecca nudged Fran in the ribs with her elbow in the hope that she would stop trying to be so insensitive, but Fran persisted even further;

"Just because you're their only child, doesn't give them the right to make you feel guilty for having your own life. Besides, it was *their* fault that you decided to pursue such an ambitious career."

Melanie sliced her scone open and lathered one half of it with strawberry jam and clotted cream, before stuffing it in her mouth comfortingly. Rebecca and Fran watched as she devoured it all in one mouthful and then dabbed the sides of her lips with her pink gingham napkin.

"Do you think we can talk about something else now please?" she requested, gently.

Rebecca thought for a moment before announcing;

"Leroy's sister's getting married."

"'Stunning Suzy'?" confirmed Fran disappointedly. "I thought girls like her were never supposed to get married."

"It certainly seemed that way for a while," Rebecca smiled. "But she and her new fiancé are very much in love and they're obviously really happy."

"I think it's sweet," commented Melanie, feeling a little sorry for herself. She was usually such a sucker for romance, but when her own love-life had gone so terribly wrong, it was hard to be enthusiastic for someone else.

"So when's the wedding?"

"They're not sure yet. Suzy only called to break the news of their engagement to us last night, and they're telling her fiancé's family today."

"Leroy's parents must be excited," Melanie smiled. "A wedding *and* a new grandchild to look forward to."

Rebecca looked down at her pregnant bump and stroked it protectively, at which point Melanie's phone rang and interrupted them.

"Your father's been asking for you," announced her mother abruptly as soon as she held the phone up to her ear.

"Is he speaking now?" Melanie clarified, standing up and stepping away from the table so that Fran and Rebecca could continue enjoying their refreshments in peace.

"He's very weak but he was definitely trying to say your name when I visited him this morning," her mum explained, encouraging Melanie's stomach to plummet with guilt.

"I might be able to book a flight at the end of the week," she explained, sounding reluctant. "I can't take Josh out of school and I need to make sure Richard's available to look after him over the weekend."

"Your father may not last that long!" retorted her mother, hurtfully, at which point a tear escaped from the corner of Melanie's eye and rolled down her cheek before she had a chance to wipe it away with the tip of her finger.

"Please don't say things like that mum," she begged. "You know I would come and visit him tomorrow if I could but I've got Josh and my job to think about. Besides, I can't talk about this right now; I'm out with Fran and Rebecca."

"Well I can see you have far more important things to deal with," complained her mum, before hanging up the phone.

❖

Friday 17th May 2019

By the end of that week, Melanie was no closer to convincing Philip that she needed to go and visit her father. Her workload had rocketed beyond belief and she was having to work until 10pm every day to keep on top of it. She tried to get into the office by no later than 7am every morning, and was absolutely exhausted by the time the welcome relief of Friday afternoon eventually arrived. The pile of paperwork on her desk was slowly beginning to go down, and at the bottom of it all was a sheet of paper confirming the flight details for her trip to the south of France later that evening. She was planning to stay there for two nights while Josh was at Richard's house for the weekend, and then fly home again on Sunday afternoon. She had stayed up until midnight packing the night before, and couldn't wait to fall asleep on the plane the second it had taken off. After all, she didn't expect to be getting very much rest once she arrived at her parents' house.

At the top of the pile of paperwork was a handwritten note from one of her colleagues, asking her to phone someone called Miss Newton. She put the note to one side and decided to forget about it for the time being because she had more than enough work to be getting on with already. Besides, she had a feeling that Miss Newton had tried calling her before, and if it was *that* important then she would no doubt call again at some point.

At 5pm, as the rest of her colleagues started packing up their desks and retreating with the promise of after work drinks in the bar down the road, Melanie sighed at the thought of a nice cool glass of white wine out in the beer garden. The early evening sunshine cast a stripe of light over her desk as all the lights in the office started going out, and eventually the only sound that she could hear was the distant hum of Brenda's vacuum cleaner in the post room across the corridor. Eventually the sound got louder and louder, before switching off abruptly, causing her to jump a little in her seat.

"Are you working late again?" said a concerned voice from behind her. It was Brenda. "It's Friday; you should be heading off to the pub with everyone else."

"I wish I was," chuckled Melanie, remembering her glass of wine again. "But I'm actually flying down to the south of France to see my father later this evening."

Brenda smiled encouragingly. "You're going then; that's great news. How's he getting on?"

"No improvement," Melanie replied, before realising that it was already 5.25pm. "In fact, I ought to get going. My flight's in a couple of hours and I still need to get a cab to the airport."

"Don't let me hold you up," insisted Brenda loudly, turning the vacuum cleaner on again. "I'm only working tonight so that I don't have to come in early on Monday morning; we're taking the grandchildren away for a long weekend. Have a safe trip."

"Thanks," smiled Melanie, appreciatively, as she frantically started clearing her desk of paperwork, before locating her handbag on the coat stand next to her. She couldn't believe that she was managing to get away from work so promptly for a change.

She slung her handbag over her shoulder, switched off her computer and her desk light and started walking towards the door, when Gill suddenly caught up with her.

"Mr Delaney needs to see you urgently," she explained, looking stern. "Apparently there's a problem with the accounts that you've been working on."

Melanie's heart plummeted. She looked at her watch and it was 5.35pm. Her flight was due to take off at 8pm and she wasn't even at the airport yet.

"Will it take long?" she frowned, sounding agitated.

"You'll have to ask him that," replied Gill, snidely. "I'm off to the pub for an extra-large glass of white wine; it's been a long week."

Melanie tried not to laugh in her face. Gill rarely started work any earlier than 8.30am and she was always out of the door by no later than 6pm, which, compared with Melanie's 15 hour long shifts, was rather pitiful. But then again, she was only Philip's PA. Philip *knew* that Melanie was hoping to leave early tonight in order to go and visit her father. She had done everything that he had asked of her and she had worked her fingers to the bone in the process. What on earth could he possibly want to talk to her about? And why couldn't it just wait until Monday morning?

"Our clients have asked for some additional figures," Mr Delaney explained, once Melanie had let herself into his office. "And they need them as soon as possible."

"No problem," replied Melanie, trying to ignore the clock on the wall behind him and remain as calm as possible. "Just email me the details and I'll deal with it first thing on Monday."

"I'm afraid they need the information before that," Philip cut in, encouraging Melanie's pulse to start pounding rapidly. She knew exactly where this was going. "Is there any chance you'll be able to prepare them before you leave tonight?"

"Well no, there isn't actually; my flight is at 8pm and it's really important that I'm on that plane."

"It's really important that these figures are prepared too," snapped Philip, angrily. "They should only take you half an hour or so. You'll still be able to make it to the airport in time."

"Not if I need to allow two hours to check-in!" retorted Melanie.

"You won't need to allow as long as that for a European flight; you've got plenty of time," insisted Philip. "Besides, these clients are really important to this firm and if they've asked for something, they're going to bloody well get it! Particularly if you're still interested in becoming a partner here."

Melanie knew he was about to play the partner card again. But she also knew that the figures would take a lot longer than half an hour to prepare. And if she didn't manage to get on that plane, she would probably never get to see her father again.

There was a long silence as Melanie tried to think of a way of getting out of it; of holding onto her job *and* her pride without having to work late. But as Philip stood up from his desk and leaned across to pass her the paperwork, she found herself snatching it from him anyway. And before she knew it she was switching on her computer and her desk light again, and hanging her handbag back up on the coat stand next to her desk.

Chapter twenty seven

November 2000

My mission to make Julia's life a misery was quickly beginning to build impetus, and by the end of my first week back at school following my tedious two week long suspension, Fran and I had managed to reduce her to a quivering heap in the girls' toilets. I still had so much anger and resentment inside me, not least because I had barely spent a single second with either one of my parents for the entire fortnight that I was off school. And when Julia's dad's car pulled up alongside us on Monday morning, and Fran and I were obliged to watch her kissing and hugging him goodbye, I actually felt physically sick. It was almost as though she was rubbing our noses in it, but I suppose I wasn't really in the position to complain about that when I had been guilty of doing the exact same thing with Craig.

Fran asked me if Julia and her dad had always been so sickeningly close to each other, but to be completely honest, I hadn't really paid much attention to it before. Her brother Christian was a proper mummy's boy, but it had never occurred to me, until that morning at least, that Julia was a real daddy's girl as well. And as she opened the car door and stepped out onto the path outside the school gates, Fran felt that she had no choice but to make a pointed comment about it.

"Well at least my dad cares about me!" was Julia's defensive reply, as she got ready to slam the car door shut. We overheard Mr Croft asking her if she was OK, before eyeing me suspiciously. Fran and I just looked at each other and laughed, at which moment Mr Parker burst through the gates and instructed us to start making our way to morning registration. I had been chewing a piece of gum at the time, which was completely against school rules, but even though it wasn't anywhere near as serious as drinking vodka, I decided to conceal the evidence from Mr Parker anyway because I knew what an old stickler he was for the

rulebook. So as we reluctantly followed Julia through the gate and heard her dad's car slowly driving away behind us, I removed the sticky piece of gum from my mouth and squeezed it into Julia's ponytail. The gum welded itself onto a chunk of her boring brown hair and just hung there, prompting Fran to start laughing again. Mr Parker, who had been walking across the car park in front of Julia, turned to look at us disapprovingly, before reminding Craig and his friends that it was time for them to stop their game of football.

Julia didn't even make it to morning registration that day because she had to go to the staff room and have the chewing gum removed from her hair. I do remember feeling a little bit guilty about it but that didn't last long when I thought about how much trouble she had got me into at the Halloween disco. And with that amount of fire in my belly, and someone as fearless and influential as Fran spurring me on, there really was no stopping me after that.

Looking back now, it's hard to believe that this kind of toxic behaviour went on for over a year. But I genuinely didn't think of what we were doing as bullying at the time. We were simply defending ourselves. In fact on one occasion Julia actually accused me of being the victim as opposed to the perpetrator, because she convinced herself that Fran was manipulating me into doing her dirty work for her. And that just succeeded in winding me up further so that I was even more determined to take revenge.

Craig and I continued to date each other for the rest of that term, but with the exception of the occasional grope behind the bike sheds, we never really spent any time together. He was always far too busy playing football with his mates. Sometimes Fran and I would stand and watch them from the side lines, and it was always very amusing whenever Julia attempted to walk past, because Craig would deliberately kick the ball at her head. A week before the Christmas holidays she ended up spilling the contents of her school bag in the process, and we all took great pleasure in watching her stoop down to retrieve it all from the ground. Just as she was about to gather up her final few items, Craig ran over and grabbed her pencil case, before proceeding to throw it to one of his mates. Eventually we were all playing a game of catch with it, enticing Julia to tirelessly run from one person to the next with her hands outstretched, begging for one of us to take pity on her and give it back. After several minutes of taunting she finally decided to admit defeat and sloped off to her next class with her head hung low. I wondered whether she was crying but erased the possibility from my mind in the fear that a semblance of remorse might set in.

Before Fran and I decided to show up to our next class that day, we emptied the pencil case onto the ground and deliberately snapped the end off each of her pencils. We also stole the lids to all her pens so that they would gradually dry up, and then used one to write 'Julia Croft loves Mr Parker' on the outside of the pencil case in fat red felt tip, with love hearts around the outside. I knew it wasn't right but it was strangely exhilarating, and every time I did anything to scorn Julia, Fran looked at me approvingly and made me feel really good about myself.

"Just remember, she deserves it," she would whisper under her breath, every time she could sense that I was beginning to lose my nerve. She really was the ultimate puppet master.

When I got to registration that afternoon, Fran had instructed me to return the pencil case to Julia in full view of our form tutor, as though I was doing some kind of good deed. I remember our form tutor actually praising me for my efforts, completely oblivious to the fact that I had been responsible for taking it in the first place. In fact, she even persuaded Julia to say thank you to me.

I actually felt quite good about myself after she apologised, much like I had when I found out how long it took for the teachers to cut my chewing gum out of her ponytail; because I really hadn't appreciated her scornful comment when she got out of her dad's car that day. She had basically implied that my dad didn't care about me, and even though I was pained to admit that there was some truth in her observation, it wasn't her right to try and make me feel even more bad about it than I did already. And I suppose that was what really motivated me to continue bullying her.

Because telling Mr Parker about the vodka was one thing, but using my relationship with my father against me, was another matter entirely. She had really touched a nerve that day and I wasn't prepared to let her get away with it.

Chapter twenty eight

Friday 17th May 2019

At 6.45pm, Melanie eventually left the office. She had arranged for a cab to meet her outside the main entrance, and as soon as she approached, the driver flung her suitcase into the boot and accelerated away as fast as he could, with strict instructions to get her to the airport as quickly as possible.

"My flight's due to take off at 8pm," she explained, tapping into her phone to find out whether there had been any delays.

"You'll never make it," announced the cab driver, bluntly. "The traffic's always a nightmare at this time of night, and it takes at least half an hour to get to the airport from this side of town."

"I *have* to make it!" exclaimed Melanie, feeling the panic rise up inside her again. "I'm going to see my father and he's doesn't have long to live."

"So why are you cutting it so fine?" replied the driver, frowning at her in the reflection of his rear view mirror. "You should have been at the airport ages ago."

"I was stuck at work," confessed Melanie, sheepishly. "I had an important deadline to meet."

"More important than visiting your dad on his death bed?" scoffed the driver.

"My boss is very strict," Melanie objected, getting defensive, but deep down she knew that both he and Brenda were right. She should have told Mr Delaney what to do with his assignment and she should have been taking this cab ride at least an hour ago.

"It will be fine," she then insisted, after a short silence. "It has to be."

Besides, she was an intelligent woman, why did she need a cab driver and a cleaner to tell her what to do? She was just about to put her phone back in her handbag when an email came through. It was from Josh;

'*Hi Mum,*

You'll be in the boarding lounge by now and probably won't read this until you get to France, but I just wanted to let you know that Dad and I are looking forward to a great weekend together. He's taking me to a football match tomorrow and then we're going to that new pizza restaurant again! I hope Grandad's OK. Have a safe flight and I'll speak to you in the morning.

Love Josh'

Melanie swallowed the lump in her throat as she read the message, and then snapped her phone case shut before exhaling loudly. It sounded like Josh and Richard were really enjoying one another's company again, and Richard had obviously put a lot of thought into their plans for the weekend. He really was a wonderful father; Josh was very lucky to have him, particularly as Josh's biological father didn't want to have anything to do with him. They had met each other at university and were very young when Melanie fell pregnant. By the time Josh was born, he had graduated and moved away, and Melanie was forced to bring up the baby on her own. Her parents were devastated because she had to leave university a year early and then re-take her accountancy exams once Josh had started school. They had been particularly unsupportive, and moved to the South of France a short while later, but by that time Melanie was dating Richard.

"So are you and your dad close?" enquired the cab driver, interrupting Melanie's thoughts.

Melanie sighed at the prospect of having to explain her temperamental relationship with her father to yet another complete stranger, but then decided to open up to him anyway because it had failed to do her any harm when she chose to confide in Brenda at work.

"My dad doesn't *do* close. He's never exactly been the 'touchy feely' type. I'm not really sure why he and Mum decided to have a child because they've spent most of my life resenting my existence. But my mum wants me to go and make my peace with him before he dies, and I feel that's something that I really need to do while I've still got the chance."

"I'll do my best to get you to the airport," insisted the driver, trying to sound positive, but just as he was about to put his foot down on the accelerator, the traffic came to a grinding halt again.

It was 7.05pm. She was never going to make it in time. She removed her tickets and passport from her handbag and stared at them despairingly, before concluding that she would simply have to rebook her flight tomorrow if she did miss the plane. After all, she would still be able to spend at least one night with her mother before returning to the UK in time for work on Monday.

"So when was the last time you saw your dad?" asked the driver, as the traffic started moving again.

"On his 70th Birthday," replied Melanie. "About two years ago. Mum held a big party for him and my son and my husband and I went over to France to visit them."

"Sounds nice," smiled the driver, encouraging Melanie to shake her head.

"Not really, no," she explained. "He and my husband have never got on very well, and my father spent the entire visit convincing me to apply for a promotion at work because he didn't feel that I was aiming high enough in my career. Unfortunately I listened to him, and my husband and I split up a year later because I was working too much."

"So that's why you're travelling solo," confirmed the driver, sympathetically. "And what's wrong with your dad?"

"He has a heart condition," replied Melanie, before trying not to smile at the irony of the situation. "Apparently it was brought on by stress because he used to work too hard!"

The cab driver chose not to say anything in reply to this particular revelation, because as he pulled up outside the departures entrance at the airport, his silence spoke volumes.

"Good luck," he smiled, removing Melanie's suitcase from the boot of the cab. "I hope you manage to get all the closure that you need."

"Thank you," replied Melanie, handing him the money for the fare and running towards the entrance as fast as she could. She didn't even bother to try and decipher what was written on the departure boards above her head, and ran straight to the nearest assistant at the desk marked Nice.

"Can I check my luggage in please?" she pleaded, whilst glancing across at the enormous clock on the wall. It was 7.30pm.

"I'm sorry madam," replied the airport assistant, studying her ticket. "This flight has already boarded and is now preparing for take-off."

It was too late.

❖

Melanie spent more than 45 minutes trying to plead with the airline to book her on the next plane out to Nice, but the earliest flight that she was able to arrange was for lunchtime the following day.

"And are you sure you don't have anything else sooner?" she insisted, sliding her credit card across the counter. "I need to get there urgently to visit my sick father. He may not make it until tomorrow!"

"I'm sorry Ms Allsopp," replied the airport assistant, sounding a little robotic. "All the outward flights are booked up until then."

Melanie knew that she was fighting a losing battle and decided to give up. She wasn't looking forward to explaining the situation to her mother though, and very reluctantly retrieved her phone from her hand luggage as the airport assistant continued to process the payment.

"Hi Mum, it's Mel. I'm afraid I've been delayed and I won't be able to get there until late afternoon tomorrow. Will you tell Dad that I'm sorry?"

"Delayed!" retorted her mother. "Is there something wrong with the plane?"

"Not exactly, no," replied Melanie, sounding guilty. "Other than the fact that I missed it."

"How did you miss it?" demanded her mum, encouraging Melanie to turn away from where she had been standing so that the airport assistant couldn't hear.

"I had to work late," Melanie explained, lowering her voice. "You know what my boss is like. He's as tough as you and Dad combined and I couldn't get away."

"Your father is getting weaker by the hour," replied her mother. "Time is running out. You should have been here by now."

"I've been up to my eyeballs with work this week, you know that!" snapped Melanie. "If anyone should relate to my situation, it's you. You were always working when I was growing up and you never had any time for me."

"So this is your way of seeking revenge is it?" snapped her mother. "By keeping us both waiting!"

"Of course not," sighed Melanie, rubbing her forehead. "It's just difficult sometimes. You and Dad always wanted me to make something of myself. In fact, it was Dad's idea that I applied for a promotion. And if I want to become a partner, I need to put the work in."

"So you're saying it's *our* fault that you've been putting your career before your family all this time?" her mother shouted, raising her voice again. Melanie put her hand over the mouthpiece of her phone in the fear that the airport assistant could hear every word.

"All I'm saying is that I feel like I can't win. Whatever I do, it never seems to be good enough..."

"Here are your new tickets Ms Allsopp," interrupted the airport assistant, placing her new flight details and her credit card in the palm of Melanie's hand. "Thank you for flying with Nice Airways."

As she turned to walk away, Melanie rolled her eyes at her overly robotic nature, before placing her phone up to her ear again in order to continue the conversation with her mum. But she was surprised to discover that the line had gone dead, and that her mother had clearly hung up on her.

"Typical," she sighed, before dragging her luggage to the exit and flagging down another taxi.

❖

When Melanie eventually arrived home, Ursula was just about to lock up and leave.

"What are you still doing here?" Melanie frowned, confronting her on the doorstep.

"You asked me to come and do a few extra jobs while you're away, so I decided to just work this evening instead of over the weekend," Ursula explained, before mirroring Melanie's expression with a frown. "So what are *you* doing here?"

Melanie was about to pour her heart out to Ursula about Mr Delaney's assignment, missing her flight, and then having a horrible conversation with her mother on the phone, but she managed to stop herself in time to simply smile weakly and shake her head;

"It's a long story; I'll tell you another time. Now I expect you're desperate to get home. It's almost 9pm."

Confiding in her housekeeper was the last thing she felt like doing. Besides, she had already shared far too many details with the office cleaner and the cab driver. This time she wanted to speak to someone who genuinely cared about her.

"Did you manage to speak to Josh about his computer by the way?" enquired Ursula, just as Melanie was about to close the door behind her. "I'm worried about him."

"I'm sure he's fine," insisted Melanie, brushing the situation off. "It's probably just teenage boy stuff."

"You should still make some time to talk to him," continued Ursula, as the door started to close in her face. Melanie really wasn't in the mood for thinking about this right now. Besides, she didn't need her housekeeper to tell her how to be a parent to her own son.

"Good night Ursula, and thanks for the advice," she then smiled through gritted teeth, before closing the front door and sinking down onto the hall floor.

"What a day!" she then exclaimed, out loud. "I wonder if Rebecca's around for a chat."

She removed her phone from her suit trouser pocket and dialled Rebecca's number but there was no reply. She vaguely remembered Rebecca telling her about Leroy's sister's engagement party but she couldn't recall whether it was tonight or not. She then thought about calling Fran, but for some reason she didn't feel particularly keen on the idea of confiding in her. She and Fran had been growing apart for some time now. They didn't seem to have anything in common anymore. In fact, it was almost as though they were staying friends with each other out of habit. So who else could she call? She didn't really have that many friends to be perfectly honest because she was simply too busy. And she had never really felt the need to pour her heart out to anyone until now. She slowly lifted herself up from the hall floor and made her way into the living room, where she collapsed onto the sofa and fell asleep within minutes.

❖

Almost four hours later Melanie awoke to find the side of her face squashed against the hard sofa arm. She pushed herself up onto her hands, rubbed her eyes and peered at her watch; it was 1am. She would have been in Nice at least an hour ago by now. Her entire body ached from having lain awkwardly so she decided to make her way up to bed. When she got to the top of the stairs, Melanie peered into Josh's empty bedroom and suddenly started to feel extremely lonely. She then noticed that his laptop was lying on the bed and remembered what Ursula had told her.

"I wonder if I can work out what Josh's password is," she thought aloud, before stepping forward into his room. She was just about to open the laptop when a ringing from her pocket interrupted her. The thought of someone calling her at 1 o'clock in the morning, confirmed who it must have been before she had even managed to slide her phone out of her pocket to check the name on the display;

"Mum?"

"It's about your father," replied the choked up voice at the other end. "He passed away half an hour ago."

Chapter twenty nine

Saturday 18th May 2019

"Can I come in?" pleaded Melanie, as Richard opened the door of his flat and rubbed his eyes sleepily.

"But it's three o'clock in the morning," he replied, lowering his voice in the fear that Melanie's very unexpected visit might wake Josh up.

"Please," she insisted. "I really don't want to be on my own tonight."

"Has something happened?" Richard frowned, looking concerned. "Why aren't you in France?"

"I missed my flight," replied Melanie as she followed him into the sitting room. "And before you ask, I was working late, so I didn't get to the airport in time."

Just as Richard was about to put his 'Mr Delaney defences' up again, Melanie held a finger to his lips in order to stop him.

"But that's not why I'm here," she continued. "A couple of hours ago, my mum called to tell me that my father had died."

"Oh Melanie, I'm so sorry," sighed Richard, putting his arms around her. They held each other for what felt like a few minutes before either of them spoke again.

Melanie sank down onto the sofa and removed a tissue from her pocket, as Richard slumped down next to her and started stroking her hair comfortingly.

"If only I hadn't missed my flight," she sobbed, resting her head on his shoulder. "I would have been there just in time to say good bye. My mum's been on and on at me to go and visit him all week, but I was determined to put my job first *again*."

Richard decided not to say anything, but his facial expression told her everything she needed to know.

"Why do I keep doing this? First my marriage and now my father's illness. What will it take for me to learn that there are more important things in life than work?"

"I wish I knew," replied Richard, raising his eyebrows despairingly. "But don't forget how influential your father was on your career. He had the same attitude towards it as you do. In fact it's probably *his* fault that you turned out like this in the first place."

Melanie smiled weakly, before wrapping her arms around Richard's neck and breathing in the warm comforting smell of the soft skin below his jaw-line. Their embrace felt so comfortable and natural. She temporarily forgot that they weren't together anymore.

"But I never had a chance to make it right with him," she reflected, closing her eyes.

"I'm not sure you would have been able to anyway," insisted Richard, encouragingly. "Even after his first heart attack, your father remained as stubborn and success driven as ever. It was him who pushed you to apply for your promotion."

"I'm sorry for letting you down," Melanie explained. "I remember how difficult my father was to live with when I was growing up; always putting his career before me. And then I went and did the same thing to you and Josh."

There was a long pause, as Melanie continued to stroke the soft skin around Richard's neck with the very tip of her lips.

"I still love you."

"So what are you trying to say?" clarified Richard, placing his hand on her thigh and closing his own eyes.

"I'm trying to say that I'll change," explained Melanie. "I don't want to end up on my *own* death bed in 40 years' time, without Josh there to hold my hand."

She hesitated "Without *you* there."

"But what are you going to do for a job? accountancy is all you know."

"Who said anything about giving up accountancy?" replied Melanie, sitting up suddenly. "As soon as I get my promotion, I'll be able to take more time off because I won't need to try and prove myself anymore. And I won't have to answer to Philip anymore either."

"You really think so do you," replied Richard, sitting back against the sofa looking disappointed. "Because I think you'll end up being even busier than ever once you're a partner."

Melanie could sense that the atmosphere in the room had completely changed, persuading her to stand up and walk over to the door.

"I shouldn't have come," she concluded. "I just couldn't think of anyone else who I wanted to confide in as much as you."

"You don't have to go," insisted Richard, wearily. "You can spend the rest of the night on the sofa and then we can both tell Josh about your dad in the morning."

"Thank you," Melanie smiled, as Richard went to find a spare pillow and a blanket from the cupboard in the hall.

She had fallen fast asleep again within minutes, at which point Richard snuck back into the sitting room in order to prevent the blanket from slipping off the sofa and onto the floor.

"I still love you too, but unfortunately it's not enough," he whispered, before switching off the light.

❖

The following morning, Melanie awoke early and crept into the kitchen to make herself some fresh coffee. As she slowly pushed the plunger to the base of the cafetiere, and breathed in its delicious aroma, she sat back in her chair and closed her eyes. The smell reminded her of her father. He used to drink a lot of fresh coffee, particularly when he was stressed. In fact, excessive amounts of caffeine and stress were two of the main reasons why he had ended up with heart problems. As well as the fact that he had been rather partial to a cigar of course. He was by no means overweight. Far from it; he always claimed that he was simply too busy to eat a proper meal. But there was no denying that his poor lifestyle had been responsible for cutting his life short, despite him having sold his business and moved down to the South of France following his first heart attack. It had all been too little too late.

Melanie didn't want it to be too late for her too, but when she thought about what Richard had said the night before, she wasn't sure whether she was inclined to agree with him or not. After all, being a partner was all about being able to delegate the work to someone else; just like Mr Delaney does. As she lifted the cafetiere and started to pour its contents into her cup, she was interrupted by Josh, who slumped into one of the chairs opposite her and scratched his head.

"What are you doing here mum?" he frowned. "Is Grandad OK?"

"Melanie hesitated, and then reached across the table to hold his hand.

"I'm afraid not darling, no," she explained, gently, as Richard entered the room and placed his hands on her shoulders supportively. "Granny rang last night to tell me that he had passed away."

Josh's frown softened slightly as he began to process what she had just told him.

"So are you still going down there?" he eventually enquired, looking a little perplexed.

Melanie nodded "I've re-booked my flight for this lunchtime," she explained. "But I might need to reschedule it again so that we can all fly down there together for the funeral."

"Does that mean I get to take some time off school?" Josh clarified, his facial expression brightening.

"A couple of days perhaps," replied Melanie. "I'll pop in to see your form tutor on Monday morning and explain."

"You can just send a note," insisted Josh. "You don't need to go in."

"It's no bother," continued Melanie. "I need to go into the office on Monday anyway and explain why I won't be back at work until later in the week. I can pop into your school on the way."

Josh was just about to protest when the sound of his phone vibrating across the kitchen table interrupted them. He picked it up and looked at it, before standing up abruptly and almost knocking the cafetiere over.

"I need to go," he suddenly announced, looking uneasy.

"Careful mate; what's the hurry?" replied Richard, grabbing the handle of the cafetiere as it started to topple.

"It's nothing!" Josh snapped, as he reached the kitchen doorway. "Why do you and Mum have to be so interfering?"

"Interfering?" Melanie frowned, looking at Richard. They both jumped as Josh slammed the kitchen door behind him, encouraging Richard to place his hands on Melanie's shoulders again.

"He's probably just in shock because of my dad," she concluded, closing her eyes and rolling her head back, as Richard started to gently massage her shoulders and neck. "You know what 12 year olds are like; he's practically a teenager"

"I think there might be more to it than that," replied Richard. "He's been particularly sensitive about his phone and his laptop recently."

"That's what Ursula said," agreed Melanie. "In fact I was tempted to check his laptop last night before my mum rang but I didn't know the password."

"You can't invade his privacy like that," Richard insisted. "If he needs to open up to us about anything, then we've got to make ourselves more available."

"You mean *I've* got to make myself more available," clarified Melanie, defensively, tensing herself up again. "You're not even his real dad and he spends more time with you than he does with his own mother."

"Well that's not my fault is it," snapped Richard, removing his hands from Melanie's shoulders and folding his arms across his chest.

"I wish everyone would stop telling me how to be a parent to my own son!" she shouted, standing up from her chair and walking over to the kitchen door. "Thanks for letting me stay last night but I don't need you to decide what's best for me; we're not even together anymore!"

"Well that's a relief," retorted Richard, following her through to the hall. "Give my regards to Mr Delaney."

The sarcastic expression on Richard's face encouraged Melanie to huff loudly as she picked up her handbag from the hall table and opened the front door.

"Goodbye Richard," she snapped, before retreating down the path towards her car. He made her so angry sometimes. But as he slammed the front door behind her, all she could focus on as she climbed into the driver's seat was how his warm muscular hands had felt on the soft sensitive skin around her shoulders and neck, and how she longed to be intimate with him again.

❖

Monday 20th May 2019

As Melanie prepared herself to go into the office that Monday, all she could think about was what Mr Delaney's reaction would be when she told him that she would need to take some more time off work. Ursula was just arriving for her shift as she grabbed a slice of cold buttered toast from the breakfast table and stuffed it into her mouth.

"Not enough time to eat again?" Ursula confirmed, looking at her disapprovingly over her half-moon spectacles.

"At least I'm not skipping breakfast altogether," replied Melanie defensively, gathering her belongings and attempting to open the front door with her elbow. "Besides, I'm leaving even earlier than usual today because I need to pop into Josh's school on my way into work."

"Earlier than what?" retorted Ursula, stopping Melanie in her tracks. "You've been starting work at 6am every day for the past 3 weeks."

She looked at Melanie sternly for a few seconds and then softened a little before putting her hands on Melanie's arm;

"I'm sorry about your father," she insisted, encouraging Melanie to drop her handbag.

Melanie then removed the slice of toast from her mouth and smiled sheepishly. "Thank you Ursula; that means a lot."

What she meant to say was that it meant a lot coming from *her*, because Ursula very rarely bothered to show any form of emotion whatsoever. She was always so cold towards everyone, even Josh. Ursula sensed that she had let her guard down too much and then straightened herself up a little before removing the dustpan and brush from the cupboard under the stairs.

"Have a good day," Melanie smiled, rescuing her handbag from the floor and then closing the front door behind her with her foot.

She was just about to get into her car when a very heavily pregnant Rebecca waddled up to her.

"What are you doing here?" she frowned, squinting at the face of her watch under the bright sunshine. "Its 8.30am."

"I was on my way to my pregnancy yoga class and I wanted to see you before you left for work," Rebecca explained. "I'm really sorry about your dad; I can't believe you didn't make it to France in time to see him before he died."

"He was really ill," Melanie replied, trying to ease her guilty conscience a little. "None of us really knew how much longer he could hold on for."

"Were you OK over the weekend on your own?" confirmed Rebecca. "When I got your text message yesterday I was really worried about you. I wanted to come over here then but Leroy insisted that I stayed at home. The engagement party really wore me out on Saturday evening."

"Don't worry; I stayed at Richard's place on Friday night so I wasn't on my own *all* weekend," smiled Melanie. "So how was the party? What's Suzy's new fiancée like?"

"Never mind how the party was, what do you mean you stayed at Richard's?"

"I went over there after my mum called," Melanie explained. "I wanted to be with him."

"And did anything happen this time?" probed Rebecca, getting excited.

"I'm afraid not, no," replied Melanie, sounding disappointed. "I spent the night on his sofa, and then we ended up having another row about my job on Saturday morning."

"Speaking of which," Rebecca replied, looking down at Melanie's suit, "Why are you going into work today? Shouldn't you be on compassionate leave?"

"Not if I want to be promoted," Melanie scoffed, before looking at her watch again. "Actually, I should really get going; I need to pop into the school and speak to Josh's teacher on my way to the office. I'll give you a call at the weekend to let you know how the funeral went."

Rebecca attempted to try and hug her but her bump got in the way, so she simply leant sideways and planted a kiss on her cheek instead.

"You know where we are if you need anything," she smiled, as Melanie climbed into her car.

She watched her heavily pregnant friend waddle away down the road and thought about how supportive she was, particularly compared with Fran who hadn't even bothered to reply to her text message. She was probably propping up some cocktail bar on Saturday night and had spent the rest of the weekend in bed with her latest conquest. Melanie shook her head despairingly at the thought, put on her seatbelt, turned the engine on and started to reverse out of her driveway. All of a sudden a girl in Pinewood school uniform stepped out behind the car, encouraging her to slam her brakes on.

"Watch where you're going," she complained, winding her window down and waving her hand in objection. The girl turned to look at her. She was three or four years older than Josh, with dyed black hair and a streak of blonde down one side. Her eyes were thick with mascara, most of which had formed two watery black lines down either side of her face.

"Are you OK?" Melanie frowned softening slightly when she realised how upset the girl was.

"It's none of your business!" the girl snapped, before continuing to head down the street in the direction of the nearby park.

Chapter thirty

Julia was an easy target. She rarely defended herself, and she was unbelievably irritating. I often used to wonder how I had managed to remain best friends with her for nearly three years. And she continued to look down her nose at Fran and me whenever she caught a glimpse of us enjoying a sneaky smoke together, as though we were a bit of dirt that she had scraped from the sole of her shoe.

One day Fran suggested that I should force Julia to take a drag from my cigarette. I remember feeling a little reluctant about following through with this particular punishment because Julia's grandfather had died of lung cancer and I knew how sensitive she felt about the effects of smoking. But the next time she was obliged to make her way past the bike sheds, Fran shoved me so hard that I almost went crashing into her at full force. Julia gripped her arm in pain as it got trapped between the weight of me and the wall behind her, and I couldn't help but laugh at what a pathetically low pain threshold she had. Of course, I didn't know then that her arm was in pain before I had crushed it, which was why I then proceeded to grab hold of it tightly and drag her to where Fran was waiting.

Julia struggled and squirmed, but there was no chance of her escaping our tight little triangle until she had succeeded in coughing up a lungful of smoke, and as Fran forced me to push my cigarette between Julia's tightly closed lips, she was choking and hacking within seconds.

"I bet you wish your precious daddy was here to save you now!" laughed Fran, tossing her long red locks of hair over her shoulder.

I remember throwing the cigarette down on the floor and stepping on it suddenly when I thought about what our punishment would be if Julia decided to confide in her dad about what we had just done. And from that point onwards we decided to try and be a lot more calculated in our approach because we didn't want to get ourselves suspended again. We had to ensure that everything we did couldn't be traced back to us in any way. After all, even if Julia had her suspicions about who was responsible, she wouldn't be able to actually prove anything, and that gave us the upper hand at all times, as well as providing the rest of the children in our year with enough ammunition for Fran and I to retire on anyway.

One particular example of this was during the autumn term of year 11, when our PE group were getting changed for a hockey lesson. Julia made the rather foolish mistake of leaving her kit bag in the changing rooms whilst she went to the toilet, giving Fran and me the perfect opportunity to steal her tracksuit bottoms from it. To this day, I don't actually know what Fran did with them, but when Julia returned from the toilet and discovered that they were missing, she was obliged to wear her PE shorts instead and it was absolutely freezing out on the school field. There was practically a frost on the ground.

Mr Parker was far from sympathetic when he realised that Julia was the only member of his class who was wearing the incorrect hockey kit. He told her that he would have expected better from her and that she would be obliged to stand out on the field with bare legs as a punishment, despite the fact that the lost property cupboard was full of plenty of spare pairs of tracksuit bottoms. Julia tried to insist that she had packed the right kit that morning, but he just wasn't interested. And Fran and I knew that she would never be able to prove otherwise so we skipped out onto the field together feeling very pleased with ourselves. It really did feel very exhilarating watching someone else suffer; particularly someone as irritating as Julia. Back then I truly believed that she had no one to blame but herself for being so self-righteous and condescending. And every time Fran patted me on the back for assisting her with her latest prank, it made me so happy, because all I really wanted when I was growing up was approval and acceptance, and in the absence of either of my parents, it didn't really matter who it was from.

Fran and I laughed all the way to the hockey pitch. I remember watching the clouds of our warm breath cutting through the cold air ahead of us as we continued to skip along the muddy grass together. We were eventually joined by Craig who slipped his arm around my shoulder in his usual cavalier fashion and then pointed with glee at the sorry sight of Julia as she trudged across the field towards us. Her teeth were chattering together in the cold and she had her arms wrapped around herself protectively in a futile attempt to keep warm.

"Nice legs," observed Craig, sarcastically, before crouching down to study them more closely.

My elated expression subsided slightly as I tried to pull him back up from his crouched position, but it was too late.

"Ergh, your legs are really hairy!" he laughed, drawing everybody else's attention to them too. "They're disgusting."

I knew how self-conscious Julia was about the dark hairs on her legs. When we first hit puberty she used to roll her tights down after school and obsessively scrutinise each and every little hair as though it was an ugly imposter and had no right to be there. I always felt rather sorry for her for being so dark, when my own hairs were barely detectable blond strands of fluff in comparison. She told me that she tried shaving her legs once but the hairs just seemed to grow back even thicker and faster as a result, and she was also covered in a red itchy shaving rash which simply succeeded in making her feel even more self-conscious. When we were in year 9 her mum bought her a home waxing kit but she found it far too painful. So she decided that she would always stick to wearing tracksuit bottoms for PE, even in the hot summer months when the rest of us couldn't wait to put our shorts on instead. That day out on the hockey field was the first time she had been forced to bare her hairy legs, and I hadn't quite appreciated how guilty it would make me feel until Craig decided to draw attention to it.

Julia's eyes filled with tears as she looked at me pleadingly, but the damage had already been done, and before I knew it she had thrown her hockey stick on the muddy ground and fled across the field towards the changing rooms again. Mr Parker contacted her parents after that, which prompted Mrs Jenkinson to instruct all the girls in our particular class to empty our kit bags out onto our desks later that afternoon, so that she could try and work out who had stolen Julia's tracksuit bottoms. Of course, there was no sign of the missing kit in anyone else's bags because Fran had managed to leave no trace of what we had done anywhere. And all the bag search succeeded in doing was humiliating Julia even further. Most of the other girls in our class were quite annoyed about having to empty the contents of their PE kit bags out onto their desks, particularly when many of them were concealing feminine hygiene products, amongst other personal items. And they resented being treated like potential suspects in what they believed to be a very petty crime. No one knew who was really responsible for stealing the tracksuit bottoms, so they lashed out at Julia instead for subjecting them all to such a public invasion of their personal property, and I actually found myself blaming her as well even though I knew that it was Fran who had stolen them.

Meanwhile, the boys, who were spared the humiliation of having their bags searched because they didn't share a changing room with us, had latched on to Craig's observation about Julia's hairy legs, and she didn't live it down for months after that even though she did her best to avoid having to bare them to anyone again. And every time we had a swimming lesson in the school pool, she always seemed to manage to get out of it somehow. But looking back, and knowing now what I didn't know then, I suspect she was trying to conceal rather more than just the hairs on her legs.

Chapter thirty one

Monday 20th May 2019

When Melanie arrived at Josh's school a few minutes later, her stomach sank a little. She didn't exactly have the fondest memories of school, particularly secondary, and she always hated having to step foot in such an undesirable environment. She knew that most of the teachers would be preparing for their first classes of the day and that she would therefore need to head straight to reception in order to request an appointment with Josh's form tutor. The receptionist looked up at her unenthusiastically and then lifted up the phone in order to dial through to the relevant department once Melanie explained who she needed to speak to.

"Josh Williams' mother is in reception to see Miss Newton," she confirmed to the person at the other end of the phone.

For some reason, Miss Newton's name sounded familiar, although Melanie couldn't recall whether Josh had ever mentioned her or not. He never talked about school. In fact, Melanie really struggled to get any kind of information out of him at all. But she wasn't really around often enough to ask him.

"Mr Langley's coming to see you," the receptionist confirmed. "Take a seat over there and he'll be along in a couple of minutes."

"Who's Mr Langley?" Melanie frowned.

"He's the Acting head teacher," replied the receptionist, sighing dramatically, as though it was a huge inconvenience to her that she was obliged to answer so many questions, as opposed to simply chewing gum, flicking through her magazine and staring dreamily out of the window like she was usually used to doing. At that moment, a young man in an immaculately tailored navy suit entered the room, prompting the receptionist to sit upright and pretend to start tapping something on her computer keyboard.

Melanie watched him walk towards her and hold out his hand, at which point she stood up from where she had been sitting and greeted him with one of her firm, businesswoman handshakes.

"Mrs Williams?" the young man clarified. "I'm Mr Langley. Would you like to come through to my office for a chat?"

"Of course," smiled Melanie, politely, before starting to follow him towards the door that he had just entered through. "But *I'm* actually here to see you, not the other way around."

"Forgive me," replied Mr Langley, straightening his tie and showing her through to the office marked 'head teacher'. "I assumed you were here in response to Miss Newton's letter."

"What letter?" Melanie frowned, feeling suspicious.

"The one she sent home last week; didn't Josh pass it on to you?"

"No Mr Langley, I'm afraid he didn't," sighed Melanie, sounding disappointed.

"Miss Newton's been trying to get hold of you," Mr Langley explained, inviting Melanie to sit down in the chair opposite him. "She's left you messages at work but when you didn't call her back, I advised her to write to you instead."

Melanie started to feel a little uneasy when she realised how remiss she had been. But a phone message from someone whose name she didn't even recognise was never likely to be top of her list of priorities as far as her job was concerned. If only she had realised that Miss Newton was the name of Josh's form tutor.

"I'm so sorry," she explained, feeling her face flush. "I've had a lot on at work recently, and we've also had a few family issues, which is why I'm here to talk to you actually."

Mr Langley sat back in his chair, adjusted his tie again and unbuttoned the top of his shirt. He really was very young to be an Acting Head, Melanie thought.

"My father passed away at the weekend," she explained. "I'm here to ask you if Josh can be excused from school for a couple of days in order to travel down to France for the funeral."

"Please accept my sincere condolences Mrs Williams," insisted Mr Langley, before looking at her expectantly. Melanie had been hoping that he would confirm that Josh would be able to attend his grandfather's funeral, but instead it appeared as though he was waiting for her to say something else. After what felt like a particularly long and uncomfortable pause, he eventually decided to speak again;

"You mentioned that there had been some family issues; care to elaborate?"

"Not really, no," replied Melanie, defensively. "There's been a bereavement in the family; that's all I meant by that."

"Josh mentioned to Miss Newton that you work a lot and that he tends to stay at his father's house at weekends," continued Mr Langley, unfazed by Melanie's defensive reaction.

"I've already told you that I'm particularly busy at the moment," protested Melanie, feeling a little annoyed at this point. "He usually stays with my husband every other weekend, but Richard's just been helping out a bit more recently. He's not even Josh's biological father."

"I see," replied Mr Langley, nodding. "And where is his biological father?"

"I'm not sure that's any of your business!" retorted Melanie, standing up and snatching hold of her handbag. "And I didn't come here today to be interrogated like this. I don't even understand why you're asking me all these questions. Why has Miss Newton been trying to contact me?"

"Sit back down and I'll explain," insisted Mr Langley, apologetically. "I'm sorry if I've embarrassed you with my line of questioning. Pinewood only has Josh's best interests at heart."

Melanie hesitated and then decided to reluctantly return to her seat. She held her handbag on her lap as though it was some kind of protective shield and then braced herself for what he was about to say.

"I'm afraid Josh appears to be suffering from cyber bullying," Mr Langley explained, softening his voice a little. "He's also been caught truanting a couple of times recently. I'm not surprised that he didn't pass Miss Newton's letter onto you. I'm just sorry that I had to be the one to tell you about it."

Melanie's head started to spin when she thought about the couple of occasions recently when Josh had behaved rather uncharacteristically around his laptop or his phone. She had been tempted to try and access his account, but only because she was determined to quash any of Ursula's seemingly ridiculous suspicions. If only she had actually bothered to listen to her housekeeper. If only Josh had felt the urge to confide in her in some way. But Melanie knew that if she hadn't have been working so much, he probably would have done. When she and Richard were still together, Josh used to confide in her about everything. But right now she felt as though she barely knew him at all.

"Are you alright Mrs Williams?" Mr Langley confirmed. "You look very pale. Can I get you a glass of water?"

But before Melanie was able to respond, she passed out.

❖

When Melanie came round, she was lying on the floor of Mr Langley's office with her legs sprawled out in front of her.

"Mrs Williams, can you hear me?" urged Mr Langley, sounding concerned. "Mrs Williams?"

"Actually, you can call me Ms Allsopp," Melanie smiled groggily before slowly opening her eyes. "I've always been known as Ms Allsopp at work and I haven't used my married name since my husband and I separated."

"Well your husband is on his way in," Mr Langley replied, helping her back up into her chair and handing her a glass of water. "He said he was already in the area because he has just dropped Josh at school."

"What did you call him for?" complained Melanie, rubbing her head. "I'm fine. I can look after myself."

"I wouldn't advise it if I were you," insisted Mr Langley. "You need someone to take care of you. You're grieving and you've just had a terrible shock about Josh."

"Can we talk about it a bit more please?" Melanie pleaded. "How does the school handle this kind of thing?"

"Well as we've learnt from a similar case recently, we start by talking to the parents," explained Mr Langley, peeling off a post-it note from the block on his desk and writing on it.

"But we also have a qualified psychologist who has recently started working here, and she runs a counselling programme for some of the students affected by bullying. You may wish to consider contacting her directly."

He then handed Melanie the post-it.

"You could send her an email if you like."

"Well can't I just speak to her in person?" frowned Melanie, as they were interrupted by a knock on the door.

"I'm afraid she's busy dealing with another case this morning," explained Mr Langley, as Richard entered the office.

"What happened; are you OK?" he asked, sounding concerned.

"I'm fine, I just fainted that's all. You didn't need to come," insisted Melanie, trying to stand up.

"It's no problem, I was here anyway," replied Richard, kneeling down beside her chair. "Besides, who else would you have called? One of your best friends is about to have a baby and the other one's an alcoholic!"

Melanie rolled her eyes in protest and then eventually decided to cling onto his arm for support. He slowly lifted her up to a standing position and then slipped his hand around her waist in order to help her to the door.

"I'm still a bit light-headed," she confessed, once they had thanked Mr Langley for his time and returned to where the receptionist was busy pulling a string of chewing gum out of her mouth with her thumb and index finger.

"Come on," Richard insisted, taking Melanie by the hand "We're going to the park for some fresh air."

❖

Melanie decided not to confide in Richard about Josh until they reached the park, in the fear of overwhelming herself too much again. They found an empty bench and sat down together, at which point Richard removed a bottle of water and a packet of biscuits from his jacket pocket.

"How do you always manage to come so prepared?" Melanie smiled, weakly.

"I need to in my line of work," replied Richard, reminding Melanie to look at her watch again.

"It's almost 10am!" she announced. "I was supposed to be at the office an hour ago."

"And I was supposed to be starting a new job today," explained Richard. "But some things are more important than work. You've been through a lot recently and your body's telling you to slow down."

"At least let me call Philip and explain," insisted Melanie, rummaging around in her handbag for her phone.

She was just about to dial the number, when a Spaniel came bounding up to them. The elderly couple who were walking it, could tell that Melanie was wary of dogs and immediately managed to entice it back to where they were standing before its presence unnerved her any further. Just at that moment, Richard managed to snatch her phone out of her grasp.

"What are you doing?" she complained, turning to face him. "Give it back!"

"Not until you agree to stay here in the park and rest for half an hour before you even so much as think about calling Mr Delaney," dictated Richard, whilst slipping the phone into the inside pocket of his jacket.

"Well it doesn't look like I have any choice in the matter, does it," complained Melanie, looking at him huffily. She then slumped back on the bench and took a bite out of her biscuit.

"Why won't my own son confide in me?" she sighed.

"What do you mean?" frowned Richard, turning to face her. "Are you still referring to his behaviour yesterday morning?"

"Partly yes," explained Melanie, reluctantly. "But according to Mr Langley, there's a lot more to Josh's mood swings than meets the eye."

She swallowed before continuing to explain; "Apparently he's being cyber bullied."

Richard remained silent once Melanie had finished explaining, almost as though this particular revelation was of no great surprise to him, encouraging her to eye him suspiciously.

"You already knew, didn't you?" she concluded, raising her voice slightly. "Why didn't you tell me?"

"Because I wanted Josh to tell you himself," replied Richard, sounding defensive. "Besides, I only had my suspicions. We talked about it during our camping trip and I told him that I wanted us to go into school and speak to the teachers, but he insisted that it was nothing and that he didn't want to burden you with it."

"He's been bunking off school!" retorted Melanie. "That's how serious it is."

"Well I didn't know *that*," insisted Richard. "And besides, you're the one who lives with him; if anyone should have picked up on how serious it's become, it's *you!*"

"I've had a lot on my plate recently," explained Melanie, as though she was automatically programmed to tell everyone about her promotion and her father's death, every time she started to find herself feeling the slightest bit guilty. But then she realised that she didn't need to explain her situation to Richard because he was probably fed up with hearing it by now.

The two of them sat on the bench together in complete silence, before Richard eventually decided to speak; "So what are we going to do?"

"Mr Langley's given me the contact details of a woman called 'Dr Jules'," replied Melanie, removing the post-it note from her pocket. "Apparently she's some sort of anti-bullying counsellor."

"Sounds good," replied Richard. "Why don't you give her a call."

"Maybe I will," agreed Melanie, nodding slowly. "But I'll need my phone back first"

"Not yet," smiled Richard, teasingly, as Melanie tried to make a grab for his jacket. He placed his fingers around her wrists and held onto them tightly.

"What did I ever see in you?" she laughed, feeling a little flirtatious.

"Do I really need to remind you?" replied Richard, looking at her intensely, loosening his grip on one of her wrists and then sliding his hand up her thigh. She stared deep into his eyes, and before she was able to process what was happening, they were kissing each other again. This time it felt a lot more intense than it had done in her hallway. Something had been building between the two of them over the past couple of weeks; something that had never quite had the chance to escape from the shattered remains of their marriage. They still loved each other, and this was her opportunity to prove to him that they belonged together.

Just at that moment, her phone started ringing, forcing them to break out of their embrace. Richard removed the phone from his pocket and the two of them sat and stared at the name that was flashing up on the display screen: 'Philip Delaney'

"Don't answer it," insisted Richard. "You can tell him you're still in France."

"But it's more than my job's worth," replied Melanie, snatching the phone out of his hand and holding it up to her ear.

"Goodbye Melanie," Richard sighed, sounding disappointed. "You're obviously feeling much better now so I'll give you a call later to talk about Josh."

Melanie nodded distractedly and then turned her attention to her phone call again, as Richard stood up from the bench and slowly walked away.

Chapter thirty two

Monday 20th May 2019

Mr Delaney's PA, Gill, insisted that Melanie went into work as soon as possible. By the time Melanie had managed to hang up on Gill, Richard had gone. Now she was on her way along the corridor to Mr Delaney's office and she could feel a knot of nerves in the pit of her stomach. She needed to tell him that she would be taking the end of the week off work in order to go to her father's funeral, but she knew that it wasn't going to be easy. Gill was sitting at her desk as Melanie approached, and once Melanie was within hearing distance of her, she tutted loudly and peered at her watch over the top of her spectacles.

"Ms Allsopp's here to see you," she then announced, pressing her long taloned index finger down onto the intercom button.

Melanie swallowed as Gill then gestured towards his door before reluctantly stepping inside. As usual, Philip Delaney failed to look up from what he was doing when Melanie entered the room, and she knew better than to attempt to say anything until eye contact had been achieved. So she simply took a seat in the chair opposite his desk and waited for his permission to speak.

"So how was your holiday?" he enquired, sounding particularly sarcastic.

"It wasn't a holiday," replied Melanie, feeling her blood boil. "I was visiting my terminally ill father. But I'm sorry to report that he passed away before I got there and I have therefore had to re-schedule my visit."

"What do you mean 're-schedule' your visit?" retorted Philip. "I need you *here*! I already allowed you to leave early on Friday, you haven't done any work whatsoever over the weekend, and you've arrived late today!"

"I think you'll find that I didn't leave early on Friday actually," insisted Melanie, asserting herself a little. "Which is why I missed my flight and didn't get to France in time to say goodbye before he died."

"I sympathise with your loss Ms Allsopp," replied Philip, continuing to sound stern. "But what happens in your private life is of no concern to me. You're here to work, and right now this company needs your experience more than ever. So I'm afraid you won't be able to go back to France at the end of the week."

"But I didn't even make it there in the first place!" Melanie pleaded feeling pools of tears flood her eyes. "I can't miss my own father's funeral."

"I'm a very busy man," Philip snapped in reply, before summoning Gill through to his office. "Will you ask Ms Allsopp to leave now please."

"Don't worry, I'm going," replied Melanie, as Gill attempted to place her hand on Melanie's arm. Melanie shrugged her off and then stormed out of the office in defeat.

"Do you want this promotion or not?" Philip scolded, confronting her from his doorway.

"Actually, I'm not sure that I do anymore," Melanie mumbled, a little under her breath, before throwing her handbag onto her shoulder and marching towards the main entrance. "I'm going to take an early lunch"

"But you *never* have a lunch break," scoffed Gill, looking concerned.

"Well maybe it's about time I did."

❖

As soon as Melanie had left the office, she sent Josh a text message, offering to pick him up in half an hour so that they could have lunch together. She sat outside the school gates in her car and waited for 12.30pm to tick round. By 12.45pm she started to get a little worried. What if he refused to come and meet her? She was just about to remove her phone from her bag in order to send him another message, when a boy in school uniform appeared at the car. He leant over to look at her, encouraging Melanie to wind down the window.

"Aren't you going to get in?" she smiled, trying to sound as laid back as possible.

"What are you doing here mum?" Josh frowned, ignoring her question. "You know I'm not allowed to leave the school grounds at lunchtimes."

"I just thought I would come and have lunch with you," she replied. "We don't need to go anywhere. You can just eat your packed lunch in the car while we have a chat."

Josh sighed and then walked round to the passenger side. As he reluctantly opened the door and sank down into the seat next to her, Melanie felt her stomach twist with nerves. She was surprised at how anxious she was. Confronting Josh was almost as terrifying as her meeting with Mr Delaney this morning.

"How are you?" she enquired, as Josh removed his packed lunch box from his bag and clicked the lid open.

"Fine," he replied, unwrapping his sandwich and biting into it. Melanie tried a different tack;

"Are you upset about your grandad?"

"I guess so," explained Josh, through a mouthful of bread and cheese. "But I didn't really know him did I. He and Granny moved to France when I was a baby and you've hardly ever taken me to visit them."

Melanie experienced a sudden pang of guilt; an emotion that she appeared to be becoming all too familiar with.

"I'm sorry," she soothed. "I should have encouraged you to get to know him a bit better."

"It's OK," insisted Josh, removing a handful of ready salted crisps from their packet. "I know you didn't like him very much. And besides, he could have come back here to visit us."

"That's true. But two wrongs don't make a right." Melanie conceded, before staring at the packet of crisps in Josh's hand. "Did Richard give you those?"

Josh nodded, licking the salt from his fingers. "Why?"

"Because he knows that I prefer you to take healthy food to school with you," replied Melanie, rummaging through his packed lunch box and unearthing a chocolate bar. "Where's the fruit?"

"Ursula makes me this kind of packed lunch all the time," explained Josh, defensively. "Maybe you would already know that if you actually bothered to take an interest in me every once in a while."

"You're right," insisted Melanie, unfastening her seatbelt and turning to face him properly with a sincere expression on her face. "From now on I'll make sure that *I* prepare your packed lunches."

"It's not about the bloody packed lunches!" retorted Josh, raising his voice.

"Please don't use that language," replied Melanie, trying not to lose her temper. She then breathed deeply before asking the question that up until that point she had been far too afraid to ask; "So what *is* it about?"

There was a long silence as Josh finished his sandwich and then stared out of the car windscreen in deep thought.

"You know you can talk to me about anything don't you?"

Josh still refused to open up to her about the bullying. Eventually he shoved the rest of his lunch back into his bag and then started to open the car door.

"Please don't go yet," pleaded Melanie, leaning over and grabbing hold of his arm. "Tell me what you were just thinking about."

"Well if you *really* want to know," replied Josh, scathingly "I was thinking about why you and Grandad didn't like each other. He was always too busy to spend any time with you, and you resented him for it. Does that remind you of anyone?"

"You're referring to me aren't you," Melanie sighed. "But I'm nothing like your grandad. You're my son; I'll *never* be too busy for you. That's why I came to meet you for lunch today. From now on I'm going to be around more."

"Maybe it's too late for that," snapped Josh, trying to control his emotions.

"What do you mean?" Melanie frowned. "It's never too late to talk to me Josh. Tell me what's been going on at school. If you talk to me, I'll be able to help you."

Josh hesitated and then made a reach for the door again, before turning back to face his mother for one last time;

"I was never part of the plan was I mum?" he confirmed. "You fell pregnant with me by mistake and then Granny and Grandad disowned you because they knew that you wouldn't be able to live up to their expectations. You've resented me ever since and that's why you work so hard. Because all you've ever been interested in is making a career for yourself!"

"That's not true," insisted Melanie, as Josh opened the car door and stepped out.

"Well why do you think Dad had enough of you?" he replied. "As long as you're still at that accountancy firm, you'll never be any different. And that's why I'm going to live with Dad from now on!"

Before Melanie was given the chance to say anything else, Josh slammed the car door and stormed away.

❖

Melanie refused to return to work again after lunch, claiming that she was on compassionate leave. She went straight home and told Ursula to take the rest of the day off, while she curled up on the sofa with a tub of ice cream and a box of tissues. As soon as Ursula had tidied away the cleaning products that she had been using, she quietly let herself out of the house, at which point Melanie burst into tears. Warm wet streaks cascaded down her hot cheeks and down the back of her throat, as she sobbed her way through half a tub of ice cream and at least a quarter of the box of tissues. She seemed to have so much to cry about; her father, Josh, Mr Delaney, and, of course, Richard. She tried sending text messages to both Richard and Josh, by way of an apology for her behaviour recently, but every time she attempted to draft something it sounded flippant or insincere, so she threw her phone down onto the coffee table and then noticed a piece of paper that had fallen out of her pocket when she got home. It was the contact details for the anti-bullying counsellor that Mr Langley has passed onto her. She then picked her phone up again and began to type out an email;

'*Dear Dr Jules,*

I've recently discovered that my son is being bullied and I just don't know how to deal with it. Every time I try and talk to him about it, he completely shuts down. I could really do with some advice and I'm hoping that you might be the right person to help me.

M Williams'

A few seconds later a reply flashed up on Melanie's phone;

'Dear M,

Thanks so much for your email. You've already made the first step by contacting me. Why don't you begin by telling me a bit more about it?

Dr Jules'

Melanie thought for a moment and then typed a reply;

M Williams: 'What sort of details do you need?

Dr Jules: *'How did you find out that your son was being bullied? Do you know what kind of bullying he's experiencing? Have you noticed any changes in his behaviour recently?'*

Melanie put her phone down in frustration. It was too overwhelming, she would just have to continue their conversation later on.

❖

A few hours later, Melanie had managed to call her mother in France, arrange the flowers for her father's funeral, prepare a delicious dinner for Josh ready for when he was due to get home from his friend's house, book their flights to Nice at the end of the week, pop to Mr Shah's shop down the road in order to stock up on some more ice cream, and decide which gift to buy Rebecca's baby when he or she finally arrived. She had even managed to get a few chores done once she had located all the laundry products in Ursula's cupboard. And she had her work phone switched off the entire time so that she could avoid any unwanted calls from Mr Delaney. Dr Jules had emailed her again as well, but she had been too busy preparing Josh's dinner to reply to her straight away, so she waited until it became clear that Josh had no intention of coming home from his friend's house anytime soon, before concluding that she needed Dr Jules more than ever. And at 7pm she eventually drafted a reply;

M Williams: *'My housekeeper told me that he was being bullied and suggested that I checked his computer. Apparently other children have been posting nasty comments about him all over his Facebook page. But it wasn't until today that one of his teachers confirmed what has been going on and gave me your contact details. I'm ashamed to admit that I hadn't been aware of anything until my housekeeper told me about it. I've been really busy at work recently.'*

Dr Jules: *'Every mother blames themselves but what's happening to your son isn't your fault. And it certainly isn't your son's fault. In fact, it's not even the bullies' fault. It's just important to remember that he will get through this and that you'll always be there for him. So what do you do for a living?'*

Melanie sat back against the sofa and frowned. Asking her what she did for a living seemed like a bit of an unusual question, with little or no relevance to the situation at hand. Perhaps she was just trying to build up a sense of trust between them. So Melanie eventually decided to indulge her curiosity;

M Williams: *'I'm an accountant. I'm currently being considered for a promotion, which is why I'm having to work such long hours at the moment. My boss is a bit of a task master. He's been telling me to put the rest of my life on hold recently. He won't even give me permission to travel down to the south of France for my father's funeral at the end of this week.'*

Dr Jules: *'I'm sorry to hear about your father. Were you very close to him?'*

Melanie rolled her eyes. Not that question again. But at least this time she was talking to a trained psychologist, as opposed to just a taxi driver or the office cleaner.

M Williams: *'Not particularly, no. When I was growing up, he was always working and so was my mum. I ended up having to just look after myself most of the time.'*

Dr Jules: *'That must have been tough. I hope you managed to make it up with him though. I'm sure he was very proud of you. Becoming a successful accountant, and settling down to have a family.'*

M Williams: *'Not exactly'* typed Melanie, taking a deep breath before deciding to elaborate. It was, after all, quite refreshing to have someone impartial to confide in. Particularly someone whom she had never met.

M Williams: *'I fell pregnant with my son just after I finished university and I was about to begin my accountancy exams. As I'm sure you can probably imagine, my parents were not very pleased about that and they had very little to do with me while my son was a baby. My dad had a heart attack and they decided to move to France. I wasn't with the baby's father anymore so I was forced to look after my son all on my own; life was pretty tough.'*

There was a long pause before Melanie eventually received a reply;

Dr Jules: *'I realise I haven't really spent very long getting to know you yet but reading between the lines, I can't help but conclude that your son isn't the only person who is being bullied. Has it occurred to you that you yourself have in fact been suffering at the hands of a bully over the past few months and years? And not just one bully but two...'*

Melanie's heart leapt into her throat as she read Dr Jules' reply, and as she reluctantly leant over to begin typing a message back, the realisation of what Dr Jules had implied suddenly dawned on her. She clutched her mouth in disbelief as five little words appeared on the screen;

Dr Jules: *'...your father and your boss.'*

Melanie had never even thought of it like that. She had certainly never considered herself as a 'victim'. She had always just assumed that bullying was something that took place on the playground at school. Or that involved physical or verbal abuse. With trembling hands, she immediately decided to look up the dictionary definition of a bully on the internet:

'Bully, noun. *A person who uses strength or influence to harm or intimidate those who are weaker. Someone who hurts or frightens someone who is smaller or less powerful, often forcing them to do something that they do not want to do.'*

Mr Delaney was constantly forcing her to put her job before anything else, by corrupting her conscience and telling her to perform impossibly unreasonable tasks. But he was her boss, and she needed to be challenged in order to prove to him that she would make a worthy partner. Besides, wasn't that what bosses were *supposed* to do? And as for her father, well, he had always been very strict, but that was only because he wanted the best for her, wasn't it? Melanie felt sick.

Dr Jules: *'Are you OK?'*

M Williams: *'Would it be alright if we meet to discuss this further?'*

Dr Jules: *'Of course. A face to face chat about your son would be a lot easier. When did you have in mind?'*

Melanie sat back on the sofa again and smiled as she decided what to type in reply. She really liked the sound of Dr Jules, and was beginning to feel as though she had finally found someone with whom she could really confide in.

M Williams: *'Are you free first thing tomorrow morning?'*

Part three

Chapter thirty three

Julia

Tuesday 21st May 2019

When Jules arrived at work the following day, she prepared herself a mug of strong black coffee and slowly carried it into the office with her. It was 8.30am and she was expecting a visit from Josh Williams' mother first thing, but before she had been given the chance to place her coffee mug down on the desk in front of her, a woman in a grey tailored suit and blonde hair managed to catch the handle of her door as it slowly started to close itself in her face.

"Sorry," smiled Jules, reaching to catch the door from the other side, but as she did so she looked up into the woman's eyes and then failed to keep hold of the handle of her coffee mug properly, causing it to fall and hit the carpet-tiled floor in between them. Black coffee cascaded everywhere, including the woman's suit trousers, and as her visitor looked up from the dark brown puddle that was beginning to engulf her expensive looking high heeled shoes, she smiled reassuringly at Jules.

"I'm so sorry," Jules apologised, feeling mortified.

"Honestly, it doesn't matter. It's the least of my worries at the moment. Besides, I have half a dozen suits like this one," the woman replied. "Are you OK by the way? You look like you've seen a ghost!"

"I'm fine," insisted Jules.

But she was far from 'fine'. And Josh Williams' mother was far from just a woman in a grey suit who had contacted her about some counselling for her son. *She* was the reason why Jules had decided to become a psychologist in the first place. In fact, she was at the very heart of Jules' entire career, because if it hadn't have been for Melanie, Jules would never have felt the need to turn her life around in such a radical way. Seeing Melanie again after nearly 20 years was like being struck by a bolt of lightning. And she looked exactly the same as she had when they were 16; slim build; blonde, wavy, shoulder length hair; the same confident expression on her face, if somewhat more business-like in her appearance than she had been at school; a wide mouth full of perfectly straight teeth; and piercing blue eyes. She hadn't always been that striking of course; at least not until she had managed to tame her seemingly unmanageable mop of frizzy hair and had her brace removed.

And it had been from that point onwards that Melanie had decided to set out on a mission to make Jules' life as miserable as possible for her. When they eventually parted ways in February 2002, Jules vowed never to put herself through the ordeal of having to see Melanie again; until *now* of course. As she slowly stepped over the puddle of coffee and made her way to the seat opposite Jules' desk, Jules wondered how long it would take for Melanie to recognise *her*. Perhaps once she had, they could part ways again. After all, how were they supposed to conduct a serious conversation about bullying, based on the past that they had shared with each other?

"Are you sure you're alright?"

Jules hesitated; "I'm just embarrassed that's all. First impressions are so important and I'm supposed to be giving you some professional advice this morning."

"It was an accident," Melanie insisted. "And besides, I could really just do with an informal chat with someone. No professional airs and graces are necessary."

Jules still couldn't believe that Melanie didn't recognise her; unless of course she was just pretending. In fact, it was possible that Melanie had contacted her on purpose in order to set her up.

She probably didn't even have a son or a recently deceased father, and certainly not an over-controlling boss. She couldn't imagine Melanie being controlled by anyone, other than Fran of course. Having said that, she did remember how busy Melanie's parents always were. Perhaps she wasn't sure whether Jules recognised *her*, and she was waiting for her identity to be acknowledged? The genuinely vacant look in her eyes would certainly suggest otherwise though.

After a long pause, Melanie smiled awkwardly, as though she wasn't really sure what to say. Her facial expression then softened a little when Jules eventually thought of a way to get the conversation started.

"I understand why this might be difficult for you. But you have taken a very important step by contacting me. Can you start by telling me a little more about your son?"

"His name's Josh, he's 12 years old. He's been coming to Pinewood School for almost an entire academic year and I swear I had no idea that he was being bullied," Melanie explained. "I don't know how long it's been going on but now that I know about the cyber element of it, I've started trying to think back to all the occasions in recent months when he might have reacted unpredictably, particularly when using his laptop or his phone."

Jules couldn't help but feel a little overwhelmed by how bullying had evolved over the last two decades due to social media; now school children could be tormented anywhere and at any time, as opposed to just within the confines of the school gates. Information could be spread very quickly and to lots of different people. Not only that but cyber bullying had the potential for being a lot nastier as it wasn't face to face, and it could also remain anonymous leaving the victim to wonder whether someone they knew and regarded as their friend could be responsible.

"What type of cyber bullying has he been experiencing?"

"I wasn't aware that there was more than one type?" Melanie frowned. "Can you give me some examples?"

"Well cyber bullying can take place through chat rooms. Bullies can send viruses to your computer. They can set up websites where people can vote for the ugliest, fattest or stupidest person at school. They can post nasty messages or memes on social media, or they can upload embarrassing photos of the victim and share it with all their contacts..."

"OK, I don't think I want to hear anymore," insisted Melanie, holding her hand up. "It sounds as though there could be all kinds of things going on in Josh's world that I haven't even got the first idea about. If only I had been more supportive. Maybe he would have opened up to me before it started to get out of hand."

"Don't blame yourself," replied Jules reassuringly, shaking her head. "Some children choose not to confide in their parents in spite of the circumstances. Besides, it's possible to push your child away by *over*protecting them too." And that was something that Jules was all too familiar with.

"So what do I do now?" asked Melanie rather helplessly, as Mr Langley's receptionist discretely snuck into the office and placed two fresh mugs of coffee onto the desk in front of them.

Jules actually started to feel a little sorry for her. After all, it was clear that she really loved her son and that in spite of all the pain that she had inflicted on Jules in the past she certainly didn't deserve to be dealing with a situation like this.

"A facilitated meeting with you and Josh would probably be the best place to start" Jules explained. "I could act as mediator and we could try and persuade him to open up to you a bit more. He might even be prepared to show you his Facebook page."

Melanie rolled her eyes.

"I doubt it," she scoffed. "But I guess it has to be worth a try. So should we do this at home or at the school?"

"Wherever you think he might be most comfortable," replied Jules. "I work with a lot of students from Pinewood, but many of them don't feel safe or comfortable enough to have the meetings at their home."

She paused before thinking about Caitlin and then continued;

"It sounds to me as though your home would be the best place for Josh though. And I might be able to pop over after school this afternoon if that's convenient?"

Melanie sighed loudly and then smiled;

"Thank you Jules. It means a lot to have someone to talk to about it. Someone who genuinely understands about bullying."

Jules looked down at the desk as Melanie's eyes lingered on her, as if she was waiting for some kind of reaction. *Of course* she knew about bullying; she was an anti-bullying counsellor, but Jules couldn't help but feel as though Melanie was referring to their mutual past instead.

"Have we met before?" Melanie hesitated, refusing to take her eyes away from Jules' face. Jules' cheeks flushed as she slowly looked up from the desk and maintained eye contact with her. But she failed to give anything away.

"You look vaguely familiar."

"I must have one of those faces," smiled Jules uncomfortably, before changing the subject. "So what about your husband?"

"What about him?" replied Melanie, defensively.

"Will he be attending the meeting?" Jules clarified.

"I suppose I ought to tell him about it," Melanie sighed. "But things have been a bit awkward between us recently."

There was another long silence as Melanie started staring at Jules across the desk again. Jules could feel her eyes burning into her as she gazed out of the window and tried to remain as casual as possible.

"Can I tell you something?" Melanie eventually announced, breaking the silence and making Jules jump a little.

"Richard, my ex-husband, and when I say 'ex' I mean we're not divorced yet, we're just separated. I only use my maiden name at work. Anyway..." she smiled uncomfortably before continuing "We kissed yesterday, and not for the first time. I still love him but he refuses to give our marriage another go because he knows I'm too devoted to my job..."

Jules listened patiently to everything Melanie had to say, and when she had eventually finished, she made some handwritten notes on the pad of paper in front of her and then smiled encouragingly;

"Do you want to know what I think?" she replied, taking a deep breath as Melanie nodded.

"I think you're allowing your past to get the better of you. Your parents were workaholics and they managed to instil the same work ethic in you. But whether that's because you're a chip off the old block, or because you have a pathological urge to try and please them all the time, remains to be seen. What *is* obvious is that your parents, particularly your father, have bullied you into being the kind of person that *they* wanted you to be, as opposed to allowing you to find your own way in life. And in doing so they have driven you into the arms of yet another over-controlling role model: your boss."

Melanie listened intently.

"No one should be expected to work the ridiculously long hours that you've been working, promotion or not," continued Jules, as Melanie remained fixated on what she was saying.

"You should put a complaint in to Human Resources about the way he's been treating you. I'm sure you've worked very hard to get to where you are now, and it's clear that you have had to make a lot of sacrifices along the way, including your marriage to Richard, who, by the way, sounds like he completely broke the conventions of your usual male relationships. But you should not have had to do that. You should have qualified for that promotion on your own merits."

"You're absolutely right!" exclaimed Melanie, raising her eyebrows as though the concept was finally beginning to sink in. "And I don't understand why I've failed to realise it myself. It's so obvious. It's been staring me in the face all this time."

"What has?" enquired Jules, deciding to rein herself in a little, as she had allowed her opinions to get the better of her.

"Thank you again for all your help," insisted Melanie, failing to elaborate. "I'll see you at our facilitated meeting later; you'll have our address on your system. But right now there's something I need to do."

And before Jules was given a chance to advise her that she needed to check with Josh that he was comfortable about having the meeting in the first place, Melanie had stood up from her chair, downed the rest of her mug of coffee, and had rushed out of the door.

Chapter thirty four
Melanie

When Melanie arrived at Richard's flat 20 minutes later, he opened the door wearing nothing but a towel tied around his waist. He was just about to get in the shower when she phoned ahead to find out if he had left for work yet, and as soon as he gave her permission to go over there, she couldn't wait to rush round and tell him about her meeting with Dr Jules. Not to mention the very important decision that she had just made as a result. She didn't expect him to be quite so revealing when she arrived, and as her eyes were drawn to his broad chest, which was still dripping with moisture from the shower, she couldn't help but smile to herself in the hope that he was inadvertently trying to seduce her.

"So what was so urgent that it couldn't wait until after work?" he frowned, running his hand through his scruffy wet hair and rubbing his eyes.

"You know that psychologist woman that I was telling you about yesterday" Melanie explained, following Richard through to his living room. "Well I decided to arrange to go meet with her at the school first thing this morning."

Richard nodded, whilst inviting her to take a seat on the sofa.

"She was really nice, and we've arranged to have a facilitated meeting with Josh so that we can try to get to the bottom of what's been going on."

"That sounds like a good idea," replied Richard. "As long as you can persuade Josh to agree to it. And when are you hoping that this meeting might take place?"

"After school today," explained Melanie. "We need to get it done before we go to France for my father's funeral."

"But what about your job?" Richard frowned, rubbing his eyes again and looking down at her coffee stained suit trousers. "You'll never be able to fit it in this week. In fact, shouldn't you be at work right now?"

"Well that's the other reason why I wanted to come over and see you," Melanie smiled, edging closer to him on the sofa. "I've decided to hand in my resignation."

Richard took a few moments to process what she had just said, during which time Melanie had placed her hand on his leg in what she hoped would be a sufficiently understated attempt to express her feelings towards him. They had shared two rather passionate kisses with each other recently, and she knew that Richard still loved her. The only thing that had been stopping them from getting back together was her overriding commitment to her job, but now that she had decided to resign, they had no reason to be apart anymore, and Melanie wanted more than anything to be able to run her hands over his bare torso again.

"What do you mean you've decided to hand in your resignation?" he suddenly retorted, before removing her hand from his leg and standing up from the sofa. "What about your promotion?"

"I thought you'd be pleased," Melanie frowned, feeling crestfallen. "I thought it was what you wanted."

"Well what about what *you* want?" replied Richard, tightening the towel around his waist and pacing the room. "You're in no fit state to go making decisions like that. You've just lost your father."

"I want *you*!" insisted Melanie, standing up and facing him head on so that he was forced to stop pacing for a moment. "I love you Richard and I want us to be a proper husband and wife again."

"I think you should go," Richard concluded, folding his arms across his bare chest protectively.

"Can we at least just talk about this?" Melanie suggested, feeling desperate. "I'm lonely and I miss you."

Richard simply looked down at the floor and shook his head, before leading her back through to the hallway.

"I know you feel the same," she pleaded. "Why else would you have come to the school to collect me yesterday? Why else would you have agreed to let me come over again just now? And why else would you have kissed me? Twice."

There was a long silence during which Richard refused to make eye contact with her.

Melanie sighed "Will you at least come along to the facilitated meeting, if not for my sake then for Josh's?"

"I'll think about it," replied Richard, before showing her out of the door.

❖

When Melanie returned home, she discovered that her company phone was still lying on the table in the hall where she had left it. Her heart started beating rapidly as she reluctantly picked it up. It was switched off. She didn't know what to expect when she turned it back on again. After all, she had walked out on her meeting with Mr Delaney the day before and had failed to turn up for work again since. But she didn't care anymore. Because rather than allowing herself to be distracted by any of the incoming messages or emails that began flooding her phone as soon as it was switched on, she decided instead to open up a new email, where she rather zealously found herself typing the word 'Resignation' into the subject box.

Half an hour later she read the email back to herself. It sounded perfect. And before she had been given the opportunity to over think it, she entered Mr Delaney's email address into the 'to' box and then pressed 'send'. As soon as the email had been successfully delivered, she wandered into the kitchen and flicked on the kettle in order to make herself a cup of tea, her company mobile weighing down heavily on the inside of her suit trouser pocket as though it was some kind of fragile explosive device and she was just waiting for it to go off. She then placed it on the worktop in front of her and pulled herself up onto one of the barstools as the kettle gradually started to come to the boil.

Just as the steam began to shoot out of its spout, her phone vibrated suddenly making her jump. But it wasn't her company mobile, it was her personal one. She hoped that it might be Richard, reassuring her that he had reconsidered her proposition, but the only new message that appeared once she had swiped the screen open, was from her mother. She was simply asking Melanie to give her a call, which she reluctantly did as soon as she had poured her tea.

"I wanted to apologise to you for being so blunt when you didn't manage to make it here in time to see your father," her mother explained once the overseas dial tone had connected them.

Melanie's mouth hung open in disbelief as Mrs Allsopp continued;

"I know how difficult it is for you to get away from work at short notice, and it's not as though you and your father were ever particularly close."

"No," Melanie conceded, sounding disappointed. She had always been perfectly aware of how painfully non-existent her relationship with her dad had been, but for some reason hearing her mother confirm it, made it feel a lot more tragic.

"I've been doing a lot of thinking over the past few days," her mum explained. "And I've realised that I need to get to know the family properly. Your father was all I had and now that he's gone, I've been feeling rather..." she hesitated, before reluctantly continuing "...rather, well, lonely I suppose."

Melanie was speechless. She never thought she would hear her mother admit to something like that. But grief did strange things to people, and even someone as emotionally stunted as her mum was entitled to show her vulnerability every now and again. She didn't quite know where her mum was going with this conversation but she decided to let it run its course anyway, in spite of her reservations.

"So I was wondering," explained Mrs Allsopp, hesitating again. "Would it be alright if I came back to England with you after the funeral? I think I need a bit of a holiday, and it would be good to get to know my grandson a little better."

"Of course!" exclaimed Melanie, clapping her hand to her mouth in disbelief. "You can stay at the house with us. It would be lovely to have you here."

"Don't be ridiculous darling," scoffed her mother, bursting her bubble slightly. "I'll stay at that wonderful 5 star hotel in town. I can't possibly stay in your pokey little house."

And before Melanie knew it, she had gone back to being the mum that she had always known and loved... to hate.

Their conversation didn't last very long after that, at which point Melanie decided to send two text messages; one to Dr Jules confirming their appointment later that afternoon, and one to Richard, letting him know what time the facilitated meeting was due to take place. She hoped that he would be able to join them, but she knew that there was a strong possibility that he probably wouldn't, even if he was available to do so. She would just have to wait and see if he showed up.

❖

Later that day, when Josh returned from school, Melanie was waiting for him in the kitchen.

"You frightened the life out of me!" he complained, when he opened the kitchen door and found her standing behind it. "Why aren't you at work?"

"I'm taking some time off," Melanie replied, failing to enlighten him about her resignation. After all, Richard's reaction had been very disappointing, and as Mr Delaney had still failed to acknowledge her email, she was beginning to wonder whether it had actually managed to get through. Perhaps she would return to the office when she got back from France and find out whether they would be prepared to overlook her erratic attendance recently.

"Anyway, why didn't you come home last night?" she then retorted, putting her hands on her hips disapprovingly.

"I told you I was staying at a mate's house," snapped Josh, throwing his school bag on the floor. "I sent you a text."

"Which 'mate'?" Melanie continued, looking suspicious. "You didn't mention it when I came to have lunch with you at school yesterday."

"That's because it wasn't arranged then," Josh complained, attempting to leave the kitchen again. Melanie stuck her foot out and managed to stop the door from closing as he turned to try and slam it behind him.

"Since when did you turn into such a stroppy teenager?" she demanded. "You're only 12."

"Since my mum stopped caring enough to notice," replied Josh, cuttingly.

Melanie paused for a moment and then moved her foot out of the door.

"Well as a matter of fact I *do* care," she insisted, following him into the hall. "I care enough to take some time off work. I care enough to come and have lunch with you at school. And I care enough to..." she hesitated.

"To what?" frowned Josh dubiously on his way up the staircase.

"To arrange for a bullying counsellor to come over and talk to you," she replied quickly, in the hope that the faster she said it, the less likely Josh would be to over react.

"What?" Josh shouted. "I don't need *counselling*!"

"It's just an opportunity for us all to sit down and talk about things with someone impartial," Melanie insisted. "She works at your school and she's really nice"

Josh hesitated; "Dr Jules?" he then confirmed, sounding as though he might actually be coming around to the idea. "When are we seeing her?"

Melanie looked at her watch and then smiled sheepishly. "In about 20 minutes actually."

There was a brief silence as Josh appeared to be considering her proposal, after which he muttered something that vaguely resembled the word 'fine' before continuing to stomp up the stairs.

Melanie smiled to herself. Everyone was full of surprises today; first her mother and now Josh. Perhaps things were finally beginning to fall into place.

❖

Twenty minutes later there was a ring at the doorbell. Melanie's heart did a quick somersault in the hope that it might have been Richard on the other side of the door when she went to open it, but it was of course Jules, punctual as always. For some reason Jules' face seemed more familiar to her than it had done when they met at the school that morning, and she hesitated slightly before letting her in.

"There's something familiar about you," she frowned, inviting her into the living room. "Have we met before?"

Jules shifted uncomfortably as she selected which armchair to sit in and then shook her head;

"I shouldn't think so," she insisted. "Unless you've seen me at school"

"I doubt it," concluded Melanie. "I'm usually too busy to give Josh lifts. You obviously just have one of those faces."

"I guess so," smiled Jules, looking down at her lap.

Melanie couldn't help but observe that she had a surprising lack of self-confidence for someone who specialised in counselling and nurturing other people. But she could already tell from their initial meeting that Jules was very good at her job, and she was looking forward to introducing her to Josh.

"I'll go and get my son," Melanie smiled, before opening the door into the hall and then shouting upwards. Eventually Josh emerged on the stairs looking particularly despondent.

"Dr Jules is here to help you," she whispered before he entered the living room. "At least try to be nice."

"Whatever," replied Josh, sinking down into the other armchair opposite Jules.

"Hi Josh," Jules smiled warmly, reaching her hand out to shake his.

Josh lent forward and obliged, encouraging Melanie to breathe a small sigh of relief. She then looked at her watch anxiously, aware that she had advised Richard to turn up at least 10 minutes before Jules did so that they would be able to talk to Josh together in advance of the meeting. But he was now at least 15 minutes late, persuading her to conclude that he had probably decided not to come.

"Will your husband be joining us?" Jules enquired, interrupting her thoughts.

"I don't know," replied Melanie, a little defensively. "I guess we should start without him."

Just as she was about to sit down on the sofa, she heard a key turning in the lock, and as the front door swung open, she turned to face the living room doorway with her heart in her throat. A pair of slow heavy footsteps made their way through the hall and then eventually Richard emerged, looking as handsome as ever.

"I'm sorry I'm late," he smiled leaning across to shake Jules' hand. "And I hope you didn't mind me using my key; I didn't want to interrupt the meeting."

He and Melanie made eye contact at which point there was a slight pause.

"Of course not," she then insisted, as Richard sank down onto the sofa next to her. "Besides, this is still your home."

Her latter comment went unnoticed as Jules reluctantly decided to commence the meeting, but Melanie could still feel it hanging in the air, reminding her of all the times that Richard had unlocked the front door and greeted her as his loving wife, as opposed to the virtual stranger that she had eventually become.

He helped himself to a mug of coffee from the cafetiere that Melanie had placed on the table in front of them, and then sat back and listened to everything that Jules had to say. Melanie even found herself feeling slightly jealous of Jules because she appeared to have Richard's undivided attention from the second he walked through the door. And because Richard had never met her before, Melanie started thinking about the very first time *they* had met, before she had been given the opportunity to ruin everything between them. If only they could have a clean slate.

Jules was an attractive woman, who, despite her apparent lack of self-confidence, conducted herself in a surprisingly confident and professional manner. There was something rather genuine and almost *vulnerable* about her that seemed to creep through every time she allowed her professional guard to fall slightly, and Melanie knew that she could trust her. But then she also noticed Richard's eyes wander slightly when he caught sight of the slit in Jules' pencil skirt as she crossed her legs. Melanie's chest started to fill with a jealous rage that she found difficult to suppress, at which point Jules decided to interrupt her thoughts suddenly by directing a question at her, and it was only then that she realised that she hadn't actually be listening to a word Jules was saying.

There was another long silence as Melanie attempted to work out what the question could have been, prompting Richard to push in and rescue her;

"Why don't you let Josh answer that one," he suggested. "After all, he's the reason why we're having this meeting in the first place."

Everyone looked at Josh.

"It's OK," Josh replied standing up from his armchair. "I'll go and get my laptop so that you can have a look." at which point he left the room.

"We really appreciate you coming over to the house like this," Richard smiled, as his eyes found themselves drawn to the slit in Jules' skirt again. "Mel tells me that you work at the school."

"That's right," smiled Jules, tucking a strand of her chocolate brown hair behind her ear in what could only be described as a flirtatious manner. "The students are a great bunch."

"It must be lovely to be able to do something so worthwhile," Richard continued scratching his neck. Melanie knew that

Richard always scratched his neck when he was attracted to someone because it was one of his nervous habits.

"I can't imagine doing anything else," explained Jules. "It's so rewarding."

Melanie felt as though she was intruding on a first date or something, and couldn't help but exhale loudly in an attempt to mask her jealousy and frustration.

Richard and Jules both turned to look at her, just as Josh re-entered the room carrying his laptop. He opened it up and placed it on the table in front of Jules, enticing her to sit forward and remove a pair of reading glasses from her handbag.

"Are you sure you don't mind me looking at this?" she confirmed.

"It's fine; do what you've got to do," replied Josh dismissively, bracing himself for Jules' reaction.

Melanie was overwhelmed with how Jules had managed to get through to her son in such a short space of time. She found it virtually impossible to persuade Josh to open up to her about anything these days, and his laptop and phone were always completely out of bounds. She longed to be sitting in Jules' seat so that she could see what was displayed on the screen in front of her. But Josh wasn't ready to show her yet, and felt more comfortable confiding in a complete stranger instead. Jealousy started to rise up inside her again as she watched Jules' eyes scanning the screen. She refused to give anything away in her facial expressions and simply nodded her head in understanding.

After a few more minutes, Melanie stood up in exasperation, breaking the agonising silence that had fallen in the room.

"So is anybody actually going to show *me* what's on that screen?" she complained. "I'm his mum, I have a right to know!"

"Sit down Mel," Richard insisted, grabbing her hand and pulling her back towards the sofa. His hands were warm and a little rough.

Melanie flinched at the touch of them but then did what he said, after which he placed his hand on her leg instead in the hope of steadying her nerves a little.

"Just let Dr Jules do her job," he smiled softly as Melanie let out a deep sigh.

"I know you're frustrated Mrs Williams," Jules explained, removing her reading glasses and looking up from the screen. "But it's taken Josh a lot of guts to show me the content of his Facebook page. Sharing this with me is a big step and I'm sure he'll confide in you when he's good and ready."

Jules then looked at Josh and smiled. "Is there anything else?"

Josh nodded before passing her his phone. Melanie had absolutely no idea what they were dealing with. Embarrassing photos, unpleasant comments, threats; her mind was flooded with the possibilities and she was powerless to do anything about it.

"Do you mind if I talk to Josh on my own for a while?" Jules enquired, looking across at Melanie and Richard.

"But I thought this was supposed to be a group discussion?" Melanie retorted. "You're just here to mediate. *We're* the ones who need to talk to Josh!"

"The point of the meeting is to get to the bottom of Josh's concerns," replied Jules, trying not to sound too defensive. "And I get a sense that he would prefer to speak to me on his own first."

Jules and Melanie both turned to look at Josh expectantly.

"She's right Mum," he agreed. "Can you and Dad go and sit in the kitchen for a bit?"

Richard stood up to leave but Melanie was resolute.

"Whatever you've got to talk about you can talk about in front of me," she insisted. "After all, I'm the one who invited Dr Jules here in the first place."

"Don't be so stubborn Mel," sighed Richard walking towards the living room door. "You're not helping the situation as usual."

"And what's *that* supposed to mean?" Melanie retorted feeling her skin prickle with rage. She was just about to put an end to the meeting when they were interrupted by the doorbell. Sighing heavily she stormed through to the hall, grabbed the handle of the front door and pulled it towards her before stopping suddenly when she discovered who was standing on the other side of it. It was Mr Delaney.

Chapter thirty five
Julia

One day I had my pencil case stolen and all the contents of it were vandalised. When Melanie handed it back to me during registration that same afternoon, I was obliged to actually say thank you to her for returning it, even though I knew that she, Craig and Fran had been responsible for stealing it from me in the first place. They had also drawn a huge love heart on it in red felt tip pen, with Mr Parker's name inside, and when I realised I hastily removed my compass from it and began to try and scratch the graffiti out using its sharp tip.

Two of the girls who sat in front of me in registration turned around and sniggered over their shoulders as the scratching sound also started to attract the attention of our form tutor. Having Mr Parker's name written on my pencil case was so embarrassing, particularly since I had replaced my crush on Craig with our attractive young PE teacher instead. But as well as being young and athletic looking, he was also rather unpopular with the majority of children in the school, due to him being so strict and unsympathetic. Once, Fran and Melanie managed to smuggle some vodka into school on the night of our Halloween disco, and as soon as Mr Parker had been tipped off about it, he escorted them off the premises immediately before proceeding to tip the entire contents of the Evian bottle into the gutter outside the school gates.

There's another reason why I remember that night so much. I watched Mr Parker do it because I was standing outside the hall at the time with my witch's cape pulled up over my head. I remember my mum going to so much effort to make my Halloween costume for me and I didn't even get a chance to enjoy the disco. Melanie had written me a note earlier that week asking me if we could be friends again. She arranged for us to meet each other outside, and I genuinely believed that she was keen to make up with me, but it all turned out to be an elaborate ruse in order to make me look foolish, because as soon as I arrived she and Craig started kissing each other in front of me. I couldn't believe that I had fallen for it.

And after that night she was suspended from school for two weeks. I thought about contacting her during her suspension but my parents talked me out of it because they were disappointed with how far downhill Melanie had gone since making friends with Fran. Or 'that bully from the private school' as my mum used to refer to her as. And they were relieved that I hadn't made it up with Melanie because they didn't want me to get involved with smoking and alcohol as well. But the trouble was, Melanie had been my best and only friend, and after she became best friends with Fran instead, I didn't have anyone else. It was a bit like being back at Acornfields again.

During the months that followed the Halloween disco, I was determined to try and make amends, even though a large part of me hated Melanie for abandoning our friendship for no good reason. I just wanted everything to go back to how it had always been before Fran came along and ruined it all. And that was another reason why I decided not to tell any of the teachers who had been responsible for stealing my pencil case; or for putting chewing gum in my hair. I didn't even tell anyone that Melanie had forced me to take a drag from her cigarette; because I just wanted us to be friends with each other again.

In some ways I didn't blame her for doing all those things to me anyway because I was beginning to despise myself almost as much as she did. I used to look at my reflection in the bathroom mirror and feel physically sick at the sight of my repulsive face, covered in large red clusters of acne. One morning, when I was standing there digging my fingernails into the soft flesh on my forearms, I decided that I had desensitised myself to the pain because I had been doing it for so long. It felt a little raw and tingly afterwards but the sensation was almost undetectable. In fact I often had to run the tips of my fingers over the nail marks afterwards in order to check if they were actually there. So I opened the bathroom cabinet and found a pair of nail scissors. But rather than using them to cut my fingernails into sharp points in order to make the pain that they would potentially be able to inflict a little more intense, I found myself digging the tip of the scissors into my forearm instead. And as they gradually pierced my skin, unleashing a tiny spot of blood, the relief was overwhelming. It was as though the burden of all my emotional pain had come pouring out of that one tiny little hole in my arm, and I had finally found a way of being in control of something.

On the day that my pencil case was vandalised and I had fruitlessly attempted to scratch the graffiti off, I ended up taking my compass to the girl's toilets with me and locking myself in a cubicle so that I could use it to scratch my arm instead. I remember how satisfying it felt once I had managed to draw blood again, and it quickly became a bit of a habit after that. I just felt the need to punish myself for not even being worthy of Melanie's friendship anymore; and for feeling like a complete and utter failure at absolutely everything. Of course she wanted to be friends with Fran instead. Fran was popular and talented. Fran was pretty and 'cool'. But I wasn't any of those things. And I couldn't even dream of being any of those things. Melanie on the other hand had been wasted on the likes of me. Being popular suited her. Having a boyfriend and playing in a band suited her. Even smoking and drinking alcohol suited her, not to mention the tattoo of course. I wondered how painful it must have felt to get the tattoo done, as I jabbed the tip of the compass into my arm again. It must have been quite a satisfying sort of pain, much like the one I was inflicting on myself. But my sort of pain was shameful and weak and only succeeded in making me despise myself even more. The only trouble was, once I had started it I found it very hard to stop, and by the time I had reached the day of that fateful hockey lesson, the monster inside my head that had driven me to start doing it, was getting bigger and bigger.

After the teachers had conducted a thorough search of all the other girl's PE kits, I felt utterly humiliated. Everyone was understandably very annoyed with me for compelling Mr Parker to rummage through their personal belongings, particularly when tampons and other types of sanitary hygiene were amongst them. Nobody wanted someone as sexy as Mr Parker to handle their intimate products although I remember observing how unperturbed he seemed to be about it all, and how completely oblivious he was to the various shades of crimson that each and every girl in my PE class appeared to be turning when it was their turn to empty the contents of their bag out in front of him. Of course, a male teacher wouldn't be allowed to conduct such an investigation these days, although I later discovered that Mr Parker was gay anyway and that my subsequent infatuation had therefore been wasted on him.

He felt like a bit of a hero to me that day though, despite the distinctly unpleasant feeling that the bag search generated between me and the rest of the girls in my class. I could tell that Fran and Melanie were particularly pleased with that outcome, and I also suspected that they were the ones who had been responsible for stealing my tracksuit bottoms in the first place, but it was never actually proven. And they probably would have got away with it anyway, had it not have been for my interfering mother, who insisted on complaining to Mrs Jenkinson as soon as she discovered that some of my PE kit had been stolen. I was very angry with Mum for reacting like that. I told her not to be so overprotective of me all the time and to let me have some space. We ended up having a huge row and the next thing I knew I had locked myself in the bathroom and was removing the pair of nail scissors from the cabinet again. Despite my mum's rather suffocating parental skills, she failed to pick up on what I was doing to myself for several months. But I knew that I wouldn't be able to get away with it forever.

Chapter thirty six
Julia

Tuesday 21st May 2019

It was difficult to make out who Melanie and Richard were talking to out in the hall so Jules and Josh fell silent in the hope of identifying their visitor's voice. All of a sudden a look of recognition swept across Josh's face, which was quickly replaced by anger and frustration.

"Are you alright?" smiled Jules feeling concerned for him.

"It's mum's boss," he replied. "He always seems to end up getting in the way of everything."

"How do you mean?" enquired Jules trying hard to sound like a concerned acquaintance as opposed to an over-inquisitive counsellor.

"She works a lot," explained Josh, looking down at his knees. "And her boss always manages to make her forget about her family. He phones her late in the evening and tells her to go into the office at weekends. She even missed my birthday meal the other week because she had to work late."

"It sounds like she's under a lot of strain," acknowledged Jules doing her best not to take sides. "She's hoping to get promoted and she needs to put a lot of extra hours in to prove that she's worthy of the position."

"Why can't she just stay at home a bit more?" Josh frowned, shaking his sandy brown hair out of his eyes.

"Have you told her how you feel?" suggested Jules, removing her reading glasses and placing them on the table in front of her.

"I shouldn't have to tell her," complained Josh. "She's my mum; she should just *know*."

There was a brief silence.

"If it's any consolation I think she *does* know and it sounds as though she's trying to support you a bit more," explained Jules, gesturing towards Josh's laptop. "I don't think she would have met you at school yesterday or arranged this meeting with me if she didn't care. But it would still help to talk to her about your feelings."

"I guess," mumbled Josh, rolling his eyes a little. "But she's not always around long enough for me to talk to her."

"Would you have told her about the cyber bullying if she was?" asked Jules.

"I don't know," shrugged Josh. "Maybe."

"So how long has it been going on?"

There was another silence as Josh considered Jules' question. Jules took the opportunity to put her reading glasses back on and reach for her notepad and pen; her counsellor status firmly reinstated.

"You've taken the most important step by agreeing to speak to me," she added encouragingly when it started to become clear that Josh was not proving to be quite as forthcoming as she had at first hoped.

"And showing me your laptop and phone took a lot of guts. I really appreciate you opening up to me like that."

"You seem nice," smiled Josh reluctantly. "And it's a lot easier to show someone like you than it is to show my mum."

"What is it that you're afraid she might say if she saw it?" urged Jules, shifting towards the edge of her armchair.

Josh seized up again and scratched his head uncomfortably before attempting to change the subject;

"So who else are you counselling at the moment? That Caitlin girl in year 10 seems like a bit of a nightmare!"

"I can't discuss my other cases with you," replied Jules defensively, pushing any thoughts of Caitlin to the back of her mind.

"Is that all I am to you, a 'case'?" complained Josh sounding deflated.

Jules decided to adopt a more gentle approach with him.

"You can talk to me in confidence Josh and I will promise you that it won't go any further than these four walls."

"You mean you won't even tell my mum?" clarified Josh looking more responsive.

"Not if you don't want me to, no," insisted Jules sensing an encouraging shift in Josh's body language. He looked directly into her eyes and swallowed before opening his mouth to speak, at which point the living room door burst open.

"I got the promotion!" announced Melanie sounding elated. "Mr Delaney just popped round to tell me that as of today I am the new partner at 'Drummond and Delaney Chartered accountants'. Apparently he received my resignation email and panicked because he didn't want to lose me from the firm. I should have just threatened to leave ages ago."

Josh and Jules were completely dumbstruck, and Richard, who had been standing in the hall behind Melanie, simply sighed heavily before retrieving his jacket from the back of the sofa and then storming towards the door.

"It was lovely to meet you Dr Jules but I'm afraid I can't stay here a minute longer," he complained. "I'm sorry Josh; I'll call you tomorrow."

"Dad, wait," insisted Josh, tripping over the coffee table in an attempt to get to the hall before his stepfather had managed to reach the front door. "Can I come and stay with you tonight?"

Melanie looked crestfallen;

"But what about our meeting?" she protested.

Josh hesitated before turning to face his mother "So you've accepted it then? The promotion."

"Of course I've accepted it," replied Melanie half smiling. "I've been working so hard for it. You can't possibly expect me to turn it down."

"I don't know what to expect anymore," concluded Josh, hanging his head in disappointment as he made his way into the hall and picked up his overnight bag that was still sitting there from when he had returned home from his friend's house less than an hour earlier.

"I'll see you tomorrow; unless you're too busy celebrating with your work colleagues."

"Josh, wait. Let's at least talk about this," insisted Melanie following them to the front door. But before Jules had been given the opportunity to gather her thoughts, the door slammed and Melanie returned to the living room again with a very frustrated expression on her face.

"They've gone," she announced sinking down onto the sofa. "I thought they would be pleased."

Jules couldn't quite understand *why* Melanie thought they would feel that way about her promotion, particularly since her strict working ethic had caused so many problems as far as both her marriage *and* her relationship with her vulnerable son were concerned. But in an attempt to give Melanie the benefit of the doubt, perhaps she truly believed that things would get a lot easier now that she was partner.

"I should get going too," announced Jules, making a reach for her handbag. "We can't really continue this meeting without Josh."

"Please stay for a glass of wine," insisted Melanie, placing her hand on Jules' arm. "I could really do with the company right now."

Jules' stomach twisted when she thought about sharing yet another uncomfortable drink with the woman who had caused her so much pain and misery 17 years ago. Perhaps she should tell Melanie who she really was before the situation got out of hand any further. She wasn't really supposed to drink alcohol with any of her clients, even though the end of their meeting with Josh had also confirmed that she was officially off duty for the rest of the afternoon.

Having said that of course, she wasn't supposed to provide her services to someone she knew, due to the possible conflict of interests. But it wouldn't have been fair on Josh to refuse because he was entitled to the same amount of support as all the other students at Pinewood were. And besides, she had already fully immersed herself in his case when she was in the process of emailing M Williams yesterday evening, and that was before she even knew that it was Melanie at the other end of all the messages. Yesterday evening at Drew's house felt like such a long time ago already, but that was probably because she had spent the entire day just willing for him to contact her.

"Of course, some wine would be great," she eventually nodded.

Melanie's face lit up and she left the room again to collect a bottle and some wine glasses from the kitchen. Jules looked at her watch. She couldn't believe it was only 4.45pm in the afternoon. Bright sunlight flooded the sitting room and the birds were singing tunefully outside. When Melanie returned and placed the glasses on the table next to the cafetiere of coffee, she reached over and opened the doors onto the patio so that a burst of fresh air filled the room.

"It's a beautiful day," she smiled, closing her eyes and shaking her hair back over her shoulders.

Jules didn't respond because she was too busy thinking about when and how she would eventually disclose her true identity.

"When I think about what Josh is going through, I feel like the universe it trying to punish me," Melanie suddenly confessed, opening her eyes again.

"What do you mean?" frowned Jules, pouring herself a large glass of red. "Because you've been working so hard?"

"No," replied Melanie bluntly, before taking a deep breath. "Because of what I used to be like at school."

Jules' heart skipped a beat but she decided not to say anything in the fear of interrupting Melanie's confession.

"Many years ago I did something terrible," she explained. "And I've never forgiven myself for it."

Jules eventually decided to speak although her voice sounded squeaky and uncomfortable.

"What did you do?"

"I bullied someone; one of my very best friends in fact," Melanie replied, hanging her head in shame. "And I made her life so miserable that she ended up hurting herself really badly."

Jules' legs turned to jelly as she self-consciously pulled at the sleeves of her blouse in the fear that her scars were on show. She could feel some beads of sweat appearing on her top lip and her heart was pounding rapidly.

"I never found out what happened to her after that," Melanie continued. "When she was discharged from hospital she didn't come back to school and then my parents sent me away to finish my education elsewhere. Do you think the horrible things that have been happening to Josh are karma or something?"

She looked at Jules with a pleading expression on her face; almost as though she was willing her to insist otherwise. Jules was silent. She suddenly started to panic about the possibility that Melanie *did* recognise her after all, but that she was pretending that she didn't know who she was in the hope that Jules would provide her with some kind of retribution.

"You do, don't you," Melanie concluded, when Jules still failed to speak. "You think I've got what's coming to me."

Jules didn't believe that at all. She wasn't even sure whether she believed in karma anyway. But even if she did, she wouldn't have predicted that Melanie's innocent son would get punished for a crime that his mother had committed years earlier. Where was the justice in that? Jules had spent many years despising Melanie for what she had done to her at school. And for the extreme lengths that she had been driven to. And whilst she knew that her experiences during her childhood had inspired her to become a psychologist, and she had been able to turn all those negatives into many positives, she also knew that the scars on her arms were not the only ones to leave their mark. She had suffered from low self-esteem and social anxiety all of her life and she had the likes of Melanie, Fran and Barry to blame for that. Emotional scars never heal completely.

Having low self-esteem can be so contradictory; on the one hand, you assume that everyone is looking at you and judging your every move, but on the other hand, you feel completely invisible. Jules wished she was invisible now as she felt Melanie's eyes bearing into her. And she knew that the only thing left to do was to tell her the truth. She swallowed hard and leant forward in her chair as Melanie braced herself for what she was about to say;

"You know when you asked me if we had met before," she whispered, barely able to get her words out.

Melanie nodded.

"Well..."

At that very moment her phone interrupted her confession, encouraging both women to groan. Jules was tempted to cancel the call but when she discovered that Mr Langley's name was appearing on the display, she looked at Melanie apologetically and then pressed the green receive button.

"You need to come quickly," he urged, sounding fraught. "It's Caitlin. She's in hospital; her stepfather's assaulted her!"

Chapter thirty seven
Melanie

Jules threw her phone down in a panic and then started rooting around in her handbag for her car keys.

"I'm really sorry but I need to go," she announced. "Something terrible has happened. I have to go to the hospital right away."

"Are you OK?" frowned Melanie, feeling concerned. Jules' face had turned as white as a sheet and she was clearly shaken up.

"I'll be fine," Jules insisted. "I just really need to be there."

"Of course," replied Melanie, pulling the patio doors shut and grabbing her own bag from underneath the coffee table. "I'll give you a lift."

"I'm perfectly capable of driving myself," snapped Jules, ungratefully, at which point Melanie raised her eyebrows disbelievingly.

"You are in no fit state to drive; you're obviously in shock. And besides, I haven't drunk any of my wine yet and it's not like I have anything better to do."

"You could stay at home and work out how you're going to manage to be a partner in an accountancy firm *and* do a half decent job of being a mother to your 12 year old son," suggested Jules, as Melanie followed her out to the road where her car was parked.

"I guess I probably deserved that," concluded Melanie, referring to the cutting tone in Jules' voice.

Jules shrugged nonchalantly as she opened the car door, sank down into the driver's seat and then turned the key in the ignition.

Nothing happened. After a few more attempts she looked up at Melanie and sighed.

"My car won't start. Is there any chance of a lift?"

The two women smiled before making their way to where Melanie's car was parked in the driveway. And as Jules climbed into the passenger seat next to her, Melanie suddenly remembered that Jules had been in the middle of trying to tell her something before the phone had rung.

"What was it that you wanted to tell me by the way?" she gently enquired as she began to reverse out of the driveway.

Jules shifted awkwardly in her seat and then shook her head;

"It doesn't matter; it was nothing," she insisted rather unconvincingly. Melanie could sense that she obviously didn't want to focus on anything other than getting to the hospital as quickly as possible, so she decided not to pursue the subject any further, but she was a little intrigued as to why Jules seemed so familiar.

They drove to the hospital in silence. Neither one of them felt like making small talk, and Melanie found herself growing increasingly overwhelmed by thoughts of what had happened back at home. Mr Delaney had offered her the promotion that she had always dreamed about, but now Richard and Josh had formed a united front and both walked out on her. And she hadn't even begun to get to the bottom of Josh's cyber bullying. Not to mention the fact that she was due to fly out to France in less than 48 hours time in order to attend her father's funeral.

"Thank you for the lift," smiled Jules, as they pulled into the hospital car park. "I'll arrange for the breakdown team to remove my car from the road outside your house as soon as I've sorted everything out here."

"No worries," replied Melanie as Jules opened the car door. She was just about to slam it shut when Rebecca's husband suddenly appeared beside her.

"It's Julia isn't it? Christian's sister," he smiled, holding his hand out in order to re-make her acquaintance.

"Leroy?" Melanie frowned, opening her own door and stepping out of the car. "Do you two know each other?"

"I could say the same about you," he replied, before rushing over to Melanie's side of the car in order to give his wife's best friend a hug.

"Julia's brother is engaged to Suzy," he explained. "We're practically family."

"And what are you doing at the hospital?" Melanie probed, observing how frantic Leroy appeared to be.

"Rebecca's just given birth," he announced. "A baby girl! It all happened so quickly that I didn't have the chance to get her maternity bag out of the car when we arrived at the hospital."

"That's fantastic!" beamed Melanie, giving him another hug.

"Congratulations," smiled Jules, stroking him on the arm. "Now if you'll excuse me, I need to get to A&E as soon as possible. Give my best wishes to your wife."

Melanie opened her mouth to speak, but Jules was already out of earshot by the time any sound started to come out, prompting her to close it again in defeat.

"So how do you know Christian's sister?" Leroy smiled, grabbing her attention again.

"Christian?" Melanie frowned. "Is that what her brother's name is?"

"My future brother-in-law," confirmed Leroy. "And the new uncle to my beautiful baby daughter."

He seemed incapable of doing anything other than smiling like a Cheshire cat, and Melanie didn't have the heart to burst his bubble by burdening him with her problems, so she decided to take a deep breath before kissing him on the cheek and then assuring him that she would pop up to the post-natal ward later on in order to visit Rebecca and the baby.

"There's just somewhere I need to be first," she explained, before following Jules towards the entrance to A&E.

❖

Inside the hospital, Jules was pacing around outside the resus room in a complete state of panic. She appeared to be on the phone to Mr Langley when Melanie stepped up behind her and placed her hand on her shoulder. Jules swung round in surprise and then frowned when she realised that Melanie had followed her.

"I appreciate the lift," she smiled uncomfortably. "But you didn't need to come in with me."

"Rebecca and the baby aren't ready for visitors yet," explained Melanie. "But I don't want to leave the hospital without seeing them so I thought I would come and make sure that you're OK."

Jules' facial expression softened.

"That's kind of you," she insisted "Particularly considering everything you're dealing with at the moment. And I'm fine, really I am. This is a rather sensitive matter and I'm afraid I couldn't discuss it with you, even if I wanted to."

"I understand," nodded Melanie, sympathetically, before remembering the *real* reason why she had been so intent on catching up with Jules in A&E.

"Leroy told me that your brother's name is Christian," she explained, at which point Jules started to look very uncomfortable again. "Are you *sure* we haven't met before?"

Jules was just about to open her mouth to speak when the door into resus burst open and a concerned looking nurse stepped out.

"A woman from Social Services has just arrived," she announced. "She's in the relative's room talking to Caitlin's mother. I'm afraid we can't let you see Caitlin without her mother's permission so you'll have to go and wait in the waiting room until she's ready."

"OK, thank you," Jules nodded, brushing her hair out of her face in an exasperated fashion before turning to Melanie again. "It sounds like I'll have to wait a while; shall we go and have a chat?"

"Yes please," Melanie replied, following her out of the building again.

❖

They bypassed the waiting room and managed to find themselves a bench on a small patch of grass that overlooked the car park. Jules refused to look Melanie in the eye as they sat down next to each other and took stock of their surroundings. The car park was busy and noisy and Melanie wasn't sure whether she felt entirely comfortable about having a confrontation with someone in such a public space, but inside the hospital building had been even worse, and she needed to get to the bottom of who Jules really was, once and for all. She didn't even need to probe Jules again in order to receive the confession that she had been waiting for. Jules ran her hand through her hair and took a lungful of polluted air before sitting forward and resting her elbows on her knees.

"My full name is Dr Julia Croft," she explained sounding guilty.

Melanie felt her head go giddy and she grabbed onto the bench in order to steady herself.

"How long have you known who I am?" she frowned, trying not to panic too much.

"Since the second I saw you," replied Jules, staring at the ground in front of her. "Which is why I dropped my mug of coffee."

"Well why didn't you say anything?" demanded Melanie, frustrated with Jules' composure. All she wanted was for Jules to look her straight in the eyes so that she could confront her properly.

"I couldn't tell whether you recognised me or not," Jules explained, finally looking up. "For all I knew you could have arranged to meet up with me on purpose. It wasn't until I met Josh this afternoon that I realised how genuine your enquiry had been, and by that point I wanted to be able to help you without our past getting in the way."

"*You* wanted to help *me*!" Melanie scoffed "I suppose you've been secretly loving all of this. 'Evil Melanie Allsopp' gets her comeuppance at last?"

"I'll admit I'm annoyed with you for not supporting your son," Jules confessed. "And for allowing your pushy parents and your promotion at work to take priority. But it's not my job to express my opinions."

Melanie slumped back against the bench and put her hand to her forehead.

"Never mind whether it's your job or not!" she complained. "You gave up the right to be impartial the minute you realised who 'M

Williams' really was. Your conduct has been completely unprofessional."

"You're absolutely right," Jules nodded, feeling tears spring to her eyes. "And I did try to tell you on a couple of occasions but we kept on getting interrupted."

"How convenient!" laughed Melanie sarcastically, at which point both women fell silent for a few seconds as they tried to make sense of what was happening.

Melanie took the opportunity to scrutinise Jules a little more closely. She really had changed over the past 17 years. The 16 year old version of Julia that Melanie remembered from school was exceptionally plain to look at, with dark straight hair that hung limp around her shoulders, thick plastic rimmed glasses that persisted in sliding down her greasy nose, and a forehead covered in acne. *This* version on the other hand was really rather stunning. Her hair was now a velvety chocolate in appearance, with voluminous waves that flatteringly framed the milky clear complexion of her flawless skin. Her large almond shaped eyes which had previously been hidden behind her very unfashionable spectacles were now accentuated with exactly the right amount of eye makeup, and her cheeks had a natural glow to them which complimented the soft rouge colour of her lips.

Jules was the first to break the silence; "I can't believe you didn't recognise me," she sniffed, tracing the underneath of her eye with the tip of her finger in order to remove any hint of a tear before it had the chance to escape down her cheek.

"You've really changed," insisted Melanie, snapping herself out of the trance that she appeared to have fallen into. "I mean, *really* changed. I thought there was something vaguely familiar about you, particularly when you put your reading glasses on earlier, but you look absolutely nothing like you did at school."

"Well, is this proof enough for you?" scolded Jules, rolling the sleeves of her jacket up and shoving her scars under Melanie's nose.

Melanie stared at Jules' arms in disbelief. She had been so busy blaming Jules for concealing her identity that she had overlooked what a lasting affect her treatment of Jules all those years ago had left.

"I'm sorry," she whispered, feeling a surge of emotions rise up inside her. "I told you how sorry I was when we were talking about it back at my house. I've never stopped thinking about what I drove you to do to yourself."

Jules folded her arms across her chest and then shrugged, before attempting to try and make light of the situation a little;

"Well at least I've made a career out of it."

"You became a psychologist because of *me*?" Melanie frowned.

"You and Fran, and Barry Harper, and all the other people who have ever bullied me or anyone else for that matter," explained Jules. "Because being bullied doesn't just affect you when it's actually happening, it stays with you for the rest of your life. And I wanted to do something to help other people to deal with its effects before they go too far."

"I think it's amazing," insisted Melanie. "You've turned a negative into a positive. And you're clearly a completely different person now to who you were back then. You're so much more confident."

"I'm more outgoing," retorted Jules, encouraging Melanie to close her mouth in disbelief because she hadn't been expecting such an aggressive reaction. "But I'm still not very *self*-confident. I've just managed to get a lot better at hiding it."

"Well you're obviously a successful psychologist," replied Melanie, in an attempt to make her feel better. After all, she had a lot of making up to do. "Mr Langley thinks you're amazing."

"I'm not sure he would agree with you based on the reason why I'm at the hospital right now," sighed Jules turning to face her. "I've really messed up."

"We've broken a lot of professional boundaries already," smiled Melanie, nudging her in the arm. "Why don't you tell me who Caitlin is. A problem shared is a problem halved."

Jules laughed. "I never thought I would see the day when Melanie Allsopp used that phrase!"

"Well maybe you're not the only one who's changed," replied Melanie. "Although I'm afraid you could be right about my pushy parents. They've bullied me all my life and now I'm allowing my boss to do the same."

"So what are you going to do about it?" enquired Jules, grateful that she no longer felt obliged to talk about Caitlin's situation instead.

Melanie's face brightened suddenly. "I'm going to quit my job," she announced. "And properly this time. Mr Delaney can stuff his promotion. I want to win my husband back."

"Do you really mean that?" confirmed Jules, removing a tissue from her suit jacket pocket and dabbing her nose with it.

"I was seriously considering it before we had this discussion," replied Melanie. "But now that I know who you are, I'm absolutely certain that it's the right thing to do. Richard and Josh are the two most important people in my life and I don't want to lose them."

"I'm really pleased for you," smiled Jules weakly. "Josh is a great kid. And Richard seems lovely too. I wish I could find a man like him."

"Don't you have a special someone in your life?" Melanie probed, determined to convince Jules to confide in her about *something*.

After all, it was clear that Jules had no intention of sharing any details about Caitlin anytime soon.

Jules sighed heavily and started rolling a small stone along the ground in front of her with the sole of her shoe.

"Well up until last night I *thought* I did, but I'm afraid it didn't work out," she replied, refusing to elaborate.

"What went wrong?" enquired Melanie. "Maybe *I* can give *you* some advice for a change."

Jules turned to face her and raised her eyebrows disbelievingly encouraging both women to smile.

"Fair enough," Melanie conceded, laughing. "So can you at least tell me what his name is or where you both met?"

Jules could tell that Melanie was really trying to take a genuine interest in her life, and that she was determined to try and put the past well and truly behind them, so she kicked the stone into the grass and began to open up a little;

"His name's Drew," she explained. "We met here at the hospital while he was treating one of my other students and then we kept bumping into each other. We even ended up going to the same speed dating night!"

"It must have been fate," Melanie smiled. "So what does he look like?"

The sides of Jules' mouth curled up at this point encouraging Melanie to nudge her in the arm again.

"He's drop-dead gorgeous then." she concluded. "*And* he's a doctor. He sounds perfect."

"My friend Amy calls him Dr Dish!" Jules confessed, trying not to blush. "And yes, he *is* perfect. It's *me* that's the problem. I seem to be incapable of sustaining a relationship with a member of the opposite sex. I get frightened of being hurt and then I push them away."

"Because of your lack of self-confidence?" clarified Melanie feeling a little guilty. If she hadn't contributed to Jules' damaged past, perhaps Jules would have been happily married by now.

"And because of these," explained Jules tentatively rolling the sleeve of her jacket back up and drawing Melanie's attention to her scars again.

"Do you mind me asking what happened to you afterwards?" Melanie enquired hesitantly. "You didn't come back to school again and all they would tell us is that you had to move away."

"As soon as I had been discharged from hospital, my mum took me down to the south coast to stay with my grandparents for a few weeks," Julia explained. "She thought the sea air would help to clear my head but I needed her to understand that it wasn't as simple as that. It was almost as though she was in denial or something, which is strange in a way when you consider how over-protective she was of me."

"Perhaps she felt guilty for not protecting you enough," mused Melanie. "And what about your GCSEs?"

"I was home-tutored for the rest of year 11 and then sat them at the same time as everybody else, but my grades had really slipped and I didn't do well enough to get onto the A-level course that I had been hoping for," continued Julia, only looking up at Melanie long enough to swallow the lump in her throat.

"It was a blessing in disguise though," she then concluded. "Because during what I later decided to describe as my 'premature gap years' I discovered that I wanted to change my A-level options anyway."

"Why?" frowned Melanie, feeling encouraged by the positive way in which Julia portrayed this particular revelation.

"Because I discovered psychology."

"And how did that come about?"

"I arranged for myself to have some counselling," explained Julia. "Some local youth workers were offering it free of charge to young people under the age of 18 so I decided to sign up and it was the best thing I have ever done."

Julia's parents were initially unaware of her decision to have counselling because it was something that she knew they were never likely to particularly approve of, but as well as providing her with an absolutely invaluable support network, which she used to work through her issues with bullying and low self-esteem, she was also incredibly inspired by the type of work they were doing. And that's why she decided to try and pursue a career in counselling herself.

"Mental health issues, especially in young people, were virtually unheard of in those days," she explained as Melanie continued to listen intently. "But it's such a hot topic now with all kinds of different therapies and medication available."

"Have you ever taken anti-depressants?" asked Melanie reluctantly.

Julia shook her head and then fell silent for a few seconds as her brain continued to go over the rest of the events that bridged the gap between that fateful day in 2002, and the present. She had managed to drag herself up out of the depths of despair but the process had been very slow and incredibly painful.

"Did you..." Melanie paused and then swallowed before attempting to begin her sentence again. "Have you ever attempted to take your own life?"

"I don't think so, no," replied Julia, stroking her arm protectively. "In some ways the self-harming was a way of suppressing the urge to do anything more serious to myself. But whether it was my intention to put my life in danger or not, I certainly came dangerously close to it that day."

By this point Melanie was crying.

"I'm so sorry," she pleaded, her voice choked with tears as she wiped her face with the back of her hand. "This is all my fault and I'll never forgive myself for what I put you through."

"It's OK, really it is," insisted Jules. "You can't spend the rest of your life feeling guilty. Besides, I know something that will make you smile."

Melanie sniffed and then tried to compose herself a little as Julia endeavoured to lighten the mood by changing the subject for a while.

"I bumped into Craig Riley when I went speed dating last weekend. He was one of my dates and he didn't recognise me either. He asked me to go to a party with him; can you believe it?"

"No way!" Melanie laughed. "Although I'm not surprised he didn't recognise you. I was completely oblivious to your true identity until about 10 minutes ago too."

Julia smiled and the two women fell silent again.

"He was the worst snog I've ever had!" Melanie eventually smiled. "So what does he look like now? Is he still a hunk?"

"Not at all!" emphasised Julia. "The aging process has been very unkind to him, which I couldn't help but feel a little smug about. What goes around, comes around."

Melanie's expression fell flat at that point and it took Julia a few seconds to pick up on why.

"I keep telling you it wasn't your fault," Jules insisted, before wrapping her arms around Melanie tightly. "It was a combination of different factors which just happened to come to a head that day. But if I hadn't have gone to hospital then I wouldn't have got myself sorted out."

"It should never have got that far in the first place," retorted Melanie.

"Well it's not always that easy to ask for help. Or to accept that you actually need it in the first place. I knew deep down that cutting myself was wrong, but it was also making me better in a strange sort of way. The pain and the bleeding was like a release and it was one of the few things that I felt in control of at the time, even though the self-harming was actually in control of me."

"I had no idea you were going through all that," sniffed Melanie, removing a tissue from her handbag. "And even if I wasn't entirely responsible for driving you to do that, I still played a pretty integral part in it. I deserve everything I've got," she blubbed, trying to resist the urge to wipe her runny nose on the shoulder pad of Jules' suit jacket. "My husband hates me, my boss is an even bigger bully than I was, and I didn't get the chance to make amends with my father before he passed away."

"But it's not too late to make things right with Richard," Jules reminded her. "Learn from what's happened and go and sort it out. Besides, you need to talk to Josh about the cyber bullying. I get the impression that there's more to his situation than meets the eye."

"And what about you?" frowned Melanie, as Jules broke free from their embrace. "Will you go and talk to Dr Dish about your past?"

Jules looked back at the hospital building and sighed again. "I suppose I probably should," she agreed. "But I need to sort the situation with Caitlin out first."

"Good luck," smiled Melanie encouragingly, holding out her hand. "Let me know how you get on."

Jules stood up from the bench and shook hands with her. "I will. And good luck to you too."

❖

Melanie decided not to hang around at the hospital long enough to visit Rebecca and the new arrival. She needed to talk to Richard as soon as possible, and besides, it was only fair that Leroy and Rebecca enjoyed some time alone with their new baby daughter before any other visitors attempted to descend on them. So she climbed into her car, sent Leroy a quick text message, and then drove as fast as she could to Richard's flat across the other side of town. When she pulled up outside, she took her phone out of her bag again, scrolled down her contacts list and then stared at Philip Delaney's name on the display screen for a couple of minutes, before switching her car engine off and taking a deep breath. Removing her keys from the ignition and pressing the call button, she then peered into the front window of Richard's flat and smiled at the outline of Josh and Richard playing computer games, laughing together and sharing a big bowl of crisps, as though no one else in the world mattered. Josh looked so happy.

When Philip picked the phone up, Melanie refused to give him the opportunity to say anything before she launched into the reason why she was calling;

"I won't beat around the bush," she announced. "I appreciate you coming to my house this afternoon to offer me the promotion, but I am calling to inform you that my resignation still stands. And because of all the unpaid overtime and unused annual leave that I have accrued over the past few months, I will be standing down from my post with immediate effect."

"How dare you!" retorted Philip, sounding as though he was about to erupt. "I refuse to accept your resignation and I will expect to see you here in the office bright and early tomorrow morning."

"I'm going to France tomorrow," replied Melanie, remaining resolute. "It's my father's funeral on Thursday and I want to go and make peace with him."

"Fine," scoffed Philip, reluctantly re-evaluating the situation. "I can see that I'm not going to win this one so I am willing to negotiate some terms with you."

"Such as?" smiled Melanie, rolling her eyes.

"Such as extended annual leave and a substantial pay rise for a start," replied Philip.

Melanie's smile widened, but not at the thought of a larger salary or more holidays. At the realisation that Mr Delaney was not prepared to let her go without a fight. She was obviously a highly valued member of the team, even though it had taken her several years of hoop jumping for him to actually offer her the promotion and the terms that she so clearly deserved.

"You could triple my salary and offer me all the incentives in the world, but I wouldn't want to work for a bully like you for a moment longer than I have to!" Melanie replied, her heart thumping in her chest. "And if you don't accept my resignation, I will make a complaint to Human Resources about the way I've been treated over the past few months. I'm sure they'll be more than happy to initiate a disciplinary with the senior partner of the firm."

"You wouldn't dare!" shouted Philip. "It's your word against mine."

"I wouldn't be so sure about that if I were you," replied Melanie, before smiling at her reflection in the rear view mirror. "You've totally abused the Working Time Directive by forcing me to work such long hours. Even our office cleaner can vouch for that. And don't get me started on Compassionate Leave! I'm confident that I can build a very strong case against you."

There was silence at the other end of the phone line, which was eventually broken by the sound of Mr Delaney pushing a pile of paperwork off his desk in a rage.

"Have it your way!" he then bellowed. "But don't expect a reference."

"Well that's just fine by me," replied Melanie sounding smug. "Because I don't *need* a reference anyway. I'm not planning to join another accountancy firm after this because I've decided to spend some time with my family instead."

At that point the phone line went dead and it was clear that Mr Delaney had hung up on her. Melanie filled her lungs with air and then breathed out through pursed lips in an attempt to slow her heart rate down again. She couldn't believe what she had just done, not because of the sudden realisation that her career as an accountant was in tatters, but because it had felt so good. So *right*. She was a hard worker and she was good at her job, but she had only really ended up following that particular path because that was what her father and mother had pushed her to do. If recent weeks had taught her anything, they had taught her that there was so much more to life than work, and as she stepped out of the car and reluctantly started to make her way to Richard's front door, she decided that it was now time to try and begin proving that to the rest of her family.

Chapter thirty eight
Julia

February 2002

During the weeks that followed our humiliating hockey lesson and its subsequent search for my tracksuit bottoms, which was equally mortifying, I began to develop a heightened awareness of everyone around me. And despite having been subjected to such humiliation on more than one occasion in my past, this time felt a lot more challenging because I was also experiencing the true intensity of adolescence.

Skidding on a raw egg at the year 4 sports day, or even wetting myself in front of a dormitory full of immature 10 and 11 year olds at that fateful field trip, had felt like the worst experiences of my life back then. But over five years later, and combined with all the extra pressures, expectations and hormones that being a teenager brought with it, an experience like the one I had out on the hockey pitch was enough to scar anyone for life. And that is exactly what happened to me in the literal sense because I was so unbelievably devastated about the memory of everyone seeing my hairy legs that day that I decided, one Saturday morning, to go out and buy myself a home waxing kit. I then waited until my mum and dad had gone out before I made a dash for the microwave in the kitchen, barely stopping for long enough to read the instructions on the packaging properly. Whilst the microwave was busy spinning my pot of wax around and whirring loudly, I remember looking across the kitchen at my mum's notice board which was absolutely covered with postcards from Christian. He and his girlfriend at the time had decided to spend the year between their A levels and university travelling around the world, and my mum was missing him terribly. In fact, I couldn't help but wonder, if it hadn't have been for his gap year, whether Mum might have spent less time thinking about him and more time concentrating on me instead.

After all, we lived under the same roof as each other and she seemed to have a far better idea about what Christian was up to in South East Asia than she did about the turmoil that I was going through right under her nose.

Having said that of course, I deliberately kept my feelings buried because I hated it when she made a fuss. And even though a small part of me wanted her to stop pining for her prodigal son and actually concentrate on me for a change, a much larger percentage of me didn't. Which was why I had waited until she and Dad had gone out that day, before I decided to try out my new home waxing kit. I had been absolutely mortified when she arranged for Mr Parker to conduct the search of everyone's PE kits, so there was no way that I was going to give her the opportunity to interfere with this too. Just as the microwave was about to ping, I suddenly heard a key turn in the front door. She and Dad had been out of the house for less than the time it had taken for me to run downstairs and heat my pot of wax up. Somehow I managed to retrieve the wax pot from the microwave and return to my bedroom before they had finished taking their shoes and coats off, and as I slipped past them in the hall, clutching the burning hot pot with the cuffs of my jumper, they barely even looked up long enough to inform me that they had decided to pop out after lunch instead.

I can't even remember where it was that they had been planning to go that Saturday morning, or why they changed their minds at such short notice. All I remember is the panic and disappointment because I had a pot of freshly heated wax in my hands and I was only prepared to use it when they weren't around to interrupt me. It felt like such a wasted opportunity though, and I had a 'do not disturb' sign on my bedroom door, so I decided to risk it anyway. The temptation was simply too hard to resist as I dipped my wooden spatula stick into the pot of wax and stirred it around tantalisingly. The colour and consistency was like runny caramel and it was still bubbling and sizzling wildly as I gently placed the heat proof pot down onto my dressing table and then started removing my jeans.

There was a long string of melting hot wax hanging from the spatula stick as I pulled it over to where the first patch of hair was and then pressed down. I couldn't feel anything at first – it must have been so hot that my nerve endings were numb to the pain – and it wasn't until I had dragged the spatula across a large area of hairy skin just above my left knee that I was compelled to scream out in agony.

I remember my mum bursting into my bedroom within a few seconds, almost as though she had been standing right outside the door. I later discovered that she frequently used to check up on me whenever I chose to hang the 'do not disturb' sign on my bedroom door handle, because she was concerned that I might have been crying about Melanie. Little did she know until later of course, that I was probably trying to inflict some kind of physical pain on myself in order to take the edge off the emotional pain that I was experiencing. I hadn't intentionally set out to hurt myself that particular day though. I was genuinely attempting to just remove the ugly hairs from my legs because I was so ashamed about having to bare them to my PE class. But the sensation of the burning hot wax on my skin took my breath away, and even though I had been obliged to scream out in agony, there was something even more compelling about it than drawing blood. It was almost as though I could feel my skin melting.

As soon as my mum realised, she dragged me through to the bathroom across the landing where she proceeded to fill the bath tub with cold water.

"Didn't you read the instructions properly Julia?" she panicked, as I peeled off my jumper and T-shirt and then reluctantly lowered myself into the tub with my underwear still on.

I remember soaking my leg for what felt like an eternity whilst we waited for the wax to go hard, and after that she drove me to the Urgent Care clinic where they gradually removed it all using a pair of tweezers, before covering my entire thigh with a heavy lint dressing. Apparently I had removed several layers of skin and would need to keep the wound covered until it had almost completely healed. My mum asked them if I would have a scar, but all I was interested in was whether I would still be allowed to wax the rest of my legs in order to get rid of all the hairs. The nurse who had been treating me advised that I made an appointment at the beauty salon next time, rather than attempting to do it myself again. She also confirmed that I was likely to have a scar, much to my mum's dismay.

On the rare occasions that I chose to confide in anyone about my scars, they always expect me to just show them my arms. But it's actually my legs that tell the real story because they are covered with painful memories. From the tiny little scar on my shin that I sustained on sports day when I fell over during the egg and spoon race, to the much larger ones on my knees from when they bashed the handle bars of the undersized bike that Mrs Greaves forced me to ride during our field trip to Wales, to the home-waxing kit disaster which caused my left thigh to blister. They all remind me of being bullied in some shape or form, even though I was never actually physically abused by any of the people who bullied me.

I wasn't punched or kicked. I didn't have stinging nettles shoved down my school shirt. I didn't get my glasses broken or have cigarettes stubbed out on me. I wasn't even obliged to recover my head from the inside of a toilet bowl after it had been flushed. Yet somehow, my body had ended up just as damaged. So much for sticks and stones.

Chapter thirty nine

Tuesday 21st May 2019

As Jules walked back towards the entrance to A&E, she felt strangely calm. Now that she had talked everything through with Melanie, she suddenly found herself believing that she was actually capable of *anything*. Besides, she had asserted herself in all the right places, and she had been firm but fair with regards to illustrating her point about the self-harming scars. It was a conversation that she had practised in her head many times, determined to get everything *just* right in the hope of clawing back some semblance of justice for the pain that she had experienced all those years ago.

But two things surprised her about their confrontation. The first being the fact that Melanie was so in awe of how much she had changed since their school days, both in her appearance and in her professionalism and career achievements. And the second thing that surprised her was how much *Melanie* had changed. She was a lot more sensitive now, vulnerable even. And whilst a very small part of Jules had been finding it difficult not to feel a little smug about their change in circumstances, she also genuinely wanted everything to work out for Melanie. In fact, to a certain extent, she wanted the two of them to be able to remain friends.

She floated along the busy corridor allowing the feeling of serenity to wash through her, and when she reached the door into resus, she closed her eyes, took two deep breaths, and then slowly pushed it open. The first thing she expected to find was a concerned looking nurse sitting vigil at Caitlin's bedside, determined not to allow anyone to enter the room without Mrs Murphy's permission. Or two social workers holding clipboards and ushering her straight back to where she had just come from. But the room was completely silent with the exception of the heart rate monitor that Caitlin was rigged up to, the sound of which immediately catapulted her back to the resus room 17 years ago as she drifted in and out of consciousness. She gripped her left arm protectively as the door swung closed behind her and she reluctantly started to approach Caitlin's bed. Caitlin was either asleep or unconscious; she wasn't sure which, and her injuries were a lot more extensive than she had expected them to be. Her face was swollen and bruised and her arms and abdomen had been bandaged up. In fact, in the absence of her signature dark eye makeup, she would have been barely recognisable if it wasn't for the thick streak of blonde in her otherwise black head of hair.

"I'm so sorry Caitlin," she whispered, making a reach for Caitlin's hand, at which point a voice from behind her cut through the silence and startled her.

"You will be sorry!" the voice bellowed. "Sorry that you made me do this to her."

"Mr Murphy!" Jules cried turning around and finding herself confronted with Caitlin's violent stepfather, Steve. Any feeling of serenity that she had experienced before she entered the room, evaporated rapidly as her heart started to pound loudly in her chest. She composed herself long enough to confront him about what he had done.

"So you admit that you did this to Caitlin?" she confirmed through a clenched jaw.

Steve's nostrils started to flare angrily as he stepped towards her. Jules discreetly attempted to fumble about in her handbag for her phone, which she removed from the inside pocket of it with shaking hands. "I'm calling the police."

Steve grabbed her wrist and slammed it against the hard metal frame of Caitlin's hospital bed causing her to drop the phone on the floor. She let out a shriek of pain, at which point two hospital security guards rushed in and forced Steve to put his hands behind his back. All of a sudden the room was full of people. A social worker was marshalling Mr Murphy and the security guards towards the door, Mrs Murphy was standing beside Caitlin's bed shouting abuse at him, and three members of the medical team were checking to make sure that Caitlin's condition hadn't been compromised even further by her stepfather's unexpected visit. Jules recognised one of the nurses who smiled at her reassuringly before looking down at her wrist and frowning.

"Would you like me to take a look at your arm?" she then offered, sounding concerned.

"It's OK nurse, I'll do it," insisted the doctor on duty, who Jules also recognised rather well. She looked up into Drew's warm eyes and burst into tears.

"Caitlin's condition is stable so unless you need me to stick around and deal with the fall-out from this, I'll go and treat Miss Croft in one of the cubicles," explained Drew, turning to the nurse again. She nodded in agreement and then led a tearful Mrs Murphy out of the room, followed closely by the other social worker.

Drew waited for Jules to make her way towards the door as well, but she was too busy staring at all the equipment around Caitlin's bed.

"Let's go and get your wrist looked at," Drew insisted putting his hand on her shoulder. Jules flinched slightly at his touch and refused to move.

"I need to tell you something first," she began to explain, failing to take her eyes off Caitlin's equipment. "I need to tell you why I ran out on you last night."

"Not now," insisted Drew. "This isn't the time or the place."

"But that's just it," continued Jules, as a tear rolled down her cheek. "This is *exactly* the time and the place. Because 17 years ago the girl lying in this bed surrounded by all this equipment, was *me*!"

Drew's face dropped and he ran his hand through his hair uncomfortably before offering her a chair to sit on. He then pulled up a chair beside her and made a reach for her hand.

"Please, let me look at your wrist," he smiled gently, before pushing the sleeve of her suit jacket up a little further than she would have usually felt comfortable with. And instead of examining the injury that she had just sustained, he ran the tip of his index finger over the scars further up her arm and then lifted them to his lips before kissing them softly.

"It was bullying that caused me to end up here," Jules explained, as warm salty tears continued to roll down her cheeks and gather at the sides of her mouth. "But it wasn't another person who caused my injuries. I did it to myself."

Drew leaned forward and wrapped his arms around her protectively.

"Why didn't you say anything before?" he whispered as she reluctantly relaxed into his arms.

"Because I was ashamed," Jules replied, breathing in the warm familiar scent of his neck. "And because the scars make me feel ugly. I couldn't bear the thought of someone as sexy as you seeing me without my top on."

Drew broke free from their embrace and then looked deep into her eyes.

"You're beautiful," he insisted. "And the reason I didn't come after you last night is because I'm falling in love with you."

Jules' stomach did a summersault as she processed what Drew was saying.

"Me?" she then clarified, sounding a little sceptical. "Are you sure?"

Drew smiled and brushed a strand of hair away from her tear tracked face. "I've never been more sure about anything in my entire life."

"And even in spite of what I've just told you?" Jules frowned, looking down at her arm.

"Why should your past have anything to do with how I feel about you?" Drew explained. "We all have a past that we would probably rather forget. And I'm completely in awe of you for turning your experiences at school into such a positive career. You're a fantastic counsellor, not only because you're caring and sensitive, but because you actually *understand* what your students are going through."

"I only understand from the victim's point of view," Jules replied, looking across as Caitlin in the bed beside them.

"And I thought Louisa was the victim in this scenario, but it turns out that Caitlin was being bullied as well. By her own stepfather."

"You've really made a connection with this girl haven't you," Drew smiled, squeezing Jules' hand again. "She's going to be OK you know. Her injuries are mainly superficial. Her head CT was clear but we had to sedate her in order to treat her facial lacerations, so she's just sleeping it off now."

"She's not in a coma then?" clarified Jules, feeling relieved, and as Drew shook his head reassuringly, she suddenly found herself leaning forward and kissing him on the mouth.

"What was that for?" he smiled, as she eventually pulled herself away. His warm soft lips had encouraged her to get a little carried away with herself again.

"Thank you," she confessed. "For looking after Caitlin. And for putting up with me."

She then looked down momentarily and shifted uneasily in her seat before making eye contact with him again.

"I think I'm falling in love with you too."

"I'm glad to hear it," Drew laughed, pulling her into his arms for another passionate kiss.

It had been such an overwhelming day and Jules couldn't wait to tell Drew all about her reunion with Melanie, but she would save it for when they had their next date because she didn't really feel comfortable discussing it in front of Caitlin.

"So what is it about *your* past that you would really rather forget?" she smiled. "Don't tell me *you* were bullied as well?"

"I *was* actually," replied Drew, persuading Jules to sit back in her chair in disbelief.

"I don't believe it!" she retorted. "Surely you were the boy that all the girls fancied at school?"

"Far from it," Drew explained, whilst removing an old photo from the inside of his wallet. "In fact, I was about 3 stones heavier than I am now."

Jules was absolutely speechless, and found herself snatching the photo out of his hand in disbelief because she just couldn't imagine someone as gorgeous as Drew being so overweight.

"That's a photo of me with my mum and dad when I was 21," he explained. "I had just qualified as a paramedic."

Before they had chance to say anything else, a very croaky sounding voice interrupted them from the hospital bed.

"Where am I?"

Caitlin had woken up.

Chapter forty
Julia

I often wonder why I never chose to open up to my dad about what I was going through, despite claiming to be a bit of a 'daddy's girl'. And it wasn't as though I never had enough opportunities to confide in him, because even though he was at work during the day, in the evenings the two of us would always sit and watch TV together for at least an hour after my mum had gone to bed. Mum never seemed to manage to make it through to the end of whichever TV programme we were watching, without falling asleep on the sofa. And she was frequently obliged to drag herself up to bed by about 9pm every evening, leaving me and my dad alone in our living room.

He often took the opportunity to ask me if I was OK, particularly following the incident with the missing tracksuit bottoms, when he chose to rephrase his question a little by asking me if I was 'happy'. I was never aware of how convincing my happy facade actually was, but I had certainly become very practiced at it over the years. It didn't have anything to do with trying to deceive anyone into believing that there was nothing wrong. I just didn't want them to worry about me, particularly my mum. Ever since Melanie and I had fallen out with each other, she seemed to look at me differently. Sometimes with worry in her soft brown eyes, and sometimes with something far worse than that; pity.

But Dad didn't do that. Dad was supportive without being overbearing about it. And one evening I came really close to telling him that I had deliberately been hurting myself, but for some reason I just couldn't seem to find a way of saying it out loud. Because by saying it out loud – by admitting to another living being what I was doing – I would be making it real. And as long as I could continue concealing it from everyone around me, I could pretend that it wasn't really happening.

As the blister on my leg started to heal, I really had to try and resist the urge to pick at it because my mum had arranged for me to go and have my legs waxed at the beauty salon. And I continued to wear long trousers for PE during the weeks that followed, despite the fact that it was unseasonably warm for February. Of course, I hated our PE lessons, regardless of what the weather was like, because I had still failed to develop any kind of affection for anything that was in the least bit sporty, despite continuing to have a rather inappropriate crush on our teacher.

Swimming was the worst because I had no way of keeping my body hidden from everyone. I used to wrap myself in an enormous beach towel until the last feasible moment, and then lower myself into the water as quickly as possible before anyone had a chance to notice my unsightly combination of hairs and scars. On one occasion Fran and Melanie managed to swipe my towel from the side of the pool so that I was unable to wrap myself up in it again after I got back out of the water. So the next time we had swimming, I told Mr Parker that I had my period and he allowed me to sit the lesson out altogether. It was only after I got home from school that day that I discovered that I had a tampon tied to my rucksack, and that I had obviously been walking around the school campus with it dangling there all day. Of course, I knew exactly who had been responsible for tying it there, but I had very little chance of being able to actually prove it, and that was what was so unnerving about the way Fran and Melanie treated me. It was all so underhand; calculated even, because they knew that they would probably never get caught.

The only time they ever actually got into trouble was when they smuggled the bottle of vodka into the Halloween disco. And that was only because someone had reported them to Mr Parker. Fran had been expelled from her previous school and she knew that she had too much to lose by being indiscreet about her treatment towards me. I just hated how she seemed to manipulate Melanie into doing her dirty work for her, and knowing what I know now, it's clear to see that Melanie was being bullied by Fran just as much as I was, but in an even more underhand way.

As well as PE, I also disliked most of the creative subjects like music and drama, not least because music was the main reason why Melanie and Fran became friends with each other. My favourite subjects at school were English, maths and the sciences, and in particular, biology, which ended up standing me in very good stead for my psychology qualifications. During one of our biology lessons we started learning about the body's ability to fight infection. Of course, we were only secondary school students so we didn't really go into it in any great depth, but I was fascinated by the human body back in those days, and I wanted to learn as much about it as possible. Perhaps it was my ability to think of my own body in the same way that enabled me to disrespect it to such a great extent. It was simply a vessel; a shell to experiment on, rather than something to cherish and to care for. And it was always letting me down. My legs were covered in ugly black hairs and wouldn't run fast enough. My oversized feet tripped me up. My arms were gangly and unfeminine. My face was inflicted with craters of puss filled acne. My eyes weren't in focus anymore, confining me to an adolescence of wearing thick rimmed spectacles. Everything about my body was wrong or inadequate, even the bits of me that weren't, like my hair and my teeth. I simply despised it all, every last part of me, and that's how I was able to punish it so zealously, without any consideration whatsoever for the consequences.

Of course, I never expected to get caught, having managed to get away with it for so many months. My parents were none the wiser, and I lived under the same roof as them. And since Melanie and I had parted ways, it wasn't as though I had any close friends to keep an eye out for me either, which was one of the other reasons why Fran saw me as an easy target; because I had no one to stand up for me. So when I did eventually get caught, the last thing I expected was for Melanie, of all the people in Heathmount Comp, to be the one to uncover my dreadful secret.

❖

We had just been subjected to one of those painfully boring assemblies which every school child dreads, because sitting amongst an entire assembly hall of students felt a bit like being trapped in the worst kind of hell, with no means of escape. And unless you were fortunate enough to be seated on the end of a row, which was something that I had persistently favoured throughout adulthood whenever I visited a theatre or a cinema, then you just couldn't get out until the nightmare was over, and that was something that used to make me feel very uneasy indeed.

Fortunately, on the day that my secret was revealed, I had been lucky enough to find myself sitting at the very end of the row, and whilst I pretended to try and listen to what Mrs Jenkinson was talking about, I gradually started to feel light headed. I had been feeling sick all morning. In fact, I was convinced that I must have been coming down with some kind of nasty virus because I just hadn't been feeling very well at all over the past couple of days. But my mum refused to allow me to take the day off school because she thought I was making it up in order to just avoid seeing Melanie and Fran. Life had become pretty unbearable since the hockey lesson fall out and their gang appeared to have tripled in size, with Craig Riley at the helm whenever either of the girls weren't available to taunt me instead. That day there had been a rumour circulating that Craig and Melanie had broken up. Part of me was actually relieved that she had managed to cut one of her ties with that group, although I had given up any hope of forming a reconciliation with her at that point, so I knew it wouldn't really make any difference. Particularly not with Fran still hanging around like a bad smell.

My form tutor was rather hesitant when I asked her if I could be excused in order to go to the toilet, because trying to avoid mind numbingly boring assemblies like that one were fairly common practice, but when she realised how pale I looked, she excused me from the assembly hall quite willingly. And when I got to the girls' toilets and gasped at my ghostly complexion in the mirror, it was easy to see why. I looked absolutely dreadful.

I locked myself in one of the toilet cubicles, placed my rucksack on the floor, and then attempted to open my bladder, which was something that I wasn't actually that used to doing at school. The main reason why I usually visited the school toilet cubicles was so that I could make use of the pair of nail scissors which I kept in a little blue makeup bag, piercing the skin on my arm, and alleviating the pressure inside my head which had been brought on by one of Melanie and Fran's latest vendettas. But that day I had been attempting to alleviate a very different kind of pressure, and that was my rather unexpected inability to pass urine. In fact, I had been unable to go for a wee since the day before.

I remember squatting on the toilet for what felt like forever, but aware that the noise from the assembly hall was still yet to erupt, signalling the end of Mrs Jenkinson's speech. And the longer I sat there, the worse I started to feel, until eventually my entire body started shaking irrepressibly. The sensation made me panic so much that it got to the point where I wasn't sure whether I was just shaking with anxiety instead, and that familiar anxious feeling spurred me to reach for my little blue makeup bag and remove my nail scissors from it. As I slowly peeled the left sleeve of my school shirt up and folded it in place above my elbow, I noticed that the plaster from my previous cut was beginning to peel off. It was also feeling a lot more painful than usual, and as I lifted up the peeling plaster in order to peer underneath, I discovered that it was very red and swollen, and there was a cloudy pus seeping out of it which smelt really stagnant.

I decided to splash it with some cold water, but when I emerged from the cubicle and started to make my way over to the sinks, my legs began to buckle beneath me and I felt as though I was about to throw up. As I stood there with my face in the sink, staring at the plughole and shaking and retching with fear, all I could think about were the symptoms of an infection that we had been discussing during our biology lesson a few days earlier, and it quickly became apparent that the reason why I was feeling like this was because the cut on my arm had become septic.

Chapter forty one

Melanie

Little did I know, that when I walked into those toilets after assembly that day back in February 2002, my life would change forever. At first I wanted to just turn around and head back out the way I came in, because being in the same room as Julia was the last thing that I felt like dealing with, having just been dumped by Craig in one of the most humiliating ways possible. But there was something about Julia's demeanour that encouraged me to hesitate. She was slumped against the sinks as though she was no longer capable of supporting her own body weight, and her body appeared to be shivering uncontrollably.

"Helf mah," she pleaded, peering up at me from beneath her hair, which hung limply in front of her face. I was then able to observe that her complexion was very pale and clammy.

"What's the matter with you?" I panicked, reluctantly edging a little closer to where she was standing. "Why are you speaking like that? You're slurring your words."

At first I wondered whether she was drunk, and instinctively inspected the floor of the toilet cubicle in which she had abandoned her rucksack. There was no evidence of any alcohol, but what I did notice was a small blue makeup bag with some of the contents spilling out of it. Perhaps she had been taking drugs instead?

"Have you taken anything?" I demanded picking the makeup bag up off the floor.

I examined its contents more closely; an old pair of nail scissors, a packet of pocket sized tissues, and some plasters were all I was able to find. It was only then that I realised that Julia was wearing one of the plasters on her left forearm; it was hanging off slightly and the sleeve of her school shirt was rolled up to her elbow. There was also a little bit of blood and pus on her cuff.

"Have you hurt yourself?" I frowned, beginning to get frustrated with her for failing to answer either of my previous questions. "I can't help you unless you tell me what's been going on."

"I think I'm ill," Julia replied, managing to control her slurring. "I feel sick and I can't breathe properly."

I gently placed my hand on her forehead and discovered that it was burning hot. She tried to maintain eye contact with me but her head was floppy and her eyelids seemed heavy. I'll never forget how terrified I felt when it began to dawn on me how serious the situation was.

"My arm hurts," explained Julia, as slowly and coherently as she was able to manage, but the sheer effort of speaking seemed to use up every last little bit of strength that she had, because no sooner had she said it than her legs started to buckle beneath her and she ended up in a slumped heap on the floor. She rested her head gently against the pedestal of the sink that she was nearest to, and her breathing started to become more and more shallow.

"What have you done to it?" I urged her, crouching down. "Why is it so painful, and what has it got to do with your other symptoms?"

"I cut it," she eventually confessed. "With the nail scissors."

I looked down at the blue makeup bag in my hand and then realised what she was telling me. She had used the scissors to cut her arm deliberately.

"But why would you do that to yourself?" I demanded, as Julia's head started to become floppy again.

"Becauth of you," she slurred. "Becauth you're a bully."

The word 'bully' resonated against my ear drums, creating a high pitched ringing sound in my head. But rather than staying to help Julia, and to try and atone for what I had driven her to do to herself, I simply stood up from my crouched position and ran, as fast as I could, out of the door of the girls' toilets and across the school grounds, as though the only person whose life depended on it, was mine.

Chapter forty two
Julia

February 2002

I remember it being one of those uncharacteristically warm days for the middle of February, almost as though spring had burst into bud a few weeks early. The sound of birdsong was amplified and pretty bulbs were beginning to open up between blades of dewy grass. My face glowed from the warmth of the sun and the air smelt fresh and clean. It was one of those beautiful days that cut through the bleakness of winter and awakened everyone from hibernation.

It was one of those beautiful days that would have put a smile on my face and a spring in my step had it not have been for the sheer hell of the situation in which I had found myself in. Because rather than a warm, soft glow in my cheeks, they were burning red hot with fever. My entire body trembled uncontrollably as I slipped in and out of consciousness. Two paramedics gently lifted me onto a stretcher and carried me to where an ambulance was waiting for us, and I found myself aware of lots of people standing around watching as my eyelids started to become heavy again.

"Stay with us Julia," urged a voice, but all I could make out as I squinted to identify its owner, was a blurry outline of a dark haired young man with a round friendly face and a wide smile.

"I'm Andy," he then explained, gripping my hand tightly as he spoke. His voice was soft and kind. "I'm a trainee paramedic and I'm here to look after you. Everything's going to be alright."

As my eyes opened and closed again, I could see the bright blue lights from the ambulance flashing through my eyelids, and before I was able to make sense of what was happening I had been lifted into the back of it and the doors were slammed shut. The sound of all the concerned voices from the crowd outside were immediately replaced by sirens as the ambulance began to move.

"It hurts," I croaked, swallowing hard and raising my right arm – the one that wasn't in excruciating pain – and feeling on my face for where my glasses should have been in the hope of being able to focus on the kind paramedic more closely.

"Your glasses got broken when you collapsed," Andy explained when he realised what I was doing. "Try not to move; you've got a nasty infection and we need to keep your arm nice and still."

I licked my dry lips and swallowed again. The pain in my left arm was unbearable and I could hear my heart pounding in my ears as the ambulance swayed from side to side.

"What happened?" I sobbed as he gripped hold of my hand again and brushed a few stray strands of hair away from my tear tracked face. As he lent forward, I was just about able to read his identity badge properly as it swung against the pocket of his paramedic's uniform:

'Andrew Trent, Trainee Paramedic'

Deep down I knew what had happened though. I just didn't want to admit it to myself. Before we arrived at the hospital I lost consciousness again.

Epilogue

Sunday 17th November 2019

"I still can't believe you're moving out next weekend," exclaimed Amy, linking arms with Jules on their way through the park. It was a beautiful autumn day. The ground was littered with leaves, the gold and red hues of which were glowing in the mid-morning sunlight.

"We need to do something to celebrate; we've been flat mates for nearly 8 years!"

"I'm only moving down the road," Jules reminded her as they waded through piles of leaves. "We'll still see each other all the time."

"But it won't be the same," complained Amy. "I'm really going to miss you."

"I'll miss you too," smiled Jules, rubbing the sleeve of Amy's coat reassuringly and then giving her friend's arm a squeeze. "It's the end of an era."

A smile crept across Amy's face at that point.

"What's so amusing?" Jules frowned, starting to get suspicious.

"I can think of *one* advantage to you moving out," laughed Amy sounding sheepish. "At least I won't have to put up with listening to you and Dr Dish having it off in the next room!"

Jules blushed and covered her face in her hands with embarrassment as Amy nudged her affectionately. Jules and Drew had been together for 6 months now and she had never seen her best friend so happy. Not only were they the perfect couple in every possible way, but Jules had finally discovered how wonderful sex could be, having covered her body up and hidden it away for so many years. And now Jules and Drew were moving in together, leaving Amy alone in their flat.

"So how long will it be before you agree to let Tim move in?" asked Jules, turning the attention back on to her friend.

"It depends how long it takes him to set a date for our wedding," retorted Amy, as they reached the end of the main path through the park and weaved their way out of the gates.

"And I can't think of a better place to get married than in a building like that," Amy pointed.

Across the road stood a beautiful old church with steep steps leading up to a large wooden door. The tall bell tower to the right of the building was chiming loudly, signalling the start of the Sunday morning service, and at the foot of the tower lay a collection of poppy wreaths which had been placed there at the Remembrance Day service the weekend before.

"We were wondering how long it would take you two to catch us up!" teased Drew from where he and Tim had been patiently standing to wait for them.

The four of them ascended the stone steps together and then pushed open the heavy wooden door, at which moment the musty smell of hymn books and the trills and vibrations of the church organ greeted them as they stepped inside. It was the day of baby Grace's baptism and Jules and Drew, who had crossed paths with Rebecca and Leroy on various occasions since the engagement party, had decided to go along to the church to join in the service. Amy and Tim had agreed to go with them as it wasn't a private Christening, although they weren't usually accustomed to such civilised Sunday morning rituals, preferring instead to spend this particular part of the weekend either sleeping off their hangovers, or running up and down a football pitch. Christian was the first person to notice them when they arrived, and slid along the pew in the second row in order to create enough space for them to sit down at the end.

"We can just watch from the back of the church," Jules insisted, looking behind her self-consciously. "We don't want to block anyone else's view."

"Don't worry about it sis," replied Christian, casually, whilst kissing his little sister on the cheek. "Are you going to Mum and Dad's house for lunch today?"

Jules nodded unenthusiastically.

"But only because we can't go next Sunday instead," she then explained. "Drew and I want to spend our first weekend together in the new house."

Christian winked at her before turning his attention towards his fiancée who was standing at the front of the church talking to Leroy and the vicar.

"Suzy looks stunning," Jules observed. "Is she excited about being a Godmother?"

"Not as excited as she is about being an auntie," Christian replied. "She seems to have spent more time looking for a flower girl dress for Grace than she has looking for a wedding dress for herself!"

Jules couldn't help but conclude that Grace would look perfect in the beautiful white Christening gown that she was wearing today. Although Christian and Suzy weren't due to get married until Christmas, and babies always seemed to grow out of outfits so quickly. As Jules continued to sit and admire Grace and Suzy's outfits, Rebecca walked over to join them at the front of the church, and she was accompanied by the rest of Grace's Godparents; Melanie and Richard. Jules' heart did a little leap in her chest as she hadn't really seen or spoken to Melanie very much since their first couple of encounters back in May.

They decided between them that it would be inappropriate for Jules to continue to support Josh through his experiences with cyber bullying, and Melanie had managed to arrange for Josh to have some private counselling sessions instead, using some of the money that her father had left for her in his will. The rest of the money had enabled her to leave her job at the accountancy firm with far fewer financial worries than she might otherwise have had, and as well as investing some of her inheritance in Richard's thriving building company, she had also started teaching piano to some of the pupils from Josh's school, including Caitlin Murphy. Ursula was no longer working for her, providing Melanie with the excuse to enjoy many of the household chores herself, and even though Josh was continuing to behave like a typical teenager, she really appreciated being able to spend more time with him at long last.

The only person Melanie was no longer in contact with was Fran, who was showing no sign of changing her manipulative ways. It took getting back in touch with Julia to make Melanie realise that Fran was a negative force in her life and that she had only really bothered to stay friends with her out of habit over the past 17 years. They stopped having anything in common with each other a long time ago, but the guilt and responsibility of what happened to Julia back at school, was the only thing that she and Fran shared, and continuing to be Fran's friend enabled her to distribute the burden to a certain extent. It was obvious that Fran had never actually been able to feel any remorse for Julia's devastating circumstances though, and Melanie decided to conclude that she was obviously just in denial. She also felt quite sorry for Fran because she had always been on her own; to an even greater extent than Melanie had in fact. After all, Fran's parents worked abroad a lot when she was a teenager, and prior to when she was expelled and moved to Heathmount Comp, she was filed away at a private boarding school over 150 miles from where they lived. Melanie had confirmed through Facebook recently that she was now living with her step sister and was seeking help for her alcohol problem. It was a positive development, but a far flung cry away from marital bliss and mortgages.

Someone who *was* about to enjoy settling down and getting a mortgage however, was Julia. And when Melanie looked across at the second pew and saw Julia and Drew sitting there, her stomach flipped over. Julia was busy talking to her brother and didn't appear to have realised that Melanie was there, but when it was time for the three Godparents to assemble at the front of the church, Julia's attention immediately turned from Suzy to Melanie and Richard instead. And as the two women made eye contact with each other for the first time in over five months, they were both compelled to break out in a warm smile, putting each other at ease immediately.

"Right, if everybody's ready I think we can begin," the vicar suddenly announced.

❖

At the end of the service, Drew squeezed Jules' hand encouragingly as he enticed her to where Rebecca and Leroy were standing.

"We wanted to come and say hello before we head off," smiled Drew, leaning forward to shake Leroy's hand.

"Thank you so much for coming," gushed Rebecca, giving Jules a kiss on the cheek. "I haven't seen you since Suzy's hen do! How have you been?"

"Great actually," smiled Jules. "We're completing on the house next week."

"That's fantastic news," Rebecca replied, just as Suzy was about to walk up and interrupt them. She was holding baby Grace at arm's length and she had a particularly distasteful look on her face.

"Can you hold her again?" she squirmed, passing Grace back to Rebecca. "She just spat up on my designer jacket."

"Perhaps *you* would like a cuddle with her Jules?" Rebecca suggested.

"I'd love one," Jules replied animatedly, before holding her hands out and gripping onto Grace's tiny little waist. As she positioned her in her arms and admired her beautiful Christening gown more closely, Drew leant in and whispered in her ear;

"Shall we have a baby?"

Jules' caught her breath in her throat at the thought of such an exciting prospect. When she and Drew had decided to buy a house together after as little as 3 months, she just knew that they were doing the right thing because there had been no doubt in her mind, since that day at the hospital with Caitlin, that he was the man who she would end up spending the rest of her life with. And whilst she could have just moved in with him, they concluded that they would prefer to sell his Victorian terrace, cash in on the profit he had made from having had it renovated, and buy themselves a slightly larger house instead, with a couple of extra bedrooms. It was inevitable that they were upsizing with the intention of having a family, but this was the first time he had actually said it out loud. Of course, they would need to get married first. Jules prided herself on having some rather traditional values. Although they would have to get Christian and Suzy's wedding, *and* Amy and Tim's wedding out of the way before they could even contemplate setting a date of their own.

Jules still couldn't believe that she had managed to find herself someone as perfect as Dr Andrew Trent. He was the sweetest and sexiest man she had ever met and he was incredibly intelligent and successful. But more importantly than any of that, he was compassionate to the core. He genuinely understood her and what she had been through, and they had an unbreakable bond with each other which had inspired her to truly turn her life around after that fateful day in 2002. It was almost as though meeting him again six months ago was just meant to be.

"Will you join us for tea and cake in the church hall?" asked Leroy, as Jules gently pressed her face against Grace's soft chubby cheek.

"We don't want to impose," insisted Jules. "I'm sure you would rather just have your close friends and family there."

Leroy began to laugh;

"After what Drew and I went through at Christian's stag do the other week, we're friends for life!"

Jules and Rebecca eyed them both suspiciously before laughing too.

"Well in that case we'd love to join you," concluded Jules, prompting Drew to nudge her gently and then wink.

Drew had spent the past few months of their relationship encouraging Jules to try and believe in herself a little more, and to stop assuming that her company was an imposition. If someone wanted to spend time with her, then they were actually being genuine, as opposed to simply taking advantage of her good nature so that they could chew her friendship up and spit it out once they had managed to get what they wanted out of it. She also knew that she needed to practice what she preached because if the students at Pinewood School were obliged to heed her advice, it was only right that she should too. But Jules knew that she would probably always suffer from low self-esteem, and that she would find it difficult to trust other people's motives, because she had spent the first 16 years of her life dealing with the likes of Barry Harper and Kylie Sinclair; and Fran Wheeler and Craig Riley. And, of course, Melanie Allsopp.

❖

After the members of the Christening party had all moved through into the church hall, Melanie decided to take the opportunity of reacquainting herself with Julia. But just as she was beginning to pluck up the courage to approach her, Richard placed a cup of tea in her hand.

"Thank you," she smiled, before kissing him on the lips appreciatively.

He always knew how to look after her, and a cup of tea was exactly what she needed in order to steady her nerves a little before she made her approach. She softly blew on her cup whilst clasping her hands around it in order to keep warm. It was cold in the church hall and the hot steam from her tea made her nose tickle as she inhaled it's comforting scent.

"Are you OK?" enquired Richard, sensing the nervous edge to her voice.

Melanie glanced over at Josh, who was sitting in the corner of the room looking at his phone.

"We should probably go home soon; Josh is getting bored," she replied.

"But we're the Godparents," Richard insisted. "We can't leave yet. Besides, I haven't even had a chance to get myself a second slice of cake!"

Melanie smiled and shook her head at him disapprovingly as she took a sip of her tea.

"So what's the *real* reason why you want to go home?"

"Well I need to prepare the spare bedroom for mum," replied Melanie, clutching onto as many different excuses as she could possibly think of in order to avoid providing Richard with the real answer to his question.

Her mother was due to come over from France to stay with them the following day, which was her third visit in as many months. Since they had all returned to England together following Melanie's father's funeral back in the spring, Mrs Allsopp had really begun to appreciate how important family was. So much so in fact that she had even agreed to start making use of their spare bedroom, as opposed to simply retreating to the 4 star hotel on the other side of town.

"It won't take that long to get the spare bedroom ready," Richard retorted. "Even to your mother's 5 star standards!"

Melanie cuffed him on the arm and smiled again. Since Ursula left, she had become particularly house proud.

"It's Julia isn't it?" Richard then clarified, as discreetly as he possibly could. "*She's* the reason why you want to leave early."

"I was all fired up and ready to go over to her," explained Melanie, placing her cup of tea on the table beside her. "But then I panicked in case she doesn't want to speak to me. After I arranged for Josh to have some private counselling, we completely lost touch again."

"She's a reasonable person," replied Richard, reassuringly. "Just imagine how pleased she'll be to find out that you've ditched your job *and* you've ditched Fran."

"I suppose so," Melanie conceded, and before she had managed to give herself another chance to change her mind, she started to stride across the hall to where Julia and Drew were standing.

Julia, who had been holding baby Grace, had passed her to one of the other Christening guests for a cuddle so that she could proceed to feed Drew fingers full of cake. The two of them were laughing flirtatiously, and although Melanie felt very awkward about interrupting them, she also felt rather warm and comforted by their obvious affection for one another.

"I just had to come over and say hello," she smiled, as Julia pulled her fingers away from Drew's mouth and wiped the remaining cake crumbs on the napkin she was holding.

"Melanie, hi!" Jules beamed in reply, feeling her face flush a little.

She had been intending to make the first move, but that was before Suzy had passed the baby back to Rebecca, and by then she had already agreed to have a cuddle with her. Or at least that was the excuse she had decided to stick to in her own mind in order to ease her guilt. Of course, she would never have left the Christening without speaking to Melanie because she had been thinking about their reunion a lot over the last few days; ever since she and Amy had decided to drag Drew and Tim along to the service in fact, because she knew that Melanie would be there. And she had even put something in her handbag to share with Melanie when the time came, although she was beginning to have second thoughts about it now.

"How are you?" she enquired, sensing that Drew was beginning to edge away from where they were standing. He knew that Jules would probably appreciate some time alone with her.

"I'm really good actually," Melanie replied, before noticing that Drew had made his way over to introduce himself to Richard.

"Richard and I are living together again, and I've started teaching piano to some of the children at Pinewood."

"So I hear," smiled Jules. "In fact, I think Mr Langley's planning to offer you a job in the music department!"

"Caitlin's one of my students," explained Melanie. "She's very gifted. And it sounds as though she's a lot happier at home, now that her stepdad's no longer around."

Jules nodded before agreeing;

"She's doing really well. She's even managed to build a few bridges with her nemesis, Louisa."

There was a long pause. Jules wasn't allowed to elaborate any further for fear of breaching any confidences, so she decided to enquire after Josh instead.

"He's doing much better, thank you," confirmed Melanie. "And thank you for putting us in touch with the right people. Richard and I really did appreciate the advice you gave us after you came over to the house that day. I'm just sorry I didn't make more of an effort to keep in contact with you."

"Well I didn't keep in touch with you either," insisted Jules, apologetically. "Although to be honest, I guess I just assumed that you had rather a lot to deal with in your life at the time and you probably wouldn't want to hear from me."

"Of course I wanted to hear from you," Melanie replied. "I feel like I owe you so much. Meeting you again made me realise how unhappy I was with my life, and if it hadn't have been for that then I probably would have lost Richard forever."

"I'm really happy for you," Jules smiled.

"And I'm really happy for you too," gushed Melanie, looking across to where the two men were standing. "Dr Dish is gorgeous!"

"I still can't quite understand how I ended up with someone as perfect as him," Jules confessed.

"Well he obviously adores you," replied Melanie. "And he's lucky to have you too."

"Thanks," Jules blushed.

She still found it very difficult to accept a compliment. After that there was an awkward silence, as Jules started to rummage in her handbag for the special item that she had brought to the church with her.

"I wanted to give you something," she explained, taking hold of Melanie's arm and turning the palm or her hand upwards.

Once Jules had stepped back a little, Melanie gently uncurled her fingers to reveal a tiny bracelet made of purple thread.

"Do you remember making that for me when we were 13?"

"I do!" beamed Melanie, studying the bracelet more closely. "Why is it broken?"

"Because I wore it all the time," explained Jules. "Even when I was in the bath! But on the day that Fran joined our school, the thread snapped apart, almost as though it was symbolic of our friendship starting to unravel."

Melanie pinched the end of each piece of thread between her thumb and index finger and managed to tie the tiniest of knots in them so that the bracelet was joined together again. She then placed it back into Jules' hand and leaned forward to give her old friend a big hug.

"Can we try to forget about the past and start again? I really want my best friend back."

"Of course," agreed Jules, as a tear started to roll down her cheek. "From now on, let's just focus on the future. I have a feeling it's going to be pretty great!"

The End.

Acknowledgements

Firstly, I would like to thank my husband Michael for all the time that he spent with me reading through the completed manuscript, editing it and preparing it for self-publication. I would also like to thank my friends Rowena and Sarah for their proof reading skills, and Alex for providing me with some advice with regards to Julia's profession.

I must also take this opportunity to thank my parents for their belief and support, particularly when I first started to pursue my passion for writing all those years ago, as well as my daughter Catherine whose own flair and talent for writing has inspired me to continue with mine.

A Message from the Author

My passion for writing is something that I have carried through life with me ever since I was a teenager. I kept a diary between the ages of 14 and 28, and I also used to write short stories based on some of my secondary school experiences. Ideas for storylines came very easily to me, as well as the desire to put pen to paper, but I was never particularly good at the execution when I first started out. I continue to keep journals now, based on specific themes including getting married, having a baby and living through a global pandemic.

Writing has always been extremely cathartic. It provides me with the perfect outlet. Re-reading old diaries in recent months has also enabled me to learn a lot about myself and my insecurities. I am able to appreciate how much I have managed to overcome over the years in terms of personal struggles such as low self-esteem and social anxiety.

Writing a book about bullying has been an ambition of mine for as long as I can remember. Having suffered from bullying for many of my school years, it was important for me to convey the long-lasting effects, as well as the more obvious, short-term ones. I hope that it will provide inspiration and hope to anyone who might be going through similar experiences.

Information and Support

If you or someone you know have been affected by any of the issues raised in *Sticks and Stones*, lots of help is available. Here are just some of the organisations that can provide support for bullying or self-harm:

www.nationalbullyinghelpline.co.uk

www.kidscape.org.uk

www.themix.org.uk

www.youngminds.org.uk

www.samaritans.org

anti-bullyingalliance.org.uk

It is my intention to donate a significant percentage of the sales profits from my book to anti-bullying charities, so thank you for your support.

The 'Greener Grass' Concept

I would like to expand on my novel collection over the coming years and I am currently working on another novel entitled *The Pregnant Pause*. In a similar vein to *Sticks and Stones*, this novel follows the individual stories of two separate women living parodic lives. It explores the concept that the grass isn't always greener by comparing the feelings and opinions of the central characters, who end up envying each other's situations without really knowing the whole truth. Resisting the urge to persistently compare myself to others has been a life-long battle for me and my self-esteem, so this is an important message for me to share with my readers.

> The grass isn't greener on the other side. It's greener where YOU water it.

Sticks and Stones is part of the Greener Grass series.

The Pregnant Pause

Ellen Ogilvie lives in a large detached house with her wealthy husband Neil and their three children. Ellen's marriage isn't as perfect as it seems and she yearns for the chance to put herself first for a change. Being a housewife and mother isn't fulfilling enough for her anymore and as her 40th Birthday approaches, she decides that she's desperate for an adventure. She finds herself feeling deeply attracted to a new work colleague and wondering whether he will be able to give her everything that Neil won't. That is until she receives some news from her GP that could change her outlook on life forever.

35 year old **Cass Thornton** lives alone in a modest but modern mid-terrace and has an exciting career and a thriving social life. She's desperate to settle down and start a family before it's too late but by the time she manages to persuade her flaky boyfriend Jake that he's ready to move in with her and become a dad, Mother Nature has other ideas. Cass must then embark on a heart wrenching journey in order to try and fulfil her ultimate dream of having a baby.

When Ellen and Cass cross paths, they are unable to resist the urge to resent one another for living the life that they so desperately crave for themselves. But they eventually discover that they have a lot more in common with each other than they think, and come to realise that the grass isn't always greener on the other side.

Printed in Great Britain
by Amazon